Close to the Skin

by

Zara West

The Skin Quartet Series

Close to the Skin

Cover Art by *Angela Anderson*

The Wild Rose Press, Inc.
PO Box 708
Adams Basin, NY 14410-0708
Visit us at www.thewildrosepress.com

Publishing History
First Crimson Rose Edition, 2017
Print ISBN 978-1-5092-1643-7
Digital ISBN 978-1-5092-1644-4

The Skin Quartet Series
Published in the United States of America

The man was dead.

Her brother had killed him in front of her eyes.

Or had it all been a lie?

If anyone knew what was going on it would be Vernon. She moved back into the living room and peered out the window. The sky was still dark. The street light still burned. Dare she call him? He'd think she'd capitulated. Wanted him.

She dropped the curtain and straightened her shoulders. She wanted him all right. She wanted answers. She wanted to know why dead men were calling her and threatening notes appeared in her mail.

Hands shaking, she punched in Vernon's cell number. It rang once. Twice. She imagined him holding her, kissing her. His low, rumbling voice whispering in her ear. No, she couldn't talk to him. Not yet. She was still addicted to the man.

She tapped the phone off and curled back up on the sofa. *Tomorrow.* Tomorrow, she'd send him an e mail—a nicely worded formal request.

At that moment, the phone in her hand rang. Vernon returning her call? She hesitated. Then flicked it on.

A low pitched voice spoke through heavy static. "Does Vernon know what you did?" A frisson of fear crept down her spine and burrowed deep into her core. She tossed the cell phone onto the floor and buried herself under the silk shawls, struggling to breathe.

Forget all the reasons why Vernon was the wrong man for her. She needed him. She needed him now.

Dedication

To my sister—
My Number One Fan!

Chapter 1

The Siren

Bella lifted her foot off the pedal and laid down her Kronos tattoo machine. She picked up the antiseptic cream and rubbed it over the reddened skin. "This is getting ridiculous, Vernon. It has to stop. There's no room for another tat."

Vernon turned his head and grinned. "Ah, Bella. There's still a few places."

"Don't do faces. Or man parts." She slapped an adhesive film bandage over the mermaid with the long red hair that swam across his well-muscled left buttock. "You know the routine. No picking. No scratching. No scrubbing. No sun—well, sun shouldn't be a problem in that location." She pulled off her rubber gloves. "Now put your pants on and get out of here and take your bruiser, Gav, with you. He's scaring away my customers."

"That's his job, baby."

She pushed her rolling work cart aside and stood up. "I'm not your baby. I'm not your anything."

"Yet." He looped his arm around her waist and pulled her close. "You know you want me."

The heat of his body spiraled through her, warmed her in places that yearned for his touch. She rested her hands on his arms. She did want him, had wanted him

1

since she was a know-nothing nineteen-year-old. But too many years had passed. She was no longer the naive Greek village girl she'd once been. That girl—Sirena Stavros—had cried enough tears to fill an ocean.

Reinvented Bella Bell, with her flamboyant red wig and shoulder-to-toe body art never cried. She was a hard-nosed business woman with a thriving Williamsburg, Brooklyn tattoo studio to run. It had taken eight years from the day she arrived in New York City for her to establish herself as a top tattoo artist with a TV series deal in the offing. No way would she give up her hard-won career to please Vernon Newell. And she didn't need the complications an ex-crime boss would bring into her life, no matter how many billions of dollars he wanted to spend on her. Not now. Not ever.

Bella pushed away from him and passed through the beaded curtain that separated her tatting station with its black granite counter and maple cabinets from the waiting area. Sunlight streamed through the plate glass window, illuminating the golden walls and outrageous mermaid-themed décor she'd collected over the years.

Outside, mothers pushing baby carriages and shoppers noshing tacos and pad thai strolled by enjoying the unusually warm winter day. Bella smiled and waved at a familiar passer-by sporting one of her signature mermaid tattoos on his arm. It was the perfect location for her shop—right on Bedford Avenue, one of the main shopping streets, and just a few blocks from the subway. Yes, she was doing well.

She turned and glanced down at Vernon's bodyguard sprawled across one of her twin faux-leather sofas, a newspaper shielding his head from the sun, his huge hand petting her most recent rescue kitten, Fishtail. She yanked the paper off his head. "What happened to my next customer, Gav?"

The ex-wrestler shrugged. "I suggested you might be delayed awhile."

"Delayed?" She strode to the door and turned the door knob. "You locked it"—she looked over at the neon siren sign that hung in the window—"and turned off my mermaid?"

"Just following orders."

"Well, here's an order for you to *follow*. Get your boss out of here before I call the cops."

Gav put the cat down and pushed himself up to his feet. At six foot four and a well-muscled two-eighty, he towered over her, and she was not a short woman. He studied his fingernails. "Cops his friends, Miss Bella."

Vernon appeared through the curtain, thumbs hooked in the waistband of his unzipped jeans. He reached down and inched his fly up. "Everyone is my friend, Bella, except you."

"So go spend time with *everyone* else and leave me alone."

"Bella Bell, you're a hard woman. Can't you forgive a man a little miscalculation?"

"Miscalculation? You call what you did to my brother 'a miscalculation'?"

"He knew what he was getting into. I just hadn't expected him to be so out of practice. After all, he'd wrestled in the Olympics."

"Twelve years ago." She glared at him. "It was *vengeance*, pure and simple."

Vernon glanced away. "Well, it was his fault you whacked me with that marble statue guy. What was his

3

name?"

"Archimedes."

He rubbed the back of his head. "Still got the dent."

"Too bad I didn't knock some compassion into you at the same time."

"Please. I've changed, Bella. Look at me. I've lost thirty pounds, bulked up at the gym." He winked and pointed to himself. "I'm a damn handsome guy. You can't say you don't want me."

Bella tipped her head toward him. Of course, she wanted him. He *was* a damn handsome guy. As tall as Gav, but leaner and more elegant than the hulking bulldog of a bodyguard. Vernon Newell had the build of a boxer, long-legged, narrow-hipped, with powerful biceps and thighs. But it was his smoky, blue-gray eyes sparked with silver highlights and a hint of sadness that drew her like a magnet.

She took a step back and fisted her hands to stop her traitorous body from touching him. "I don't want you. There, I said it."

Vernon gave her a crooked smile. "So what *do* you want, baby?"

"I don't ever want to see you again. If you love me, you'll leave and never come back." She turned away and bit her lip to keep from saying more.

"Oh, Bella. You don't mean that. You're mine— heart and soul."

She spun around, the long braid of her wig slapping against her back. "Can't you hear yourself? You're an arrogant bastard who has strong-armed people to get what you want for so long you don't know how to be a normal human being. You lie. You steal.

You're a bad man, Vernon Newell."

He ran his fingers through the curly white-gold hair she loved to touch. "If I had you by my side, I could be a better man."

"I am not a miracle worker. I'm a tattoo artist with customers to serve." She clapped her hands together. "Oh, just scram, the two of you. A client's coming in three minutes, and I need to get the tracings ready."

Gav tugged Vernon by the sleeve. "Lady wants you to go."

Vernon threw his hand off. "I got the message. Wait outside. Be there in a minute."

The bodyguard nodded and headed out to the street. The door latch clicked shut behind him. Vernon glanced at Bella and then turned the lock.

She put her hands on her hips. "*Now* what are you doing?"

"Bella, you know I'm never going to give up. It took me eight years to find you. Please be reasonable." He stepped closer. "I love you."

She laughed. "*Love?* Bah. You haven't a lemon slice of an idea what love is."

He seized her hand and placed the palm against his chest. "When I think of you, my heart beats so fast I think it's going to explode."

She slid her hand down. "I rather think it's another part of your anatomy that's prone to explode."

"Well, that too." The length of his body pressed against hers, his erection hot and hard. Powerful hands that could crush bones encircled her waist with a gentleness that always surprised her. Then his mouth met hers, warm and spicy from the cinnamon gum he'd chewed while under the needle.

He licked the seam of her lips, and despite knowing it would only make resisting him all the harder, she opened to him, let his tongue sweep inside and claim her. She angled her head and tangled her tongue with his, dueling her way deeper until they were joined, breath to breath, heart to heart.

Heat spiraled through her and gathered between her thighs. His hand slipped beneath the waistband of her jeans.

She jerked her head back and broke the kiss. "No. Stop it. You know it drives me wild when you touch me." His hand kept moving lower. Cocksure man. He knew just what he was doing. She slapped him on the buttock with the fresh tattoo.

"Ow." Vernon extracted his hand and rubbed his rear end. "Why'd you do that? You were enjoying yourself."

Bella crossed her arms in front of her as if somehow she could shield herself from the desire sparking between them. "You're impossible. Look out the window. We have an audience."

Outside, Bedford Street was humming with late afternoon foot traffic. Several preteen mini-hipsters in vintage hats and wildly striped stockings, with designer schoolbags slung over their shoulders, peered in at them.

Vernon gave them a thumbs-up, and they scampered off giggling. "Sex education 101. How to kiss." He held out his hand. "Come, you have a backroom, don't you?"

Bella squeezed her arms more tightly around her. "Not anymore. I added another tattoo station." She hesitated. "I've taken on an apprentice."

His eyes narrowed. "Who?"

"Fernando Pharaoh."

"A guy? No way. Don't want no guy hanging round here with you all the time."

Bella threw up her chin and stepped toward him. "This is what I hate. You pay absolutely no attention to me when I tell you about my work and my plans. Fernando Pharaoh is Fur Tree. Remember him? He's at least seven years younger than me. A kid. One of Ari's graffiti boys. The tall one. A very talented artist. You have nothing to fear. In fact"—she poked him in the chest with her index finger—"you have nothing to fear at all. I am not interested in a relationship. With you. With your buddy Gav out there. With anyone. Some hot young movie star could cross that threshold, and I wouldn't look twice. I've enough to do running my business. Creating my art."

Vernon hooked his thumbs in his waistband and smiled. "I'm glad you wouldn't look at anyone else. You've got me. Come—let me whisk you away from all this." He swiped at her, and she danced back out of reach. "Tell me you wouldn't like to fly down to my villa in the Caymans. We could lie on the beach and enjoy each other without"—he tilted his chin at the window where Gav stood glaring at them—"an audience."

"I grew up in a villa on an island. There's always an audience. Servants know where you hide all your dirty socks."

"Then how about my castle in the Catskills? Big thick walls and five hundred acres of forest surrounding it. You can run naked around the parapet."

"Thick walls. Parapets. Sounds like something an

ex-crook like you would need. Do you have knights with swords at the drawbridge? Archers at the arrow slits? Or more thugs like Gav out there with AK-47s?"

"I'll send them all away."

"You *do.*" She pushed past him. "Go away. I have a business to run."

He grabbed her arm and brought her to a halt. "You don't need to work, baby. You can have me and all my billions to do with as you will." His voice softened. "Marry me, Bella, and I'll cherish you forever."

She stared at his hand and pretended that his touch didn't set her blood afire—that his words didn't touch her heart. She shook her head. "No. Marriage to you is out of the question. Money isn't everything, Vernon. Especially dirty money. None of what you have is really yours. Give it away to a good cause. Do some honest work. Then I'll know you've truly gone straight. Now let go of me."

Someone rattled the latch. "Bella? You there?"

"That's Fur Tree now." She freed herself, rushed to the door, and unlocked it. Her new apprentice pushed into the studio, his portfolio under his arm. He placed the leather case on the coffee table and ran a hand through the closely cropped frizz on top of his head that had earned him his graffiti-crew handle.

He looked back and forth between them. "Sorry to interrupt. But I have the sketches for Vitaria. I thought you ought to look at them."

"Sure, no problem." Bella opened the door wider. "This *gentleman* was on his way out."

Vernon kissed her on the tip of her nose. "You got it bad for me, Bella baby. Look around. There ain't nobody loves you as much as I do. And money is money. It comes clean in the wash. I'll leave now. But I'm not going to give up, you know. Take your time. Reconsider my proposal and give me a call when you change your mind."

Vernon winked at her and then headed for the door. He stopped half in, half out and waved his finger at Fur Tree. "You take care of my Bella, now. She means the world to me. I want you to treat her like a queen. And don't you ever, *ever* hurt her." Then he turned on his heel and strode out to the waiting limo.

Bella collapsed on to the sofa and pulled Fishtail into her lap. The warm weight of the kitten did little to chase away the turmoil that clawed at her insides. She gathered the gray ball of fur in her arms. Vernon had just proposed to her. The thought took her breath away.

But she could never marry him. A crook? For most of his life, Vernon had lived a life outside the law. He might say he'd quit his shady operations. Hah, no way she believed that. He liked his billions too much.

Besides, even if he had gone legit, Vernon had enemies everywhere. Ice cold fear crept down her spine. Vicious enemies. She rubbed the hidden scar under her collarbone. Murderous enemies. She'd already met some.

Bella nuzzled her face in the kitten's soft fur and absorbed the vibrations of its purr. With Vernon in her life, she'd never feel safe.

Fur Tree picked up his portfolio and plopped down next to her. "You okay?"

Bella caressed the kitten between the ears and concentrated on drawing in each breath and then letting it out, the way her therapist had taught her to do when the terror threatened. "I will be. Let's see what you've done."

"Here." He opened the portfolio and took out a sketch. "Came up with this to cover up that pimp mark. Will it work?"

She took the drawing from his fingers and studied the delicately sketched phoenix, its wings spread wide. "It's brilliant. Vitaria will love it. I'll call Mercy House and let Daniela know she can bring the girl over tomorrow afternoon. It'll take about two hours to do, I should think." She handed it back. "I'll pay you for the time."

Fur Tree tucked the sketch away. "No. I can't wait to make that *maldito* mark into something that poor girl will be proud to wear."

Bella patted his hand. "I didn't mean for you to get involved in my little side line. You're just starting out. You shouldn't be working gratis."

"What you do here—with your Transformative Ink Project. It's absolutely wonderful. Makes me feel good to be a part of it. Those girls—when they see the names and marks of their pimps and abusers turned into our tats? Worth more than money."

She rested a hand on his shoulder. "That's why I took you on. Not only are you a gifted artist, but you have soul, Fur Tree. And your skill with the machine is just amazing for someone who used to splash paint on walls."

Her apprentice straightened and gave her a one-eye look. "*Cielos.* Deco boys don't splash paint. Bombing the side of a building with a Rusto—that takes tons of skill—as much as tatting." He rolled up his sleeve and displayed the intricate cuff encircling his bicep, the black swirls and loops and shapes vibrant against his rich brown skin. "It's the surface that's different—flesh. Ya gotta work over muscles, bones while the guy twitches. That's what's hard. And if I have any skill at it, I owe that to you. You've been a great teacher, Bella. El Toro might be King of Street Art, but you're the Queen of Tatting. Your boyfriend's not wrong about that—you being a queen."

Bella leaned back against the sofa and shaded her eyes with her forearm. "Speaking of Vernon—you may have made a mistake hooking up with me. Vernon has his nasty side, and he's not too happy with me right now." She sucked in a breath. "I just turned down his marriage proposal."

Fur Tree raised an eyebrow. "You refused Vernon? Nobody refuses *El Hombre* anything. No wonder he had steam coming out his nostrils."

"I'm sorry he threatened you."

"No worries. I've had dealings with the man." He jerked his sleeve down. "Look. I may not be as bulky as Mr. Looks-Good, but I can take care of myself. You don't hang off the sides of bridges and climb up walls and not develop some muscle and street smarts." Fur Tree glanced at her. "Besides, I know what happened. I was the one who tatted the fish over that scar. The question is, does Vernon know?"

Bella pressed her lips together. "I—"

There was a rustling at the door. Envelopes and magazines cascaded through the mail slot and plopped in a heap on the mermaid-shaped welcome mat. She put the cat down on the cushion next to her and rose. "Let's see what damage Mr. Postman brings us today." She scooped up the letters, catalogs, and junk flyers, and shuffled through them. "Bills, bills, and more bills.

Here"—she tossed the Eikens catalog to Fur Tree—"dream a little. Someday, you'll be a big name and have your own tattoo studio. Be able to afford all that delicious tat equipment."

Fur Tree caught the magazine and flipped it open. "This neon ink looks cool." He turned the page. "What's this? Got your name on it." He held up a folded piece of loose-leaf paper, the edge tattered as if torn hurriedly from a middle schooler's spiral notebook. He grinned. "Got yourself a young admirer? Or maybe your jilted boyfriend's sent a love note."

"Not Vernon's style. He'd be more likely to send a case of champagne." Bella took the paper from him.

Fur Tree laughed. "Champagne? More like Grey Goose."

"Yeah, well—" She flicked the note open and stopped.

"What is it?"

She stared at him. "Did you write this? Is this your idea of a joke?"

Fur Tree pushed himself up. "Why, what's it say?"

Fear whipped through her and formed a hard knot in the pit of her stomach. She forced herself to read it aloud. "*Stay away from Vernon Newell or you'll be sorry.*"

Fur Tree's eyes opened wide. "*Dios mío.* No, I wouldn't do that to you, Bella."

She slumped back against the counter, her heart racing and ran her fingertip over the Greek frets encircling her wrist. "Who then?" She held the scrap out to him. "Recognize the handwriting?"

Fur Tree fingered the note. "Look at how it's scrawled in pencil like the person was writing on a notebook stuck against their arm. Probably some mini-teen saw you with Mr. Looks-Good and got all jealous." He pressed the paper flat against his thigh. "Isn't that what teenage girls do when they crush on a guy."

"I wouldn't know." She turned away and made a show of sorting through the bills. "I never had a chance to be that kind of teenager. I wasn't allowed to date."

"Well, you didn't miss anything. I say toss it in the bin and let's get to work. I think I see your next appointment coming down the street. Skinny with glasses?"

Bella glanced out the window. "My three o'clock. Thank goodness." She refolded the note. "Tatting a huge spider on the guy's back is just the thing I need right now. All those legs. Ugh."

Fur Tree laughed. "I'll go get my equipment set up. Girl's coming in for her first tat early in the morning. Just a little thing, but mummy's coming too. Nothing like having a backseat driver while you work."

She gave him a pat on his back. "You'll handle it fine. Just bat those badass eyelashes and use that female-swooning voice of yours, and they'll both do whatever you say."

The door opened. Bella pasted on a smile for her pimply-faced, would-be Spiderman and waved him in. "Step right this way." She led him through the beaded curtain and gestured at the padded tat table. "Take off your tee and lie face down." She tossed the note on the counter. Fur Tree was surely right. The note was nothing but a schoolgirl prank.

She took a deep breath. Then why couldn't she get her hands to stop trembling?

Chapter 2

It was later than normal when Bella arrived home. The sun had long set, and the evening turned chill. A damp breeze wafted in off the East River and crept down her neck and up her sleeves. It was time to get out the wool sweaters and winter scarfs.

Shivering, she gathered her thin jacket tighter around her, inserted the key in the ornate lock, and let herself into her apartment building. She loved the old place, dating back to the turn of the nineteenth century, with its plaster pilasters and terrazzo floor. Even more, she loved her fourth floor apartment with its view of the New York City skyline. With the current boom in the Williamsburg real estate market, she'd never find another place as perfect.

She ran her palm along the oak banister as she trudged up the stairs. Here was another thing she wasn't willing to give up. If she married Vernon, she'd end up trapped in his electronically-surveilled, steel-encased penthouse when they weren't in the Caymans or in his castle in the Catskills, always surrounded by bodyguards, always looking over her shoulder. It was what she'd fled the island to escape. She'd hate it.

Outside her apartment door, she pulled off her gloves and rubbed her hands together. The shop had been busy toward the end. Two walk-ins and a make-up appointment helped the bottom line, but left her fingers cramped and her eyesight blurry. Vernon was right about one thing—she worked too hard.

Bella fumbled in her tote bag for her apartment key. Taking on Fur Tree as an apprentice should have made things easier. But after working alone for years, his constant chatter and her worry that he'd mess up a design wracked her nerves. But she could probably stand that. The problem was he knew too much about her, and now Vernon had threatened him. If anything happened to the boy, it would be her fault.

She swiped through the bag again. Where was the key chain with its clunky brass mermaid that was supposed to make it easy to find? She'd had the keys out just moments ago. Letting out a puff of air, Bella dumped out the tote. Pens, markers, colored pencils, and erasers mixed with lipstick, hand cream, loose change, a sketchbook, her cell phone, the ubiquitous bills, and finally, her keys tumbled to the floor. She fished up the key chain, and then squatted down to gather everything back up.

Bella lifted the sketch pad and caught sight of the crinkled loose-leaf note wedged between the bills. Pressure built in her chest. Fool. She should have thrown the dratted thing in the trash bin at the studio. Her therapist would have insisted. She snatched it up, ready to toss it the minute she got inside.

Everything back into the bag, Bella inserted the key in the lock, and clicked the door open. Her orange tabby sat peering up at her with his huge green eyes. She smiled down. "Been waiting for me have you, Pussyballs?" The cat bounced up on the arm of the side chair and pawed at her. "Right-o. Dinner coming up."

She kicked off her wet heels, slung her tote onto

the brown leather sofa, and then fingered the ripped edge of the crumbled note. A kid's prank—nothing more. She squeezed it into a ball and tossed it at the cat. "There. Bat that around instead of clawing the upholstery."

Pussyballs sniffed the paper wad and then abandoned it to sit at Bella's feet, his tail whipping back and forth. "Oh, you little beggar. It's coming." She scrounged a can opener out of the dish drain and opened a can of cat food. The off-smell of processed fish filled the room.

"Dinner is served, your highness." Holding her breath, Bella dumped the foul-smelling stuff into the cat's bowl, and then leaned back against the counter. Pussyball's little pink tongue lapped up the gray goop with enthusiasm.

Ugh. Was this how she would spend the rest of her life? Coming home to an empty apartment. No husband to wrap her arms around. No children to pull her skirts. Only a cat that cared more about filling its belly than paying attention to her.

Bella surveyed her little nest, filled with all the things she loved. The mirrored Indian pillows bought at the local bazaar. The vintage silk shawls splurged on in a moment of weakness. Her picture of Eudokia, painted when she still believed she could be a better artist than her brother. And the beautiful collection of art books that weighed down her coffee table and provided inspiration for her tattoo designs.

Blast it, Vernon was not her whole life. She had her tattoo business. She had a comfortable home. She had—she glanced down at Pussyballs licking his bowl clean—she had her cats.

Bella rinsed the cat food stink from her hands, retrieved her laptop from the counter, and sprawled on the sofa. With a click, she opened her e-mail account and checked the day's messages. Nothing exciting. Ads from tattoo suppliers. Politicians asking for votes. Receipts for orders. Nothing personal. She turned to Facebook and scrolled through her feed. Her skin art buddies showed off their most recent designs. The owner of the neighboring boutique had posted a picture of her and her family on a Disney vacation in Florida, the kids sitting on either side of a girl wearing an unnaturally red wig and a mermaid costume. The fake Ariel looked stiff and emotionless, like a cardboard cutout of a woman who couldn't wait for her day posing with sticky-fingered, fawning children to be over.

Yikes. Was that how she looked? Fake? Disgruntled? Indifferent? Bella yanked off her wig and leaned back. She tapped her fingers on the edge of the laptop. No. She cared. She listened to her clients and created tattoos that made them happy. She helped abused women and saved stray cats. She loved what she did.

But she had no real friends. No past. She toyed with the wig and then tossed it across the room. She'd lived in hiding for so many years that now that she was out in the open, she was still hidden. Is that why she was so vulnerable to Vernon's touch? Why refusing his proposal had felt like a stab to her own heart?

Wait, she did have someone who cared. She opened Skype. Good, her brother was online. She clicked the call button and waited for him to answer. Funny, they'd been estranged for years and yet now, she felt closer to him than anyone else in the world. She wished she had reached out to him sooner—before Vernon had found her and all the bad things happened.

The screen opened, and there he was, smiling at her from the battered face that made him look like some defaced Greek statue. He'd been so handsome once. She leaned in and waved. "Ari, how you doing?"

"*Oraía, adelphí mou. Polí oraía.*"

"Talk English. My Greek is rusty."

"Rusty? The girl who mastered five languages says she's rusty? Ha." He shook his finger at her. "But as you wish—I am fine. And you?"

"Okay—how's the painting going?"

"No go. My hands are shot. I'm lucky to be able to feed myself. The painting might be in my head, but my fingers are too stiff to put the paint on the canvas with any semblance of skill."

"You got to keep at it. That's what the physical therapist said."

Her brother shrugged. "*Ti na kánoume.* It will be what it will be. Life's a labyrinth with twists and turns we can't predict, and we have to do the best with what we find around the corner." He held up his deformed hands. "Guess in my case, I met the Minotaur. Anyway, it doesn't matter. Melissa and I are packing for her ethnographic research in the Pindos. Going to trade this cozy sheep hut for a freezing cold, falling-down stone house on a mountainside. She's convinced me to try photography. I only need one working finger to snap digital pictures." He mimicked snapping a photo. "If nothing else, I can document her research. Maybe publish one of those coffee table books you love so much. How's this sound for a title: *The Tattooed Ladies of Greece*? And you—how are you doing? You look troubled."

She swallowed hard. She never shared her feelings, but of all the people she knew, only Ari would understand. "I refused a marriage proposal today—from Vernon."

"Ah. I wondered why you called so early."

"Oops. You in bed? I forgot the time zone. Sorry if I woke you."

"Den perázi. No problem. You can call anytime. Besides, I was awake. I've been helping the shepherd here with the milking. Tasos likes to have the sheep out grazing before dawn. We start at five thirty."

Bella gave him her patented little-sister look. "You're milking? With your hands?"

"No. I stand at the back of the milking pen and drive the ewes through the eye so he can milk them."

She smiled. "We used to do that when we were kids. I can still remember the smell—warm wool, fresh dung, spilled sheep milk, and us flicking our willow whips and shouting '*Tsk. Tsk'* so they'd move."

Ari shook his head. "We had good times together growing up on the island, didn't we?"

"Hi, Bella." Ari's new wife poked her head over his shoulder.

Drat. They hadn't been asleep. Melissa's long black hair was tangled, her lips well-kissed. Her brother draped his arm around his wife and pulled her closer.

Bella looked away. That's the kind of love she wanted. Gentle. Trusting. Safe. Not life on the edge with a hardened criminal who claimed he'd gone straight. No one would be sending Melissa threatening notes. Lucky girl. But she deserved love after that horrid day—Bella pushed the memory out of her head and smiled at her sister-in-law. "*Yia sou.*"

"Hi to you, too." Melissa snuggled closer to Ari. "How's Fur Tree doing?"

"Great. My clientele has morphed from being mainly bruisers who want to be tattooed by a Siren to sighing Fashion Institute students wanting to be tatted by a hot rapper look-alike. Some days the waiting room looks like a scene from a young adult novel. Bulky gym-nuts in muscle tees and anorexic fashion mavens in leotards. Been some strange couples walking out together."

"It's not what's on the outside that counts, Bella." Melissa kissed Ari on the scar running down the side of his face. "So business is looking up?"

She rubbed her temple. "Not really. I had to lay out a lot to upgrade the studio and set up another tat station for Fur Tree. Put a major dent in my bank account. Vernon wanted to pay, but I wouldn't let him. Maybe I should have."

Ari frowned. "No, you did right not to let him tie your business up in loans. I've never been sure he's the right man for you. He *is* a murdering bastard"—Ari shrugged—"but then so am I."

Bella rubbed her wrist with her thumb. "You did what was needed to save us."

"Still, Vernon has to hate me. But if you told me you loved him and wedding bells were ringing, I would never let bad blood stand in the way. Still, I can't say I'm not relieved you turned him down. It will complicate financial matters, but we'll figure it out."

"Financial matters?"

"Up to now Vernon's been paying the upkeep and

taxes on the villa, paying the staff, and covering the cost of the boat and helicopter. It's unlikely he will continue to do it if you've rejected him. He's not known to be a forgiving man."

"I never thought. Is the villa his?"

"Everything's in your name. At least, it better be. He promised to change the deed before I left. So the cost is all yours. I'd pay, but my money's gone. I tied up all I had in the trust to protect the village and the seals. And I'll never paint again. Not paintings worth hundreds of thousands of dollars. That much is clear. We'll have to sell the helicopter."

Bella pursed her lips. "But the villagers rely on it for medical emergencies."

"The copter's not the newest. Costs a fortune to maintain."

She wanted to scream. Damn Vernon, this was all his fault. He'd made her whole family and an entire Greek village dependent on him just to punish her brother for chasing him out of her arms and off the island all those years ago. Such arrogance. Put them at risk for his personal whim. No wonder he thought she'd just acquiesce to being his trophy wife. Well, she could do something about that.

"I'll get you the money to maintain the helicopter."

Ari's jaw tightened. "How Bella? You just said—"

She eyed the sketch book sticking out of her tote "I have an offer from a television production company. They're producing a TV drama series, *Secret Ink,* with a tattoo artist hero and have asked me to submit possible designs.

Melissa's eyebrows shot up. "You're going to be a television star?"

"No." Bella covered her mouth to stifle a giggle. "They need someone to design the tattoos the actors will wear during the show. They will not be permanent, of course. I would be drawing the sketches and producing the stencils for the makeup artists."

Melissa clapped her hands. "That sounds terrific. Something you should do, regardless of the money. A chance to showcase your creativity. Imagine, people all over the world will see your designs."

"I have to send them a complete set of sketches by the end of the month. That's only two weeks away. I wasn't sure I really wanted to do it, but now—now that Vernon's out of my life, I'll have plenty of time."

Ari tipped his chin up. "You don't have to take the job if you don't want to. I can sell the painting I did of Mother and you on the beach that's hanging in the villa."

She loved that painting—her beautiful mother with flowing black hair silhouetted against blue sky and silver sand, holding her tiny hand as she waded in the water. Her mother had been happy in that picture. "No, don't. I'm sure if I put my mind to it, I'll beat out any competition. With a little effort, the money's mine."

"You know," Ari said. "I always gave you a hard time about tattooing. That it was a waste of your talents. But I was wrong. You're a true artist."

"Big brother admitting he's wrong." Bella tossed back her head. "Will wonders never cease."

"I was such an arrogant bastard as a kid, wasn't I?"

"*Óxi.* Goodness no. You were the best brother. At least, until you left me there alone with Papa."

"I'm sorry for that."

She flicked her hand back. "That's sheep dung

under the bridge."

Ari wrapped his arm around his wife. "Melissa's been giving me an education. I never appreciated the skill needed to work on quivering human flesh while keeping everything sterile."

Bella grinned. "Didn't know how easy you had it, did you?"

Ari laughed. "Yeah, all I had to do was drag a canvas and paints down to the beach and wallow in the sand."

"And create masterpieces worth thousands of dollars. I'll never earn what you did. Your paintings were feasts for the eye. No wonder you were world-renowned."

"More dung under the bridge."

Melissa poked her head into the frame. "I've been encouraging him to use his mouth together with his fingers to paint, but he refuses."

Ari gave her a quick kiss. "I have better things to do with my mouth."

Bella closed her eyes. "Enough, guys. I'll let you get back to whatever you were doing."

Melissa laughed, then pressed her fingers together and gave the traditional palm in Greek wave.

Ari rubbed his chin. "Do the TV show, Bella. Not for the money, but because you are a fantastic artist, and you deserve the recognition. Now try to sleep, *adelphí mou. Kaliníhta.*" The Skype window closed with a ding.

Bella set the laptop aside and lay back on the sofa. Two weeks. Fourteen days to read the scripts, do the research, and then work her wig off. They wanted over seventy tattoos for chests, legs, arms, and backs, mostly for the three main actors, but also a variety of designs to be put on the customers. Hours of drawing. Between that and the business she wouldn't even have time to sleep. Not that she was sleeping all that well anyway.

Bella shoved the sketch pad deeper into the tote. If she got the job, she would need to be on the set to provide instruction for the actors who would be pretending to tat. She pushed herself up and dragged herself into the bedroom. How would she fit that into her already full schedule running the shop? She flopped down on the bed. But she had to do it. The villagers couldn't lose their lifeline to the mainland.

Poor Fur Tree. She hoped he was ready to shoulder the bulk of the work for the next two weeks.

****

Bella woke drenched in sticky sweat, her heart pounding, her throat dry from screaming. She could still see the blood and feel the zip ties cutting into her wrists. Still smell the bilious stink of the cellar in her nostrils. Still feel the knife tip piercing her skin.

She sat up and pressed her palm against her thumping heart. It was only a dream. But one that never stopped. Never went away.

More than a year had passed and still the horror of that day clawed through her like some demon eating her from the inside out. Bella rubbed her hands down her face. Post-traumatic stress, her therapist called it. She'd thought only soldiers suffered from PTSD, but according to the therapist, so did kidnap victims.

Despite her efforts to use imagery rehearsal therapy and recreate an altered version of the nightmare, the fear lay there under the surface and erupted the moment she fell asleep. Bella glanced back at the twisted, wrinkled pillowcase and threw back the sheets.

Enough. If she didn't do something, it would be another sleepless night.

She rolled out of bed, drew her favorite chenille robe over her shoulders, and wandered into the kitchen. Her feet curled against the cold tiles. Chills tiptoed up her legs and settled in the pit of her stomach. For a few seconds, she hesitated, and then she took the bottle of sleeping tablets from the cabinet over the sink and twirled it in her hand. The pills clattered inside the plastic cylinder, rattling like a snake ready to attack, the sound ominous in the dark.

Bella set the container on the counter top. She hated the dizziness the pills cast over her as much as she hated diving into deep water. If she took them, she'd sleep all night and be a zombie in the morning. It would be hours before she'd be able to tat a straight line at the studio.

She shook her head and sat down on the kitchen stool. Her customers deserved more. They expected to get amazing tattoos from the steady hands and clear-seeing eyes of the most popular tattoo artist in Williamsburg, Brooklyn. But how could they when she could hardly sleep?

Bella propped her head up with her hands and stared at the pill bottle with its blue and white pharmacy label and jaunty little white cap. Behind her, the clock on the wall ticked away the minutes. Outside, the street lay quiet. Williamsburg prided itself on its rollicking night life, but even hipsters slept in the dark hours after midnight. Everyone but her.

In the distance, a siren blared, then faded away. Well, not everyone slept. This was the time when criminals roamed the streets. Before the kidnapping—before Vernon had come back into her life—she'd never thought about the danger lurking in the grimy alleys and basements of the buildings around her. Now she thought about it all the time.

Bella flicked the pill bottle with her finger. There was danger here too. She flicked it again. The bottle, with its promise of oblivion, tipped. The white plastic cap popped off, and tiny pink pills clattered across the countertop and rained to the floor. She gave herself a shake and bent down to pick them up.

At that instant, her cell phone rang. The perky little tune, so cheery during the daytime, sent an icy bolt down her spine to meet the cold knot in her gut. For a long moment, Bella ignored it, waiting for the caller to give up or be sent to voice mail.

It stopped, and she let out the air trapped in her chest. Then it started again, and she bit her lip and pushed away from the counter.

Pussyballs wrapped around her legs. "Well, kitty, who's calling at"—she squinted at the wall clock—"two in the morning?" Her heartbeat ratcheted up. No one phoned at this hour unless it was an emergency. Every muscle in her body stiffened. What if the shop were on fire? The police calling? Vernon gunned down in an alley?

Bella jumped to her feet and tore through her tote bag searching for her cell. Her wallet, her apartment keys, her sketchpad went flying. She found the phone just as it stopped ringing.

She unlocked the screen, tapped the phone log, then stared down at the caller's name. *No.* The man with that name was dead.

He had to be.

Bella read the name again, and dropped the phone. Heart thundering in her ears, adrenaline flooding her senses, she crawled into a corner of the couch, drew up her knees, and wrapped her arms around them until she was curled as tight as a fist.

Wait. The pills. She opened her hand and peered down. Somehow she'd managed to hold on to two of them. With trembling breath, she popped them in her mouth and choked them down. Anything was better than thinking Theo Tuccio was still alive.

****

When she raised her head again, the pale gray light of dawn crept through the gaps in the drapes, and down below the early morning traffic emitted the low rumble that would soon become a roar as the city awoke.

The apartment had chilled. Gooseflesh covered her body. Only her feet were warm, thanks to the furry cat blanket curled around her ankles. She leaned over and picked Pussyballs up. "Sorry to give you such an uncomfortable pillow." He wiggled his way under her arm and rubbed against her. She ran her hand down his sleek fur. His purr grew louder. "Yeah, I know. You think it's time to eat. You always think it's time to eat."

The cat jumped down and headed for its food dish.

Bella rose to follow, shaking her head to rid it of grogginess. Her phone lay on the coffee table where she'd dropped it. She picked it up and swiped her finger across the lock screen, hoping she'd dreamed the ghostly call. But no, the name was there in the phone log like a bruise that wouldn't fade.

Her stomach roiled and heaved, and she rushed to the bathroom and hung her head over the toilet. But all that came up was a trickle of bile that burned her throat and nose.

She stood up and leaned on the sink, shaking her head. Bella Bell had faced down a lot worse than a phone call from a dead guy. She would not be turned into a pathetic weakling. She filled a glass of water and gulped it down. There had to be an explanation. The man was dead. Her brother had killed him in front of her eyes.

Or had it all been a lie?

If anyone knew what was going on it would be Vernon. She moved back into the living room and peered out the window. The sky was still dark. The street light still burned. Dare she call him? He'd think she'd capitulated. Wanted him.

She dropped the curtain and straightened her shoulders. She wanted him all right. She wanted answers. She wanted to know why dead men were calling her and threatening notes appeared in her mail.

Hands shaking, she punched in Vernon's cell number. It rang once. Twice. She imagined him holding her, kissing her. His low, rumbling voice whispering in her ear. No, she couldn't talk to him. Not yet. She was still addicted to the man.

She tapped the phone off and curled back up on the sofa. *Tomorrow*. Tomorrow, she'd send him an e-mail—a nicely worded formal request.

At that moment, the phone in her hand rang. Vernon returning her call? She hesitated. Then flicked it on.

A low pitched voice spoke through heavy static. "Does Vernon know what you did?" A frisson of fear crept down her spine and burrowed deep into her core.

She tossed the cell phone onto the floor and buried herself under the silk shawls, struggling to breathe.

Forget all the reasons why Vernon was the wrong man for her. She needed him. She needed him now.

Chapter 3

Vernon looked up at Bella's fourth floor apartment window. For a moment, a faint light shone through the blind slats. He glanced at his watch. Four in the morning. She was having nightmares again. He paced back and forth on the pavement below.

Gav leaned out the window of the limo. "So are you staying or leaving, Vern?"

Vernon rocked back on his heels and stared at Bella's window. "Think there's any hope?"

"Lady likes you right enough, but she doesn't trust you."

Vernon ran a hand down his face. "I've gone about this all wrong, haven't I?"

Gav gave him a hard look. "Well, women don't usually marry men who kidnap them."

"But she wouldn't let me near her or give me a chance to talk to her."

"And she's not talking to you now. So unless you plan to kidnap her again, let's go home." Gav got out of the limo and opened the rear car door. "We've been freezing our bums out here all night while I have a lovely wife waiting for me at home."

Vernon rested his hand on the door handle and put a foot inside. "Lucky you."

"Yeah, lucky me. Lovisa knows what's what. That one"—he tipped his head toward the window—"is too stubborn by half. Find yourself another. Plenty more women out there who'd give a rich guy like you the moon."

"But none—" Vernon's cell squawked, and he yanked it from his pocket. His heart sped up. "It's Bella." He swiped it on at the same time he waved Gav off. "Go. Just go." He spoke into the phone. "Bella baby, I knew you'd call. Buzz me in, and I'll be right up—Bella?" He looked at the phone. Hell, she'd hung up on him.

He called her back. Let it ring and ring. No answer. Her recorded voice mail came on. God, he loved her voice with its slight hint of an accent. He loved everything about her. From the moment she'd given him her virginity all those years ago, he'd been bonded to her. He had many women since. But none of them smelled right or felt right under his hands. None of them fit curled up against his body. And none of them knew just how to touch him to bring him to his knees. He couldn't live without her. All he needed to do was convince her of that fact.

He squinted up at her apartment window. She wouldn't have called if she hadn't needed him. He stuffed the phone into his pocket and pulled out his handy dandy lock pick. Something wasn't right, and no door could keep a former cat burglar from his treasure.

In less than half a minute, he had the inner door open. He slipped inside, making a mental note to have a locksmith come by in the morning and put in a high security lock. Behind him, the door closed with a soft click. He turned toward the staircase and came to an abrupt halt. Bella's landlady, clad in a silk robe covered with dragon embroidery, fluffy pink bunny slippers peeking out from underneath, stood in his way. The four-foot-tall woman glared at him, shiny black baseball bat held high over her head, the old tribal tattoos on her face vivid against her skin.

Damn. Caught in the act. He gave her his most charming smile. "Evening, Zeya Aung."

She narrowed her eyes. "How'd you get in, Vernon, sir?"

He'd have to lie his way past her. "I have a key."

"Against rules. Bella doesn't break rules. Caused a big problem last time. I have to put her out if she does that. Only tenants have keys. You're no tenant."

For a moment, he considered telling her Bella had broken the rules and given him a key. If she were kicked out, Bella might consider moving in with him. But no. His independent-minded tattoo artist would hate him for it. He gave Zeya his biggest smile and lied again. "My bad. I snuck her key and had it copied. I wanted to bring her a surprise." He pulled the velvet ring box out of his pocket and opened the lid.

Zeya's eyes widened, and she lowered the bat. "Nice surprise, Vernon sir." Then she raised it again. "Wrong time. Bella sleeps. Everyone sleeps. You want to give her that ring you come back later. *In daylight.*" She waved the bat at him. *"Ring bell. Act a gentleman. Ask her out to a fine dinner. Treat her like a lady."

He shifted from one foot to the other, thinking fast. He clasped his hands against his heart. "Ah, Zeya, I'm a man in love. I can't wait till the sun comes up."

The bat lowered again. "Okay. Love is good. But just this one time." She walked up to him and poked her finger in his belly. "You treat her right. I want to see a happy smiling Bella in the morning. Not a sad, dark-eyed girl." She stepped back. "Now go. Give her joy."

"You're an angel, Zeya." He kissed her on the forehead and with a wink over his shoulder, dashed up the stairs.

On the fourth floor landing, he hesitated, but only for a moment. Low moans emanated from the apartment. Bella's moans. Damn. He pulled out the lock pick and silently turned the tumblers. He pushed the door open a crack and peered in. In the gloom, he could make out Bella curled in a ball on the sofa, her head buried beneath a swatch of cloth like an old homeless woman sheltering from the rain.

He bit his lip. He'd done that to her. Reduced a strong, smart woman to someone afraid to sleep at night. Damn. He'd rather see her angry.

He crossed the room, and in one sweeping motion, swooped her up, and set her in his lap, He nestled his head in her hair, inhaled the enticing citrus and patchouli perfume that scented all her clothing. His mouth brushed her ear, skimmed along her jaw. "Bella, my love."

She stiffened in his arms, and made a weak attempt to push him away. "Go away, Vernon."

He clasped her tighter. "Hush. I'm here. You're safe now." He readjusted her in his arms and lowered his mouth to hers. At the touch of his tongue, her lips clamped together like a wary virgin's. "Ahhh, Bella," he whispered against her lips. "Let me in. Let me take your nightmares away." He pressed his lips against hers, licked at the seam. "Please."

He felt the moment all the fight went out of her. Her body relaxed. Her mouth opened beneath his. Gently, he deepened the kiss. He slipped his tongue inside the warmth of her mouth. She tasted like mint. She tasted like Bella.

Her hand slid up and tangled in his hair. She tugged him closer and molded her lips to his. She might say she didn't want him, but he knew better.

She was his woman for now and always. But how would he ever convince her? Words didn't work with his wild siren. He had to show her with his body how much he worshipped her. Prove that he could be gentle. Prove he could keep her safe.

He moved his mouth down, planting small kisses along her neck. With one hand, he pushed her robe back and ran his fingertips down the long smooth line of her shoulder, the vulnerable V where the clavicles met. His kisses followed his fingers, licking and blowing until she quivered in his arms. She leaned in, offering herself to him, and he murmured against the tender flesh. "Yes. That's my girl."

"Vernon." The gentle breath of his name on her lips nearly broke his control. His cock hardened and strained beneath his jeans. He wanted her fiercely. But she was too defenseless, too frightened. She needed to be comforted, not possessed. Warmed, not set afire. With trembling hands, he picked her up, carried her into her bedroom, and laid her on the bed.

He slipped her robe off and nested her in the swirl of vibrant red and orange bedding. Then he stood back and took in her slender neck, her breasts that fit his hands so perfectly, the deep rose nipples against her warm olive skin, the concave curve between her waist and her hips where he loved to rest his hand, her long toned legs, and the nest of dark curly hair between her thighs that hid his favorite place to be in the whole world. The only place he felt whole.

His cock pressed harder against his jeans. God, how he wanted her. Always wanted her. He sat down on the bed beside her and brushed his fingers down the side of her cheek. Her skin beneath his fingertips was soft. Warm. Alive. He had come so close to losing her that day in the cellar, the day that still haunted her. The day he'd let her down. She was right not to trust him.

The knot in his stomach cinched, stole his breath. He tugged the sheet over her, and tucked it around her neck. "Get some sleep, Bella. I'll sit right here and keep watch. Nothing's going to hurt you."

She peered up at him through her dark eyelashes and seized his hand. "Make me forget. Make love to me."

"Ah, Bella." He knew he shouldn't. She was too vulnerable. She wasn't thinking straight. But it had been too long since he'd sunk into her warmth and felt whole; he couldn't turn her invitation down. In record time, he shucked his jacket, pulled his T-shirt over his head. Then he was kneeling on the bed and kissing her again.

Her fingertips ran down his chest, circled his nipples. "Take me, Vernon. Take me now."

He groaned and pushed her legs apart with his knee. Leaning on one elbow, he moved his hand lower and settled his hand in her nest of curls, found the heat of her, and swirled his fingers in the figure eight pattern she loved.

Beneath him, she arched her back and made small noises of pleasure. All the while driving him crazy as she alternatively pinched and brushed his nipples. He captured her tormenting hands in his and lifted them over her head. "Don't move. Let me."

He licked and sucked his way down her neck and over her breasts. He caught each nipple in his teeth and bit lightly. She wiggled beneath him. Her breathing deepened, became huskier and more sibilant. He wanted to mark her, claim her in some primeval way, declare to the world that this woman was his, and no one dare touch her.

But she was already marked with her own designs. He ran his tongue along the lines of the siren tattoo that started above her breastbone, fishtailed between her breasts, spread across her belly, and curled into a flowing tail across the top of her left thigh.

He licked and sucked his way to her inner core. Showing her how much he cherished her. Beneath him, she gasped. He whispered, "Yes, that's my sweet, my *duššo*. Let me take you to heaven. Come now, my hot little girl, my *devojka*."

Her body trembled. Her breath hitched and then she came, convulsing against him over and over. Her hands came down and pulled at his shoulders.

"You. I want you." She arched against him. "Now. In me now."

It was all the invitation he needed. He unzipped his jeans and pushed them down. They caught on his sneakers. Damn. He bent over and fumbled with the laces. Socks. Boxers. Yanked them off and tossed everything on the floor. At the last moment, he remembered the condom. He worked it out of his jeans pocket and stared at the bright red square.

He could give her a child. She would marry him for the child's sake. Or maybe not. She was one feisty woman.

"What's wrong?" Bella's fingers swirled down his chest and touched his cock. Her hand wrapped around him and all thought fled. He tore the packet open and slipped it on.

Then he was leaning over her, breathing in the blend of warm oranges and patchouli mixed with the heady spiciness of her arousal.

He spread her legs, found her opening, and drove inside. He tried to go slow. Stick to his resolve and be gentle. But she thrust her hips against him, clamped her fingernails into his shoulders, urging him on. Her breath came in huge gasps.

Their bodies slapped against each other faster and faster. The headboard of the bed banged against the wall. Her inner muscles encircled him pulsating, sending ripples of pleasure shooting through him.

They came together with a powerful convulsion that zapped through him and left him feeling as weak as a kitten. He had just enough strength to lever off her and roll to her side.

Her overheated body still shaking with aftershocks, Bella nestled beside him, making tiny sounds of pleasure. He reached down and pulled the coverlet over them. The aroma of their mixed scents surrounded them.

He slid his hand across her back and drew small circles and letters, spelling out his love in every language he knew. Beneath his hand, she grew still, hovering on the fringes of sleep. It was at this moment, in the aftermath of sex, that she was her true self—the hard shell she showed the world cracked.

He breathed into her hair. "You are so beautiful, Bella. You don't need that awful red wig, that garish eye makeup. You don't have to hide any more. I love you. I would die for you. Marry me. Grow old with me."

She curled tighter around him and made a soft murmur against his chest. The words inaudible, a mere vibration that rippled through him. It didn't sound like no. Hope rose. "Hush, *devojka*. Sleep. I'll stand guard and keep the nightmares away, I promise—for as long as I live."

Chapter 4

Bella woke, warm and cozy, the aroma of strong, bitter Greek coffee tantalizing her nose. She pushed herself up. *Vernon.* Conjured from her dreams. He knew just how she liked her coffee. She ran her hand through the frizz on top of her head. Damn the man. He'd weaseled his way in somehow and made her forget everything. Her body trembled, her inner muscles clenched. His scent, his touch, his voice brought her to her knees—she glanced around—well, to her bed. She sat upright. Drat it all, Vernon Newell was like a drug she couldn't do without.

She slipped on one of her flowing vintage skirts in her signature rusty gold, yanked a black turtle neck over her head, pulled on her favorite nubby, turquoise blue wool sweater, and then picked up her wig. She'd worn it for over eight years, first as a disguise, then later as part of the persona, Bella Bell—the wild red-headed siren she'd created to make her business stand out from the crowd.

Siren. She touched the long red strands of the wig and then worked her fingers through the frizzy curls covering her skull. She'd always hated her hair, black as charcoal, wiry as dried seaweed. It looked nothing like the smooth sleek styles models sported in the *Vogue* and *Elle* magazines she'd pored over as a motherless teenager living with her bitter, critical father. She dropped her chin. Vernon was wrong. She was no beauty.

She plopped the wig on her head and tugged it down so it fit snugly. She straightened her neck, and the familiar weight of it settled and formed around her head like a helmet. Nothing wrong with wearing a wig. All the Hasidic women in the community wore them. She fit right in.

Now for the face. She smeared on her eyeliner, feathered the mascara over her thick lashes, and added glittery aubergine eye shadow. Holding her fingers as steady as possible, she outlined her lips in Heatwave Red and filled them in.

She stood back and glared at herself in the mirror. There. She no longer felt naked. She turned on her heel ready to face Vernon and what she'd whispered last night. She clutched her stomach and faltered.

****

In the kitchen alcove, Vernon was frying an omelet. Egg shells, milk splatters, and Feta cheese crumbs littered the counter. The aroma of toasted bread filled the room. It was far too domestic for her taste. She picked up a dish towel and slapped his butt. "Morning, Vern."

He grinned at her. "Morning, *devojka*."

She wrinkled her nose. "Speak English. None of that Macedonian crap. You're a Jersey boy. Don't try to pretend you're some exotic creature from some downtrodden place. You grew up in Upper Saddle River, for heaven's sake."

"Spent my summers with my *baba* in Huma on the Greek border. Besides, *you* speak Greek."

She slapped him again with the towel. "Never."

He took the cloth from her hand, leaned in, and gave her a kiss. "You do when you're in the throes of passion, my dear. Let's see." He tapped his finger to his lips. "I seem to remember a *palikari mou* and an *agape mou* and *akoma*." He kissed her again. "Lots of *akoma*. More. More. More. You're insatiable, darling."

"Damn you, Vernon. Maintain my illusions, at least." She squinted at him. "How'd did you get in? If Zeya—"

He held up his hand. "No, not her fault. She protected you like a she-tiger. I talked my way in." He reached into his pocket and pulled out a velvet box.

Bella's heart speeded up. "What—"

"Come on—you can't deny we can't keep our hands off one another. It's time to let me do the right thing. Go straight in the most important way. Please let me make *this*"—he gave her another quick kiss on the lips—"what we have—legal. I made a mess of it at the studio. I can do better." He opened the box and took out the ring.

It was magnificent. The huge diamond was surrounded by blue tear-drop shaped sapphires—her favorite gem stone. A diamond-studded, engraved siren encircled the wide platinum band. He held it out to her on a trembling palm.

Bella's heart skipped a beat. Nothing made Vernon tremble. On the surface, he was hard, rough, and decisive. At times, insensitive, even cruel. All the things she hated about him. But underneath was a little boy begging for approval, searching for a place to belong. That was the Vernon she loved.

For a moment, she wondered what had changed him into the vicious criminal he'd been for so many years. It wasn't something they ever talked about. Did she have it in her power to find that lost boy and heal him like he hoped she would?

Vernon was a ruthless man. He lived by trampling weaker men into the ground. He seized what he wanted when he wanted it. Command radiated off him. It was there in the way he held his finely chiseled chin, in the way his muscles flexed when he moved, in the way he placed his feet so firmly on the ground. He was a man used to owning his space. A man used to wielding power over others. As Gav said: A boss man.

She peered into his silver disk eyes. Expecting Vernon to change was like asking a mountain lion to become a house cat. What was it her mama always said when Papa had been unreasonable? That's right: "Trying to force a man's feet into one shoe was doomed to failure." No. Marrying Vernon was a recipe for disaster. But dear God, she really wanted to say yes.

"Bella." Vernon went down on one knee.

She grabbed his shoulder and tried to make him stand up. "No. You don't have to—"

He held out the ring on a wavering hand. "Marry me, Bella. Make me the happiest ex-crook alive. I'll do anything you say. You want to keep tattooing guys' butts, go ahead. I won't interfere with your business. I promise. Wear the wig. Be yourself. I don't want you to change. All I ask is that you wake up in bed next to me every morning and let me pamper you in all the ways possible."

The sulfuric reek of burning eggs filled the room. He jerked around and shoved the pan off the burner. He cast her a sad puppy look. "Besides, I have a professional chef. And neither one of us can cook." He took her hand in his and found her ring finger. "Surely a match made in heaven. Say yes."

Before he could slide it on, she snatched the ring from him, and squeezed it between her fingers. The sharpness of the stone stung. A shiver snaked its way up her spine. "Vernon. Is that freaking bastard who attacked me and Melissa and destroyed Ari's paintings, really dead and buried?"

He rose from his knee and stepped back. "What the hell question is that? You mean my brother Theo?"

"Yeah him. Who else?"

"Damn it, Bella. Of course he is. You were there."

"I didn't see the body. See him buried. You whisked him away before the police arrived. Did you hold a funeral?" She let the ring drop back into his hand.

Vernon's face flushed. "I didn't want you to see. The body was—well, in bad shape. I wanted to save you that." He wrapped his arms around her. "I'm sorry, I see that was a mistake. There was no funeral. But yes, he's dead and buried. In the family mausoleum in Calvary Cemetery over in Queens. We put him next to my father. 'Like with like' my step-mama said. We can go visit the vault if you wish."

"Take me there. I need to know."

"Now?"

She could do no more than nod. The words stuck in her throat.

"What's wrong, Bella?"

"He—he—phoned me last night."

"*No.* Impossible. He's dead."

Bella stepped across the room and swiped her phone off the coffee table. She flicked it on and held it out to him. "Here. Look."

Vernon glanced at the name. "Someone's using his phone or a phone set to his name." He took the cell from her and tapped it.

"What are you doing?"

"Ringing back. Let's see who's on the other end."

Bella bit her lip and waited, her body cold all over.

"No answer." He shrugged. "Didn't expect one. Ghosts don't make phone calls." He shook the phone. "But people trying to make mischief do, and I won't stand for that. Not when they frighten the woman I love." He gathered her against him.

She pressed back, unable to stop shaking, and concentrated on breathing in and out. She hated losing control in front of him.

Vernon hugged her tighter. "Whoever the bastard is, he'll pay." He eyed the burnt eggs. "Look, breakfast is ruined. Let's go grab something to eat, and then I'll take you to Calvary. Visiting cemeteries is not something I want to do on an empty stomach. Hate those places. Too many friends buried there."

There was a slight tremor beneath his eye. He didn't want to go, she realized. But he would do that for her. Despite his cockiness, she loved this man. She rested her ear against his chest, listened to his heart beating, and worked at tucking away her fears. "It's okay, I believe you. Theo Tuccio is dead." She wiggled out of his arms. "You're right. It must be someone pulling a prank." A little spear of fear pricked her conscience. The note. Tell him about the note—notes. It hadn't been the first. But she couldn't.

Fur Tree swore he hadn't written it, but there was something about the way he found it so conveniently in the magazine that set her on edge. Vernon would kill the poor guy if he had. Or at the least, make her fire him.

And the others? Well, even a billionaire crime lord couldn't kill ghosts.

Chapter 5

Five minutes later, they were downstairs and in the lobby. Zeya Aung stuck her head out the door of her apartment.

"Happy day, Bella." Zeya's eyes focused on her hand. "Where's the ring?"

Bella pressed her teeth into her lower lip. "Uh, it wasn't—"

"—the right fit," Vernon completed. He hitched his hand a little higher on Bella's arm and tugged her out the door. "Gotta run, Zeya."

The landlady's tiny high-pitched voice with its lilting Burmese accent followed after them. "No happy eyes, Vernon sir. No happy eyes."

Bella yanked her arm free. "What's she talking about?"

"She wants you happy. Everyone wants you happy." He puffed out a breath of air, frosty white in the morning chill. "I want you happy."

She stomped down the steps. "Happy. You want to make me *happy*? The great crime boss who only knows how to take and take? Tell me. How many people in your life have you ever made happy?"

He ran his thumb down her cheek. "*You.* I can make you happy."

She tossed back his hand. "Bedsport. That's not happiness. That's—that's lust. True happiness is living a good life. Working at a job you love. Helping others. Not lying and cheating and killing."

A muscle twitched along his jaw. "I don't do those things anymore."

"So you say. So where's all the money coming from to pay for your fancy taste in leather"—she fingered his Armani jacket—"and that penthouse you live in with *the chef* and all the rest of your entourage."

"I told you, I have financial investments." He trapped her hand flat against his chest.

Beneath her palm, his heart thumped, his chest rose and fell. He was so alive, and he could be so dead in an instant.

She stopped on the step and peered up into his face. "Investments that require you to walk around with a bruiser like Gav day and night. To live surrounded by locks and armed guards. Bah. That's not living. That won't make me happy." She pulled her hand back. "Get rid of that filthy money. Give it to a worthy cause."

"But my billions can—"

"Don't want your billions." She put a hand on her hip and tapped her toe. "You want to give me something? Give me the deed to the villa on Eudokia. Ari said you have it."

Next to her, Vernon stiffened, every muscle taut.

"You do have it?"

He looked down the street. "Yes, yes, of course. It's in my safe."

"And it's in my name?"

He rubbed the side of his cheek. "Everything is taken care of properly. Don't you worry your wig off about it. I'll make sure you get it."

"I'll hold you to that." Bella stepped onto the

sidewalk and frowned at the limo parked at the curb. Gav got out and came around their side of the car. She glared at Vernon. "Did you have this poor man waiting out here in the cold for you?"

"It's why I pay him big bucks. Right, Gav?"

"Right, boss," Gav said with a grin better suited to a close buddy than a chauffeur. For a moment, Bella wondered about the relationship between the two men. Was Gav truly a bodyguard, or was he a friend? If there was one thing she knew, Vernon needed all the friends he could get. She hoped Gav was one, despite the fact that the ex-wrestler opened the rear door with all the deference of the serving class as he assisted her inside.

Bella slid over to make room for Vernon's hulk. She studied him as he sat back on the seat. His jaw was tense, his lips pressed tightly together. He looked like a man going to his own funeral. "You don't have to do this, you know."

He rested his arm across her shoulders. "I want to set your mind at ease." He nodded to Gav. "Calvary Cemetery. You get the eats?"

"Got your favorite, boss. A box of donuts and hot coffee are in the console, and the rest of the food is in the trunk."

The limo pulled out into the traffic and headed north. Bella sipped her coffee. At every stop light, people hurried across the street, rushing to work. It was what she should be doing. Here was another day The Siren would be understaffed.

Fur Tree would be annoyed with her—blast it— more than annoyed. He'd have to deal with the morning appointments alone. She set the coffee cup in the console. "Tell Gav to turn around, Vernon. I am sure the call was just a prank. I really should get to work."

Vernon ran a finger down the side of her neck. "And waste this beautiful day sitting inside? How many blue-sky days with temperatures in the fifties do we get in December? Relax, babe. Gav packed a picnic for us."

"In a cemetery?" Memories of the bone house and the weathered photos on the graves in Eudokia set her a shiver.

"Calvary is quite some place. Has a grand view of the city skyline."

"Seeing Theo Tuccio's grave will be enough."

He tugged her closer. "Come on, relax. No one is going to hurt you ever again. I know I let you down, and I'm sorry your brother had to kill him—but if he'd just waited—"

Bella shifted beneath his arm. Thank heavens, Ari hadn't waited. She rubbed her wrist. "Yes, I know. You've apologized over and over. I forgive you."

"Good." He caught her fingers and kissed the base of her hand where her pulse throbbed. Then he licked and nipped his way up the tender skin of her palm until he reached her index finger. He drew it into his mouth and sucked. Heat surged through her, driving away the twisted knot buried in her chest.

"Mine," he whispered against the tips of her fingers. "All mine, these clever fingers." He turned her hand over and pushed up her coat and sweater sleeve. "Mine." With his tongue, he traced the line of the seal's back as it curled over her forearm, then crossed the tender inner side of her elbow and flared into its flowing tail. He tucked her closer and nuzzled her neck as his other hand crept down her thigh. "Mine. From head to toe."

His muscles flexed beneath his leather jacket, and suddenly she was lifted into his lap. He snugged her against the hardness of his erection. "I have to have you." He tugged her tighter against him. "I cannot live without you. Never. Never leave me."

"Oh, Vernon. You sound like some lovesick fool."

He pulled back his head and gave her his trademark whole face wink that made him look like Paul Hogan in *Crocodile Dundee* and rolled his pelvis under her. "That's because I am lovesick. I'm sick of these clothes between us, and this uncomfortable limo seat beneath us and Gav's eyeballs rolling at us."

She batted at him with her hand. "Then put me down and act respectable."

He caught her hand and kissed it. "Nothing respectable about me, Bella babe. That's why you love me so much."

"Is that right?" She slid out of his lap and settled onto the seat, her hands folded neatly on her knees like an errant school girl. "There. That should help you get better."

The limo turned off Greenpoint Avenue, the tires whirring on the thick asphalt, and stopped under a turn-of-the-century entrance gate consisting of two stone columns supporting a lintel of wrought iron curlicues. A cross crowned the top. Bella moved closer to Vernon, her hands clasped together so tightly she could hear the joints crack. She hated cemeteries.

"Which way, boss?" Gav asked over his shoulder.

Vernon pointed out the window. "Right. Past this mish-mosh of a building."

"A Queen Anne chapel, I think, boss."

"You an architecture expert now, Gav?"

"Just saying. Has those turret things."

Vernon settled back into the seat. "And a vinyl-sided dormer and window air conditioners. A mish-mosh, like I said."

Gav steered the limo down the cemetery drive. "Whatever, boss."

Rows of thick and thin tombstones lined the roadway, some topped with crosses, others with statues. Bella averted her head and studied the iron-spiked stone wall on her right. She didn't want to see graves, think about ghosts. She didn't want to remember knives sliding into flesh, blood pooling on the floor, the sound of bones crushing. She didn't want to be here. She put a hand on Vernon's thigh. "Please, let's go. It's okay. I believe you. He's dead."

"But I want to check it out myself—now I'm here. See if the guys I hired followed my orders." Vernon leaned over the front seat and pointed. "There. Just up that path. Pull over, Gav. We'll walk."

The limo came to a silent halt, and Vernon pushed open the door. "Come, Bella. It's a lovely day. Just imagine we're taking a walk in the park."

Bella slid over and got out of the car. A shadow loomed over her. She peered up. An angel, features eaten away by pollution, glared down, the expression more demonic than angelic. Behind the crumbling statue stretched row upon row of other worn angels guarding the graves of the long dead. She shifted from one foot to the other, chilled despite the warmth of the sun, scuffed her boot on the asphalt. "Some park."

Vernon pushed a lock of hair out of his eyes. "Settle, Bella. The dead can't hurt you." He opened the trunk and pulled out a blanket and a brown paper bag.

He slammed the hood down.

"That's the picnic?"

He shrugged. "Spur of the moment thing." He took her hand and led her up the uneven cobbles. "Come on. Just look at the view."

Bella peered over her shoulder. To the west, the spire of the Empire State Building glimmered in the sunlight, the rectangular shapes of its neighbors boxing it in. Farther down, the stepped aquamarine glass of the Citi tower rose like a glittering man-made crystal above the gray tombstones and mossy monuments stretching out in all directions. She tripped over a tuft of grass and turned to look where Vernon was leading her. To their right, a row of marble mausoleums lined the path, the fake Greek exteriors of the oldest ones as pitted and crumbling as the statues of the angels.

Vernon stopped in front of one of the newer-looking vaults, its pink granite exterior still smooth and shiny, and put down the blanket and bag. He drew out a key.

Bella huddled behind him, shivering in the shadow of the stone. Blast it, he was seriously going to open the thing. She stepped farther back and averted her eyes. But she couldn't shut out the sounds of the key grinding in the lock, the hinges squealing, and the scraping against the granite as he pulled the metal door open.

A whiff of stone cold damp and death brushed past her from the shadowed interior. He stepped inside, then turned back, and held out his hand. "Come."

Bella picked up the blanket and flung it over her shoulders. She shook her head. "Take a photo with your cell."

"Don't be a coward. Come on." He circled her

waist with his arm and pulled her forward.

Squeezing her eyes closed, she let him drag her inside. Her boot heels clacked on the granite floor and cold radiated through the soles, up her legs, and under her skirt. Her calves cramped, and her stomach clenched. It took all her willpower not to tear away and run. Run until the dead—these dead—were far behind.

Beside her, Vernon stiffened. "There. Theo Tuccio. 1986-2015." His voice thickened. "I personally guarantee his remains are inside."

Bella opened her eyes expecting dark, instead finding herself bathed in multicolored light. The morning sun streamed through a small stained-glass window featuring a large letter T surrounded by lilies. In the narrow space between the tiers of crypts, Vernon stood still as if in prayer, his hand resting atop his brother's name.

She rested her hand over his. It was as cold as her own. "I believe you." She huddled into his warmth, her breath stuck in her throat. He pulled his hand free, and touched another name.

Bella squinted at the engraving. "Cosmo Newell. Your father?"

Vernon nodded. "Yeah. You could call him that." He ran a finger down her cheek. "You're freezing. Hell, your teeth are chattering." He hustled her back outside and stopped in a patch of sun. Holding her close, he stared off at the skyline, breathing deeply. "Sorry. Shouldn't have dragged you in there—I needed you beside me." He slammed the doors closed with a clash and turned the key in the lock. "Bad memories."

She pressed her teeth together and studied the name caved over the door. "If this is your family mausoleum, why's it say Tuccio, not Newell?"

"My father wasn't the marrying kind. That's my stepmother's last name. It's her family's tomb."

"But you're a Newell. He married your mother?"

"Yeah. He did. And she's buried in Macedonia. *My* family plot is there." He picked up the basket and headed farther up the path. "At least, you can rest easy that I won't be put in there next to those two bastards." He stopped and shook out the blanket. "You know, I never thought I'd be buried. Always figured I'd end up concreted and dropped into the river. But now"—he sat down and tugged her onto the blanket next to him—"I have you." He tightened his hold. "I can see a future for me, getting old, dying a bald old man with hairy ears, a passel of grandkids circled round my grave." He pressed his lips to hers. "Marry me, Bella. Marry me and have my children." He lay back, pulling her down on top of him. "Make my dream come true."

Bella relaxed into the heat of his body. This was the man she loved. The one with hope.

His nimble hand came between them and pushed under her coat, then rucked up her skirt. With practiced ease, he slipped his hand into her panties. "Please say yes."

She let out a little breath, felt the tomb's damp and cold flee as his fingers found the heat of her and swirled round and round driving her wild, driving away her reservations. Her breath came faster. Her blood pounded in her head. This she couldn't resist. "You don't fight fair."

"Fair has nothing to do with it. I love you." He settled her over his hardness and slid her back and forth over the soft worn denim of his jeans. The feeling was exquisite. She could feel the moisture gathering, the flame building, driving the cold of the tomb away.

A bird cawed. A fire siren blared and then faded. Voices echoed from the other side of the hill. Heavens, they were outside—in public. She slapped at him. "Stop it, we're in plain view."

He gazed up at her. "All I see are angels looking down and you, my Bella are the most beautiful of them all. Besides, your coat is draped over the important bits." He grabbed the band of her lacy underwear and tore them off her. "Now"—he fumbled with his zipper and released his engorged cock, slipped a condom on in record time—"take me to heaven, angel mine."

Why did she need this man so? He was so wrong for her. He was demanding and possessive and almost irresistible. The keyword was *almost*.

At this moment, resistance was futile. She rose on her knees and positioned herself over him. As she sank down, he drove his hips up, impaling her, stretching her, filling her completely. She rocked forward and settled a little deeper.

She'd not been a saint during the years they'd been apart. She'd let other men into her bed on occasion when the loneliness got too much. But not one of them had fit her the way this man did. Only he touched her inner core and sent heat and pleasure shooting through her with every thrust. She'd never believed the stupid idea that there was one perfect man for every woman. People could learn to love each other. She'd seen it happen many times on Eudokia, where many marriages were still arranged.

But this man she had loved at first sight. His scent drove her wild. His touch wiped away every barrier she put up. This man—she rocked again—was her perfect mate.

She glimpsed the thin scar that ran from behind his ear to beneath his collar, the remnant of some shakedown gone wrong. He lived a brutal, violent life. She had to give him up. But not this minute. She leaned forward, taking him in deeper.

Vernon's chin tipped back, his eyes half closed. He wrapped his hands around her thighs. "Do your worst, my siren."

She rose and swiveled her hips slowly, languidly, each move bringing her closer and closer to heaven. Her whole body became hot, liquid. Her head fell forward, her neck boneless. Her arms flailed to the sides. She could feel her leg muscles weakening. Suddenly, his strong hands slipped under her sweater, his thumbs pressed hard on her tender nipples and he drove his hips up and up, harder and harder until she burst and floated like a cloud, every bit of her dispersed into the chill blue sky above.

"Oh, my heavens." She collapsed on top of him, the rise and fall of his chest matching her own.

"Do you hear them?" Vernon whispered in her ear.

She turned her head to the side. "Hear who?"

He sat up, bringing her with him. "The angels cheering. Even they know you are going to marry me. Say yes."

"The angels?" She stared up at the pockmarked marble faces. The winter chill from the ground seeped under her skirt. Her overheated muscles cramped. In the distance, cars whizzed like bullets over the Kosciusko Bridge. Closer, a backhoe chugged, digging a grave. She pushed herself up and gazed off at the rows of stone crosses, inhaled the scent of sodden earth and molding vegetation. Death. All this man would bring her was death. His death.

She straightened her skirt and buttoned up her coat. He dreamed of old age. The criminals he'd angered in his lifetime would never let him grow old. What were those dates on his father's crypt? She calculated the years in her head. Forty-three.

He'd been seven years older than Vernon was at this minute when he'd died. Lives lived on the wrong side of the law tended to be short. No, she refused to be one of those Greek widows dressed all in black wailing every year on the anniversary of his death.

She scrabbled to her feet and stumbled forward. "Get me out of here, Vernon. Now." She dashed down the path, pulling her coat closed as she ran.

****

"Damn it, Bella." Vernon flailed upright, and zipped up his jeans. Now what had he said wrong? He clutched the lunch bag in one hand, scooped the blanket from the ground, and willed his well-sated body to move. Her panties. He snagged them with one finger and stuffed them in his pocket. Then, breathing hard, he headed after her. God, she was beautiful. Tall, willowy, she flew down the slight slope like a soaring hawk, her brown coat spread out about her like wings.

At the bottom, she glared back at him and then banged on the limo door. Gav stepped out and looked up at him with a scornful expression as if he, Vernon, would hurt her or something. Damn bodyguard was starting to act like an overprotective nanny. Time to think about retiring the man. After twelve years together, Gav no longer feared him. He knew too many of his secrets. Besides, Lovisa would appreciate having her husband home and safe. Now, there was another woman who didn't believe he could go straight and survive.

He looked back at the mausoleum. Well, his chances were a lot better now that those two were stuffed nice and tight inside walls of stone. He leaped over a low headstone and cut across the next row, coming up behind Bella just as she slid into the car. She moved all the way to the other side and pressed her face against the window. All he could see was the mass of fake red hair.

He signaled Gav with his thumb to take a walk and slid in after Bella. He tossed the blanket and bag on the floor. "Okay, whatever I did or said, I apologize." He slid closer and put his hand on her shoulder. Her whole body was shaking. "Bella? Bella? What is it?"

She jerked around. "You can't keep apologizing for—oh blast it—for being you."

Tears streamed down her face. He ran his thumb under each eye, willing the tears to stop. "I don't get it. Why are you crying?"

She firmed her chin. "I hate cemeteries."

"Yeah, well, I'm not too big on them either, but the sex was good right?"

"Men. You think you can solve everything with your cocks." She turned and stared out the window again. "Get Gav back here and take me to The Siren. I have a business to run."

He swiped a hand through his hair. She was acting like the bimbos he'd chased and caught to fill in the empty years. Loving him one minute. Hating him the next. Making no sense.

But this was Bella. She wasn't a feather-brain. She loved him. He knew she did. Something was really wrong. He reached out to pull her close and comfort her, but her body was rigid and unyielding. He held up his palms. "Okay, whatever."

He waved to Gav, who took his hands out of his pockets and strolled back to the car. He got in the driver's side and started up the engine. "You know," Gav called back. "I didn't believe it when I heard, but that waste treatment plant over there"—he tipped his chin to the west—"Newton Creek. The steel digester egg things really do look like blue tits."

"Really?" Vernon leaned over and tried to see out the passenger side window. "The Shit Tits are over there?"

"You can't see them from here. I walked up the hill a bit. To take in the scenery as you were gone so long."

Oops. Gav'd been checking on them. Doing his job. Vernon swallowed. Seeing what he shouldn't. Guess the man had a reason to be shooting him black looks. He tapped the tips of his fingers together. "Let's drive over that way. I hear they give tours."

Bella slapped her hand on the seat back. "How old are you two? Quit acting like ten-year-old idiots over a poop plant. Take me to The Siren now."

Damn, she was angry. There was something in the set of her mouth and the narrowing of her eyes that made him draw back. She looked like one of those kerchiefed Greek women on Eudokia who'd made the sign of the cross every time he walked past.

He rubbed his hands up and down his thighs. Making love in a cemetery had probably not been the best idea. But knowing the two bastards who'd hurt him the worst in the world were rotting behind those cold slabs of granite gave him hope he'd have a normal life at last. He glanced over at Bella. Besides, she'd been chilled. He warmed her up the only way he knew how. And for a moment, he had thought she'd say yes.

He rustled down between his feet and found the bag from the deli. He pulled out the white-paper-wrapped subs and held out a crushed ham and cheese to Bella. "Want something to eat?"

She pressed her lips together and faced forward, her profile harsh in the glare of the sunlight bouncing off the limo's hood. She gave him a quick look. "Did you ever visit the cemetery on Eudokia?"

"Wasn't there long enough. Your brother was very persuasive about my leaving."

"Right. Well, there's a bone house there."

"I know about them."

Her chin flicked in his direction. "You do?"

"Have them in Macedonia too. Ghoulish custom." He slipped a little closer and patted her knee. "You think I'm going to disinter those guys back there? Don't worry. I don't intend to ever go again. I just had to make sure everything was as I ordered."

"I was there when they dug up my father and washed his bones after the five years."

"Surely you could have afforded a permanent plot for him?"

She batted her hand in front of her like she was swatting away a bad vision. "Not the village way. Everyone gets dug up and judged."

"Judged?"

Her hands twisted in her lap. "If the bones aren't clean, the flesh rotted away, then the person is judged to have done wrong in their lives." She scrubbed her face with her hands. "You will think me foolish."

Vernon placed his arm over the seat back behind her. "So your father had some gunk still clinging. So what?"

She rubbed her face again. "No, his bones were bare white. He was declared a saintly man."

"What does it matter how your father's bones were judged? That's folk foolery. Hell, when I was boy in the village, me and my buddies would play with the bones."

She huffed. "My father thought only of his standing in the world. He was an arrogant bastard. He had his body soaked in vinegar so it would rot better, and he'd be judged well. But in the end, he was a pile of bones sitting in a dusty shoe box just like everybody else."

He pulled her against him. She smelled of woman and spice and sex. "I'm not going to die."

"We all die. That's my point."

"You've lost me here, Bella babe."

She shrugged out of his arms. "No, you've lost me. I can't marry you, Vernon."

Chapter 6

The limo pulled up in front of The Siren, and without a glance back, Bella stepped out of the car and hurried inside. Through the beaded curtain separating the waiting area from the tat station she could see Fur Tree leaning over a girl, her pinch-mouthed mother hovering in the background. Tension snapped around them.

Bella smiled. Good thing watchful mom didn't know the young man tattooing the rose on her daughter's back was an apprentice and had only started working on customers three months ago.

She took off her coat and hung it on the hook in the hallway. Fur Tree would do a fine job. She trusted his skill. He was a born artist, had a gentle, delicate touch with the machine. She rubbed the scorpionfish tattoo on her neck. He'd done a perfect job covering the scar. So perfect, Vernon hadn't even noticed it. Typical male. He only noticed one thing. A wave of pleasure suffused over her. He was her candy and her poison.

She gave herself a shake, picked up the sack of cat food, and then headed to the back. Time to feed the feral cats. Hand trembling, she lifted the heavy bolt. She hated unlocking the back door. Every time, the vision of Tuccio's goon with his Taser welled up and made her feel weak and twitchy all over again.

Enough. She steadied her hand, threw the latch

back, and pushed open the door. Cats of all colors and sizes poked their heads out of the Styrofoam cooler cat houses she had built for them. She sprinkled dry food in the metal pans spread about the yard and waited. One by one they left their shelters and slunk toward the dishes.

As they ate, she took inventory. Right now there were six. There'd been more last year. All the goings-on had frightened most of her rescues off.

She bent down and rubbed the head of a battered black tom with chewed off ears. Beneath her hand, he sank down and went rigid, but didn't run. Only this one let her touch him.

She gazed around at the other cats nibbling away at the food, ready to scatter if she made a move toward them. Not that she blamed the others for being wary. Abandoned as kittens or tossed in a garbage bin, they were half-bald, scarred, and frightened. And she loved every one of them. If she could only tame them, she'd bring them all inside.

She rested her hand on the cat's back. His fur was greasy and clotted with hard bits of dirt and grime. She picked at a wad near its neck. The cat sank lower and purred.

"Starting to trust me, are you? Time to give you a better name than Blackie, I think." She squatted down and used two hands to work through the knots. "Maybe I'll get you off the streets yet. Would you like to move inside with your old bud, Fishtail?"

"There you are." Fur Tree stood in the doorway. "Figured you'd be here."

Bella rose to her feet. "Your customers satisfied?"

He stepped out and peered up at the sky. "Yeah, I

survived. But where were you? You were supposed to distract mama bear."

"I know. Sorry to be late again."

"What happened?"

"Vernon took me to the cemetery."

Fur Tree blinked. "Someone died?"

"No. Nothing like that. I asked to see where Tuccio was buried. That's all."

The boy ran a hand through his hair. "Couldn't wait till The Siren closed? Or were you just hanging with the guy?"

"Just a minute. You can't talk to me like that. *I'm* the boss here."

He sucked in a breath. "Yes. And not a very good one. Leaving me here to handle everything on my own."

"You know, in most shops you wouldn't be tattooing on clients at all for at least a year, and you'd be working for free. I've given you more practice than any other shop would. You're way ahead of other apprentices. I let you have your own clients. You're making money."

"Don't need the money. Not why I'm doing it." Fur Tree looked around the yard, his mouth scrunched up in a crooked line. "You should clean this place up. All these stinking fur bags. It's unsanitary. Good thing the clients and inspectors don't come back here."

A knot formed in her chest, making it hard to breathe. Everyone wanted to tell her what to do. Even her apprentice.

She tossed back her hair and squinted at him. "No one gets tattoos in the backyard. If you're so worried about sanitation then you just get right back in there and scrub everything down again with disinfectant."

He gave her a narrow-eyed stare.

"Hey, no dirty looks from you. Don't like being treated like a partner, then I'll treat you like the apprentice you are. I've spoiled you. I should have made you work like a dog's body just as any other tattoo artist would."

"I'm good at it. Almost as good as you. And you know it." He threw a shoulder back. "And soon I'll be better."

Enough. She rubbed her temple, pressing her fingers against the throbbing headache building behind her eyes. This had to stop. The kid was way out of line. "Daniela didn't bring her client yet, did she?"

Fur Tree kicked one of the cat pans. The metallic clang drilled into her aching head. "Not yet. It's not quite nine-thirty."

"Good. Give me your sketch. I'll do the tat."

The boy's head snapped back. "But you can't. It's my design!"

"I most certainly can. This is my shop. Everything you do here is mine. If you don't disinfect properly, and someone falls sick, it's mine. If you make a mistake on a client, its mine. It's my reputation that's on the line here. And *don't* you forget it. You don't like my treatment of you, then you can leave. I don't care what I promised my brother."

He rolled his eyes. "Touchy. Touchy. You and *El Hombre* have another tiff?"

She stepped forward and poked her finger in his chest. "My private life is *mine* too. You stick your nose right out of it, Mr. Pharaoh."

He held up his hands. "Okay. Okay. Got it. I'll go

scrub."

"Yes. You do that."

He stormed back into the shop, leaving her standing in the yard. All the cats had disappeared. Overhead, the blue sky had gone gray. A stiff wind gusted down the narrow alleyway rattling the food tins. She fisted her hands in her skirt and tried to calm herself down. She'd always had a temper. That was why she was better alone.

All morning her blood had been boiling. Blast it. Why'd Vernon have to offer her that ring? She pressed her fingertips against the sides of her head and rocked back and forth. She didn't want this choice. She didn't want anything to change.

The black tom crept out from behind the garbage can and sat down at her feet. She settled on the steps and stroked his back, flexing and releasing her shoulder muscles the way her therapist had taught her until the knot in her chest loosened. Drat, taking out her anger on Fur Tree had been a mistake. She needed to apologize.

Back inside, she stopped in The Siren's tiny bathroom and washed her hands thoroughly, annoyed they were still trembling. From the front of the shop came the sound of Daniela's Spanish accent and the higher pitched voice of the girl. Her client was here. She bent her head over the sink and took deep breaths. In. Out. In. Out. She had a tattoo to do.

Chapter 7

Waving goodbye to Fátima, Bella backed out into Mercy House's hallway with its institutional green walls. She glanced over at Daniela. Today her friend wore a yellow blouse emblazoned with some kind of fuchsia tropical flowers. In the dim, drab hall, she looked like an escapee from the Brooklyn Botanical Garden, instead of the self-sacrificing social worker she was.

Daniela pushed away from the wall. "How is she?"

"It's an allergic reaction to the dye. Nothing more."

Daniela gnawed her lower lip. "You're sure it's not an infection? Her neck looked very inflamed."

"It's not helping that she keeps picking at it. But I'm sure. However, you will need to have her see a doctor. And get it treated."

The social worker flung her hands up, fingers spread wide. "I'll put it on my to-do list." She turned and headed down the hall.

Bella trailed after her, peeking in the doorways as they swept past. In the plain dorm-style bedrooms, young girls lay curled up in balls under quilts and blankets limp from too many washer-dryer cycles. In the living room, two women sat arm-in-arm on a sagging sofa, giggling at something on TV. In the kitchen, one girl stirred a huge pot of what smelled like chili, and another pulled trays of cornbread from the oven. The aroma made her stomach growl. "You do good work here at Mercy House, Dani."

"We try. But there's never enough money. An undercover shelter for poor abused women and prostitutes fleeing their pimps just doesn't touch the heartstrings of the charitable in the same way granting a wish to a dying child or donating to a fund for wounded veterans does." She peered over her shoulder. "Not that I am against funding those things. They are worthwhile causes. My brother is a wounded vet, for goodness sake." She pulled open the door to her office. "Nobody wants to be associated with these women—have their name on our marquee. It's not their fault men have trampled on them, brought them so low. Some have been whipped, chained, starved, repeatedly raped. Why, if you saw some of the damage done to their bodies, your heart would break. And they are so young. They have all their lives to still live. But to hear some politicians, all a woman has to do to be safe is to keep her knees together." She plopped down into her chair with a huff. "They have no compassion."

"Nor imagination," Bella said. She looked around for a place to sit. The beat-up old steel desk took up most of the tiny office. Files lined the far wall and the only free chair was heaped high with folders.

"Oh, just toss those things in the recycle bin over there. They're all the grant applications I sent out that never got funded."

Bella cleared the seat and sat. "Money is really that big a problem? I would think the city or state—"

"Of course, we get funding, but it has strings attached. Yards and yards of accounting. Just what category do you think tattooing and treating tattoo infections comes under? Not to mention dyeing hair, buying concealing makeup, or a plane ticket to send a girl to a safe place to escape a man who wants to beat her to death." She shuffled the papers on her desk. "The board does its best. As I said, we get by. But what we wouldn't give for some rich donor to give us a lot of money." She shrugged. "But that I will have to leave to God."

Bella rubbed her wrist. "I am sorry about the extra cost for the allergy treatment. There was no way to know. I did ask if she'd had a reaction to the one I covered over."

"Girl probably been so drugged up, she hadn't noticed. Now enough of my problems. What's troubling you? You on the outs with your apprentice, *mi cariño*? Fur Tree was shooting daggers at you the whole time you worked on Vitaria."

Bella pressed her hand against her collarbone. "I'd promised he could do the tat. It was his design."

"Stepped on his *cojones*, yes?"

"Oh, Dani, I was angry and I took it out on him."

"Angry? Why? Your brother okay? And Melissa?"

Bella rested her hands in her lap. "Ari's taken up photography. Plans to publish a book on tattoo practices in Greece based on Melissa's research."

"It's exciting about the baby."

"Baby?"

Daniela stared at her. "Melissa's pregnant. Due in May. Didn't you know?"

Ari hadn't said. Bella squeezed her hands together. "I guess they wanted to surprise me."

"I'm happy it worked out for them. Love conquers all, as they say." Daniela rubbed her arm.

"Still having trouble from the car crash?"

Danielle pushed up the sleeve of her blouse. "The bone healed crooked, but at least everything still works. Not like your poor brother's hands. I don't like sounding bloodthirsty, but I am glad Theo Tuccio is dead."

"So am I." Bella bit her lip. "Vernon took me to see his grave yesterday."

"*Dios mío*, that doesn't sound like a fun date."

She rubbed her hands down her skirt. "He's in Calvary. Nice view."

"Should have dumped the bastard in the East River after what he did to you."

"He's dead. That's—" A chill swept over her. Her head swirled. Her stomach cramped. She gripped the arms of the chair and fought for breath.

"*Cielos*." Daniela rustled under her desk and held out a paper bag. "Breathe into this. You're hyperventilating."

Bella inhaled, but her lungs seemed to have stopped working.

Daniela pushed around the desk and thrust the bag in front of her nose. "Breathe in and out. Now." She laid a warm hand on her neck. "Oh, *chica*. I'm so sorry."

Bella stuck the bag over her mouth and nose and gasped in ham-and-mustard scented air like a drowning victim pulled out of the depths. The weight lifted from her chest and she snuggled against Daniela's plump body that felt so much like her old nanny's. She breathed in the soft, peppery scent of the woman. She wanted to stay there forever.

Daniela stroked her back. "You still being haunted

by what that man did to you?"

Bella nodded. "I have nightmares. All the time. I worry he's going to come back. And the other one. The one who touched me when I was tied up—put his fingers—will I ever forget?"

"Hush, *mi cariño*. Hush." Daniela patted her on the shoulder. "That, Bella, was abuse. You were tied up. You didn't give consent to what he did. You're suffering just as much as my girls."

"But he didn't rape me. It was cold, calculated. He wanted to see me squirm. Respond."

"Abuse isn't always physically violent. Sometimes it plays with your mind."

Bella pushed away. "It's been over a year. I keep hoping it will all go away. I feel so weak and foolish. It was nothing like what these girls here have suffered. You should be comforting them, not me." She rose from the chair.

Daniela placed her palm on her shoulder and pressed her back into the seat. "I suggested back then you get more counseling. But you refused."

She shook her head. "I can't talk to strangers about it. You're the only one I've ever told the whole story to."

"You haven't told Vernon?"

"Of course not. Besides, I'm done with him."

"Uh-oh, what's Vicious Vernon done now? Kill someone?"

"No. He proposed."

"Ah, a marriage proposal. Well, that's a death blow to be sure. And this surprised you so much you chased him away?" Daniela sat back down at her desk. "You've been sleeping with the man for close on a year. You've loved him forever. Marry him. Have a *niño* or two. Find contentment."

"I can't marry him. He's a—well you know what he is. Tuccio was his brother."

Daniela clasped her hands together. "And his brother is dead, *si*?"

Bella shivered. "Yes."

"And you love this man."

"Yes."

"So what is the *problema*?"

"I'm afraid I will lose who I am."

"Marriage doesn't have to be like that. It can be a partnership. A give and take."

"But that's exactly the problem." Bella laid the paper bag on the desk. "Vernon only knows how to take."

Chapter 8

Vernon steered his silver SUV into the tree-lined drive and brought the car to a stop in front of the entranceway. Tiny snowflakes fell and melted against the windshield. He gripped the steering wheel and looked out over the garden, the lush plantings a winter brown and gray.

Hell. He hated this place. He slapped the dashboard, and then forced himself to get out. From the backseat he snagged the gift bag and headed to the door. It opened before he could ring the bell.

"You came." Nina Tuccio peered up at him with her dark eyes.

"Don't I always?" He handed her the bag.

"Come."

He followed the expensively dressed woman who'd once been his father's mistress as she swayed her overly-wide hips down the hall and led him into the salon. Despite the extra poundage, she was still a lovely woman. Her hair, black as ebony, hung shoulder-length, in an off-kilter slanted cut suitable for a Vogue model. Her fair skin showed no wrinkles. But it was all an illusion, the product of bottles and needles, and a surgeon's knife. Nina Tuccio would never let age or anything else catch up to her.

The woman signaled he should sit. He chose the delicate velvet Queen Anne loveseat and sat on the edge, praying it would support his weight. He'd hate to have to buy her another.

She chose the harp-backed chair across from him. "Tea?" She crossed her legs and gave a little tug on the short skirt that revealed over-exercised calves and thighs. "Or something stronger?"

"Tea is fine."

She tipped her chin to the doorway where a black-uniformed maid stood at attention. "The tea tray, Felicia." The servant disappeared in silence. "Now what trinket have you brought me this time?" She opened the bag and withdrew the box. "Tiffany's. How lovely." She held the box on her palm and lifted one eyelid. "Is this what I think it is?"

He knew the ritual. Vernon nodded and said the required words. "Happy Anniversary, Nina."

She took off the lid and stared down at the diamond ring. "How many is this now?"

"Six."

"Ah, yes. Six wedding rings. One for every year the bastard's been *dead*." She slipped it onto her pinkie finger where it sparkled in unison with the ones on each of her other fingers and smiled. "Got the size perfect." She turned her hand this way and that. "I really do like this part of his will, don't you?"

Vernon shrugged. "You'll run out of fingers eventually."

She swung her leg. "There's always my toes. Got at least that many years left. Long, lonely, *expensive* years." She looked up. "Ah yes, here is our tea." The maid set the tray on the tea table beside her and stepped back. "That is all. Leave us." She focused back on him. "Black with lemon, yes?"

Vernon grunted.

"No need to be grumpy. This is a happy occasion for you." She poured the tea and handed him the cup. "I'm another year older. Just imagine one more year gone over the falls that you won't have to do this." She put her teacup down. "I had a note from Cole."

"Cole sends notes?"

She took a sip of tea. "Well, his secretary does."

"He's liking his new job at the law firm?"

"Well, no. That's the problem." She uncrossed her legs and smoothed down her skirt. "I want you to do him a favor."

"I don't do favors."

"Oh, you look so much like your father when you wrinkle your nose like that. Like you smelled something dead." She examined her new ring. "It doesn't work on me."

"I'm not my father. I don't do favors."

"You already said that. Let me reword my request. You are going to help Cole because he is your brother."

Vernon sighed. "What's his problem?"

She tucked in her chin like a woman who'd spent long hours in front of a mirror perfecting just how to move so she appeared younger, and gave him the sad little look that had always broken through his defenses. "Not sure exactly. Bored probably. He's too smart for the work they're giving him. Needs to wrap his head around something tougher so to speak."

"I told you he should have chosen criminal law for his specialty. Defend some real crooks instead of tax and real estate cheats.

"Oh, but this way he'll get to rub shoulders with the politicians and financiers. Much better for his future. But he is so young. He doesn't see that yet." She reached across and took the tea cup from his hand. "No, he needs a little excitement. Safe excitement, if you know what I mean. Let him rob a bank or do a major drug deal. Just so he feels he's part of the family tradition. Once or twice should be enough to satisfy him."

"Get one of your nephews to take him under his wing. I'm out of the business." He put his hands on the seat and went to rise. Heaven save him from the she-devil his father had saddled him with.

She wagged her finger at him. "Sit your butt down."

It was the voice she'd used on him when he was a boy and had just destroyed her favorite flowerbed. He sank back onto the loveseat.

"I want *you* to do it. He idolizes you. And I know you will keep him safe. You love him."

"I'm out of the business."

"You wish. It's in your blood. I bet you're already thinking of how you could arrange it. A small job or two. But they have to be lucrative. So he feels he's part of the family."

"My father's dead, Nina. His way of life is dead. We lost Theo. Let this boy go straight, live safe, be normal. You know I have done everything I can to give him the life denied me, denied Theo. I've supported him for six years. I sent him to that highfalutin academy you wanted. I paid for his college education and that damn expensive law degree. If he lacks excitement, then he can travel. Climb Mount Everest. Get a yacht and sail the seven seas. Or if he wants to hang around—run for political office. I'll pay for that. But no, I will not concoct criminal activity because Cole is bored and wants to be like the papa he barely knew."

"He wants to be like you, dearie. His big bad brother who has it all. Even a wife soon, I think?"

"Wife?"

She snapped the Tiffany box open and closed. "I heard you bought two rings."

Vernon shifted on the seat. "You got spies on me, Nina?"

She laughed. "Not necessary. Tiffany's called to check the size, and I chatted up the clerk." She put the box down. "Who's the lucky girl? Anyone I know?"

"No."

She patted her lips with a napkin. "That's a shame. The things I could tell her about my dear Vernie. You really should bring her around to meet your loving mamma."

Every muscle in his body tensed. Damn it. No way would he let Nina Tuccio anywhere near Bella. She'd spill just enough to give Bella a permanent disgust of him.

He shifted on the cushion. One small job to get the woman off his back. He could arrange that. Something safe to give the bored lawyer a thrill, nothing deadly, and then he'd be done, wipe his hands of them all.

Light sparked off the rings on Nina's hands. Aw hell, he'd never be done with it. His sort-of-step-mama would keep her claws in him until he was dead. A little thought niggled around the edges. This criminal jaunt for Cole could be a set up.

He chewed the inside of his cheek. Nina wouldn't do that to him, would she? She'd been his mother, at least as much as anyone had been. She'd protected him from his father with her body. Taken beatings for him. And since his father's death he'd been overwhelmingly generous with the money and the surgeries and the properties. He gave her anything she wanted.

No, he couldn't see her doing that.

And he wouldn't lose Bella over this. She'd never know.

He stood up. "Now about Cole. I'll talk to him. See what I can do about his 'boredom.' But nothing criminal. Okay?"

"Fine. But you'll see. He wants a taste of that life, and you will have to give it to him. Besides, it will be good for him to actually kill someone, I think."

He took a step back. "You're disgusting."

She kissed the ring. "No, just realistic. It's what your father would have done if he lived. So it's now up to you. Toughen him up. Cole's always been too soft. And you know as well as I do, you can never escape this lifestyle. He will always be in danger unless you show him how to survive." She rose and took his hand in hers. "It will work out just fine, Vernie. A mother knows these things."

Vernon glared at her. "What kind of mother wants her son to get involved in that hell?"

Her nails dug in deeper. "This one."

"And if he ends up in jail?" He backed toward the door. "Or dead?"

"Then"—she dropped his hand—"it won't matter what I promised your father. I'll kill you."

Chapter 9

This was a mistake. Vernon shoved his gloved hand in his coat pocket and wrapped his fingers around the gun. It had been years since he'd done his own shakedowns. He eyed his brother in his spiffy-clean Burberry trench coat, scrutinized the two toughs he'd brought for protection, and cursed himself for not bringing more.

"How much you say this guy owes you?" Cole asked as he pushed open the graffiti-smeared door of the apartment building.

"Five hundred."

"Chicken shit. Thought we were going after a big one."

"Every job's a big one." Vernon peered into the shadowy recesses of the stairwell. "The addict who owes you five hundred dollars is just as likely to shoot you as the broker who owes you a million. They just use different methods. Mr. Five Hundred is not going to be happy to see us, and he's sure to be armed. The trick is to surprise him before he has a weapon in his hand." He touched the gun again and hoped his intel was right, and the addict was home alone.

"So let's do it." His brother started up the stairs.

Vernon caught him by the collar. "*I* go first."

Cole shook his hand off. "What fun is there in that? I know how to shoot. Took lessons. Got an NRA

Marksmanship award."

Vernon's head pounded. Lessons? As if shooting a man was like target practice. He fingered his gun. He'd never won a marksmanship award, but he knew how to use a gun and when *not* to use it.

He shoved in front of his brother and tromped up the stairs to the second floor. The narrow corridor was dank and dark, most of the overhead lights smashed out, the air stinking of decaying garbage and decaying lives. He squinted in the darkness. Good. No kids playing ball. No teens with screaming babies. No junkies shooting up. He willed all the tenants to stay behind their doors for the next few minutes and headed down the hall.

Outside apartment number thirty-five, he stopped and raised his hand to knock. Instead, his brother dashed forward and shouldered the door. Wood cracked. The door bent back on its hinges and opened as far as the bolt chain would allow. A shot whizzed past Cole's head.

Cole ducked and came up shooting. The bullets shattered the door. There was a whimper and then silence.

Vernon cursed and smacked the door the rest of the way down with his boot. He felt along the wall, found a light switch, flicked it on. A woman lay sprawled on the floor, her night gown stained with blood, her fingers clenched around a battered handgun. Scraggly gray hair covered her face. Vernon knelt beside her and pushed the hair back. Years of addiction had stolen any beauty she once had, but he recognized her. She'd worked in one of his bars; always had a smile for him. He paid for one of her kids to go to college. At least, he thought he had. He hadn't given much attention to his account books in the last few years. Vernon shook his head. "What were you doing with a gun, Maryanne?"

He swallowed down the sour bile in his throat and looked up. One of his men had disappeared into the bedroom. The other stood guard at the door, gun drawn. They knew the routine. From the kitchen came the sound of curses and cans being thrown. He strolled over to the doorway. His brother was emptying a box of cereal onto the floor. Vernon raised an eyebrow. "Hungry, Cole?"

"This is where they always hide their junk in the movies." He tossed the carton and seized another from the cupboard.

Vernon clicked his tongue. "You got a lot more to hide than that old woman did, baby brother." Damn if he didn't sound like his father.

Cole looked up. "What?"

Vernon's jaw twitched. "You just killed a woman."

"Yeah."

Warning bells went off in Vernon's head and blended with the approaching sirens. He knew a set up when he was in the middle of one. Cole was no innocent dipping in his toes. The kid had spent too much time with Theo.

If he didn't have to deal with Nina, he'd throttle his brother right here, right now, and leave him for the cops to find. Let him lawyer his way out. He stared into Cole's eyes so like his own and knew he couldn't. 'Hand me your gun."

Cole shrugged. "Sure." He turned over the gun and stepped back into the living room. He tipped his head toward the body. "Guess that wasn't the piece of shit you were after."

Vernon reminded himself this was supposed to be his go-straight, stay-out-of-prison brother. He signaled Cole. "Go. Go. Follow these guys."

He sent them off down the hallway to the fire exit. Then he pulled off his gloves, zipped up his jacket and smoothed back his hair. Head up, shoulders back, he faced in the opposite direction and headed toward the stamping feet of the police, praying Detective Simmons was on this detail and would let the billionaire slumlord past.

****

Two hours later, he had everything wrapped up—the police appeased, his brother tucked safely in bed. All that was left to do was to get rid of the evidence.

He leaned over the railing and tossed the gun into the inky water of the East River.

Splash.

Done. Nina had gotten her wish. Her baby boy'd been blooded, and Maryann's murderer would never pay for the crime. "Drug deal gone wrong" the police would write in the books.

He wondered what the old woman had done to bring the might of his empire down on her. Somewhere in some dilapidated office, one of his collection do-bees would have ticked her name for a shakedown. Several of his muscle men would have been sent to rattle the message into her that nobody got away with owing Vernon Newell five hundred dollars. And she'd still be breathing, and he would have never known.

Now an old woman was dead, because he had interfered in his well-oiled organization.

Now he *knew*.

Nausea soured his stomach and snaked up his throat. He might as well have pulled the trigger. She was dead because of his actions. He forced the burning acid down. He wouldn't vomit. Couldn't. The first time he'd killed a man, he'd thrown up, contaminating the body with his DNA. His father had made him cart his sin away, cut it up and bury the pieces in the cement foundation of a new office building going up.

He'd been thirteen.

Bile rose again, creeping up his throat like a viper that wouldn't die. He swallowed hard and tightened his stomach to keep the angry snake inside. If he kept his head fairly still and didn't move fast, the urge to vomit would go away. It always did. But the nausea would cling to him for days.

Vernon sat down on a park bench and peered out at the river rushing toward the Atlantic. The inky black water roiled and swirled like liquid marble. To his right, the lights of the Williamsburg Bridge flickered over the surface, red, yellow, white. Across the river, his condo rose above the neighboring apartments and factories lining the Brooklyn shore. His fortress. His bolt-hole.

Bella was right. He rolled his shoulders. He was a target—a big one. Even now in the empty park he felt naked without Gav and a guard or two on watch. Someone'd gunned his father down in his own bathtub.

Somewhere, someone he'd crossed was gunning for him. Somehow, someone would figure out Bella was his weak spot and go after her. Eventually, someone would get around the men he hired to protect her and take her down to bring him down. No cordon of guards could defend her apartment or shop against a determined enemy. Hell, he'd almost lost her last year, and he'd had Gav on her. His best.

The phone call she'd gotten from "Tuccio" popped into his head. Damn, someone was already threatening her. She was living on borrowed time. He needed her close. He needed her inside that fortress where he could keep her safe.

He rose and strolled back to where he'd parked his BMW. Tomorrow morning, he'd get her to marry him, and then he'd never let her go.

Chapter 10

Who was knocking on her door this early in the morning? A neighbor? Bella, a piece of toast in her hand, peered through the peephole, and swung it open. "Vernon. What do you want"—she squinted at the mermaid clock over the kitchen sink—"at seven a.m.?" She took a bite of her toast. Damn, he looked so handsome standing there, all hard angles and soft lips. But his eyes were troubled like he hadn't slept well, if at all.

"Put something warm on. Bring a scarf. We're going for a drive. I have a surprise for you." He took the toast from her hand and threw it in the trash. "And we can get something better for breakfast."

Bella's voice hitched. "But I have to be at The Siren in twenty minutes. I have a client coming at eight."

"I'll get you there in time." He picked up her coat and helped her into it. "We have some unfinished business—I need an answer."

Blast it. She didn't like the sound of that. He wanted her decision. She buttoned the coat and grabbed her tote bag. Was Daniela right? Should she say yes to make him happy? Get a divorce if it didn't work out? The idea made her stomach cringe. Marriage vows meant something. The image of her mother diving into the cold, dark sea sent prickles of fear under her skin.

Sometimes they meant too much.

She touched the tattoo encircling her wrist. He had promised not to interfere in her business. She'd have to make sure of that before she said yes. Maybe demand a marriage contract and get the deed for Eudokia from him, too.

"Ready?" Vernon hooked his arm in hers and steered her down the stairs. "Now give Zeya a big smile as we go by. I told her I'd make you happy this time."

****

Gav was waiting in the doorway, arguing with Zeya to let him in. Bella smiled to herself. Bet Gav thought he was safe standing there, towering over the old woman. A lion toying with a mouse.

Except Zeya Aung was no mouse. Bella'd seen her take down a hulk of a thief with that trusty little bat she was swinging from side to side. "Always go for the jewels," Zeya'd told her with a wink. "The bigger they are, the louder they scream." Bella put her hand on Zeya's shoulder. "Vernon's asked me to marry him."

Zeya gave Vernon a hard look. "Wise man. Now you take good care of my Bella for as *long* as you live. She poked his calf with her bat. "Get rid of the guns." She bared her teeth. "Teeth that grind into old age must avoid chewing bones."

Gav laughed. "Hear the lady. No grinding your teeth at me anymore."

Zeya whirled around and tapped the bat on the floor. "You too, Mr. Gav. You love your wife? You walk careful as an elephant with those big feet of yours."

"Yes, Ms. Zeya." Gav held out a set of keys. "Brought the car round like you asked, boss."

Vernon snatched the keys, looped his arm around Bella, and escorted her outside. A candy red Boxster Spyder convertible sat double-parked at the curb.

Bella glanced at Vernon. "New car?"

"Like it?" He handed her into the passenger's seat.

She slipped inside and ran her hand down the soft tan and red leather seat. "Spending your ill-gotten gains on frivolities?"

"Transportation." Vernon sat down in the driver's seat.

"This is way more than simple transportation. You could have fed an entire village of starving people for years on what this cost. You should be ashamed to be seen in it."

"You didn't refuse to get in." He started up the engine and slipped into traffic. "Besides, it's all yours. Sell it if you want and donate the proceeds to feeding cats or whatever. But first, let's give it a whirl."

Bella wrapped the scarf around her head and concentrated on keeping her wig in place as the convertible swerved in and out of double parked vans and lumbering buses. At the corner of Nassau, he turned and headed up the I-278 West ramp to the Williamsburg Bridge.

Bella sat up. "We're going to Manhattan?"

Vernon merged into the lane. "Keep your wig on. We're almost there."

In seconds, they were on the bridge. She swiveled around and watched Brooklyn disappearing. "It will take forever to get back. It's rush hour."

"Wait." Right before the four lanes of the bridge divided, Vernon swerved into the outside lane, cutting off a Mercedes.

"Get ready." He slowed the car down. "Set."

"What the devil, Vern."

"Now. Look up."

Bella glared at him. "You can't—"

"Look"—Vernon put his hand under her chin and lifted it—"up."

She gasped. Suspended across the bridge tower hung a huge banner with *Vernon loves Bella* splashed across it in thick red letters.

"How?"

"Called T-Crew while you lay a-bed."

He braked to a halt beneath the banner. Horns blared. Drivers cursed and made obscene gestures as they fought their way around the convertible.

Bella's fingers dug into the door handle. "What *are* you doing? You can't stop dead on the bridge."

"Just did."

Vernon hit the flashers, then put his arm over her shoulders, and drew her close. "Say yes." He lowered his mouth to hers and gave her a gentle kiss. "Marry me." He held out the ring on the palm of his hand. The diamonded siren glittered in the sunlight. "I will do whatever you wish, just say 'yes'."

She peered up into Vernon's silvery eyes. There was a vulnerability there, something soft and tender he kept hidden under all the bluff and swagger. It called to her in a way that all his sexy good looks couldn't. She would probably survive without him in her bed. She would not survive knowing she'd hurt him.

Cars whizzed by, horns honked, sirens whined, drivers cursed. All the commotion around them faded into the background. She touched the curve of his cheek. Life with Vernon Newell would never be perfect. It would never be peaceful. It would never be ordinary. It would never be safe. But it would certainly be spine-tingling. She ran her hand through his hair and whispered in his ear. "Yes."

He joined his lips to hers and licked and nudged her mouth open. He thrust his tongue inside and claimed her. Bella threw her arms around him, held on tight, and kissed him back. Behind her closed eyelids, red and blue lights flashed around them. She pulled a few inches away. "You arranged fireworks too?"

Vernon looked over his shoulder and laughed. "No, sweetheart. The police have arrived."

****

Three days later, Vernon was still in shock. Bella'd said yes. He thumbed through the clothes hanging in his closet. He needed to look his best for the engagement party tonight. He glanced down at his tattooed body: the Celtic cuffs on his arms, the mermaids swirling across his chest and back and covering his legs, the clasped hands encircling his neck. He cherished every flowing line, every sweep of color on his skin, every memory of Bella's finely-honed fingers tracing her vision onto his body. Tonight, in front of her friends and business associates, would she want him to display her work or cover it up?

He fingered his cell, considered texting her, and then laid it down. No, she would be running around like the proverbial chicken missing a head, getting ready for the celebration.

He hooked a finger in the waistband of his black skintight jeans and turned back to the closet. He tugged out a black muscle shirt and his diamond-buttoned Alexander Amosu bespoke suit jacket. He pulled the tee over his head and snugged into the jacket. There. If she thought him overdressed, he could strip down to the tee and his tats. He peered at himself in the mirror and laughed. Amosu would be in a dead faint to see his ten thousand dollar jacket paired with a three dollar tee and jeans.

Who cared what he wore. She'd said yes. The words repeated in his brain like a Boomeranged video. They were getting married. Humming *The Wedding March*, he headed for the door, stopping at the marble pedestal in the foyer to pick up his wedding gift for Bella. He scooped up the new iPhone, the travel itinerary, and the keys to his Cayman villa, and dropped them in his inside jacket pocket alongside the marriage contract.

The Eudokia deed. He slapped the table top. He'd said he'd bring it. His inner snake roiled and sent chills up his spine. He should have handed it over to her months ago. He'd promised her brother. But he liked keeping Ari Stavros thinking he was indebted to him. They weren't exactly best friends.

He hesitated. The deed was in the safe. He tapped the papers in his pocket and checked his watch. Better to take care of it when they got back from the Caymans. It was a technicality anyway. Everything he owned became hers once they were married.

He pushed the button to open the sliding steel door that protected his condo and passed into the steel-clad entrance hall.

Gav was waiting for him at the elevator.

"Got my suitcase in the limo?"

Gav nodded.

"Then let's go. Don't want to be late to my own

party." He input the password in the keypad. The door slid open with a soft whir. They stepped inside, and the elevator descended.

In the dim light, Gav looked him over, picked a piece of lint from his sleeve. "Nice jacket." He cleared his throat. "You sure about this trip, boss?"

Vernon leaned back against the cool metal wall. "She'll love it. A chance to get away and relax. Take her mind off that prank call." He glanced at Gav. "Any luck tracing it?"

"No. Bastard must have tossed the cell."

He exhaled, but it did little to relieve the pressure in his chest. "Well, keep on it. Allow access to no one while I'm away. When they bring Bella's things over after we've gone, have them stack the boxes in my storeroom downstairs." He threw up his hand. "Most of it's junk. She can sort through it after we get back."

Gav's fingers hovered over the door open button. "She knows about you cleaning out her apartment and ending the lease?"

Vernon grunted. "She doesn't need it anymore. We'll be married by tomorrow morning. I've got a nice little priest down in the Caymans ready and waiting to tie the knot. White sand, blue sky, turquoise ocean. Absolute perfection. I'll send you photos.

"What about the cat?"

"Cat?"

Gav dropped his hand and stared at him over his shoulder. "The cat—Pussyballs."

"Ugh. Forgot about that. Give the flea-bitten thing to Zeya. She can take care of it."

Gav rolled his eyes. "Whatever you say boss."

****

Her red-tiered gypsy skirt flying about her, Bella spun around, taking in the transformed studio. Her brother's graffiti artist buddies had outdone themselves with the decorations. No white ribbon and baby's breath for her.

Crepe paper ribbons in orange and red hung from the ceiling. Strobe lights flashed and loud hip hop music blared from The Siren's speakers. Spray paint tags of her name intertwined with Vernon's decorated the walls—and probably every flat surface in Williamsburg. She twirled the ring around her finger. It was real. She was going to marry Vernon after all these years.

Heat gathered between her thighs and suffused her insides. Soon. No more lonely bed and sleepless nights. She fluffed the pillows on the two faux leather sofas in the waiting room. No more worries. Vernon would keep her safe and satisfied. Her mind flashed to Eudokia. She'd saved the villagers' helicopter, too. Wait till Ari heard.

She twirled the ring again. They'd need to set the date for the wedding. Not too soon, she hoped. She was meeting with all the show's pre-production team in Los Angeles day after tomorrow, and if she got the job, she'd be tied up with that project for at least the next two months. She hurried into her tatting station and pulled out her preliminary sketches. She might not need to worry about the helicopter anymore, but Ari was right. She needed to do the TV series for herself, to prove she stood with the best in the business.

She traced the flowing lines of the dragon design the lead actor would wear. Millions of viewers would see her art. It was a heady feeling.

Someone knocked on The Siren's door. She shoved her sketches away. Time to celebrate. Tucking a wild strand of her red wig behind her ear, she rushed to let the first arrivals in.

Bella threw the door wide open. The twin graffiti artists Solo and Neto pushed through, balancing a huge sheet cake between them, *Bella loves Vernon* iced across the top. They swerved past her and placed it on the counter. Fur Tree followed, carrying the banner from the bridge. He tossed it over her shoulders and pulled her close. "I wish you the happiest of marriages," he whispered in her ear. "Please don't hold what I said about Vernon against me."

Bella smiled. "Never. Vern rubs everybody the wrong way. But underneath, he's a big pussycat."

"Rabid tiger, more like." Fur Tree flicked her nose. "Whatever makes you happy, Bella. But remember I'm always here for you." He enveloped her in a hug.

There was a commotion behind them, and then someone grabbed Fur Tree by the shoulder. "Hands off my bride," Vernon said as he shoved the younger man to the side.

Fur Tree mouthed to Bella, "Told you so."

She took a deep breath. "*Vernon.* It's traditional to hug the bride. Not assault her friends."

He wrapped his arm around her waist and nuzzled her neck. "No one touches my woman."

Bella gave him a push, but he didn't let go. "You can't monopolize me. I have to greet our guests."

"We'll greet them together." His grip tightened on her waist. "Any stranger can walk in that door."

Bella's heart jumped. "You don't think—"

"We haven't had any luck tracking that phone.

Until something turns up, I plan to keep an eye on you. In fact"—he patted his coat pocket—"I have a present for you."

A tall man with the high forehead of the early balding stepped through the door, accompanied by a woman in a flame-red business suit. Bella sucked in a breath. The TV series director had come.

She gave Vernon another push. "Later." She turned her back to him and held out her hand. "Mr. Avery, I didn't expect you."

The director squeezed her hand hard. "Call me Henri, please. I hope you don't mind. I've brought our money pockets." He tilted his head toward the woman who was glancing around, wearing a puckered expression as if she'd stepped into a particularly obnoxious pigsty. "I don't make any decisions without Gloria's approval. She keeps me from going over budget. Gloria Cooper, meet Bella Bell, the best tattoo artist in the city. Gloria is the assistant producer for the show."

The woman nodded, her eyes focused on something over Bella's shoulder. Her pointy nose tipped up. "Pleased."

Bella tugged down her tube top. It wasn't like her to hate someone on sight. But she hated this woman. Everything about the five-foot-tall woman was sharp-edged, from her nose-job to the red lizard Jimmy Choo's on her feet. "Ms. Cooper."

"Gloria's never been in a tattoo parlor before," Henri said. "Thought she'd enjoy coming tonight. See the skin art up close and personal. "

A naked-from-the-waist-up man sporting a huge death's head across his muscular torso and a row of piercings in his lip pushed past. Gloria's nostrils flared. "That's awful. I cannot believe people mutilate themselves this way."

Bella sucked in a breath. Miss Pointy-Nose Cooper could ruin her chances for the job. She used her most business-like tone. "Not all the tattoos you see here are mine. I look forward to showing you *my* sketches for the show on Wednesday."

Someone in the backroom turned up the music. A rap singer's curses blared out of the speakers. Goths and hipsters bounced up and down to the beat. Crushed by the gyrating bodies, Gloria was pressed closer until she was standing almost chest to chest with Bella. "I find all this—this art as you call it—quite degrading. Nevertheless, Henri has convinced me a show with a tattoo artist as the hero will capture a younger audience. So I've agreed to foot the bill." She looked Bella over again. "However, I expect a professional presentation Wednesday. Lose the wig. Dress conservatively. Bring polished sketches. We can't afford any delays in the schedule."

Eileen, the purple-haired owner of the boutique next door, wiggled between them and gave Bella a peck on the cheek. She pointed at Vernon who was shimmying with the rest, hips swinging, eyes focused on Bella. "Good going, girl. You got a hot one there."

Gloria elbowed her way between them and shoved Eileen to the side. "I was having a conversation, Miss." The girl gave the woman a look, then shrugged, and stepped back. "Later, Bella."

The producer shook her finger at Bella. "Henri says you're the best. But as far as I'm concerned, tattoo artists are a penny a dozen. Your artwork must be ready for the cosmetic team in two weeks, or we'll look elsewhere."

Henri hooked his arm around Gloria's and spoke over her head. "You'll do fine. Just don't be late to the meeting. All our production crew will be there and several potential backers. One's flying in special from Toronto. We can tell them the story, but it will be your designs that will give them the flavor of the show."

Bella nodded. "Of course, I'm a business woman. I understand perfectly."

Solo appeared with a tray of red wine in plastic stem glasses. "We're about to toast the happy couple." Gloria turned to take a glass at the same time Vernon did.

"Nice ass on your girl," Vernon said with a wink at Henri. Then he reached out and pinched Gloria on the rump.

The producer jumped back, rubbing her bum. "How dare you—you—you brute." She threw the glass back on the tray, knocking over the rest. Wine spattered in all directions, but most landed on the producer's expensive suit. Gloria swiped at the wine stain on her jacket and glared. "If this is the lowlife you associate with, Miss Bell, I am not sure you are the right fit for *Secret Ink.*"

Henri patted her on her sleeve and spoke through his teeth. "It was a compliment, Gloria darling."

She threw his hand off. "That brute assaulted me. Make him leave."

Vernon's eyes narrowed. "Who's this presumptuous biddy, Bella?" He wrapped his hand around Bella's waist and licked the drops of wine trickling down her neck.

She yanked away. "Don't."

Gloria's nose rose higher into the air. "I certainly don't like the crowd you hang out with, Miss Bell. We are looking for someone reliable. Respectable. There's more to television production than making art." She waved her hand. "You will be in the public eye— representing us to our backers and the press." She shook a finger at her. "Your presentation had better be seriously outstanding. Come, Henri." Back rigid, shoulders straight, she marched her way through the mass of undulating tattooed bodies and disappeared out the door.

Henri took Bella's hand and brushed his lips across it like some gallant knight in a romance novel. "Don't give her a thought," he said. "I think you are perfect."

Bella pinched her lips together to keep from laughing. The man was flirting with her. Then with a quick wave, he was gone, too.

Vernon slid up behind her and pressed his hands down on her hips. He swayed to the beat of the music. "Good riddance to them—whoever they are. Come now, dance with me."

Bella whirled on Vernon. "How dare you touch another woman!"

He kissed her on her cheek. "God, I love when you're jealous."

She smacked him on the chest. "I'm not jealous, you idiot. I'm furious."

He put his hands on either side of her head. "I love you when you're furious, too." He lowered his mouth to hers.

She struggled for a brief moment, but then his lips pressed against hers, firm and soft, gentle and demanding. He teased her with his tongue, and she opened to let him in. She could taste the sweet floral of the cheap wine. She could taste *him.*

The pounding bass of the music thumped in time with her heart. Heat built between them as they swayed back and forth. She threw her arms around him. All the hustle and bustle and noise melted away. She turned her head to deepen the kiss, slid her leg up his thigh. Through half-closed eyes, she glimpsed a mass of smiling faces. Fur Tree, Solo, Neto, Daniela, Eileen, her regulars. They were all looking at them, clapping.

Gathering all her strength, she pulled away from Vernon and stood facing him, her heart pounding, her breath coming in audible gasps. Their friends raised their glasses and let out a rousing cheer. "To Vernon and Bella. True love forever."

Vernon took her hand, the one with the ring on it, and held it up high above their heads. He bowed. Bella bent her head in acknowledgement but underneath she cursed. The pointy-nosed prude was right. She had no self-control. She'd spent eight years regaining her self-confidence after the disaster on Eudokia, honing her art. She'd gotten Mr. Arrogant out of her blood.

But all he had to do was kidnap her off the street, play pretty, and touch her, and she turned into a damp dishrag ready to make love to him anywhere, even in the middle of a very public party.

She couldn't marry him. She'd lose her whole sense of self. She pulled her hand down and stared at the ring on her finger. The sapphire mermaid twinkled in the strobe light. She considered taking it off and then hesitated. She would never humiliate Vernon in front of all their friends. She lowered her hand and hid it in her skirts.

Vernon flashed her a smile, a real smile, not the cynical one he usually wore. She bit her lip. He'd done everything she'd asked. A marriage contract. A pledge to not interfere in her business. A declaration to sell off his crime empire. The deed to Eudokia. She couldn't easily retract her promise to marry him. But maybe she could get him to put the marriage off for a while—a long while.

She seized a glass of wine from an outstretched tray and gulped it down. Surely he'd understand. Meanwhile, come Wednesday, she'd be the ultimate business woman and make that little she-devil in a red suit eat her words.

****

Vernon raised an eyebrow. He didn't like that look on Bella's face. He'd embarrassed her again. But hell, it was their engagement party. Everyone knew they had a thing going. And by tomorrow night, they'd be married. He tapped his chest pocket again. He couldn't wait to see her—his Siren—lying on the beach, in her natural element of sea and sand. She didn't belong in this hard-walled, cold city cavorting with all these tattoo junkies. She'd fled her island because of him. He would take her back to where she belonged. Somehow he'd convince her to give up all this idiocy, and he would surround her with love and protection.

He glanced at the colorful tattooed bodies swirling around him. The small space had grown hot and more and more people were shedding their shirts, revealing sweat-sheened bodies covered in magical ink drawings by his Bella. Over by the counter, someone had shoved down his jeans to reveal the angel Bella had inscribed on his butt. Might as well blend in. He slipped off his suit jacket and flung it on the back of the sofa.

He looked over at Bella. She'd moved away from him and was busy hugging everyone, a sweet expression on her face, her cheeks flushed red. Someone handed her a glass of wine, and she swallowed it down. Damn, she was drinking too much. She'd be hungover in the morning. Couldn't have that. He wanted her wide awake when she said her vows. He took a step toward her.

Someone grabbed his arm.

"Vernon."

He tore his eyes off Bella and turned. "Simmons, how are you?"

"Wild party here. I hope no neighbor complains and calls the police on you. Definitely over the occupancy limit." The detective winked at him.

Vernon waved his hand expansively. "Bella invited all the neighbors. Besides"—he threw his arm over the shoulder of his buddy—"the police are already here." A girl with tattoos over every visible inch of her back pushed behind him, blocking Bella's view of him. He leaned closer. "That murder put to rest?"

Simmons studied his feet. "They found some DNA. I don't think they will drop it."

Vernon's heart skipped a beat. It couldn't be his brother's. Could it? "Whose?"

"Not sure. Not in the database." Simmons took a glass of wine off an offered tray and downed it. "May not be the shooter's. They're checking out all the tenants and local junkies."

Vernon seized a wine bottle from a cavorting girl and refilled Simmons' glass. "See what you can do, my friend, to make the DNA disappear." He dug in the pocket of his jeans and pulled out a wad of cash, and pressed it into the detective's hand. "I don't like investigators messing around my properties."

Simmons nodded and slipped the money inside his jacket.

Vernon tossed back the bottle and glimpsed Fur Tree glaring at him over the heads of a group of girls. Had he seen? The wine in his stomach turned sour. If Bella found out he was still neck deep in illegal doings, shaking down druggies, covering up murder, he'd have a lot of explaining to do. More than explaining. He swallowed and turned to face Bella at the same instant she swung around and smiled up to him. He put his hands around her waist and drew her close. To hell with it.

Fur Tree could think what he wanted about Vernon Newell. Bella had said yes. By tomorrow, she would be his wife and far, far away from here.

Chapter 11

Bella leaned back against the door and peered at Vernon sprawled across the sofa. Men. Just when you need them, they punk out. She crossed the room and gave him a shake. "Wake up. That was the last of them. Clean up time."

Vernon grunted. "Did you check the john for stowaways?"

She wiped her brow. "Yeah, and behind the counter and under the tat chair. Nobody here but us. And there's a mess of work. I have to sanitize the place."

He closed his eyes. "Some party. I'm wrung out."

"Well, you can't sleep there. I got to get The Siren ready for the morning." She tugged on his arm. "Get up, Vernie."

He gripped her by the waist and pulled her down on top of him. "Hmmm. You can be my blanket."

For a moment, she lay still, enjoying the warmth of his body pressed against hers, and then she remembered Pointy-Nosed Gloria. She had to get her sketches prepared for the meeting in LA. She feathered kisses up his neck, then rolled off him.

"Come back," he muttered, and then his eyes closed and a gentle snore started up.

"No help there." Bella laughed and went searching for the broom. She found it by the back door. Outside, the cat colony was quiet for a change. She opened the door and peeked out into the yard. A big old tomcat lapped water from one of the dishpans. On the fence, a young, long-limbed cat, probably with some Siamese ancestry, licked his paw.

She took a deep breath and sat down on the step. All was well in the cattery. The air was fresh with a hint of frost, the sky cloudless. In Eudokia, there would be a billion stars on a night like this. But all she could see above her were the blinking lights of a low flying jet coming in to LaGuardia.

When she first moved here, she'd hated the rotten air, the chlorinated water, and the closed-in feel of cement and brick all around her. Now she loved the place.

She'd never leave Brooklyn. Somehow the city had wormed its way inside her. She loved having neighbors, each one different from the next. She loved the roar of traffic on the move and the footsteps of people going places. She loved the exuberant graffiti art scrawled on doors and walls and bridges, and the outrageous clothing and the vibrant tattoo scene. This was where she belonged.

She stood up and wiped the dirt off the seat of her skirt. Her rescue kitten slipped out the open door and pushed his nose under her arm. She tickled his ears and then scooped him up. "Inside, Fishtail. Too cold a night for a little guy to be out. Come, I have treats for you."

Cuddling the kitten, she stepped back into the studio. A blast of heat and the reek of spilled wine and sweaty bodies left over from the party hit her. Vernon still snored on the sofa. She wrinkled her nose at him and picked up the broom. "Lot of help you are."

Bella sprinkled treats on the counter for Fishtail and then set to sweeping away the confetti and cake crumbs littering the floor. She gathered them up in a pile and bent down to whisk them into the dustpan.

Vernon's suit jacket peeked out from under the sofa. She dropped the dustpan and tugged it out. A white envelope with her name scrawled across it in Vernon's scraggly script stuck out of the inner pocket. He'd mentioned a gift. This had to be it.

She looked at the sleeping hulk on her sofa. So like Vernon to forget to give it to her. She sat down beside him and gave him a kiss. "I hope this is the deed to Eudokia," she said, tearing the envelope open. It was not a deed, but an itinerary. She stared at the date and destination. *How dare he!*

She gave Vernon a hard whack on the bum. "Wake up, lover boy. We got a problem."

Vernon's fingers twitched. She whacked him harder. "Explain this."

He turned over and opened one eye. Then closed it again.

She tugged on his T-shirt. "Get up."

His eye opened again. "Bella, why aren't you asleep?" He stretched out his arm. "Come here, baby."

"I'm not your baby. I am not a doll. I am not sleeping with you. *Ever again.*"

"Sweetie. What's got your panties all twisted now?"

"This sweetie is not wearing panties." Bella picked up the dustpan and dumped the entire mess on his head. "You arrogant bastard."

"What?" Vernon jerked up, coughing. He brushed the crumbs and confetti out of his hair. "What's the matter with you?"

She held the computer printout inches from his face. "Explain this, idiot."

Vernon rubbed his eyes and peered at the paper. "Oh." He grinned up at her. "That's my engagement gift for you."

"And when were you going to *give* me this gift?"

He glanced at his watch. "Gav should be arriving shortly with the limo. The plane leaves at 6 a.m."

She ran the paper through her fingers. "I noticed."

He sat up fully. "My Cayman villa is on the most beautiful beach in the world. The perfect place to say our vows. By tomorrow night, you'll be my wedded wife."

"Will I now?"

"Everything is set. The priest is waiting. The wedding dinner ordered. The ceremony will take place at sunset. And wonderfully private, exactly like you wanted. I gave all the servants the month off, including the chef. Food will be delivered daily from the local hotel."

She gave him a hard look. "You forgot one thing."

Vernon seized her hand. "What? Tell me. Anything your heart desires."

She tapped her foot. "You didn't ask *me*."

"Ask?" He frowned like a school boy accused of breaking a window. "But you said yes."

Blood rushed to her head. The man was totally obtuse. She yanked her hand from his. "I'm a bit busy here, Vernon. I have a business to open in the morning. I have appointments. I have my own life."

"Cancel them."

Her jaw tightened. "Nope. I am cancelling the

wedding. I love you, but not enough to become the wife of a slimy snake who lies to get what he wants." She twisted the ring off her finger and threw it at him.

He caught it without looking. His silver eyes darkened. "Lies?"

"Yeah. That thing about letting me run my business without interference."

"But damn. It's just a month. Let what's his name Tree Top run the place." Vernon pushed up off the sofa and came toward her. "The Siren's just one goddamn tattoo parlor among hundreds. Come here, baby."

Blood thundered in her ears. "That's it." She held the broom handle out in front of her. "Don't. You. Touch. Me."

"But Bella." He came closer.

She aimed the handle for his balls and jabbed at him.

"Witch." He seized the end of the broom and pulled her toward him.

Someone banged hard on the door. They both jumped.

Bella dropped the broom and rushed over to unlock it. She opened it wide.

Gav tipped his baseball cap. "Everything's set, boss."

"There," she hissed through her teeth. "Your ride's here. Have fun in the Caymans."

"Come on, Bella. You don't mean what you are saying."

She picked up a half-empty wine bottle from the counter and threw it at him. It missed and landed with a crash on the floor. Red wine spread across the tiles like blood. "Damn it, you must have cement in that head of yours. It's over. I never want to see you again." She seized another bottle by the neck.

Gav tugged on Vernon's shoulder. "I see you've upset the bride. *Again.*"

Vernon threw his hand off. "Look, I'll cancel the tickets, the wedding, everything. Just please—please come home with me."

"Too late. I will not be at your beck and call."

"But you love me." Vernon reached out his arms, his eyes full of pain.

She'd break if he touched her. Summoning up all her anger, she swung the bottle and let go. This time it didn't miss. It hit him squarely on the forehead. Vernon's eyes rolled up, and he jerked backwards. Gav caught him as he fell.

"Nooo. I've killed him." Bella rushed over and knelt beside him. She cradled his head in her arms. For a moment, he lay still as a corpse, and then he groaned. Thank the heavens. Bella let out the breath she'd been holding. Not dead.

Gav helped Vernon sit up. Already a lump was forming on his forehead.

"Bella?" Vernon's voice sounded like a small boy's.

"He needs medical attention." She rose and headed for the phone. "I'll call 911."

Gav flicked his hand. "Don't bother. He's had much harder knocks on the noggin. I'll take him home and put him to bed." He winked at her. "Give him some tender loving care." He slid his hand under his boss's arm and hefted him up. Vernon's head lolled to one side.

Bella rummaged behind the counter, found a towel

and filled it with ice from the cooler. She held it out to Gav. "I didn't mean—"

"Had it coming, I'd say." Gav half-dragged Vernon to the door. "He's been boss man too long. Doesn't know how to ask—only order. Let him stew awhile, Miss Bella. He'll come around. He's a good man underneath. Just loves you too much to see straight." With that, he yanked Vernon out the door, stuffed him into the limo, and jumped in after him.

The car door slammed, and the limo took off down the empty street.

Bella stood in the doorway. She'd hurt the man she loved. Ari always said she had a temper hot enough to melt rock. She rubbed her hands up and down her arms aware of her bare finger. She turned and stepped back into The Siren. It stank of sour wine and lost hope.

Gav wanted her to give Vernon time. But it wasn't time apart they needed. She'd known it wouldn't work the minute she'd said yes. They weren't good for each other.

Vernon Newell brought out the worst in her. She'd nearly smashed his head in. They would always be at each other over everything. They were like baking soda and vinegar—fizzy when things went well, explosive when they didn't. They were both too used to getting their own way.

She picked up the broom and dustpan and bent down to sweep up the broken glass. A glint of gold caught her eye. The engagement ring. She scooped it up and clasped it in her fist.

She loved him too much to risk hurting him again. Better they part. A little niggle ran up her spine. Without Vernon, there'd be no money for Eudokia's helicopter. She'd have to get that TV job for sure now, and Miss Pointy-Nose had not been too impressed.

She picked up the broom again and surveyed the mess. To work. Time to get back to the life she'd had for the last eight years—a life without the overbearing Vernon Newell. She'd put her nose to the grindstone, work hard, and Wednesday she'd wow the show's backers with her professional demeanor.

****

Vernon rolled over in bed and groaned. His head throbbed worse than when he'd been smashed into a brick wall by an outraged supplier. He ran his hand over his temple. Hell, he had a goose egg the size of a tennis ball.

"Wake, boss?"

A mass of icy cold came down on the lump. "Ow. Get that off me, idiot."

"Needs ice."

"Needs your hands off." He pushed himself up. The room spun for a moment and steadied. Must have been some party.

Party—Bella. It all came back in a flash. "Where is she?" He sat up and glared at Gav. "We're supposed to be in the Caymans. Getting married."

The bodyguard fussed with the ice. "Stay still, boss. Got a concussion. Doc's been and gone." He smacked the wrap back on the bump.

Vernon roared and seized the ice pack. He tossed it across the room. "*Where is she?*"

"Um, she was pretty angry. Especially when she got to her apartment and found you'd removed all her belongings and told Zeya to sublet it—I did warn you, boss."

His whole body tensed. "Yes—and?"

"She's left town."

His insides ripped open. He sucked in a breath. "Where to?"

Gav shrugged. "No one's saying. She didn't tell the fuzzy-headed apprentice."

Vernon's mind whirled. It had taken eight years to find her and a day to lose her. He shook his fist at Gav. "What are you doing wasting time nurse-maiding me? Get out there and start looking for her."

Gav gathered up the towels and ice pack and headed for the door. "Doc left pain killers for you. They're on the nightstand." Then he was gone with a bang of doors and a rumble of elevator.

The apartment fell silent. Vernon had given the housekeeper and chef the month off in expectation of being on his honeymoon. He flopped back on the bed and stared at the clouds floating past his window. Idiot. He'd done everything wrong from the first. Seizing her off the street and pretending she'd been kidnapped. Well, technically he *had* kidnapped her. He'd refused to let her leave until her brother showed up.

But he hadn't hurt her. He'd let her spend tons of money on fixing up his place. Then he'd got the damn villa for her from her tight-assed brother—not that she seemed to appreciate it.

He rubbed his throbbing skull. Then again, he'd failed to rescue her in time, so her stupid brother got to step in and play the hero. She hadn't been the same since then—more clingy, more fearful. He'd kind of liked that. She'd needed him.

Damn, she still did. His enemies were still out there. He untwisted the sheet from around his legs and slid to the edge of the bed. Tree Top had to know what was going on. He'd get her whereabouts from that nosy tat boy or—

His cell phone gave a shrill ring. Vernon leaned over and snatched it off the nightstand. Not a number he recognized. He hesitated. Normally, he let unknowns go to voicemail. Oh what the hell; he pressed answer.

"Bro. I'm in trouble. Need help—"

"Cole. That you?"

"I'm…"—the voice faded then came back—"injured."

"What's happened?"

"Need to talk…"

"Where are you?"

"Papa's stinkin' castle. But they won't let me in. God, sounds like wolves in the woods."

"Relax. Just the dogs. I'm on it." Vernon stood up, wobbled, caught himself on the nightstand. "I'll be there in three hours."

"Hurry, I'm dying out here, bro. It's so cold—" The line went dead.

Vernon redialed but got no response. He phoned the guards stationed at The Pines and told them to let his brother in. Then he tore through his dresser drawers and yanked out thermal underwear, a thick turtleneck and a wool sweater. It would be cold up in the mountains.

He pulled on his jeans and fought off dizziness as he bent over to pull on his heavy socks and hiking boots. He'd have to go alone. Take the Ranger. Gav was on Bella's trail and needed to keep at it.

Besides, his long-time bodyguard was becoming annoying. Mollycoddling him. Always sticking his nose in with unwanted advice. It was time he took command again. He blinked his eyes against the pain shooting across his scalp. He could handle his little brother on his own, concussion or no.

He considered sending Gav a text message and decided against it. Let the man do his job. He'd only be gone a day at the most.

Then he headed out the steel door of his penthouse and rode his private elevator to the basement. The throbbing in his head increased as he stepped into the brightly lit parking garage. He gave himself a shake and signaled the attendant to bring the Range Rover.

He checked his watch—four p.m. At this hour, it would take a little over three hours to reach his father's monstrosity in the Catskills. The Rover squealed to a stop in front of him. He tossed the boy his tip, climbed up into the SUV, and revved the engine.

Hold on, Cole. He was on his way. He stepped on the gas and roared up the ramp into the dwindling daylight.

Chapter 12

Bella strode out of the production meeting, struggling to keep a straight face. She'd done it. Wowed them with her competence. She studied her reflection in the mirrored tiles lining the wall of the office hallway. Blast it all, Vernon taking all her clothes had done her a favor. She'd had to rush out and buy a whole new wardrobe. So she'd taken advantage of an early arrival in Los Angeles to go shopping. The royal blue Albert Nippon suit from Neiman Marcus fit her like a glove, and her expertly cut and shaped curls formed an elegant cap around her head. She could never wear this suit with her red wig. Vernon might be right. It might be time to drop the brassy-lady look.

Vernon. She hoped he was okay. She ran her fingers up and down the handle of her tote. He hadn't called since "the incident," as she was calling it. Not that she wanted him to call. Still, she'd like to know he'd recovered from the knock on his head.

She stepped into the elevator. Henri Avery hadn't taken his gaze off her the entire presentation, and Miss Pointy-Nose hadn't taken her eyes off Henri. There had been real appreciation in Henri's eyes, maybe even more. She wasn't surprised Gloria Cooper felt threatened. Bella smoothed down her skirt. It was pleasant to have the attention of a *gentleman* for a change.

She stepped out of the elevator and strolled across the foyer. Not that Gloria Cooper had anything to worry about. She was done with men. From now on, she'd pour all her passion into her art. She tucked her sketchbook into her tote and headed out into the LA sunshine. She had so many ideas for the tattoo designs now that she'd met the screen writers.

Already her fingers were itching to get started. But first, she would enjoy her stay in LA. Then she'd head home and get her life back to normal.

Normal. She reached in her pocket and fingered her phone. Had Gav and Vernon returned her belongings to her apartment yet? Heck, did she still have an apartment? Places like hers didn't remain on the market more than a few days.

Fur Tree could find out. She crossed the street and stepped inside a small pastel-colored coffee shop. Fortified with a pink-iced *petit four* and a large hazelnut cappuccino, she settled back in a cramped seat outside under the awning and dialed The Siren.

The tattoo artist's voice came on the line, a bit breathless. "Bella, where are you? That bruiser of Vernon's has been all over me for days. What the hell happened?"

"Long story. Look—I have a favor."

"Yeah?"

"Find out if my apartment's okay."

"Okay?"

"Yeah, like all my stuff's there, and it hasn't been sublet."

"Don't understand."

"A thing between me and Vernon. Run over there and check and get back to me. There's a spare key hidden in my ink drawer."

"Sure, Bella. Whatever. Get right on it." There was a brief hesitation, the sound of a door closing. "Where did you say you were?"

"I didn't. I'll be at The Siren in the morning." She hung up and sipped her coffee. It was a balmy day, the temperature in the upper sixties, the sky pure cerulean. Overhead, the fronds in the palm trees rustled. On the sidewalk, people ambled by in casual dress. She leaned back and enjoyed the parade. Tattoos peeked out everywhere, below a sleeve, encircling an ankle, beneath an open collar. What a change from a few years ago, when wearing tattoos was still outside the mainstream.

An elegant woman sauntered by, a blurry lopsided shamrock tattooed on her neck. Bella frowned. Unfortunately, there were still enough hackers in the field to keep tattooing from being recognized as art. She pulled out her pad and thumbed through her sketches and notes. Once people saw high level tattoos on television stars, they'd never put up with shlock like that. She took another sip of her coffee.

"Bella."

She squinted into the sun. Henri Avery waved and headed in her direction. Tall, rangy, with the western ruggedness and kind eyes of an old-time cowboy movie star, he'd done a remarkable job explaining the need for a professional tattoo artist—for her—on the staff. She lost sight of him for a moment, and then he was there, pushing his way past the line of coffee lovers snaking out the door.

"What are you doing sitting here all by yourself, Miss Bell?"

"Loving the sun and the people. Thinking about moving here."

He slid into the seat across from her and tilted his head. "Not until our series is done." He patted her hand. "And I hope it will go on for many, many years. I live in New York, you know." He gave her a long look. "I think you would come to hate the superficiality of the people here."

He flicked his hand at the steady stream of tourists and would-be-stars passing by. "I rarely sit in public. In a few minutes, someone will recognize me, and I'll have to take cover behind you."

"People are that rude?"

"When you direct successful TV series, every would-be actor memorizes your face. It is far easier to lose yourself in New York."

"No actors there?"

"They're too busy working to pay the exorbitant rents. Don't have time to spend stalking me. Though once we start filming, they'll appear out of the bushes."

He leaned over, took her sketchbook, and spun it around to face him. "There was a design you showed the production team that I particularly liked." He thumbed through the sketches. "This one." He held out the screaming dragon she'd thought might be perfect for the lead. He examined it for a moment. "There's something about the expression on the face." He peered up at her. "I was wondering. Could you do a version of this on my back"—he picked up her hand—"with your gifted fingers?"

Heavens, the man was flirting with her again. Bella studied him through her eyelashes. He was an attractive man even with his receding hairline. She imagined running her tat machine over his skin. Having him at her mercy. Yes, maybe with a little effort she could force Vernon out of her mind.

She took a swallow of coffee. The bitter liquid trickled down her throat and pooled in her stomach. No, she was fooling herself. Getting Vernon out her heart wouldn't be so easy.

She contemplated the dragon Henri was holding. She'd been thinking about Vernon when she drew it. Large, scary, covered in tough scales, but underneath lonely and lost. She pressed her lips together. Vernon would hate to be thought of that way.

Bella flicked the cake crumbs on her plate. It would be a long time, if not forever, before she got Vernon out of her system. Toying with another man would be unfair. This was business, nothing more. She professionalized her voice. "It's a very large design. It would cover most of your back. Take at least five sessions."

"Five times having your hands on me. Sounds delightful. When we get back to New York, set up an appointment for me on"—he pulled out his cell— "Monday at ten."

She checked her own calendar. "That works. But if you change your mind, let me know." She liked this man with his gentle eyes and long tapered fingers. She imagined him touching her. A brief affair might not cleanse Vernon from her heart, but it might prove an interesting distraction.

She sipped her coffee. "So you don't like LA?"

Henri shrugged. "Grew up here. I think people often flee their childhood haunts for the unfamiliar. I like the mystery and anonymity of New York. Drugs, crime, kidnapping, murder. The city has it all. It's what excited me about this series." He handed her back the sketchbook. "You're a New York transplant. Don't you feel that pull of the dark, that feeling of being in the underbelly of a ravenous beast ready to swallow you up? Always looking over your shoulder?"

A chill tiptoed down her spine. Surely, these were merely his fantasies. The man knew nothing about her. She turned and peered out at the sun-filled street. "Yes, I understand what you mean. But LA—it has that darkness, too. All cities do at night. But here—during the day—there's this California sun. The warmth of it reminds me of Eudokia."

Avery twisted his tongue around the name. "E-doh-kee-a. That where you grew up?"

Bella hesitated. She rarely shared anything about herself. But the sunshine was warm and the colors pastel, the pace easy, and the man listening. She felt more relaxed than ever. She leaned back and looked over the rim of her coffee cup. "Yes. It's an island in Greece. Quite lovely. No darkness at all."

Avery crossed his legs. "Tell me about it."

From across the street, she glimpsed of flash of red. So much for a quiet talk getting to know each other. Miss Pointy-Nose was heading their way.

Bella pointed. "Your associate is coming our way. She looks unhappy."

Avery's head jerked up. "Gloria. Always unhappy about something. Won't give me a moment's breathing room." He rose and pushed back the chair. The metal legs screeched on the pavement. "When do you fly back?"

"This evening."

"Fine. Fine." He glanced in Gloria's direction as she battled her way across the traffic. "I'll see you Monday morning then." He peered down at her hands. "It will be enlightening to know what our actors should be experiencing while under the needle. Let's call it research." He gave her a quick wink and turned to face the woman charging toward them.

Huffing, Gloria pulled up short. "Henri, I didn't know what happened to you. We were supposed to—"

"Yes, my dear. I see you found me. No harm done, I'm sure." Henri gave her a peck on the cheek.

"It's been a real pleasure." He gave Bella a brief nod, then turned and gave the producer a smile that dripped conciliation. "Come, Gloria darling." He put an arm around Miss Pointy-Nose's waist and steered her in the direction of the hotel.

Bella took another sip of coffee. So much for that fantasy. Gloria Cooper had her claws buried deep, and Henri Avery would follow wherever her pointy nose led.

She couldn't help it. She called after him. "You can bring Miss Cooper to watch if you like."

The woman spun around and glared at her. "Watch what?"

Henri murmured something in Gloria's ear. She slipped her arm in his and pranced off—the victor. Bella laughed. Henri Avery was too much a milk-toast for her. Vernon would never have put up with being dragged around by that woman.

She wondered if the director would cry under the needle. On second thought, she hoped Miss Pointy-Nose did come to watch the sessions.

Chapter 13

Bella pushed open the door to The Siren and sucked in the familiar scent of ink and disinfectant. She parked her suitcase and set down the pet carrier. Then she unslung her tote bag, and dropped it on the coffee table. With a sigh, she glanced around at all her favorite things—the painting by Ari of Eudokia's beach that hung behind the counter, the weird Aladdin's Lamp phone from the '80s she'd found in a flea market, the eyeball-shaped paperweight or *mati* her dying grandma had pressed into her small six-year-old hands.

She rubbed her aching head. Everything seemed dull and washed of color since her return from LA, even her beautiful Siren. She gave the suitcase a kick. It wasn't helping that she would have to sleep here and live out of her travel bags for the unforeseeable future.

The worst had happened. Her apartment had been snatched up the second it went on the market. Zeya had been apologetic, but helpless. The property manager had been thrilled to have such a prime piece of real estate to sublet at double the going rate. Finding a new place equivalent to the one she'd had wouldn't be easy.

Bella opened the wire door on the carrier. Pussyballs bounced out, gave a sniff, and wrapped himself around her legs. "Welcome to your new home, sweetie." She knelt down and ran her hand over his soft fur, taking comfort in the gentle purr under her hand.

They'd faced a lot together, Pussyballs and her. Poor guy was ancient. He'd been old when she'd found him—all skin, bones, and matted fur, one leg broken, a gaping wound in his chest. She'd nursed him day and night even though the vet had called the case hopeless. He'd been her first rescue and given her hope when the world had seemed a very cruel place.

She chucked him under the chin and glanced around. Despite her exuberant tattoo flash and the golden yellow paint on the walls, the studio felt cold and commercial, fine for slinging ink, but not to live in. From the bathroom came the plunk of a dripping faucet. She made a mental note to get it fixed pronto. She'd never be able to sleep with that steady drip, drip, drip drilling into her brain.

She wrinkled her nose. Sleep here? In The Siren? She didn't even have any bedding. She added that to her mental list and picked up Pussyballs. At least, her old companion would still be with her.

Pussyballs stiffened in her arms. His purr turned to an angry hiss.

"What's wrong—you see a rat?" Bella asked looking in the same direction as the cat. There'd better not be rats in the place. But it was Fishtail come looking for treats and finding a rival instead. The silver kitten stood dead-still half-way through the beaded curtain that separated the waiting area from the tat stations.

Bella put a reassuring hand on the hissing Pussyballs. "That's Fishtail. He's a little guy."

Fishtail took a slow-mo step forward. Pussyballs growled louder and struggled in her arms. She set the cat on the sofa. "Now you two be friends." But

Pussyballs was having none it. He leaped to the floor, and the chase was on as he pursued Fishtail from one corner of the shop to the other.

Bella pressed her palms against her ears. She knew the yowling and hissing sounded worse than it was, but the screeching made her skin prickle more than a tattoo needle. She had to do something before they tore each other apart or her head exploded. She went in search of the broom.

There was a loud crash behind her.

"Oww. What *idiota* left a suitcase in the doorway?"

She stuck her head through the beaded curtain. "That you, Fur Tree?"

"You're back. *Gracias a Dios!* If that in-your-face Gav guy showed up one more time looking for you, I planned to bop him on the head." He stared at her. "Nice hair."

She glanced back to where Pussyballs had the kitten trapped in the bathroom and headed up front. "Vernon's bodyguard been giving you trouble?"

"Yeah, him." Fur Tree rubbed his shin. "It would have helped if you'd let me know where you'd gone."

Bella forced down the lump in her throat. "I—couldn't. I wasn't sure—"

"So how was the wedding?"

"What?"

"Remember—Vernon? Your fiancé? The engagement party? Gav said you took off to get married, but when you didn't show up in the Caymans, he figured you went somewhere else."

Bella shook her head. "I broke up with Vernon. No Caymans. No wedding." The words sounded so final.

"No wedding?" Fur Tree stepped closer as if to

examine her for craziness. She *so* didn't want to explain. A particularly loud screech came from the bathroom. She looked over her shoulder. Pussyballs wouldn't eat the little guy—still…

Fur Tree grabbed her by the arm. "Forget the cats. So what happened with Vernon?"

"Huh? He went home from the party in a snit."

"Right." Fur Tree put his hands in his pockets and glanced around. "Well, I'm glad you're back. Did the best here, but I really wasn't ready to take over on such short notice. I had to cancel several appointments. Not much money came in. Is there going to be enough to finish my tat station? We can't keep sharing."

"We'll survive. In fact, I have a customer coming who wants a dragon across his whole back—five to seven hours' worth. That will make up for what I lost." Bella gripped her hands behind her back. "But the revenue will be lower for a while." She did a quick calculation in her head. "We may have to wait a bit on finishing the other station."

Fur Tree looked out the window. "I can get my own station at Freddie's place anytime I want. He's no artist, but I would earn twice as much there. I'd rather learn from you, but…"

Her apprentice was right. She really couldn't afford to keep him, especially if she was going to be living here for the foreseeable future. She frowned at the sofa. Ugh. Thousands of butts had sat on that old thing. The last thing she wanted to do was put her head on it. "There's something else. I've lost my apartment."

He cocked his head. "How do you lose an apartment?"

She waved her hand. "I will have to camp out here

for the next few weeks until I find something."

He blinked. "Live here? No. There's no privacy in the place. Plus it's unprofessional *and* illegal. "

"But I have no choice."

"There's always a choice. Hook up with a friend. Try a shelter." He rolled his shoulders and stood up straighter. "But it doesn't matter. You make too many stupid decisions. I'm out of here. Time to get my own clientele. I'll go collect my stuff." He seized an empty box from behind the counter.

Bella fisted her hands. "I'm sorry. I wanted it to work."

"The hell you did. You've been pussy footing around setting up the station for me for months now." He pushed through the beaded curtain and started throwing his belongings into the carton.

"I didn't have the money and—"

"Vernon would have bankrolled it if you'd really wanted me. All you had to do was ask."

"No. I—I won't take his filthy money."

"Why the hell not? Guy loves you to death. He'd do anything for you. You're too damn independent for your own good, Bella Bell."

"I thought you didn't like him."

"I'm not the one in love with him." He bent down, pulled out drawers, and carefully placed his tattoo machine and needles in the box. "We would have made a great team."

Two cats streaked by them, a blur of gray and orange. Fishtail leaped up on Bella's shoulder and dug in his claws.

"Ow." She tried to dislodge him and came nose to nose with a snarling kitten. At her feet, Pussyballs scratched at her leg trying to reach his prey. She blinked back tears and worked at extracting the kitten's claws from her skin.

"Damn cats. Belong outside." Fur Tree set the cardboard box on the coffee table and helped her remove the kitten. Bella gingerly carried the snarling animal to the bathroom, dropped it in, and closed the door.

She rubbed her shoulder. Spots of blood stained her white silk shirt. She bent down and picked up Pussyballs, who had quieted now that his rival was out of sight, and carried him out front.

Her apprentice gave her a long look. "Take care of yourself, Bella." He hefted the box and headed for the door. "You don't want to hear this, but you'd better watch out." He nodded at the cat. "You're well on the way to becoming that dreaded thing—a nasty cat lady."

"How dare you!" She seized the Royal Copenhagen mermaid figurine Vernon had given her from the counter and hurled it at him. It bounced off Fur Tree's arm and landed on the floor, breaking into ten thousand pieces. He pushed the door open with his hip. "*Adiós*, Bella."

Through blurred tears, Bella peered out the window and watched him head down the street. What had she done? She needed Fur Tree not only for the work and extra money, but because he kept her spirits up, made her laugh. She'd promised Ari to give the kid a hand getting started in the field. Her brother would be disappointed in her.

Wait. She tilted her head to see better.

Fur Tree had stopped dead on the pavement. She crossed her fingers. Perhaps, he would change his mind.

She stepped to the door and opened her mouth to call to him. But he wasn't turning around. No. he was shifting the box to the other hip and scooping up something from the sidewalk. He looked back, caught sight of her, and dashed away like the cops were after him. She slunk back inside and collapsed on the sofa. Pussyballs jumped up and curled up in her lap. She ruffled his fur.

Cat Lady. Right.

She set Pussyballs on the floor and grabbed the tote from the top of the coffee table. No more feeling sorry for herself. She'd been on her own for years. She didn't need Vernon. She didn't need some street artist psychoanalyzing her. She had a job to do. TV actors to decorate. Big money to earn. Once she submitted her designs, her finances would be back to normal in no time. And Fur Tree would come back. He'd tire pretty quickly of tatting butterflies on fat ankles and skulls on skinny teen biceps over at Freddie's two-bit tat parlor.

She reached for her tote and yanked out the scarf and her makeup case, then felt around for her LA production notes and sketches. Damn. Where was her pad? She turned the bag over and dumped it upside down. Wallet, hair brush, lipstick, cell phone tumbled to the floor. But no sketchbook. Panic gripped her belly.

She shook the bag again. It had to be here. She'd had it on the plane. In the cab. She'd been going over her notes while they sat in traffic on North Conduit Avenue and shoved it back in the bag when they got to Zeya's. She straightened up. At least, she thought she had. She closed her eyes and tried to remember. Blast it. She'd been so angry—in a tiff over the apartment and her missing belongings, in shock at the exorbitant taxi fare—she hadn't checked the seat when she got out of the cab here at the studio. She fell back on the sofa.

She'd never find it. No cabbie would save a plain-covered notepad. It didn't even have her name in it. But it did have everything about the TV show: all the important names and numbers of people she needed to be in contact with, the suggested designs for each actor, her fee schedule, the dates everything was due by.

And most importantly, the sketches. All her ideas done in that creative moment, gone. She ran her hand through her hair, her neat LA coif long turned to NY frizz. No way could she recreate all those details from memory. She curled her legs under her and rested her head on the sofa back. She was screwed.

Chapter 14

Vernon slid the spatula under the eggs in the pan and lifted them on to the plate. He peered out the kitchen window at the thick stand of trees that surrounded The Pines. Off in the distance, he could see the top of Eagle Mountain peeking over the treetops. Damn, he loved this place. It brought back memories of childhood, playing hide and seek with his little brothers, fishing for trout in the creek. His step-mom baking cookies and playing Scrabble. Weekends at the Catskill castle, during the few years Nina thought his bastard father loved her, had been the only time the Newells had ever behaved like a normal family.

The toaster popped, and the stench of over-toasted bread filled the room. He grabbed the burnt edge with his fingers and flipped it onto the plate next to the eggs. Damn, it was hot. He stuck his seared fingers in his mouth and rustled around the drawers for a knife with the other hand. It had been a long time since he'd cooked anything, except for his botched attempt at Bella's.

He ignored the pinching in his stomach and stared at the plate. Burnt toast. Leather-looking eggs. Well, it would have to do. He hadn't taken time to call in a staff in his rush to get to his brother.

He cut the bread into triangles like his step-mom used to do and slathered butter on top to cover the black bits. He placed the plate on the tray alongside the mug of steaming coffee and trudged up the stairs, struggling to balance the dishes and not spill anything. This was so not him. Vernon Newell didn't wait on people. People waited on him.

He reached the second floor and headed for the room half-way down. Only for his little brother would he do this.

He pushed the door open and pasted on a smile. "Good morning, Cole. I've brought you breakfast in bed, like we used to do for Mom in the good old days."

Cole looked up at him through swollen eyes. His face looked even worse in the daylight than it had last night. "Thanks, bro." A bit of blood trickled from the split in his lip. He leaned to one side and attempted to sit up.

"Hold on." Vernon rested the tray on the dresser and hurried to stick a pillow behind his brother's back. "There, that's better." He reached over and brought the tray to rest in Cole's lap.

His brother gave the food a once-over. "Definitely not gourmet."

Vernon grinned. "But made with love."

Cole looked up sharply. "That's Mom's line."

"Yeah, she used it to cover up her bad cooking. Thought it would work for me, too."

His brother took a bite of toast. "Ain't a stick of love in you, Vernie."

"So I've been told." By a wild siren with the most kissable lips in the world. *Bella.* He would win her back. But first, he needed to get to the bottom of what was going on with his brother. He put his hands behind his head and leaned back in the chair. "So who beat the pulp out of you?"

"A misunderstanding."

Vernon leaned forward. "Does this misunderstanding have a name?"

Cole shrugged and then winced. "Forget about it. Nothing broken."

"Nobody does this to one of us and gets away with it."

"Really." Cole's mouth twisted. He put down his toast. "Where's all this brotherly love coming from? You let Theo go down at the hands of that beast. Now you're sweet on the murdering bastard's sister." He jerked his head at Vernon's arms. "You're covered in her girly tats. No real man would wear curlicues and simpering mermaids."

He seized his brother by the shoulder. "Don't go there."

Cole's expression hardened. "Gonna shake sense into me like you used to? Take advantage of me being flat on my back and at your mercy?"

Vernon dropped his hand. His little brother always knew how to jiggle his chain. Even when they were kids, he'd always sided with Theo—two little guys against the big bad brother, making him look cruel in front of Nina.

But it was time to dump all that childish nonsense, bring little brother back onto the right side of the law. Get him set up straight and safe. But first, he needed to know what had happened.

"I'm asking again. Who did this to you?"

"A big, fat cop. Said he was sending you a message. Knew I killed that woman. Wants a bundle of cash to keep it quiet."

Vernon chewed his lip. No cop he knew would beat up his brother. Arrest him, yes, but not torture him and let him go. More likely, one of Maryann's neighbors had decided to try a little blackmail.

He should never have involved Cole in that shake down, no matter what Nina threatened. "Don't believe you. What's the man look like?"

"It was a mistake to come here," Cole said. "Never could talk to you. Your head is still stuck up your ass. Theo had your number. He sure did. Besides, the food service stinks." He tossed down the toast and shoved the tray to the side.

"Hold on, bro." Before Vernon could stop him, Cole swung his legs over the other side of the bed and stood. The sunlight creeping over the mountain illuminated the lean muscular body.

Vernon winced at the sight. Every part of his brother's skin was covered in dark bruises. Whatever they'd hit him with had been intended to bruise, but cause no major internal damage or broken bones. But he hadn't succumbed easily. His chest and arms bore numerous knife slashes where he'd tried to defend himself, and his wrists were chafed from where he'd been bound while subjected to the beating.

Vernon hurried around the bed. No way his brother was walking out of here on his own. "Get back under the covers." He put a hand under Cole's arm as gingerly as he could.

His brother jerked away, wobbled like a drunk, and then fell back on the mattress, groaning. He landed on the corner of the tray. It tipped, and coffee spilled across the comforter and splattered in Vernon's face.

"Damn." He swiped his face with his sleeve and

yanked off the soiled cover. He turned back to Cole. His brother lay curled into tight ball, clutching his stomach, his face a sickly gray. "I'm gonna barf."

"You stay put." Vernon looked around the room, saw his great-grandfather's WWI helmet hanging on the wall, seized it, and shoved it in his brother's face.

Holding his breath against the stench, he patted Cole's back as his brother vomited. He wasn't made for this. This was woman's work.

He looked over at the framed portrait of Nina on the bureau. She should be taking care of her son. Getting him involved in the underworld had been her idea. He held the hat closer as Cole vomited again. He'd call her the minute he got free. He looked down at the bruised and battered body. Or maybe not.

It would kill her to see her baby looking like this. Cole had always been her favorite, the smart colt in a family of head-strong bulls. Coddled and cosseted, sent to the best schools, a law degree from NYU. He'd never been intended for their father's crime syndicate.

"Done." Cole drooped back on the pillow. "Nothing left."

"Don't move. Got to clean things up." Vernon carried the stinking helmet into the bathroom and set it down. Then he wet a towel and filled a glass of water.

Cole looked a bit better when he got back to the room. Vernon swabbed the sweaty face, helped him sip some water and covered him with a clean blanket from the closet.

His brother's fingers found his. "Did I ruin Grandpa's helmet?"

"Nah. I'll give it a good scrub. I'm sure Grandpop spilled his guts into it a time or two." He smoothed back Cole's hair. "Feeling better?"

"Yeah. But damn, it hurts."

"What'd they use? Knucklebusters?"

Cole's eyes widened. "How'd you—"

"Been there. And speaking from experience—you'll need several days of bed rest before you can go bounding out of here feeling like your nasty old self."

"Will you stay with me, bro?" The muscle along Cole's jaw trembled, and despite the swelling and the two black eyes, he looked like the little boy who once cowered under his bed in thunderstorms. "I need you."

"Sure. Nothing pressing right now, anyway." Just one missing fiancée. He picked up his brother's hand and held it tight until Cole fell into a restless sleep. Then, drawing the blinds, he tiptoed out and headed for the bar in the huge living room. Vernon poured himself a tumbler of his father's twenty-five-year-old scotch. Nothing pressing. Just a big empty hole where Bella should be.

He took a sip of his drink. The rough liquor burned down his throat and flamed in his stomach. *Bella.* Where was she? Whose butt was she tattooing? Damn. Merely thinking about her got his innards twisted into knots and gave him a hard on he couldn't relieve. He stepped out the French doors onto the balcony. Down below, he could see the glow of cigarette tips from the two guards at the gate.

Bella was right. This was no way to live, surrounded by armed men day and night. It was better she'd broken the engagement. There wasn't room in his world for marriage. No man he'd crossed would ever accept he had gone straight. His back would always have a bullseye on it. He'd always be in someone's crosshairs.

Vernon placed his tumbler of scotch on the balcony railing and stared out at the fading sunset. Somehow he had to get Nina to see reason. Being on the wrong side of the law was a one-way ticket to a living hell. Cole was young. He had a good degree. He had a good job. And one thing was certain. He didn't have the fighting skills needed to deal with the vicious men who trolled the bottom. This beating was a warning.

Cole and Nina would want to get even. He couldn't let that happen. It would drive his brother deeper into crime. Might even land him in jail, and once you were a jailbird, no one trusted you. He'd learned that lesson young.

Vernon downed the rest of his drink. The scotch burned all the way down. He'd have to take care of the blackmailers while Cole was laid up. He took out his cell and pulled up his step-mother's private home number from Contacts. She could come up in a day or two when the swelling had gone down, and nurse Cole. Then he could get on the trail of the thugs who'd done this to him.

Somewhere nearby, one of the guard dogs howled. The lonely wail dug into his brain, unearthing the fear he didn't want to recognize. What if this beating was not directed at his brother? What if it had been a warning to him?

He'd stepped on a lot of people in his race to the top of the garbage pile. A bad taste filled his mouth. If that were true, then everybody close to him could be in danger. He slipped the phone back in his pocket without making the call. Nina was safer in the well-guarded, gated community where she lived.

But Bella was unprotected. Only a few months ago, she'd been zapped by a Taser and taken from The Siren easy as a fast food pick up. Damn it all. He picked up his glass and tossed it over the balcony. It tumbled down three stories into the courtyard below and landed in a shatter of glass.

The men at the gate stepped out from under the arched entry way, their faces bleached white in the light from the windows, guns at the ready. Vernon cupped his hands and called down. "At ease. Glass fell."

He needed to get her here—to The Pines—where he could protect her while he took out whoever was after his brother. He pulled out his phone again and held his finger over her mermaid icon. No. He shook his head. She'd never answer his phone call.

Poor Gav. He'd have to bring her, convince her to come somehow. He hit Gav's number and was surprised when the line rang and rang and finally went to voicemail. He tried again. No go.

A slow, snaking chill wormed through him. Gav was hooked to his phone. It was his job. Never in the last eleven years had Gav not picked up instantly no matter what he was doing. Even in the throes of love, he'd answered. It's what he got paid big bucks for.

Something was very, very wrong.

Chapter 15

Bella jumped at the knock on The Siren's door. She sat up on the sofa and rubbed her aching head. Heavens, Henri Avery was here for his tattoo. She stashed the bedding in the bathroom, ran her fingers through her tangled hair, and hurried to unlock the door.

The director popped his head inside. "Good morning, Miss Bell. All set for our session?"

She waved him in, aware that she did not look her best. She'd barely slept in days. The sofa was hard and lumpy. Pussyballs chased Fishtail around the studio all night. And nightmares came back every time she looked at the back door. She would have barricaded it closed by now if it weren't against the fire laws. As it was, she had it illegally chained and bolted.

She rolled her shoulders back and put on her professional smile. "This way." She held back the beads and let him pass through to her tat station. "No Miss Cooper today? I was sure she'd want to watch."

"She thinks I'm being foolish." He turned his dark, steady gaze on her. "Am I?"

She ignored the hidden message in his eyes and turned to pick up the sketch. "Not at all. Tattooing has become quite mainstream. The reality TV shows like *NY Ink* have brought tattooing into the public eye. Your drama, with its focus on the artistry, will further propel it into the art form it is meant to be." She winked. "Besides, you can do stand-ins for your lead actor—except your tattoo will be real."

"Ah. Now that's an intriguing thought." He sat down and took the design from her hand. His forehead creased with frown lines. "This is not quite the same."

Bella bit her lip. She'd done her best to replicate the dragon he'd seen in LA, but it wasn't exact.

"Something around the mouth—before—it looked—well, less like the lizard guy wanted to eat up a fair maiden." He handed it back to her.

"Let's see." She took out her pencil and played a bit with the curve of the mouth. She darkened one of the lines. There, that was better. She gave it back and nibbled the end of the eraser while he studied it.

"This is more like it. But still—there's something missing."

Time for her sales talk. "Skin is different from paper or canvas. The design will change as your skin moves over the muscles." She pushed up her sleeve and twisted her arm with the seal tattoo one way and then the other. "Your dragon will look angry or sad with a twitch of your shoulder. I think this one will satisfy—that is, if you still want a tattoo?"

He gave a little shrug. "I can't say that I'm not a little nervous."

"Perhaps we should start with something smaller. To get you accustomed to the needle. How it feels?"

He looked at her with half-lidded eyes. "No. I'm sure you're right." He unbuttoned his shirt. "Do your worst."

She put the sketch in the thermo-fax and waited for the stencil to roll out. Then after a quick check of her sanitized prep tray, she washed her hands, pulled on her gloves, and patted the plastic-wrapped table. "Lay down on your stomach with your arms at your sides."

He jumped up and spread out on the table. Beneath his weight, the plastic squished and slid.

Bella tore open an alcohol wipe. For a moment, she hesitated, studying the man lying before her. Unlike Vernon's scarred back, Henri's was smooth and unblemished. The faint scent of soap and deodorant rose as he adjusted his position on the table. Gray at the sides, his hair darkened to its original chestnut brown at the neck, the ends curling under like commas.

Henri tucked his arms alongside his body. "Like this?"

"That's right." She swabbed the alcohol pad across his shoulders and down his spine. Beneath her fingers, his skin rippled and tensed. "Now turn your face away from me. And relax."

He lifted his head from the table and winked at her. "You mean I don't get to watch the lovely artist at work?" He smiled at her, the tilt of his mouth so much like that of Eudokia's patron saint *Agíou Georgiou*, her breath caught. She'd kissed that icon a million times as a child. What would it be like to kiss this man? Could he set her afire like Vernon or would he leave her as cold as the chill silver of the icon?

She bit her lip. "For this design I need full access to the back of your neck."

"Just my neck?"

"And back, of course." She unwrapped a disposable razor. The man was hitting on her for sure. Nothing wrong with that. But she needed to pump him for the information she'd lost, and it had to be during the stencil transfer because inking required her complete concentration. She drew the blade across his back in long, clean strokes. Then she swabbed again with an alcohol wipe. Her canvas was ready.

She picked up the stencil. "First, I will transfer the design to your skin. Then you will approve it. If it is satisfactory, I will outline in black today. In the next sessions, I will add shading and color. It is similar to how the temporary tattoos will be applied on the set, except those will be stenciled on with that special ink I recommended."

His head lifted. "I believe you said at the meeting they would last about a week. That means we will need to schedule the studio shots all at once. If we get enough clips, we can photo edit later when needed."

"Too bad we can't convince the actors to let me give them permanent ones."

Henri laughed. "That would be good for your business and mine, but what happens when they have to play a billionaire in their next gig?"

"Some billionaires have tattoos."

"You know a tattooed money mogul?"

"One." Vernon. She ran the pads of her fingers over his back, feeling for the conformity, determining the best placement. The skin was smooth and warm, the muscles long and defined. A nice back. But not Vernon's.

She pulled her hands away. Time to be the professional. "I need your back to be as flat as possible. Extend your hands up so they're parallel to your head and relax your shoulders. Take slow, deep breaths."

She dampened the skin with her favorite disinfectant solution, placed the stencil across his back, and pressed down hard. His spine stiffened beneath her hands. After a few seconds, she lessened the pressure and rubbed outward toward the edges. She picked up a damp wipe and wet the back of the paper.

The stencil flattened and clung to the contours of his back. Good, no wrinkles. She picked up a corner of the paper. The blue lines of her dragon sketch appeared. Success. She lifted the rest off. Easy part done. She tapped Henri on the shoulder. "It takes about five minutes for the design to dry. Would you mind some music?"

"Uh, no. Not at all."

Bella spun her chair around to the counter, pulled off her gloves, and flicked on the CD player. The lilting voice of Enya filled the studio.

Behind her, Henri chuckled, the deep-throated sound muffled by beat of the music. "New Age. Not what I expected."

"I find it relaxes newbies." Bella brought her notepad closer. "Speaking of newbies. When exactly do you expect to have everyone on set?"

"Don't ask me. I can't keep track of all the comings and goings. Not my job. I'm the tell-people-where-to stand-guy. Gloria keeps the schedule."

No way she'd ask Miss Pointy Nose. Bella tossed the notebook down. So much for mining the info from Henri.

Maybe she could find out more from one of the crew? The body makeup artist had seemed like a friendly person. "Do you think I should contact—Helen—I think her name is—about the ink purchases?"

"Ellen. Ellen Blake." He ran his hand over his neck. "All that was discussed at the meeting. Didn't you take notes? I saw you writing everything down—because I was kind of hoping you'd be keeping me on track with all the ins and outs of the tattooing side of things."

She scrubbed her hands at the sink. "Yeah—just making sure. My notes are a bit messy.

"No problem. You can e-mail Gloria about all that stuff. She's very efficient—among other things."

"You seem to know her well."

"Daughter of an old family friend. She has wishes I don't feel like fulfilling."

Bella couldn't help herself. "Sleeping her way to the top?"

He raised his eyebrows. "Exactly. She's on the make to be executive producer of her own hit show."

"With you as the director?"

He pushed up on his elbow. "You're not jealous, are you?"

She wanted to kick herself. It wasn't like her to be snide. He'd think she was competing for him. Men loved that. But she didn't play that game. Not ever.

She examined the blue-black dragon outlined on Henri's back. "It's dry. You can sit up now." She picked up the hand mirror and handed it to him. "Stand with your back to the wall mirror over there and see what you think."

He bounded off the table and stood wide-legged as he peered at the design. She couldn't help peeking out the corner of her eye. Without his shirt and business jacket, and despite the gray hairs covering his chest, he looked healthy and vigorous. He obviously worked out regularly. He might not have Vernon's bulk or six-pack, but his lithe runner's body was attractive in its own way. She wondered how it would feel to lie in his arms.

"Beautiful work, Miss Bell." Somehow he had slipped up beside her.

She peered at his lips. They sure did look kissable, and he was no Vicious Vernon. Upright and straight-forward. A real gentleman.

Maybe a little hot sex with someone new would wipe Vernon from her system for once and for all. She glanced down at the bulge in his pants. He had the hots for her, for sure. Wouldn't take too much convincing to set up a one night stand—or two.

Right. Like she wanted to share him with Gloria.

Back to business. She fussed with folding up the sketch and putting it in his file. She slammed the drawer shut. "So are you ready to take the next step?"

Henri's mouth turned up like he knew what she'd been thinking. "Yes. Let's do it."

"Then back on the table with you." She pulled on a new pair of gloves, and popped the individual ink bottles from their sterile wrapping. She picked up her Kronos and dipped it into the ink.

He turned to look at her. "But before we start—"

"Yes." She rolled her chair closer and held the needle points a hair's breadth above his skin.

"I thought we could have a quiet dinner tonight at my place. Just the two of us with maybe a night cap to follow?"

She'd asked for it, showing interest in the man. Still, she was tired of take out, and they could talk about the show. But she wasn't ready to jump into bed with him. Not until she knew Gloria was out of the running. She gave him a soft smile. "Maybe—dinner to start."

He broke out in a huge grin. "That would be a delightful start, Miss Bell."

"Bella, call me Bella." She lowered the needles and swept into the first line of the design. Henri flinched. They all did. The first stroke hurt the most. But then he settled, and beneath her skilled fingers, the dragon outline darkened and took form.

Her mind whirled as she worked. She'd agreed to go out with this man. Vernon would kill her if he knew she had a date with someone else. She peered over at Henri's handsome face. Kill him, too.

Heavens. Who needed a lover who made you scared he'd do something violent to you or your dates? Forget Vernon. She'd been true to him for years, and it had gotten her nothing but heartache and sleepless nights. Time to explore having a good time with a normal man.

She bent over Henri's back and worked at giving him the best tattoo she'd ever done.

****

An hour later, the outline of the dragon was done, and Henri was no longer a tattoo novice. He winced as he shoved his arm into his jacket sleeve. "You were right. It is sore." He tipped his head. "I might need some tender loving care tonight from those talented fingers."

Bella's stomach turned over. *Tonight.* Was she going to let him coax her into his bed? Every nerve in her body twitched in warning. She kept her voice steady. "You might skip the jacket."

"Good idea." He slung it over his arm. "So dinner tonight. Seven?"

She gazed up at the gentle face. "Nine. I close at

nine."

"Perfect." Henri bent down and pressed his lips to hers. "Nine it is, Bella. I'll pick you up."

"Bye." She stood in the doorway and watched Henri stroll down the street toward the subway. She should have refused. But blast it, it would be the perfect opportunity to get all the info she had lost, and somehow she'd wiggle out of the "night cap."

"Already forgotten Vernon, have you?"

Bella spun around. Fur Tree leaned against the doorframe with his hands behind his head, giving her one of his you're-an-idiot looks. "He's just a satisfied client."

Her former apprentice huffed. "*My* clients don't kiss me. Thought you insisted on keeping personal stuff and work separate. Seems like that was one of those rules you drilled into my head."

"Henri's a friend." She stepped back and let her former apprentice pass by her into The Siren.

He tossed his ball cap and leather jacket on the sofa. "Henri who?"

"Henri Avery. I'm tattooing a dragon on his back."

He rummaged around in his backpack. "Where you know him from?"

"Around." She turned away. She hated to lie. "So how are you been? Freddie getting enough work to support you?"

"Yeah, different clientele but it's working out—all *bueno*." He hesitated for moment, then shut the flap and dropped the pack on the floor. "I—er—came to get the rest of my stuff."

"No problem." She drew the beaded curtain aside for him.

He headed to the back. Something rattled. A door slammed shut. He came back into view. "You still living here?"

She played with the strings of beads. "Yeah. I looked at few places, but they were stinky. The windows looked out at air wells or bus stops."

He came forward carrying a stack of sketch pads and a set of watercolors. "I'd offer you a place in our building, but Toro and Hanger are just back from Greece, and all the other places are let." He shrugged. "Not up to your style anyway—no view."

"I know. I'm being silly. I really just want my old place back." She let the string of beads fall and followed him into the waiting room. "Toro and Hanger are back? Ari never mentioned they'd be coming. When did they get in?

"Last night. They're sleeping off the time change." He smiled. "Toro's finally out of the wheel chair. T-Crew's planning a welcome back party tonight. We are going to paint graffiti all over their apartment walls. You want to come?"

She twisted her hands together. "I have a dinner engagement."

Fur Tree shook his head, his brow furrowed. "A date? Does Vernon know? Your engagement party was just five days ago. You may want to tell whoever the guy is to come armed."

"I'm not engaged anymore, and I will not let Mr. Boss Man dictate my life." She bit her lip. "I am moving on."

Fur Tree squinted at her and then shrugged. "Whatever. But I can't believe Vicious Vernon's given you up without a roar or two. Sure he's all right?"

"The man's a violent criminal. I don't care if he is being eaten alive by zombies or walled up in a dungeon. I hate him."

"Uh-oh. Have you told Vernon that?"

She picked up Fur Tree's jacket and hat and threw them at him. "Enough. I never want to hear the name of that rotten, lying crook again."

He stepped back. "Don't go all female-bonkers on me, Bella."

"Female-bonkers? What the heck? I'll give you bonkers."

Fur Tree stuck the ball cap on his head. "Anything you say, Bella." He hefted his backpack halfway, fingered the tie. "I have a confes—"

"Go. Get out." She looked around for something to throw. "Enjoy working for Freddie. I'm sure you won't have to deal with any wild-eyed, gone-bonkers female *there*."

"*Bueno.*" Fur Tree straightened up to his full height. At six three, he towered over her. "Got the message. Take care, Bella. Enjoy your new life." He slung the pack over his shoulder and stormed out of the shop. The door slammed behind him.

Bella threw herself down on the sofa and pressed her hands against her cheeks. She was losing everything she cared about. She was losing herself. The red-wigged, in-your-face tattoo persona she'd created eight years ago was unraveling, and she didn't know how to pull herself back together.

Her stomach knotted. Her head throbbed. She beat the arm of the sofa with her fist. She didn't want to be that lost little girl again.

She seized the papers and after-care pamphlets on

the coffee table and tossed them across the room. They floated down and blanketed the floor. Fishtail popped out from under the sofa where he'd been hiding from Pussyballs and leaped into the mess, rolling and kicking up his little feet. She shook her aching head. "At least someone is happy."

A streak of orange dashed from behind the counter and jumped on the kitten, pinning him to the ground, digging in his claws. The cats hissed and rolled toward her.

"No, Pussyballs. Don't hurt the little guy." She pushed herself off the sofa and leaned down to separate them. Fishtail leaped up and clasped onto her arm. The kitten's claws dug into her skin. Its teeth sank into the tender flesh of her biceps. Blood welled.

She grasped the kitten by the scruff of his neck. "Let go, Fishtail. Let go." But the teeth and claws just dug in deeper.

The door slammed open, and someone rushed in. "*Qué diablo!* Stop! You're making it worse."

Through pain-blurred eyes, she glimpsed Fur Tree. "Thank heavens, you came back."

"*Gatito malo!*" He seized a towel from the shelf and threw it over the kitten. Then he wrapped it around the hissing creature.

Under the cloth, the kitten calmed but did not let go. With one eye focused on Fishtail, Fur Tree extracted each claw. Then he carried the kitten to the bathroom and closed it in.

He stomped back into the waiting room and loomed over her. "You and your damn cats. You got to have a doctor check that. It's already swelling."

She looked down at the huge gashes and puncture

wounds on the inside of her arm. Her bicep where Fishtail had bitten her was puffy and red. She shook her head. "No, I'll be okay."

"Don't be an idiot. Cat bites are the worst. You could get cat scratch fever. People die from it." He helped her over to the sofa. "Besides, I already called 911. They're on their way. Listen."

The tell-tale beep of the ambulance came down the street.

"Blast it. Why'd you do that?" She collapsed back on the cushions. The emergency room would make her wait there for hours. No date tonight. No names, no phone numbers, no schedule for the TV show. No sketches ready for the first shoot, whenever that would be.

The EMTs, when they arrived, treated her as if she has been attacked by a lion instead of a seven inch high kitten and insisted on putting her on a stretcher and carting her to the ER.

Fur Tree held her hand as they wheeled her out. "I'll take care of everything. Don't worry."

****

Ten hours, an antibiotic shot and a tetanus shot later, Bella was back on the sofa. She tossed her sketch pad onto the coffee table and peered through the rain-streaked shop window. Outside, the street lights glistened on the wet pavement like reflections on a still sea. The street lay deserted. Bedford Avenue hummed with traffic and pedestrians during the day, but not much of anything passed by at three in the morning, especially in a downpour. She looked at her last sketch. There was no way she could duplicate all the designs in time.

Henri had been kind, picking her up from the hospital, taking her to a Japanese tapas bar, hand-feeding her, and delivering her to the door of her old apartment. She hadn't had the courage to tell him she was all but homeless and holed up at The Siren. He left her with a gentle kiss and a reminder to be ready with the sketches for their first New York meeting on Monday.

She curled up in a ball and pulled the blanket around her. It was useless. Bad enough her drawing arm was bandaged from the palm to the shoulder, but her brain just couldn't recreate the designs she'd whipped out so easily at the meeting in LA. She could remember the subject and the form for most of them, but it was impossible to capture the free spirit that had so appealed to the production team and the actors.

Creativity couldn't be turned on and off like a tat machine.

She got up and went into the bathroom. The prescription from the ER stood on the back of the toilet. It was early yet to take another pain pill. She picked up the bottle. She'd been lucky. So far there'd been minimal swelling. She peeked under the bandage and winced. Fur Tree had done the right thing calling the ambulance.

He must think her a fool, rescuing her twice from a pint-sized kitten. She knew better than to get between spatting cats. They'd drilled that into her in her training for the Spay and Neuter Project. Throw water on them. Twist a towel around them. Use a broom. Anything but try to grapple with them barehanded.

She set the bottle down. She deserved the pain for being so stupid. Her arm brushed the edge of the sink.

White hot fire shot through her. Blast it. She seized the bottle and twisted off the cap.

Thump. Something hit the back wall of the building.

The bottle flew out of her hands, spewing pills everywhere. She held absolutely still, her breath jammed in her throat. Please. Please let it be a cat. Not someone coming for her. She closed her eyes and stood in place like a marble statue, the pain in her arm forgotten, her ears alert like a rabbit listening for the whirring wings of an owl.

The silence stretched in the dark. Blood pounded through her head, louder than any motorcycle. She gave herself a shake. Nothing. It was nothing. Just her imagination. She squatted down and began gathering up the pills.

Thump.

The hairs rose on the back of her neck. Someone was trying to get in through the back door. *Again.* Every muscle in her body tightened. She flicked off the bathroom light and huddled in the corner of the tiny room. They were coming for her again. She curled up tighter and waited for the nightmare to start all over.

****

Bella woke icy and stiff, as if she'd spent the night in a freezer. She opened her eyes and groaned. She'd fallen asleep in the yucky bathroom. She pushed herself up from the cold tiles and stretched to get rid of the kink in her back. A glance in the mirror made her wince. Hair frizzed out around her face like steel wool, and her eyes were puffy with dark circles under them. Her cat-torn arm felt like someone had slashed her with a razor. She peeked under the bandage. One good thing—at least the swelling had gone down.

She moved to the door and stopped at the threshold. Bright sunlight shone in the front store window illuminating dust motes. She forced herself to look in the other direction. The rear exit door was as securely bolted as ever. She tiptoed down the hall and undid the lock. The sunlit yard was peaceful. Cats nosed at the empty feed dishes. Someone in a neighboring apartment had hung out a line of underwear to dry. Farther down, a neighbor's dog rattled its chain.

Okay. She had to stop staying at the shop before she went crazy. She fed the cats, then went back inside. In the bathroom, she turned on the tap and waited for the water to come in hot. The old pipes gurgled. Lukewarm water spurted out. Quickly she stuck in the plug. She slipped out of her sweats and filled the sink with water. She didn't have the time, but today she needed to do serious apartment hunting, and looking scruffy wouldn't endear her to a potential landlord.

Bella grabbed her washcloth and started scrubbing. It was time to face reality. As long as it had a hot shower and a good lock on the door, any apartment would do.

When she was clean as she could get, she wiggled into her leggings and a tunic, her bandaged arm aching every time she moved. She'd have to cancel all her appointments for the day. Clients would not appreciate getting tattooed by a wounded woman. She threw back her head and rubbed her forehead. More lost revenue. At this rate, she'd not make the rent payment on The Siren this month.

She choked down two pain pills and strolled into

the waiting room. The sketchbook lay open. She flipped through the empty pages. Everything depended on the TV job. If she didn't have the finished sketches by the meeting with Henri and Pointy-Nose, she would not only let Ari and the villagers down, she'd soon be out of business.

Bella thought for a moment of calling Vernon. He'd lend her the money for sure. No. That would just get him started up again. It was better to do it herself.

Still, it was surprising he hadn't called her yet. It had been almost a week since the disastrous party. She took out her cell phone and rechecked. Nothing. She shrugged. Mr. Arrogant probably went to the Caymans on his own. For a moment, she wondered if she'd made a mistake. She shoved the phone back in her pocket.

Okay. Enough self-pity. She called her clients and rescheduled their sessions, cleared off her work counter and started to draw. She could do this.

Chapter 16

Vernon looked up from the page he was reading. His brother stood in the archway. He snapped the book closed and rose. "Should you be out of bed? You need rest."

Cole sauntered over and sprawled down in the chair in front of the fire. "I'll rest here."

Vernon pressed his lips together, nodded. There were more important things for them to battle over. "Sure. Can I get you something to eat?"

"A drink. Some of Pa's fine whiskey would hit the spot." His brother's breathing was ragged.

"I don't think—"

"Then don't. Just get me a tumbler. It'll dull the pain."

"You really should have a doctor examine you."

"I don't do *should*."

Vernon let out a quick breath. "Stop trying to be a badass. You're in pain. You need painkillers."

"Yep, I need some whiskey. Best painkiller in the world. Get that drink"—he sat up with a groan—"or I'll have to."

"Okay. Okay." Vernon moved to the bar running along the far wall of the expansive living room and poured a finger of his father's best single malt into the glass. He handed it to his brother with a grimace. With two black eyes, a swollen nose, and bruising the color of moldy mustard, he looked like something out of a zombie movie.

Vernon tried for a light tone. "Your face is looking better. The swelling's gone down some. Might need some work on the nose."

"I peeked in the mirror." Cole gulped down the drink and held out the empty glass. "Why fix the nose? Want to put me back the way I was?" He bared his teeth at him. "Good luck. I'm not like our brother Fancy-Man Theo."

Vernon wanted to smack him right in those provoking teeth. But he knew it would do no good. "Nina would—"

"You still talking to her after what she did to Pa?"

Vernon turned away. "We've reached a mutual arrangement. It wasn't her fault."

"That's right. It just *happened.* She had no inkling who those guys she let into the house were? Tell me another fairy tale."

Vernon hissed. "Bastard got what he earned. End of story."

Cole looked at the empty glass in Vernon's hand. "I'm waiting for that refill."

Vernon stalked over to the bar and poured another, then filled one for himself. So what if it was only nine in the morning. Dealing with his family would drive any man to drink before noon. And Cole was the toughest of the bunch to deal with. He loved him.

Vernon handed Cole the whiskey and sat down. Time to find out what was going on. The boy hadn't had the best of childhoods, had hated his guts for sticking him in the military school Nina had picked out, but he'd thought they'd gotten past that. He'd done fine in college. Was poised to become partner at a renowned law firm. That was until his rotten brother Theo had stepped into the picture and taken Cole under his wing and exposed him to the high life of the ruthless criminal.

He glanced at his brother. Everything about Cole screamed defiance, from his god-awful teeth to the gold earring in his ear. Trying to unearth what happened would be like picking a scab off a wounded beast. He took a sip of whiskey and let it burn down his throat. "So tell me how you landed in this condition."

"I had a disagreement."

"Obviously. With whom?"

A silly grin rolled across Cole's face. "*Whom*? A guy who never graduated high school, and whose only A was in woodworking, now uses words like *whom*?" He emptied his glass and lolled his head to one side. "Your little red-haired slut teach you that?"

Vernon's hand tightened on the glass. "Shut your trap."

"Oh, that's right, she's not a red-head. She's a curly brunette. Everywhere. Peachy keen breasts too. Nice rosy tan nipples. Lovely little seahorse tattoo on her inner thigh."

Vernon turned icy cold. The vein in his neck throbbed. His ears rang. He set down his glass carefully. And dove at his brother. He put his hands to either side of Cole's neck and leaned in. "And you come by this information how?"

Many men had shit their pants under his stare alone. Cole rolled his lips and stared straight into his eyes. "Personal observation."

Behind him, a log shifted in the fireplace. The

grandfather clock ticked in steady rhythm. Vernon leaned over Cole. "Did. You. Touch. Her?"

"You'll have to ask Miss Bella Bell." He ran his tongue over his teeth. "Oh, but she's broken off with you, hasn't she?"

"If you did anything to her, I will kill you."

"No, you won't. I'm your flesh and blood. Your special project. The sweet little brother who's going to make good." He reached up and grabbed Vernon by the wrists. "Now."

Someone captured Vernon from the back by the arms. A black bag descended over his head. A rope came around his neck, and he was hauled backwards, cutting off most of his air. Gasping, he put up his hands to yank the noose over his head, and his hands were seized and forced behind his back. *Click*. Handcuffs snapped around his wrists.

What the hell? He bent his knees and threw his shoulder into the unseen assailant. The man grunted and punched him in his kidney. Acrid pain blossomed up his side, and he stumbled forward. He landed against Cole's chest.

His brother whispered in his ear, "What do you think of your project now? All I had to do was let myself get beat up a bit, and I caught me a world-class criminal a lot of law enforcement types would love to have their hands on. Did I do good or what, big brother? I'm going to be ridding the world of a major crime lord." He pressed his hand against Vernon's chest and pushed him back. "God, I've always wanted to say this. Take the prisoner to the dungeon, my brave knights."

"Bastard!" Vernon roared and threw his body

toward where he thought his brother was standing. Something hard came down on his head. And everything went black.

Chapter 17

Bella shaded in the tip of the serpent's tail and laid down her pencil. Done. She rubbed her eyes as she flipped through the pages. She couldn't help thinking she'd forgotten one. But for the life of her, she couldn't recall an actor she'd missed. The dragons were for the lead. The Celtic cuffs for the sidekick apprentice. The hearts and sayings for the bitchy heroine. The rival tattoo artist got to wear the best of all in her mind—a huge snarling needle-toothed gryphon on his chest with wings that wrapped around the actor's shoulders so they gave him the appearance of an angel from the back until he turned around.

She gathered the sketches together and slipped them into her portfolio. She'd arranged to have dinner with Henri in the evening. She'd show him the designs. If something was missing she'd be able to complete it before the meeting tomorrow morning. She ran her hand over the leather case. She'd prove to Miss Demon-Pants that Bella Bell was not a fly-by-night.

She hurried into the bathroom, combed her fingers through her frizz, straightened her white sweater. Now she was off to sign the lease on the apartment she'd found. It was cramped and low-ceilinged, stank of dog, and had a view of a brick wall, but she couldn't stay here a day longer. A chill rattled down her spine as she remembered the noises in the night. Too many ghosts.

As she headed for the door, she spied the portfolio sitting out on the counter. Those sketches were worth everything to her.

A bad feeling hit her. Anyone could break in and find them there. She glanced out at the sunshiny street. Heavens, she was being paranoid. But hell, worse things had happened. For a moment, she considered taking it with her, but she'd already lost the first sketches in the cab. She couldn't risk that again. She looked around for a place to stash them. Her metal file cabinet. It locked.

She wedged the portfolio in the bottom drawer and turned the key. She pushed it back against the wall. Perfect. No one would think of looking in there.

She stepped out of The Siren and locked the place up behind her. The owner of the boutique next door was standing in the entrance sunning herself. Today the perky pixie was wearing a glitter-covered halter top and black and white checked leggings. "Beautiful day."

"That it is, Eileen." Bella smiled. "Hard to believe it's almost Christmas."

"Yeah. You got plans?" She slipped her sunglasses down her nose.

Bella shook her head. "All my family's in Greece."

"Not spending it with your guy?

"We broke up."

"Oh, I wondered why I hadn't seen his watchers around."

"Watchers?"

"Yeah, his spies or whatever. There's always one on every corner. Kind of liked it. Made me feel safe when I closed up in the evening. But they've been gone a week or so."

Bella bit her lip. Vernon had been watching out for her safety, and she hadn't even known. But if his men were gone, he really had given up. A gaping hole opened in her chest, and she caught a sob in her throat.

"You okay?"

She managed to nod.

"Didn't mean to upset you. Miss him, huh?" Eileen's arm wrapped over her shoulder, her multitude of bracelets jingling. "You'll get—"

Boom.

Boom.

Whoosh. The ground shook under Bella's feet. Glass shattered and flew past her. Tiny shards cut into her skin. Her ears rang. She clung to Eileen as they hurtled against the door frame of the boutique. The world filled with dust. Fiery heat scalded her nose. Someone was screaming.

There was a large thud. Something heavy landed on top of her. The air pressed out of her lungs, and she slid down, choking, struggling to breathe. Far, far away sirens wailed.

Then silence.

****

Minutes or hours later, sound roared back into her ears. Men shouting. Engines screeching. Snapping and popping. A thunderous crash.

Bella opened her eyes to a world flashing red and white. Blurs of color moved around her in slow motion. Intense heat struck her face. She tried to suck in a breath and couldn't. Something heavy pressed against her chest. She looked down and gasped. The boutique owner lay atop her, crumbled up like a broken doll, her pink hair singed black. Bile rose in her throat and lodged there.

Bella struggled and pushed to free herself from the dead weight of her friend's body, but she had no strength. She flopped back, her hands sticky and wet with blood.

Voices yelled, "Over here!" Glass crunched under heavy boots. A black shadow hung over her. She peered up into a face masked like a Darth Vader look-alike.

He bent over her and spoke calmly. "Stay still— lady—you're hurt—" Each word was separated by a breathy hiss.

The weight on her chest lifted, and she sucked in roasted air that tasted of hot metal and burnt wood. She coughed, and pain shot through her lungs.

"Take—it easy—the medics—are coming," he said in that same strange half-hiss voice.

She sucked in another mouthful of ash and dust and coughed again, her throat raw, her stomach roiling. More footsteps crunched in the glass. More shadows came round her.

"No—" Her voice came from a distance, swallowed up by a jet-engine pitched roar that stung her ears and made the very air vibrate. She struggled to get up—a scream building inside.

Someone clasped her head between two thickly-gloved hands while another squeezed her fingers and toes and asked questions. She tried to free her head. She had to see—see what had happened. But whoever held her head was strong.

"Superficial wounds. Maybe broken ribs. Okay to transport."

The hands were replaced with a hard collar, and she was rolled onto a backboard. For a moment, as she tipped sideways, she saw a wall of flame, then a mask came over her mouth and nose, and plasticized oxygen entered her lungs. She sucked it in greedily and suddenly thought screamed back into her head in full clarity.

The Siren had exploded. She'd almost been killed. She jerked against the straps holding her down.

Her cats—

Her sketches—

Her tattoo shop—

The blurred colors and shapes solidified into men in yellow-striped, black slickers and FDNY helmets. Out of the corner of her eye, she glimpsed flickering flames and black smoke shooting up into the sky. She moaned, and a fireman came into view. "My cats—"

But the man shook his head and turned away. The stretcher bumped into the ambulance, and for the second time in a week, she was off to the emergency room.

****

Bella opened her eyes into a blazing white overhead light and closed them again. Her throat burned with every breath, and her face throbbed like it had been stabbed with a thousand pins.

Something jostled her, and she forced her eyes open again. A gigantic face, less than an inch away, stared down at her. She screamed.

"She's awake."

"Get the hell off her, Hanger."

The mattress shifted, and the face disappeared.

"Sorry. The kid has no patience. He didn't hurt you, did he?"

"No," Bella rasped. "Just startled me." She peered

up. The speaker was Toro. The young graffiti artist's skin was deeply tanned, his posture straight, his legs firmly planted. The stay on Eudokia had been a healing one. The last time she'd seen the boy, he'd been a limp body, more dead than alive, lying in a heap on the cellar floor with a fractured neck.

Behind him stood the rest of T-Crew—Fur Tree and the twins Solo and Neto. Hanger clasped the bed rail and bopped up and down.

She lifted a hand. It took more effort than she expected. She let it drop back on the cotton blanket and glanced around. Blue-and-white patterned curtains surrounded her bed. Voices and clangs and rolling wheels sounded from the other side. "Where am I?"

"At Bellevue ER," Fur Tree said, moving to the front. "You've been out a while. But they said there are no major injuries. Concussed, cut up, and bruised all over though. They'll be sending you home shortly. After the doctor signs the release papers. We here to take you to our place."

"You'll stay in our apartment," Toro said. "Hanger can sleep on the sofa."

"I don't want to put you out."

Toro frowned. "None of that nonsense. Your brother gave us the building. The least we can do is take care of his sister."

Hanger peeked out from behind his brother. "Besides, you look like you've been fighting zombies. Can't have you walking around scaring people."

Toro put a hand on his little brother's shoulder. "Stop it, you're frightening her."

Bella ran her fingers over her face and down her neck. There was a large bandage on her forehead and smaller butterflies on her cheeks and chin and neck. Touching them stung. She dropped her hand onto the blanket. It could have been much worse. Eileen's body had shielded her from the flying debris.

Bella looked from face to face. A gaping pit opened in her stomach. "The Siren?"

Fur Tree picked up her hand. "A total loss."

"My cats?"

"I didn't see any sign of them. But they won't let me past the curb. Place isn't safe."

"You've been there?"

Fur Tree nodded. "I got a tweet on my phone there'd been an explosion, and rushed over. They'd already taken you away. Complete destruction inside. At least there were no tenants upstairs. Looked like the ceiling fell in."

"Good thing you got your kit out."

"Yeah. Yours is a total loss." Fur Tree gave her a squint-eyed look and something turned in Bella's stomach. They'd parted with bad feelings—he wouldn't have bombed her studio—would he?

Bella closed her eyes and sucked in a breath. She refused to believe the apprentice she'd taken under her wing would do something so horrid. Bomb The Siren— that was more like something one of Vernon's cronies would do. Air scraped down her raw throat and sent her into a coughing fit. Toro handed her a glass of ice water. She took a sip. "Was it a gas leak or something like that?"

The graffiti artist shrugged. "They said suspicious explosion on the news. They wouldn't have said suspicious if they knew for sure it was an accident."

A chill ran through her body. "Noises. I heard

noises last night round back. That could have been someone setting a bomb." She collapsed against the pillow. "*Heavens*. If I hadn't stepped out at that moment, I would have been *killed.*" The glass wobbled in her hand.

Toro snatched it up and set it on the tray table. "But why? Who would bomb The Siren?

Bella's heart clenched. The person who sent those threatening notes. Made those phone calls. One of Vernon's enemies.

She squeezed the hospital blanket in her hands. It could have been anybody inside that stone tomb. Was Tuccio still out there? Had Vernon lied?

Vernon. Where was he? He might be angry at her, but he'd have come if he knew she'd been hurt. She peered up at the T-Crew members. "Has Vernon—does Vernon know?"

Fur Tree shrugged. "An explosion at The Siren? It's been all over the news. Front page of the *Daily* this morning. He'd have to be in Timbuktu to not have heard."

There was a commotion at the doorway, and Henri Avery strode in, carrying a huge bouquet of pink roses. Miss Pointy-Nose, in her signature fire-engine red suit, trotted in after him, her spike-heeled boots clicking on the tile, a gaily-wrapped gift under her arm.

"Forget Vernon." Fur Tree jerked his chin toward Avery. "See, even your pity-date heard."

Bella sent him a warning look and reached out to take the flowers. "They're beautiful."

Henri bent down and kissed her cheek. "I am so sorry, my dear." He stared at her for a moment. "Your poor face."

Bella buried her nose in the roses. She must really be a fright.

"The nurse we talked to says the cuts will heal without too much scarring," Toro said. "Might need some plastic surgery for the one on the forehead."

Henri turned to Gloria. "The gift."

She held out the box with a smile as false as her nose. "This is from all the crew of *Secret Ink*."

"That's so kind of you." Bella untied the ribbon and ripped off the paper.

Hanger leaned over the bedrail. "Yummy. Godiva chocolates. Can I have one?"

Toro grabbed his hand. "Manners."

The kid slipped out of his hold and sat down on the edge of the bed. His fingers pried at the lid. "Pretty please with feta cheese on top? *Parakalo.*"

"Learned some Greek, did you?" Bella handed the box to him. "Help yourself."

Hanger plopped a large chocolate into his mouth.

Miss Pointy-Nose pinched her lips together. "This your kid, Miss Bell? You must be older than I thought."

Bella's jaw tightened. The bitch thought she'd scored on that.

Hanger popped another chocolate in his mouth. "Who are you, lady?"

Cooper gave him a scrunched-up look and yanked the box away from him.

Henri stepped between them. "Tsk Tsk, Gloria. Taking candy from babies. I'm surprised at you."

"That is no baby."

Henry shrugged and turned to Bella. "The nurse at the nursing station says they won't release you until the doctor has been by again. The wounds are minor. But I wouldn't expect you to make this afternoon's launch meeting—I thought—if you had the sketches—could tell me where to find them, I could present them."

The sketches. A huge weight pressed against her chest. "They were in the studio. In the metal cabinet." She glanced at Fur Tree. "Could you see? Could the file cabinet be okay?"

"The whole inside is smithereens and ashes, Bella. Nothing survived. *Nothing.*"

Henri's mouth twisted. "I was afraid of that."

"I told you." Gloria said stamping her foot. "You should have made copies of her prelims. But no, all you were interested in was flirting and getting a stupid tattoo." She gave him a big plastic smile. "And who's gonna finish that idiot thing on your back now?

Fur Tree moved closer. "What sketches?"

"Miss Bell *had been* contracted to do the tattoo designs for a new television series we are producing," Gloria said. "Now we'll have to hire a replacement ASAP."

Bella's throat seized up. She had nothing left. No home. No tattoo studio. No income. And now—no TV series. Because of her, the island would lose its helicopter. Injured villagers and premature babies would die.

She closed her eyes, suddenly weak and hopeless like the naïve child she'd been the day her mother sank below the waves and abandoned her to her merciless father. She'd wanted to crawl into a dark cave and hide, the way she'd done that day. Only this time, no big brother would be coming to save her. No Vernon would arrive, bringing his luscious kisses to restore her desire to live. She rubbed the scars on her wrists carefully hidden beneath the band of curving waves and Greek frets. Her first tattoos. Done by her mentor. The man who'd taken her in and taught her to take joy in her art—joy in transferring beauty from her mind to a canvas of skin.

The last eight years of hard work and determination had been for nothing. She was a *Has Been* in every sense of the word.

Toro laid a hand on her shoulder. "*Qué diablos.* Bella you've turned white as a sheet." He turned to Hanger. "Get a nurse. *Rápido.*"

Fur Tree waved in Henri's direction. "Come. She's in shock. Better we talk outside. I think I can help." He escorted the director through the curtains and out the door, Pointy-Nose trailing behind them.

Bella watched them leave, her stomach hollow, her brain whirling. It was like her future was disappearing. "Wait." She pushed herself up and swung out her leg to get out of bed. It was asking too much of her abused body. Every bone and muscle screamed in pain. For a moment, the world blackened, and then she fell back in defeat.

Chapter 18

Vernon woke cold, hungry, and in the complete dark. They'd left the hood on him. Not a speck of light peeked through the cloth. Damn his brother. What the hell did the idiot think he was doing? Even the lowest street criminal knew you didn't take the man at the top captive and give him time to think about how to escape. You took him out. *Wham. Bam.*

He rolled onto his side, the handcuffs cutting painfully into his wrists. They'd taken his socks and boots and stripped him to his underwear. Chill damp soaked through the thin cotton from the rough cement underneath him. His muscles quivered with the cold. Every part of his body ached as if he'd been dropped over a cliff. He sucked air in and out, choking on the stink of the hood as it pressed against his nose and mouth. It had obviously held old rags or worse and never been washed.

He couldn't stay like this, a landed fish waiting for his brother's goons to come filet him. Using what little strength his half-numb body could summon, he rolled and twisted like a snake until he reached a wall and levered himself up to a half-prone position. Just having a wall behind him made him feel more in control. If Cole wanted to take him out, it wouldn't be from the back.

He took stock of his injuries. His head throbbed

where they'd clubbed him. His wrists were raw from the cuffs, his fingers stiff from where he'd been lying atop them. He probably had bruises on his back, hips, and thighs from being manhandled. But nothing serious. His brother didn't mean to kill him, then. This was a holding maneuver of some kind.

Which meant he didn't have long to wait. If there was one thing his father had made clear to his boys, it was never take more than a few minutes to make a decision on someone you held captive—especially someone who knew you well.

He had no idea how long he'd been unconscious. Time was of the essence. Cole would be coming through the door any minute now.

He leaned against the wall and tried to get his feet under him and raise himself to a standing position. And for a moment, he managed. But not for long. Dizziness overcame him and he wobbled, tipped over, and fell, hitting his battered head on the cement.

He lay still on his stomach, his cheek pressed against the prickly burlap bag, the clammy cloth sticking to his face. Every breath tasted like dirty socks. He had to get the hood off or go crazy.

But first, the cuffs. He strained against the metal, ignoring the hard edge cutting into his wrists. Good quality. Probably from the stash under the kitchen sink. The Pines had been one of his father's torture houses, back in the old days.

He jerked with all his strength in an attempt to break the chain. No luck. Still, there wasn't a pair of cuffs made he couldn't get out of. But hell, in the condition he was in, it was going to hurt. Cursing, he flipped onto his back, bent up his knees and began the tortuous process of bringing the cuffs over his butt and legs. The position brought back memories.

When he was a kid, he'd been a champion at getting out of handcuffs. It was a game he and his brothers played every time they'd come to The Pines. And he'd been the best.

But he was a heck of a lot bigger and more bulky than he'd been at thirteen, and his head hadn't been concussed. Shaking off the constant pounding beneath his skull, he arched his back and brought the cuffs down lower. The sides of his hands scraped against the concrete. His own weight drove the metal of the cuffs deeper into his wrists. His arm muscles stretched past bearing. His shoulders cramped. He stopped struggling.

Damn, Bella was right, he *was* getting old and stiff. He let his body fall limp. Now, if Bella had put these cuffs on him—heat flowed through him as he pictured his beautiful temptress kissing his helpless body, starting at his neck and working her way down. Yes, that was what handcuffs were for.

Hell, he missed her. He'd meant to call and apologize when he got back to the city. Now he might never get back. Would she care if he disappeared forever?

He rolled his shoulders and winced. Didn't matter. He cared. There were things to do to keep her safe, before he was sent to whatever hellish place murderers went when they died.

There was a clanking sound. He pressed his ear against the freezing wall. A slight vibration told him someone was opening the castle gates. Maybe something was about to happen.

Enough playing a dead fish.

Arching his back, he used his cuffed hands to push up into a sitting position. He began again to work the cuffs down his backside. Damn. Now the stupid things were stuck in his underwear.

He turned his wrist so the inside rested against his back and, ignoring the pain shooting up his arm, felt around the cuffs. The cloth of his briefs was twisted in the bar chain. He took a deep breath and jerked hard. Fire radiated through his muscles and exploded in his head. He stopped and waited for the dizziness and nausea to pass.

He started again. Using his fingers, he worked the thin cotton free. There. He exhaled, put one foot flat on the floor and raised his butt and finagled one leg through his cuffed hands. Getting his other leg through after that was as easy as taking down a competitor horning in on a piece of real estate he had dibs on.

Hands now in front, he tore off the hood and blinked. It was as dark as it been inside the bag, and smelled worse. The place reeked of mold and the kind of damp that infected the lungs. He took a shallow breath. The sooner he was out of here the better.

He stretched out his fingers and pressed them against the wall, reaching in all directions. As he expected: bare concrete. It had to be the wine cellar. Not that it had ever held any wine.

Papa had no use for namby-pamby drinks, and the eccentric who'd built the place in the late '40s had never actually lived in it. Too isolated and cold for the man's California-born starlet wife.

Vernon's bare feet curled against the frigid floor, and he shivered. Right now his sympathies lay with the wife.

He gave himself a shake and concentrated on the handcuffs. It was time he got out of this freezing pit. Putting his wrists together, he twisted and turned. *Snap.*

He smiled. Something Papa never learned. Good quality cuffs were easier for a strong man to break than cheapo ones. He rubbed his sore wrists and stretched his cramped muscles. Time to get into position. Cole had used the element of surprise against him. Now he'd surprise him back.

Keeping his hand against the wall, he took a step forward. Yep, had to be the unused wine cellar. No shelves like in the other basement store rooms. He followed the wall to the corner and continued around. There was a door somewhere—a big, heavy, metal monstrosity covered in raised bumps like in a TV movie dungeon—and he'd eventually find it.

He rounded the next wall and inched forward. No door. He continued on, came to the next corner. Had that been four turns? He rubbed his aching head. Had he miscounted? He stumbled forward. There had to be a door. Heart thumping, he ran his palm along the wall, moving faster, counting out loud. "One—a long wall. Two—a short wall. Three—a long wall. Four—a short wall."

His voice dropped to a whisper. "Zero. No door."

Vernon let himself slip down to the icy cold concrete. He wasn't in the wine cellar. He was in the only place in The Pines that had no doors—the cistern. The dark, scary place his father had always threatened to lock him and his brothers in when they got too vicious with each other.

He blinked up into the blackness. The only way out was a heavy metal plate high up in the vaulted ceiling.

Cole didn't mean to just kill him. He meant to torture him first.

Vernon sank down on to the floor and settled in to wait.

It didn't take long. Just minutes later, a metal plate grated overhead, confirming his guess. He pulled his feet under him and forced himself to stand. Every muscle screamed in agony. Those few minutes had been long enough for his sweat-covered muscles to stiffen in the cold.

The grating sound stopped and a blinding beam of light flooded the pit, moving around the floor until it found him and halted.

"Comfortable, brother?"

Vernon grunted. "Why don't you come down and find out?"

"No, I think not. You're the one who's been the bad boy. Not me."

"Enough silliness. What do you want?"

"Everything."

"So there's a whole world out there. Go help yourself."

"Let me clarify. I want everything that's *yours*. My due."

"Your due?"

"Yeah. Papa didn't have the right to hand his empire over to you and leave Theo and me out."

"Stop whining, kid. You got plenty, plus an education. You're a fucking corporate lawyer living on Sutton Place. You have half of Mother's holdings. How much money and power do you need?"

"You betrayed Theo. Got him murdered because he demanded you give him what he was owed."

"Yeah, and that worked out great for him, didn't it? What makes you think I will give you what I refused to give Theo?"

"Take a good look around. As long as you hold one penny of the family money, you are not leaving this hole."

Vernon put his hands behind his head and tried to imagine he was sunning himself on the beach in the Caymans. "Yeah, well then, I'd best get comfortable. You'll have a long wait."

The metal cover rattled. "I could just let you die down there with no food or water. Wouldn't take long."

"*Wimp.* If you are going to kill me, do it face to face. Like a man. None of this weakling stuff—starve a man to death? Papa would be laughing in his grave."

"I'm no *weakling.* You tried to make me one so I wouldn't challenge you." There was the click of a gun being cocked. "I could shoot you right now."

Vernon stood up and shading his eyes walked to the center of the cistern. "Making idle threats, little brother, is the sign of a weakling, too."

The gun came up again. "Don't. Call. Me. That."

Vernon stared up at the muzzle of the gun pointing down at him. He took in a breath and expanded his chest. "You want to run a criminal empire? Be my guest. Shoot. We all have to die sometime. Never expected to live very long myself. Not in my line of business. But I'll tell you a hard truth, Cole. Shooting me won't put you at the top of the pile. You'll have to fight the rest of the cutthroats out there for Pa's crime empire. And it ain't worth one drop of anyone's blood." He threw back his shoulders. "Put me out of my misery and go make your own way. I did my best to set you straight, but if you want to be as crooked as your damn teeth, go ahead. I'm not stopping you."

"What a touching speech, big brother, and here I always thought you a man of big fists and few words." Cole peered down at him. "But you're wrong. I think a few signatures on some papers and a few Swiss bank account numbers and passwords will go a long way to setting me up in a style where I can compete out there. Got me a take on where to sell a lot of armaments to some hungry guys in the Middle East. And I hear you own a private Greek island with a helicopter pad. Sounds like the perfect place to set up my headquarters."

Bella's Eudokia. Vernon's stomach cramped. Cole would destroy the place. He wanted to wring the brat's neck. "Don't own any island."

Cole laughed. "Well, not officially. But you pay for its upkeep. Have a lovely villa. I *am* a property lawyer—a good one—and I do know how to find out about people's holdings. I'm sure I could convince your little red-headed bed warmer to sign it over to me. She's not feeling too good right now." He waved the gun. "Do you wish her a short life, too?"

Vernon's stomach twisted into a tight knot. "What have you done to Bella?"

Cole dropped a bag down the hole. It plopped at Vernon's feet. "Not much yet. Just gave her a little scare. She's out of the hospital now"

Vernon's heart sped up. "Hospital! She's hurt?"

"I'll save the details until our next visit."

Vernon shook his fist. "Damn you."

"Yep, I am as damned as you, big brother. But there's a difference. Tuccio told me a secret about you.

He says you have a tender heart. While me, I have no heart at all. You destroyed it the day you killed Papa."

Vernon peered up at his brother. "I *did not* kill him."

"Not what Mama says."

"And you believe her?"

"Mama'd never lie to me. But you would." The light disappeared, and the lid slid across half-way, then stopped. Cole's head filled the space. "So I'm going to kill what you love first. Before I kill you."

Chapter 19

Bella stood outside the yellow police tape and covered her nose with her scarf. It had rained during the night, and the stink of wet ash and melted plastic and singed metal hung over the street in a noxious fog.

There was more of the building standing than she expected. The two-story structure was old, probably from the turn of the century when people built solid. Most of the brick walls stood except in the front where the shop windows had blown out. She narrowed her eyes and strained to see into the black hole that had once been The Siren—a hole that matched the one in her stomach. Had anything survived?

Light glinted off something surprisingly blue in the blackened rubble. She stood on her toes to see better. Could it be? Was that her eyeball paperweight? Her grandma had insisted it would protect her against the Evil Eye, but only if she kept it close.

She moved in to get a better angle and crooked her neck to the side. It was. It had to be. She pressed against the police tape. Just a few more feet and she could reach it.

"Step away, lady." A broad-shouldered fireman with a rosy-cheeked, boyish face put out his arm and herded her back into the small crowd of onlookers. He turned to go and jerked back. "Bella Bell? That you?"

She glanced at him again. Of course, he'd been a

customer. "Eddie Green, I didn't know you were a fireman."

He gave her a little smirk. "The fact that you tattooed a large flame on my chest didn't give you a hint?" His lips turned under. "I'm sorry about your shop."

"Is there any chance I can get in and see if any of my belongings survived?"

He shook his head. "No one's allowed in. Fire is under investigation. And there are concerns the whole second floor could cave at any minute." Two men in protective gear carrying clipboards stepped under the tape and began measuring the debris area. Eddie nodded toward them. "The inspectors have just arrived."

Bella peeked around him. "Have you seen any cats? Two—a big old orange tabby and a small gray kitten were inside."

The fireman tipped back his hat. "Nothing alive would have survived the heat of a fire like this one."

The pit in her stomach sank deeper. "Any idea what caused it?

"Nothing official. But to me, it looks to be a homemade job. Something small and cheap. Whoever did it wasn't aiming to bring the building down. Just do a lot of damage inside your place. I hope you have insurance?"

Insurance. *Sweet koulouria*. She hadn't updated it in years. There was some. But not enough to replace all her supplies and equipment. To get started again. She chewed her lip. And insurance couldn't replace Pussyballs and Fishtail and her sketches.

The fireman patted her on the shoulder. "It's hard

to lose pets, but at least you survived."

She swallowed the bitter lump in her throat and stared at the paperweight. It was the only thing left. That had to mean something. "See that bluish ball over there by the corner of the building. It was a gift from my grandmother. Do you think you could get it for me?"

Eddie looked over to where the inspectors were comparing notes. "Well, it's outside the building. Sure, why not? Anything for my favorite tattoo artist." He strolled over and pried the bit of glass from under the twisted piece of metal that had probably been part of the file cabinet that held her sketches.

He handed it to her. The blue ball with the white swirl and yellow eye was intact but riddled with cracks, just like her life. She clenched it in her hand and nodded. The lump in her throat prevented her from voicing even a thank you.

She dropped the *mati* in her pocket, turned to go, and ran smack into the back of a tall woman in a lime green suit wearing an expensive perfume so strong it overpowered the reek of the fire. "Sorry."

The woman spun around. "Oh. Miss Bell. Just the woman I need to see."

Bella stepped back. The last time she'd seen the woman staring back at her, she'd been clinging to Theo Tuccio. "You're—you're that big mouth who was Tuccio's—*thing.*"

"*Thing?* Well, yeah. Whatever." The woman put out her hand. "Jana Firth, Banker Hudson Real Estate Brokers. We got business, you and I."

Bella took another step back. "I want nothing to do with you. You—betrayed Melissa."

Jana's lips twisted into a crooked line, and she dropped her hand. "Yeah, made some bad choices. But that's neither east nor west of Manhattan. We still need to talk. Vernon Newell owned this building, and I have to assess your culpability in this destruction of his property. For insurance purposes."

Bella shuffled her feet on the pavement. "Vernon Newell owned The Siren?"

"No." Jana turned and looked down the row of shops. "Actually, the whole block. Mr. Newell owns a lot of Brooklyn real estate. But you must know that, being you two were so close."

Blood pounded in Bella's head. "He never said."

Jana shrugged. "Yeah, the big guys like their little secrets, don't they? Still, no reason to get your panties in a twisteroo."

"But I've been paying rent to Banker Hudson. You're saying he was my *landlord?*"

"He probably didn't even realize it. Banker Hudson manages the properties for him." The real estate agent glanced at the blown-out shop. "He might make the connection now. Newells don't like people doing nasty things to their belongings. Then again, he may not. He's got a financial empire that pretty much runs itself." She tapped her expensively-clad foot. "Speaking of belongings, where is Mr. Newell anyway? Thought you two were a number. Can't believe he'd let his fiancée walk around looking like"—she gave her a once over—"a rag-mop. He likes his women classy. The wounded-warrior look can't be helped, I guess. But what *is* that you are wearing?"

Bella grimaced. She'd borrowed the ratty jeans, paint-splattered sweatshirt, and too-small winter jacket from Toro in her rush to see the results of the explosion. She'd planned to hit the thrift store after here. "All my clothing was in there." She pointed at The Siren. "Some of my brother's friends lent these to me until I could go shopping."

Jana reached out and touched the spray paint stain on the sleeve of the men's quilted down jacket she was wearing. "Oh, I thought maybe you did street art on the side." She narrowed her eyes. "And no wig? I almost didn't recognize you. But those wrists are so distinctive." She leaned in. "But wait a minute. Did you just say all your clothes were inside the shop?" She tapped her fingers together. "*Were you living in there?*"

Bella closed her eyes. Living in the shop went against the terms of the lease. She was in big trouble, but she had to say something. "I'd just got back from a trip, and my suitcase was inside." There, that was close to the truth.

"You *were.*" There was a triumphant note in Jana's voice. "The famous Williamsburg tattoo artist, Bella Bell, whose photo has graced a number of local mags and blogs and even the *New York Times* could not fit all her clothes into a suitcase—or two." She clapped her hands together. "You broke the terms of the lease. Didn't you? So what happened? You were cooking with a portable gas stove and it blew up?"

"No. I wasn't even inside when it happened."

"Ah, so you admit leaving the shop untended." Jana did a little shimmy. "You, my dear, are heading to court. You owe my client for the damages."

"Vernon. He would never—"

"Never what?"

"Sue me."

"Who knows what the man will do? My agency will recommend a lawsuit. I'll send a field agent around to get more info. I don't usually do my own inspections anymore. I came when I saw your name. Give me your address where you're staying. The old one didn't work."

"Wait a minute. *Your agency*? How did you end up owning a huge realty firm like Banker Hudson? Just a year ago you were a lowly sales agent, busy messing up my sister-in-law's life."

"Don't you know? Vernon was such a sweetheart after that bloody mess with his brother Tuccio. Felt bad, I guess, the way he treated me. Well, anyway, he set me up on my own. Gave me his properties to manage."

"I don't believe you. He would never have helped you—you nearly got my brother killed."

"I had good reasons for what I did." The woman straightened. "As I said, Vernon Newell is a lovely, sweet man who knows how to forgive and forget. Something you seem to have trouble doing." She tapped her lips with her finger. "In fact, I heard a rumor that you and he are on the outs." Jana looked her up and down. "Hadn't believed it. He was gaga over you. But that would explain a lot of things. Hmm, I might just mosey over to his place and console him on his loss." She stepped to the curb and waved down a cab.

Bella fisted her hands. The woman was poison. No way would she let Jana Firth console Vernon. She dashed to the curb and seized the Firth woman by the shoulder. She spun her around. "No, I *will* tell him. And *you* will be out of business."

Jana gave a little smile and shoved her hand off. "Go ahead. I do believe that sweet man will enjoy discussing his interests with me more than with you, Miss Scar Face. However, do as you wish."

Bella fell back. She slapped her hands over her face and clawed at the bandages. Jana was right. How could she face Vernon looking like this? He'd think her a monster.

Chapter 20

Bella wrapped the scarf around her head and drew it over the lower half of her face. It was cold and frigid out—a typical December night. She pulled the scarf higher. After three days, the cuts and bruises around her mouth and nose were looking worse than ever. Normal healing, the doctor said when he'd removed the bandages. But even Hanger On wouldn't look at her.

It would be months before she could have plastic surgery to repair the slash on her forehead. That is, if she had the money to pay for it. She didn't want Vernon to see her looking like this. But she couldn't wait any longer. She needed to know where he'd stashed her belongings. She needed the deed to the Eudokia villa handed over to her.

"You sure you want to go now?" Toro asked. "It's dark out."

Bella looked over at the street artist sitting on the sofa with his brother, eating popcorn and watching a very loud action movie. She wasn't used to explaining her actions, especially to two kids. "I can't get that woman's voice out of my head. And where has Vernon been, anyway? We may have broken up, but you'd think he'd at least call to see how I'm doing."

"You could call him." Toro took a handful of popcorn and stuffed it in his mouth.

"Tried that. He's not picking up the phone for me.

Better face to face anyway. Besides, it's not late. Only six. I'd just be hitting my stride if The Siren was up and running." She gathered up her tote bag and tossed her cell phone inside. "I'll take a cab, have my say with the bastard, and be back before you're both in bed." She twisted the tote strap around her hand.

Toro looked up. "He'll let you into his penthouse fortress?"

Bella reached into her bag and pulled out her key ring. "I'm the former fiancée. I have an entry key and the passcode. I plan on walking right in."

Toro shook his fist. "Then go get him, girl." He scooped up another handful of popcorn. "But if you're not back before Hanger's bedtime, I'll send T-Crew after you."

Bella blew air through her teeth. These guys were great, but they were smothering her as much as Vernon had. Still, Hanger's bedtime—eleven—was hours away. She didn't have *that* much to say to Vernon. She tipped her head. "Deal."

"Sure. *Adios.*" Toro and his brother gave a wave and turned back to a wild gun battle scene.

Bella hurried down the steps and out the door of the apartment building her brother had bought for his graffiti artist friends. It had taken a good chunk of his money—money he could never replace with his art career destroyed. Damn Vernon. That was his fault, too.

She glanced at the boldly-lettered sign over T-Crew's storefront: Big Bad Brooklyn Art Tours. Inside, the twin brothers, Neto and Solo, were handing out brochures to a group of tourists. T-Crew had done well for itself over the past year running street art tours. She rubbed the spray paint spot on the jacket sleeve. Not that it had stopped them from plastering their graffiti tags all over Williamsburg, risking arrest every time. Her brother would be disappointed to know that. He'd hoped they'd go straight when he'd set them up in business.

She shifted her tote to her other arm and strode down to the corner. She understood why they took the risk. They were artists. And the urge to create, no matter what the consequences, was as compelling as the urge to eat or to make love.

T-Crew was driven to see how the world would change if you splashed color and form over a cement wall or across a bridge span. She was driven to needle her art into all the varieties of human skin and see her creations flow over muscle and bone like a living thing.

Her hands curled into tight balls. She missed tattooing with a vengeance. Not just for the art of it, but also because Daniela's girls needed Transformative Ink up and running again as soon as possible. She had enough money in her bank account to rent equipment and a station at Freddie's or some other run-of-the-mill tat shop. She shivered and pulled the scarf tighter. As soon as her face looked less monstrous, she'd ask around.

She peered down the street. Not a taxi in sight. But a bus was coming. Heavens, no sense waiting until a cab came along. She hurried to the bus stop and joined the line.

Two hulky men came up behind her. She glanced at them and a little prickle crawled up her neck. Unshaven, shifty-eyed, dressed all in leather they looked like the goons who had worked for Tuccio.

For a moment, she considered waiting for a taxi.

Then she gave herself a shake and moved a little closer to the kerchiefed elderly woman in front of her. She was being overly dramatic. She'd ridden buses before. It was rush hour. Besides, it couldn't be those men—Vernon had sworn they were long gone. She clasped her tote against her chest and faced forward.

Vernon had rewarded Jana after she'd betrayed Ari and Melissa. Had he really run those men off?

****

Five minutes later, Bella stepped off the bus and peered down the street toward the river. She'd forgotten she would have to walk three blocks to Vernon's place. He'd always driven her there and parked in his private parking garage.

Should she forget about seeing Vernon? She glanced back. The bus had already pulled away. Who knew when another one would arrive? It would be quicker to go to Vernon's. She'd get him to call a cab to take her back to Toro's.

She set off down the street, her thrift shop sneakers pinching her toes and the wind snapping around her, carrying the foul scent of the East River to her. It seemed particularly strong tonight. A chill trickled down her back and settled in her lower belly like a broken piece of concrete. The image of a dank basement and blood-splattered floor sliced through her memory, and she was there again, bound hand and foot, a knife tip at her throat, a man with shark teeth leering at her.

Her heart thundered in her chest. Blood pounded in her ears. Her wrists burned as the zip tie dug in.

No. She gave herself a hard shake and increased her stride.

The stink of the river had brought back that horrid night, and she would not succumb to that torment again. She pressed the scarf against her nose and willed herself into the present. She flexed and released her fists and concentrated on pushing the nightmare into a box and slamming the cover the way the therapist had taught her.

She looked around. It was early evening. The neighborhood hummed with activity. People hurried home from work. Traffic zoomed by—a BMW, then a limo, followed by a police car. This was a good neighborhood. Wealthy people—billionaires like Vernon Newell—lived in these condos, paying millions of dollars just to have a prime view of the Manhattan skyline. A high-class gym occupied one side of the street. Inside under lights brighter than daylight, people sweated on treadmills and lifted weights.

It was perfectly safe. But fear kept seeping out from under the lid of her boxed memories. She bit her lip and lengthened her steps.

One block down. Two blocks to go.

She crossed the street and stepped up on the curb. The tap of footsteps sounded behind her. Her body tensed, ready to run. She sucked in a breath of the noxious air and blew it out. She was being foolish. Several well-dressed people had gotten off the bus with her and were also heading toward the high rises lining the river. If anything, she was the one out of place, dressed as she was in washed-out jeans and a shabby down jacket.

She quickened her pace. Two blocks done. One more to go. She was almost there.

The footsteps behind her came closer. She glanced

over her shoulder. A man in a business suit, briefcase under his arm, was hurrying toward her, his gaze fixed to his cell phone. He looked innocuous. Still, it paid to be alert anywhere in the city. She cut across to the other side of the street, where the streetlight was brighter, and sped up, her rubber soles slapping against the pavement.

Vernon's building loomed ahead. Just a little farther and she'd be there. She turned down the brick-paved promenade leading to the main entrance and pulled open the glass door. She risked a quick glance back. The businessman had disappeared.

Bella released the grip on her scarf, let out the breath she'd been holding, and stepped inside. The monsters on the street had been imaginary. But now she had to face the real monster: Vernon Newell.

She waved Vernon's key fob in front of the sensor, waited for the inner door to slide open, and then entered the huge lobby.

The white marble floor stretched the length of the building. A few blue and aqua upholstered sofas and an array of potted plants gave the space the appearance of a mid-class hotel quite out of character with the extravagant cost of living here. An armed guard clad all in white approached her, his hand on his gun, an eyebrow raised.

Her heart beat sped up. Vernon wouldn't have put her on a no-admittance list would he? She lowered her scarf. "I'm Vernon's Newell's fiancée."

The man thumbed through his tablet and nodded. "Apologies, Miss Bell. Hair's different from your photo." He studied her face and frowned. "You been in an accident?"

She slapped her hand to her cheek. She'd completely forgotten the cuts and bruises. "Uh—yes. Got hit with broken glass."

"I'm so sorry." He moved back and waved her to the private penthouse elevator. "Say hi to Vernon for me. Hasn't been through the lobby in quite a while."

"Sure thing." She managed a small smile, hoping it didn't look more like a grimace, and entered the code. The door opened instantly, and she stepped inside. Her battered face, crisscrossed with healing cuts, stared back at her off the highly polished steel walls. She really didn't want Vernon to see her looking like this.

She pulled her scarf up higher, and searched for the anger that had propelled her here. Instead, desire flowed through her body. Her pulse pounded. Heat built between her thighs. Fool, she still wanted the man, and her stupid, needy body seemed to sense she was getting close. She pressed her lips together and relegated her lust to the pit where it belonged. No way would she let Vicious Vernon back into her heart.

All too soon the elevator opened to the penthouse, and Bella stepped into the fortified entrance hall. She looked around, surprised to find it empty. One of Vernon's men, a cute young guy with brilliant blue eyes, always guarded the door when she'd stayed there the year before.

But maybe that was because Vernon hadn't wanted her sneaking out while he negotiated her "ransom" with her brother. Not that she'd been interested in fleeing. They'd been so hungry for each other after eight years apart that they hadn't left his bedroom for days.

She blinked away the vision of the two of them in his huge bed, his magnificent body wrapped around hers, and placed her hand on the palm reader. The door slid open, and she stepped inside. The room was dark. Too dark. A shiver crawled across her shoulders and down her back.

Bella found the wall switch and flicked on the lights. The overhead spots lit up the living room. She studied the space. Everything looked the same since her last visit. Vernon hadn't changed the décor she'd created with his money. The marble column coffee table, the Greek weaving over the sofa, the *flokati* rug on the floor all made her heart ache with homesickness. She ran her hand over the infamous bust of Archimedes with his broken nose standing on the pedestal in the vestibule. Vernon had insisted they bring the sculpture back when they'd gone to Eudokia for Melissa and Ari's wedding last summer.

Eudokia. Bella reached into her pocket and squeezed the glass paperweight. They should have stayed on the island and never come back. They'd been happy there, spending their days lolling on the beach as the waves ebbed and flowed, and their nights making love under the stars.

But that was before her lover turned into Mr. Boss Man, before his dead brother called her on the phone, and before The Siren blew up—destroying her business, killing her cats, and nearly killing her. She couldn't help, but believe it was all related.

She bellowed Vernon's name. Her voice echoed in the unnatural silence. She looked down the hall toward the kitchen and servant's quarters and called again. "Anyone here?"

Trickles of cold sweat ran down her back. Something was very wrong. It was dinner time.

Vernon's much-touted French chef should be rattling the pans in the kitchen. The fussy Swedish housekeeper, Lovisa, should be greeting her and showing her to a seat. And pain-in-the-ass Gav *never* left his side.

Bella peered down the opposite hall toward the bedrooms and called again. No answering voice came from the dark corridor.

He wasn't here. Nobody was. Damn the man. He *did* go to the Caymans without her. She pictured him lying on the beach with some floozy he'd picked up at a bar, and her blood boiled. She should turn on her heel and leave.

But she couldn't resist one last chance to wallow in self-pity for what Mr. Arrogance had tossed away with his I'm-In-Charge-Of-You attitude. She flicked on the hall lights and headed to the bedroom.

She opened the door and peered in. Through the wall of windows across from her, the lights of Manhattan shone, illuminating the super king-sized bed in the center of the room covered in tussled silk sheets. How many times had they made love in that bed, her hands discovering every part of his hard, hot body as he explored hers, teaching her to feel again, to trust again, to love again.

She threw herself face down on the bed and sucked in Vernon's distinctive citrusy cologne and the masculine scent that was uniquely his. She hated how she thirsted for him, how he made her feel weak and out of control.

She crawled under the silk top sheet and pulled it over her head, swaddling herself in an ocean of Vernon. Bitter tears gathered in the corners of her eyes. He'd ruined her. She'd never be able to make wild, abandoned love to another man. She was like one of *Baba* Eleni's baby chicks, firmly imprinted on the criminal bastard. Vernon Newell had taken her virginity and left her an aching puddle of need only he could fill.

She rubbed her face against the sheets and let her body sink into the bed, her stomach nestled in the cushiony foam mattress, and imagined Vernon kissing her, making her blood sing.

A tear ran down her cheek and pooled on the sheets, a dark stain against the white. Chill air settled over her and she gathered the cloth around her, the fine silk a mockery against her healing cuts and bruises.

She lay there staring up at the ceiling and regretted not kicking Vernon out the door when he'd shown up at The Siren a year ago, wearing his silly grin and a skin-tight T-shirt that showed off a body worthy of a Greek god.

Fool. She'd been so swept up rediscovering the man she'd thought lost forever that she'd let him keep her here for weeks, living in a dream world all their own. Just the two of them making love, eating, sleeping, and making love again, consulting with interior designers, redecorating his condo, and making love again and again and again.

All the while, her brother was in a panic, thinking her kidnapped, raising the ransom, spending his fortune to protect the island, and poor Melissa—her abandoned friend—was risking her life to find her.

She sat up and ran her hand through her hair. It had grown in the last few weeks and was now a mess of tangled curls. She finger-combed it as best she could. Then, her body shaking, her knees weak, she pushed her way off the bed and stood.

Ari had been right all those years ago when he'd chased Vernon Newell from her bed. She had fallen in love with a hard-hearted criminal. And now he had the nerve to just disappear. Bella tightened her fists. Blast it. She couldn't take her anger out on him if he wasn't here, and her body wouldn't let her forget him.

She straightened her jeans, tucked in her shirt, thought a moment about making the bed and rejected it, then strode from the room. The door to his office was cracked open a few inches. He'd never allowed her in there when she'd shacked up with him.

She stopped and gave the door a slight push. It swung a little wider, revealing a huge glass desk heaped with papers and on the wall above it, one of Ari's paintings. It showed a young girl standing on the cliff edge. Her back arched, her long, dark hair streaming behind her. Hands wrapped in ruby red bracelets stretched outward in a graceful arc like some Greek maiden contemplating diving into the sea. Below, a horse-headed, fish-tailed creature waited.

Drawn, she moved into the room, tiptoeing as if a noise would awake the sea monster of her childhood, and the *Hippocampoi*, Poseidon's sea horse, would come springing out of the painting, seize her in its teeth, and draw her down into the water and keep her there until she drowned.

Bella stopped a few feet away and sucked in her breath. She'd never seen this painting before. It wasn't like Ari's other works, his soft clinical landscapes of women's bodies. This painting was smaller, the paint colors rougher. He must have done it right after he got out of prison and had hidden away on the mountainside like a tortured hermit.

Despite its small size, the painting was powerful. Wild strokes of paint and quick dabs of color shivered with emotion. The sea below the girl roiled and splashed, dark and threatening. The sky above swirled with gray and purple storm clouds. And there was no mistaking the girl—it was her, curly headed, olive skinned. And the marks on her wrists weren't bracelets. They were bloody wounds.

She rubbed the tattoos encircling her wrists, felt the slight bump of the scars. Another reason she'd fled Eudokia eight years ago. She couldn't bear the pity in Ari's eyes. Like he had the right to judge—he was the one who shamed the family by being sent to prison for killing that boy. Anger flared and then died.

But he *had* understood. He'd forgiven her in the only way he knew how—through his art. She reached up and took the picture down off the wall, turned it over, and found the inscription she knew would be there: *For Sirena, beloved sister, 2009.*

She rested the painting on the desk. Vernon must have stolen it when he was on the island like he'd stolen everything else of hers—he and Tuccio, his bastard of a brother. Well, she would steal it right back.

She lifted it off the desk, sending papers flying to the floor. She stooped down to gather them up and stopped. Vernon's passport lay sprawled open on top of an itinerary for the Cayman trip.

She picked it up, her hand trembling. The silence deepened around her. So he hadn't left the country. He wasn't on a beach with a bimbo. She tossed the passport on to the desk. And he wasn't here.

Bella tucked the painting under her arm and headed

for the door. Maybe he'd gone to his stepmother's. Now there was a relationship with hidden depths. She stepped into the waiting elevator.

Tiny little goosebumps crept up her arms. Could he be in trouble? She held her hand over the elevator buttons. Then she pressed the one for the garage. It wouldn't hurt to check and see which car he'd taken.

The elevator came to a stop, the door slid open, and she moved into Vernon's private garage. *Click.* Motion-activated lights came on bathing the central area in brilliant light but leaving the walls in shadow. She crooked her neck and counted four vehicles. Closest to her was the big black limo she'd ridden in so many times. Next to it was Vernon's prized motorcycle. In the space beyond was a silver BMW and just beyond, the shiny new Spyder. One car was missing—Vernon's big SUV. So he'd motored off somewhere. Well, goody for him.

She shifted the painting to her other hand, and stared at the red convertible. He'd said it was hers. The thought struck her. She could sell it and use the money to get The Siren started up again. But she'd never thought to ask for the key or the papers. She's been so wrapped up in planning the engagement party,

She hurried toward it, her footsteps echoing in the cavernous space. Maybe this would be her lucky day. Perhaps Vernon had done the right thing for once, and her name was on the registration. A dealer could get her a key. She leaned the painting against the rear bumper and moved around to the side door. It was unlocked. For a moment, she hesitated. No one left a car worth almost a million unlocked, even in a private garage. But then, Vernon was made of money, and he'd kill anyone who touched it. Bella glanced around. And he would know if they did. There were security cameras everywhere.

She pulled the door open, and the sickly sweet odor of something rotten hit her full in the face. She slapped her hand over her nose. Vernon must have forgotten the left-overs from their last dinner out before the engagement party in the luggage compartment. That would be just like him. And they'd had Zakuri's black cod. The stink would never come out.

Blast it, this was her car.

She pulled the hood release and moved to the front of the car. The foul odor was stronger here. She flicked up the hood and jumped back. The hall guard lay wedged in the tiny four by four space, his face green in death, his limbs at odd angles, his body swollen with the gases of decay.

Bella slammed the hood shut, bent over, and threw up, gagging and retching until her throat burned and her stomach muscles cramped. Finally, nothing more would come up. She swiped at her mouth with her sleeve and swallowed to clear the foulness from her throat.

She peered around, her whole body twitching. The poor man had been dead for several days by the look of it. Was the killer still here? Was he waiting outside for her? And where the hell was Vernon? She felt in her pocket for her cell phone, drew it out, and dialed 911.

Chapter 21

Vernon rolled onto his stomach and groaned. The sound bounced off the walls of the cistern like a chorus of taunting ghosts. He stood, swayed from side to side in the dark, and steadied himself. Damn his brother. He couldn't survive much more of this. He'd always thought that being blind and deaf would be like being buried alive. Instead, fireworks and streaks of colors shot off in different directions every time he moved his head.

His ears, too, were overly-sensitized, picking up odd sounds that changed direction when he tipped his head to listen more closely. He'd spent quite a bit of time searching for the source of an ear-jarring buzz that sounded as if something were drilling through the wall, only to turn up nothing. Once a bird sang in his ear. Then again, maybe seeing stars and hearing imaginary drills and chirping birds was just an aftereffect of the two concussions, combined with sensory deprivation.

Every once in a while though, he heard Bella calling him, her voice low, warm, and as enticing as one of Odysseus' sirens. And despite everything—despite all the abuse his body had sustained, despite the damp cold that numbed him to the bone, and despite the regret that tore through his heart—the sound went directly to his cock. His crazy brain would recreate her scent, her silken skin would rub against his own, her

199

arms would wrap around him, and he'd lie in pain with the want of her.

When that happened, all he could do was curl up in a ball on the freezing concrete, curse himself for hurting her, and dream of ways of winning her back until he fell asleep.

If he had his way, he'd stay in those phantom arms forever. But he couldn't. It was too cold, too damp, too agonizing.

He sat up and rubbed his hands up and down his bare arms and legs, in a futile attempt to get warm. How long had it been since his brother threw him in the cistern? Minutes? Hours? Days? In the perpetual dark, who could tell?

Vernon pushed himself to his feet, his stomach grumbling with the effort. Well, he was awake now—he'd call it morning—and he was hungry. The fast food burger Cole had tossed down was long gone. He swayed, swallowed, and came up dry. His mouth and throat felt like sandpaper. No water or drinks had accompanied that soggy bun and un-chewable meat.

Lightheaded, he fought to keep himself upright. His stomach gurgled louder. Forget food, he told his complaining belly. A person could go weeks without food, but if he didn't get something to drink in the next day or two he'd be dead.

He steadied himself, lifted his arms over his head, and began the series of exercises he'd devised to keep his body in some semblance of working order. Up and down he swung his arms, his legs wobbling, his shoulder muscles protesting every stroke. Up. Down. Up. Down. Up. Down.

"Ow." Pain radiated up his biceps and cramped his

shoulders. He stopped, his heart racing, every breath burning his throat, and braced himself against the wall. Only three swings this time. Damn, he was getting weaker. He lifted his arms again, straining to get them over his shoulders.

Screech. Above him, the metal grate moved with a high-pitched squeal that tore through his head and sent chills rippling down his spine. He slapped his hands over his ears and glanced up. The dark silhouette of his brother, framed in a halo of blinding light, peered down.

Cole leaned in. "Been hoping it would rain and fill the cistern a bit, but all we've had is snow and ice. Then I remembered we had this trusty old hose." He wiggled the nozzle end he was holding. "Thought you might be getting thirsty."

Freezing water poured down on Vernon. He snorted and stumbled to the side, but the water caught him, pelting his skin, puddling beneath his bare feet. Head tucked, he crossed to the other side of the cistern. The tormenting water followed.

Cole cupped a hand around his mouth and called down, "There's no way out."

Vernon kept moving, barely staying ahead of the spray of water. There was always a way out, and he'd find it.

"You're a rat. Caught in a barrel. My rat"—Cole adjusted the direction of the hose—"who needs a little cleaning up."

A powerful burst of the water hit Vernon full in the face. His head flew back. Water flooded his eyes and shot up his nose. Coughing, he threw up his arms and covered his head. Needles of icy water pounded his shoulders and streamed down his legs. The freezing spray moved lower, hitting his belly, then his feet. Then up again. Attacking every inch of his skin with water so cold every droplet stabbed like the tip of a knife. He turned away, cowering against the wall under the onslaught. Air turned to water, tearing at his raw throat, slicing away all his will to fight. He'd say anything as long as he got out of this freezing hell. Of course, once he was out—

He forced the words past his swollen tongue. "Enough. Enough. I'll sign—"

The spray stopped. For a moment, all he could do was shiver. Then he blinked the water from his eyes, wiped his face with his palms, rubbed his hands over his arms, and waited for his brother to haul him out.

The hose slid out of the hole, and Cole peered down at him. "There we go, bro. Can't complain about the accommodations, now can you? You're nice and clean. Have plenty of water to drink."

Vernon sloshed through the ankle-deep water until he stood under the open grate.

Cole sniffed and pulled back. "Maybe not so clean after all. Sorry for the lack of toilet facilities. But I see you made do. Afraid there's no way to clean that out. It's a cistern, after all. Quite waterproof."

Vernon peered up into that shadowed face. He'd never thought his younger brother cold-hearted. The boy had once doted on him, more a son than brother. Then again, he hadn't had contact with him in recent years. Crime lords and corporate lawyers didn't mix socially. He raised his hands. "I said—enough. Let me out. Let's talk. Settle accounts." His voice gurgled like it came from a drowning man.

Cole rocked back. Disappeared. Then reappeared, paper and pencil in hand. "Glad to see you calming down. Becoming reasonable, bro. Tell me the foreign account numbers and passcodes, and I'll haul you straight up."

Vernon wasn't that stupid. He swallowed hard to clear his throat. "Can't. You know I have no head for numbers. They're in my Williamsburg penthouse." He stopped to cough. "Throw down a ladder or something." He rolled his shoulders to cover the chills shaking his whole body. "Only my palm works the security lock. You'll need me to get in." He wiped away the water dripping down his face.

"Need you?" Cole rubbed his chin. "Seems to me I'm a lot safer with you down there. You didn't happen to break papa's rules and give access to someone else? Have you been foolish in love, big brother?"

Vernon took a step back. Bella. He'd given her clearance in preparation of her moving in.

"Oh dear, I see you have." Cole moved out of sight and then came back. He held out a bag and let it fall. It plopped in the water at Vernon's feet. "Oops. Lunch time. Enjoy while I go renew my acquaintance with that lovely tattoo artist of yours. She ever tell you about our first encounter? Such a sweet thing. So obliging."

Adrenaline flooded Vernon's body. He forgot he was cold. He forgot he was trapped. He forgot everything, except the fact that Bella was unprotected, already injured, and at the mercy of the monster his brother had become. He kicked the lunch bag. It landed with a plop in one of the deeper puddles and sank.

"I guess not." Cole started to slide the metal door closed and stopped. "I'll be gone awhile, dear brother.

So chill out." He laughed. "Get it? *Chill out.*"

The cistern lid closed with a click, leaving Vernon standing in the pitch dark, ankle deep in freezing water awash with his own filth.

Cold and silence swirled around him and filled him with dread. Teeth chattering, he folded his arms against his chest and forced himself to imprint the memory of the location of the inlet pipes designed to let rain water flow in from the roofs. There was one in the center of each wall coming in at the ceiling line, at least ten feet above his head. No way he could ever reach them. No way to know if he could squeeze his body through even if he did. Still, it gave him a twinge of hope. Not that he needed it. Hope meant that he had to drink the foul water to survive, stand in it as it rotted the flesh from his feet, and imagine Cole manhandling his Bella.

"Beware what you wish for," his Macedonian grandmother's voice whispered from the grave. Minutes ago, he'd been dying of thirst. Now he was more likely to die of hypothermia. But dying wasn't an option anymore. Vernon sank to his knees. Freezing water sloshed around him. He sucked air into lungs that rattled with growing congestion and lowered his mouth to the stinking water. As long as he was alive, there was the chance he could save Bella.

Chapter 22

Bella straightened her '50s wool swing coat. On the earnings she was making at her new tattoo job, she'd managed to put together a striking wardrobe out of cheap vintage finds. The brilliant blue coat might have come from a thrift shop, but it had been well-designed six decades ago, and it still packed a punch. Underneath, she wore a flowing green silk skirt, the fabric frayed in spots at the hem, and a black velvet blazer, worn at the elbows, but still elegant in cut. Around her neck, a Florentine silk scarf in ultramarine and emerald tones, dug out of a pile at a rummage sale, added the splash of color that said *Bella Bell is back*.

Nevertheless, she bit her lip as she entered Orange Man's tattoo parlor. She hated to beg.

Early in the day, the shop was quiet, the Paradiso staff busy prepping their stations. She tucked her portfolio under her arm and headed to the back. Her old mentor looked up from the stencil he was working on and gave her one of his huge smiles, his teeth white against his dark skin. He put down his pen and opened his tattooed arms. She set her portfolio on the counter, and let him sweep her into a strong embrace. Breathing in the familiar scent of tattoo ink and disinfectant, she let the heat of his body warm hers.

Orange Man might look like a badass with his piercings, full-body tattoos, and waist-length dreadlocks, but underneath he was the sweetest of men, kind and caring and wise. Being snugged against him felt like coming home. For the first time in weeks, she felt safe.

"Having a rough time, I hear, *ma belle*." His arms tightened around her. "Keep seeing you in the newspapers. And your poor face." He feathered a finger along her jaw.

"Yeah, The Siren's a complete wreck—I'm a complete wreck." She pressed her face against his chest, afraid she'd cry if she saw pity in his eyes. Orange Man had turned her life around years ago, given her the courage to set up on her own as a tattoo artist. She didn't want him to know that all the bravado he'd imbued her with when she'd arrived, a lost and frightened Greek village girl in a city of strangers, had fizzled in the aftermath of the bombing and in the shock of finding a dead man in Vernon's garage.

But somehow he knew. Orange Man rubbed her back. "It's okay, Bella. Sometimes, when our life path gets twisted up into knots, we have to admit that we're human and seek help untangling it. I remember when you tatted your first line on me." He pushed up his T-shirt sleeve and revealed the small diamond design on the underside of his arm, her first tattoo. "Your hand was shaking like a drunk going cold-turkey. I trusted you to do the job, and you did it." He patted her shoulder. "You can trust me."

She sucked in a breath. "I've been a blind idiot. The dead guy I found—the cops took one look and pronounced it a mob execution. So much for Vernon's going straight. My brother was right. He's a horrid, vicious man who gets his employees killed."

Orange Man squeezed her tighter and then set her away. He peered into her face. "I know you love the guy, but a man like that, he's never going to give up all that illegal power and money. It's like asking a tattoo junkie to stop getting tattoos. It's in the blood."

She put a hand on his shoulder. "Don't worry. I'm done with the man. The police want him for questioning about the murder. But he's disappeared. Either he's hiding or he's dead. Either way, Vernon Newell's out of my life for good. No more excuses. He, and what's left of The Siren, can rot."

"The Siren?"

"Turns out the building belonged to him. What a joke. I've been paying my billionaire lover rent for years, and now his property agent's threatening me with a lawsuit for damages. Like I'd blow up my own studio. Destroy irreplaceable equipment and artwork." She stamped her foot. "Well, Miss Firth can stuff the damage lawsuit right up her tight ass."

"Firth? Melissa's friend?"

Bella hesitated. Last year's kidnapping of Melissa and her by Tuccio was one bit of news that hadn't ended up in the newspapers. She settled for a gloss. "They're on the outs. But that's another story."

"One I have a feeling you're not going to tell me," Orange Man said. "So who bombed The Siren? Any likely suspects?"

Bella bit her tongue. "I thought, for a while, it might have been my apprentice. We'd had a major fight. But I can't imagine Fur Tree taking revenge in such a destructive way. The police say it was an amateur job. Maybe kids or a gang trying out something they'd picked up off the Internet. But with my luck, probably a dissatisfied customer."

"Did a lot of damage, whoever they were."

Bella blinked away her tears. "The rescue cats out back took off, but my pet cats were inside. Pussyballs. He'd been with me forever. And a tiny kitten I'd just nursed back to health. I can't bear to think—"

Orange Man smothered her in another hug. "You've always loved your cats."

She nodded and then pushed away. "I'll get over it. There are always more abandoned kitties in need of rescuing."

"You're a caring soul, Bella. Sometimes too caring. In fact, what's this I hear about you renting a station at Freddie's crappo place? You feel sorry for his customers or something and decided to waste your talents there?"

"He had an opening. My former apprentice had been working there, but he's moved on."

"I'm hurt you didn't come here."

"But you're full up."

"Yeah, but I would have made space, changed some shifts."

"I couldn't ask you to do that. Freddie's is okay for right now. Clientele has rotten taste, but there's tons of work. I'm doing all right. The thing is—I do have a favor to ask."

"Anything, Bella girl."

"I have some clients. They need a little more privacy and ambiance than Freddie's can provide. I was wondering. Could I set up here for an hour or two once in a while to work on them?"

"These your Transformative Ink ladies?"

She jerked her head up. "You knew about Ink?"

He rubbed his chin. "Yeah, I've known. The word's out on the grapevine. I sent you that scoliosis patient. Lovely girl with long black hair. You did a terrific job on her spinal scar. Looked like a watercolor painting of heaven. She came back to show me."

"Why didn't you do it? You're the master."

"Some of these damaged souls need a woman's touch. They need you, Bella."

A tremor ran through her. She tapped her fingers on the counter. "The thing is most of them can't pay. I do them gratis. It wasn't a problem before, but—I couldn't pay very much for the space here."

"Don't even think about it. Consider it my donation to Transformative Ink."

Bella let out a sigh of relief and clasped his hand. "You're a wonder, Orange Man. Underneath all those tattoos, there's a beautiful heart."

"Aw Bella, you know how to make an old guy blush."

"You're not old, Orange Man." She ran a finger down his cheek and wondered why she couldn't have hooked up with a man like him, instead of Vernon Newell. They'd known each other for years. They both shared a love for art. He'd done her tattoos, given her a start in the business. But nothing had ever blossomed between them. No heat. No fire. They were just great friends.

He caught her hand, lifted it to his lips and gave her a soft kiss. "No worries now. You're going to be fine. Nobody can knock Bella Bell down for long. Just stay away from bastards like that Newell guy."

Bella couldn't miss the pained look in his eyes. Well, maybe there was some heat on his side. But she was done with men, even good ones. She stepped back and picked up her portfolio. "Yeah, I'll call when I know my clients' schedule." She headed toward the outer door.

Orange Man called after her. "You do that, *ma belle amie*. You do that."

****

Out on the sidewalk, Bella took a deep breath of the icy air and drew her scarf around her face. She was getting herself together. She looked better. The cuts marring her skin were less raw—more like smears of lipstick under the foundation she spread over them. She had a job. She had a plan. She had a place to stay until she found an apartment. Yep, she was on the rebound—she glanced back at the Paradiso—but it still felt good to be hugged by a friend.

A hulk of a man clad in black leather like Tuccio's goons had worn came up behind her, and she scooted between the parked cars and crossed the street. Her fingers tightened on the portfolio. He looked familiar.

All senses on alert, she edged into the doorway of a flower shop and pretended to be studying the rows of multicolored bouquets wrapped in festive plastic ruffles. The guy had stopped and stood motionless on the pavement. She reached in her coat pocket and squeezed the glass paperweight she taken to carrying with her everywhere. If only she could believe in its magical powers the way her *Yiayia* Patras had done.

But she couldn't. Evil seemed to find her no matter what she did. She tightened her grip on the *mati*. A piece of glass—that was all it was. A souvenir sold to thousands of tourists. But it would make a good weapon.

Across the street, the biker guy turned to greet a ponytailed girl. He gave her rousing kiss, and then strode off with her, arm in arm. Bella let out the breath she'd held tight in her lungs.

Okay, maybe that one was an innocent lover boy, but somewhere out there were murdering criminals. They'd killed that sweet-faced young bodyguard who'd always had a smile for her. What was stopping them from coming after her, hoping she'd lead them to Vernon?

She adjusted her portfolio. Not happening. She was done with Vernon Newell. Except—a tiny worry niggled in her brain—she hadn't gotten the deed for the villa on Eudokia. One last confrontation with Vernon, she feared, still awaited her.

Still holding tight to the cold glass ball, she strode out of the flower shop and glanced around for a taxi. There. A cab. She flagged it down and jumped inside, clutching her portfolio at her side.

She'd spent the last week perfecting her designs. She tapped the stiff binding. Next step on the Bella-is-Back agenda: telling Henri Avery she had the sketches redone and was ready to present her work to the cosmetic artists.

****

Twenty minutes later, Bella stood in the waiting room of one of Steiner Studio's glass-walled offices staring out at a view of the East River. The wall behind her was plastered with posters advertising all the TV shows produced in the sprawling Steiner Production complex occupying the old Brooklyn Navy Yard— *Blindspot*, *Gotham*, *Hip Hop Squares*. All the shows she never had time to watch.

"You!"

Bella spun around.

Gloria Cooper, her nose wrinkled as if she smelled something foul, drew herself up to her full five foot one and glared at her. "Avery Baby's not here. Gone to LA to see his divorced wife. Some emergency with his kids. I'm handling all the details."

Bella took a deep breath. Surely Cooper would acknowledge the quality of her designs, no matter how jealous she was. "Well, then"—she held out her portfolio—"I have the sketches done."

"Don't need them."

Her mouth dropped open. "*What?* How can you produce *Secret Ink* without them?"

A smile spread across Cooper's face. "Got another tattoo artist to fill in when you left us in the lurch."

Bella's stomach clenched so tight she could hardly breathe. Her hope of selling the Spyder had been dashed when the police impounded it. Now, without the income from *Secret Ink*, Eudokia surely would lose its helicopter. "Another artist? But I'm only a few days late."

Cooper wagged a finger at her. "Days are like years in this industry. The pilot must be ready to be filmed by March. The actors are hired. The cosmetic crew is already getting in the supplies. We decided to go with tattoos designs done by a professional." She tipped back her head. "Not you."

"But—"

Behind them, the phone rang. The secretary answered. She looked up. "The meeting is starting, Miss Cooper."

"On my way." Miss Pointy-Nose looked Bella up

and down. "Sorry it didn't work out, but really—you just weren't the right type for the job." She signaled the secretary. "Show Miss Bell out, please." Bella turned to follow the officious underling, but looked back just before leaving the office. Miss Pointy-Nose was still standing there, her hand palm out, fingers spread wide, in a gesture that looked a lot like she was casting the Evil Eye.

Chapter 23

Bella leaned against the bridge railing and peered out across the East River. Wind whipped the surface stirring up white caps that looked phosphorescent in the moonlight. She glanced at the metal arch spanning the pedestrian walkway. Hanger On was literally hanging on as he dangled by one hand and spray painted T-Crew's tag on the highest point of the span. She had to have seagull feathers for brains for agreeing to do this.

"There." The boy pushed himself up and held up his spray can like a trophy. "Done."

Bella swiveled her head and checked the walkway in both directions. She yelled to be heard over the rumble of the cars and trucks speeding past, "Great. Get down. Now. Toro is going to kick me out of your place for helping you with this."

Hanger put his hands on either side and wiggled his bottom along the beam. Bella held her breath and tried not to look. At the lowest point, he gave a kick, pushed off with his hands and landed flat on his feet beside her in a perfect gymnast's stick. She extended her hand to steady him, but he jerked away and tossed her the can. "Toro will never know."

Bella stuffed the can in the battered duffle bag and tipped her head in the direction of the shiny new red and silver tat in the shape of a crown and a sword adorning the girder. In the middle of the crown was a prominent H. "He will when he sees that. You stuck your initial in the middle."

"Yeah, he'll know I've been here. That's the point. I just proved I'm no toy. Made my mark. Notched my belt. It's my Christmas present for him." Hanger patted her on the shoulder. "But no way anyone will figure out you were here."

Two figures came into view on the Manhattan side of the bridge. "Time to move." Hanger hefted the duffle and started walking toward the Brooklyn end.

Bella was only too glad to go. This whole situation made her nervous. When Hanger had woken her in the middle of the night and asked her to help him with a project, she'd thought he needed help on a homework assignment he'd forgotten to do, not stand look out while he did his first solo tat.

She glanced over at the fourteen year old. Little imp. The minute she'd said yes, he'd hustled her out the door so fast, she hadn't even taken her purse or cell phone with her. She trailed after him as he headed down the curved walkway, duffle bag banging against his back.

Hanger looked like the mischievous graffiti kid he was. Short for his age, barely topping her shoulder, but thin and wiry—the same acrobatic build as his brother Toro. Both had dark complexions, straight black hair, heavy-lidded black eyes, and sharp-pointed chins that always reminded her of the gypsies she'd seen begging in Greece. It was easy to imagine them leaping across rooftops and sliding down drainpipes. Maybe it was the smooth, quiet way they moved, like Siamese cats. Or the fact that they actually did scale buildings and swing from gutters like urban circus performers.

Her brother called them his death-defying pain-in-the-asses. And after watching the kid climb up the bridge beam and hang suspended over the side, she had to agree.

But such gifted artists. She imagined spray painting a picture, even with the special nozzle they used, and doing it while hanging upside down. Bella wiggled her fingers. No way. Give her fine-pointed needles in a vibrating tat machine any day.

In front of her, Hanger bounced along, the duffle slapping against his shoulder. She hurried to catch up as he scampered down the walkway and headed up Driggs Avenue. In the middle of the street, he jumped a sewer cover and spun around, walking backwards, his face bright with success. "Thanks for coming, by the way." He pulled out a pack of gum and offered her a piece.

Bella took one and popped it in her mouth. Her whole mouth flamed. "Yuck, what flavor is this?"

"Red Hot Chili Pepper."

"*Yuck.*" She ran over to the gutter and spit it out. "That was awful." She rubbed the roof of her mouth with her tongue, spit again. "Are you trying to kill me?"

Hanger shrugged. "It tastes good to me. All my friends like it."

She glared at him. "Well, there's no accounting for taste."

He gave her a lopsided smile and strode away grinning.

A dark-colored car turned the corner and headed toward them.

"Police." Hanger spun around and tossed her the duffle. "Grab me by the ear. Pretend you're my mother dragging me home."

She caught the bag and shifted it to her shoulder. "Mother? I can't—"

He tipped his head toward her. "The ear. Give it a hard pull and don't let go. It's what my mama would have done if she caught me acting bad." The police car slowed down as it came abreast of them and a window rolled down.

Her hand brushed the skin of Hanger's ear, soft and tender as a baby's. Yank on it? What kind of woman had his mother been? She'd never do that to a child.

Hanger rubbed his head against her and whispered. "Do it."

Bella pinched his ear, surprised at the hard shell of it, and yanked as gently as she dared. Hanger let out a piercing scream and stamped his feet as if the ear would detach any minute. "Mama, let go, will ya? Let go. I'm coming home."

The uniformed officer leaned out, his teeth gleaming in the streetlight. "Trouble, ma'am?"

Bella avoided looking at him. "No. Just rounding up my son. School tomorrow, you know." She re-cupped her fingers around the ear and held on.

Hanger bellowed and scrabbled at her hand. The cop laughed. "Seems like you've got him under control." He leaned a little farther out and glared at Hanger. "You mind your mom, boy. Stay off the streets. All kinds of crazies out here. Had a call about some idiot swinging from the bridge. On my way to see what's doing." He tipped his hat, rolled up the window, and motored off toward the bridge.

Bella let go. "I didn't hurt you, did I?"

Hanger rubbed his ear. "Hell no. My mama would have dug her fingernails right in."

Bella peered over her shoulder. "He seemed nice enough."

Hanger scowled. "It's an act. He was casing us over but good. So get a move on before he puts two and ten together and comes back asking questions." He snapped his fingers at her. "I got paint on my hands. And you look way too different to be my mother."

"Oh." Bella's stomach sank into a tiny ball. "What did your mama look like?"

"Sick." Hanger stomped ahead.

"I heard she was very ill before she died. But I am sure she loved you."

He looked back at her, his mouth a rigid line. "You weren't there." He spun on his heel and strode down the block widening the distance between them.

"I'm sorry," she called to his retreating back. She stopped and watched him disappear around the corner. The kid acted like he hadn't a care in the world, but underneath he was a ball of hurt. The two Vargas brothers had been homeless, their mother dead in a shelter, when Ari found them and took them under his wing.

She'd promised her brother she'd watch out for them. Bella pulled the duffle off her shoulder and gave the bag a shake. Inside, the paint cans rattled. The thing weighed a ton. And now it looked like she was stuck carrying it all the way back to T-Crew's.

She hefted the bag and slipped it back over her arm. Some job she was doing. Helping the kid break the law and stirring up bad memories. Blast it, she knew how that felt. She hated remembering her mother's death. Up ahead, Hanger looked over his shoulder. She gave a wave and raced to catch up and tell him she was sorry. Suddenly, a huge man tore out of an alley and stopped dead in front of her. He was a mountain of a man, tall, dark, clad in shiny black leather and holding a knife. She skidded to a halt, eyes glued to the sharp tip of the blade glinting in the street light.

"Don't make a sound and your deco boy will just go on his merry way, Mama."

Bella drew in a breath and held herself rigid. The man turned the blade so the point was aimed at her eye. "Good girl. Now put down the bag. Slowly."

Once upon a time, when they were carefree kids in Eudokia, Ari had taught her a whole series of defensive moves using elbows and fingers and knees, but with the knife pointed at her eye, every one of them fled her brain and left her a trembling bag of bones. She'd never save herself, but she could save Hanger. She nodded and let the duffle fall to the ground in a clank of metal.

"Smart lady. Now you come with us. Turn around. Nice and easy."

Shaking from head to foot, she turned about and came face to face with a familiar sharp-toothed smile. It was her tormentor from the cellar. Kiro. She opened her mouth to scream, but the man behind her stuffed a rag in her mouth, yanked her wrists behind her back, and crushed them together in his massive hands.

She froze, every muscle rigid, waves of uncontrollable shaking rolling over her. The nightmare was happening again.

"Hello, Bella," Kiro said in the wheedling tone she remembered so well. He took one of her curls, wrapped it around his finger. "I like what you've done with your hair. Now your head matches that lovely nest below." He leaned in and gave her a kiss on the forehead. "You never told your lover Vernon about that little *tête-à-tête* we had? Did you?" He ran his fingers over her breast. "You're amazingly responsive to a knife."

She jerked back and came up against the bruiser behind her, his body hard as a brick wall. She glanced toward where the patrol car had disappeared. Where were the cops when you really needed them?

Thunk. A huge board smashed Kiro on the shoulder, knocking him half-way to the ground.

The goon behind squeezed her wrists together even tighter as he yanked a gun sporting a muffler out of the waistband of his pants and shot up at the roof. There was a small yip and another board tumbled down on Kiro, driving him completely to the pavement.

She peered up. Hanger. It had to be. The stupid kid was trying to save her. All Ari's training came back in a flash. She threw her head back and whacked her attacker in the nose. He grunted in pain, but didn't let go. Instead, he took another shot. A cement block tumbled over the eave, just missing her and caught the goon on the gun arm. The dull crack of breaking bone smashed through her, a sound she'd hoped never to hear again. His grip loosened, and she shook off the overwhelming desire to crumple on the pavement and instead, stamped on his instep, kicked him in the balls. The man howled

"Go, Bella." Suddenly, her hands were free, and Hanger was pushing her forward. "Run."

She yanked the rag from her mouth and took off down the street, Hanger's sneaker-clad feet thumping in rhythm with her own.

Behind her, someone shouted. She glanced back. The Kiro character was getting up, fumbling inside his coat. There was a flash of metal.

She screamed, "Gun!" and pushed Hanger to the side just as the thud of the muffled shot rang out.

"This way." Hanger seized her hand and pulled her into an alley closed off from the street with a heavy iron gate. In one smooth, rapid motion, he put a foot on the hinge and taking a giant leap, wrapped his hand over the top rail and hauled himself up. He reached back and offered her a hand. "Come, we got to get up above them."

Bella looked over her shoulder. The two attackers were close enough she could see their teeth and the glittering fury in their eyes. Whatever they wanted with her, it wasn't for something pleasant.

She'd never been much of an athlete. Nothing like her wrestler brother, but she had grown up climbing the cliffs of Eudokia with the son of the local goatherd. She seized Hanger's hand, placed her foot flat against the gate and used her momentum to push herself up and over. Her belly scraped across the metal bars, and her shin smashed hard into the iron rail. Then she was flying over the top. For a second, she thought she'd land on her head, but somehow Hanger blocked her tumble and righted her.

He was grinning. "Brilliant leap. I'll make a deco girl out of you, yet, Miss Bella." He seized her hand and tugged her toward a rickety looking fire escape. "Here." He cupped his hands. "Foot."

She looked up. The bottom rung of the ladder had to be ten feet off the ground. There was no way the kid could boost her that high. The gate behind them rattled.

"Foot. Now."

Bella put her sneaker in his hand and reached

toward the rung. It didn't bear thinking what it would feel like if she missed and fell to the pavement below. Suddenly she was tossed up in the air. The rung grew larger. She stretched out her fingers and caught hold with one hand. She swayed, unable to catch the bar with her other hand. Behind her, there was a noisy commotion that sounded like all the trash cans in Brooklyn had just fallen down, and then Hanger was above her, gripping her by her other hand and pulling her up the ladder until her hand caught a crossbar, and she could climb on her own.

Up they went until they reached the top of the fire escape. Bella looked down. Four stories below, the men were untangling themselves from bags and cans of garbage. She could smell the rank odor rising, hear the men cursing.

Hanger tapped her shoulder. "We're sitting pigeons. Got to get on the roof. Watch where I put my feet."

The street artist swung up on the railing, put a foot on the lower window sash, gripped the top edge with the fingers of one hand and stretched up to grab the overhanging cornice with the other. One handed, he pulled himself up and over the edge and belly flopped on to the roof.

Bella shook her head. She was no Spiderman. No way could she cling to the side of a building.

"Come on." Hanger hung over the edge one hand extended toward her. "You're a foot taller than me. It'll be a piece of cake." She looked down at the pavement. Some cake.

"Railing. Look at the railing," Hanger yelled.

A muffled gun shot rang out and zinged off the

metal. One of the guys shouted up. "Freeze. You can't escape."

Bella sucked in a breath of air and glanced up at the edge of the roof. Where were the police? The neighbors? Didn't anyone hear the gun shots? Another shot rang out. She was going to die one way or another. She put her foot on the fire escape railing, gripped the window frame, digging her fingernails into the wood molding. Blindly, she searched for a place to wedge her other foot. Nothing. She pressed against the window. Tried again. No way she would make it.

"Grab this." A piece of green cloth hung down toward her, flapping in the breeze. She narrowed her eyes: Hanger's jacket.

Compared to the thin molding and crumbling brick wall, it looked like a rescue line. She latched on with both hands and held on.

"Use the sash."

Keeping one foot on the railing, she flailed around until her sole caught the edge of the sash. Heart banging against her ribs, she pushed up, found a toehold on the top of the window frame, then a projecting brick. With a final tug from Hanger, she flopped up and over, the air whooshing out of her as she landed with all the gracelessness of a hooked fish, her face scraping on the rough tar of the roof as she slid to safety.

Hanger smacked her on the bottom. "You did it, Deco Girl."

She wanted to shake the kid. Bella rolled over and sat up. "Those men are shooting at us, and you're acting like this is a game."

He squatted back on his heels. "It *is* a game, Miss Bella. Life's a game. Sometimes you win. Sometimes you lose. But you can't stop playing."

There was a clanking from down below. He hunkered down on his hands and knees and peered over the edge. He signaled her to come abreast. "Watch."

Shark Tooth had hauled himself up onto the fire escape. His buddy stood below aiming his gun up at them, his broken arm pressed against his side.

Bella put a hand on the boy's back. "He's coming. We have to hide." She looked around. But all she saw was a flat roof leading to other flat roofs.

Hanger smiled and held out his hand to her. "Be my guest."

She stared at the round red object in his hand.

"What is that?"

"A cherry bomb."

"Does Toro know you have that? Hell, kids blow their fingers off with those things every day."

"T-Crew all carry them, Miss Bella. Never know when you need a diversion."

Below, the fire escape shook. Kiro was half way up.

He winked at her. "Safer than a gun."

She bit her lip. "I assume you have matches, too?"

"Got my whole escape kit." He dug into his jeans pocket and took out a cigarette lighter. He held it out to her with the other hand.

Bella peered down again. "He's stopped."

"Yeah, he's reached the spot where I pulled out the bolt. We do it all the time to stop the police from following us."

"What? But I climbed up behind you."

"No biggie. You're lighter than him by half." He glanced at her. "We put them back later so no worries for the people in the apartments. Okay?"

She peeked over the eaves again. "He hasn't moved."

"He's wondering what else I did." He looked down. "Thing is pretty rickety. Absentee landlord probably. Don't do the upkeep they should. Good time to drop this."

She glanced at the small round object in his hand and then down at the man who'd been torturing her sleep for a year. "Yeah."

Hanger handed her the fire cracker and the lighter. Gingerly, she held the flame to the wick, waited for it to catch. Then with a curse, she tossed it down. Hanger yanked her down flat to the roof.

Seconds later, the explosion rocked the air around her. The boom was ten times louder than the muffled gunshots. Her ears rang. The stink of sulfur filled the alley. Windows flew open. People shouted. Off in the distance, a police siren squealed.

"Now what?" she whispered. At least, it sounded like a whisper to her deafened ear drums.

Hanger mouthed back, "We wait." He rolled onto his back and pointed up.

Chapter 24

Bella lay on her back, exhausted, every bone and muscle weak from the gut-wrenching exertion of climbing to the roof. She folded her arms under her head and looked up where Hanger was pointing. Through the dissipating smoke from the firecracker, she could see only a single star. A moving star. She blinked. Not a star, a jet, taking off from LaGuardia.

For the first time in a long time, she let herself just stop. Stop thinking. Stop worrying. Stop running. Somewhere below, the police were doing what they were paid to do, mop up the bad guys.

For now, there was just her and this wild gypsy boy lying on a roof in Brooklyn. Nothing else mattered. Gradually her muscles relaxed, her brain stopped whirring, her nightmares grew distant, her problems floated up and dispersed like the smoke.

She inhaled and exhaled. Let the winter chill air surround her and fill her and didn't fight it or try to escape it. The kid was right. Life was a game, and it had been a long time since it had been fun. She thought about how she'd clung to Vernon, made love in desperation, trying to find peace in the bonding of their bodies.

When here it was. Peace. On a rooftop. Just her and the vastness of the heavens. She peered up into the night. A snowflake glinted as it floated down. Then another. The flakes twisted and curled in slow motion. One landed on her cheek. She spread out her arms and legs, opened her mouth, and welcomed them in—tiny kisses from heaven. She closed her eyes.

The next time she opened them, she was blanketed with glittering snowflakes and freezing cold. She sat up and glanced around. Hanger was gone. Panic zipped through her, and she jumped up and ran to the edge of the roof and peered down.

The alley was empty. The men had disappeared. Only a mess of trash cans belied what had happened. She stared down at the fire escape. There was no way she was getting on that thing again by herself. Besides, there was the missing bolt. And to think she thought Hanger an innocent kid. She'd forgotten that he'd spent much of his young life running from social workers and cops.

Ari had told her some of Toro and Hanger's story, but she hadn't paid much attention. She'd been too besotted with Vernon.

Bella peered over the edge again. The Kiro character had it in for Vernon for some reason. But why? It was Ari who'd killed his boss Tuccio, not Vernon.

Mr. Cocksure Crime Boss had arrived late on the bloody scene, sauntered into the cellar where Tuccio had held her captive and where her brother had nearly died, and acted like nothing major had occurred. She'd never forgiven him for that fact nor that he'd let Shark Tooth Man and the other brutes Tuccio employed escape the cops. Not after what Kiro'd done to her. She rubbed the small fish tattoo beneath her collarbone. Not that she had told him.

"Hey."

She swung around.

Hanger clambered up onto the roof. "Those guys left before the police got here. I think you can come down now."

"Where'd you go?"

"I went back for the duffle."

"What? You went back for a bag of spray paint. Why?"

The kid suddenly looked very young. "Toro'd kill me—"

"Idiot. Those men will really kill you. They were shooting at us, for heaven's sake."

"Nah. They're just pisspots." He scrubbed at his nose, trying not to cry. "Look, Bella, I am really in trouble. The duffle's gone. Bastards must have took it."

"I'll buy you new spray paint."

"It's not the paint," Hanger said. He sank down on the rough tar paper and rocked back and forth. "I had our mama's photo in it. I—I put it in for luck. I thought she'd be with me. See me make my mark. Be someone."

Bella slid closer and slipped her arm over his thin shoulders. "You must miss her."

Hanger's head jerked up. "What would you know about it?"

"My mother died when I was about your age." She rubbed her wrists. "I felt—I felt so useless. There's a big hole inside me where she used to be."

Hanger pulled away and stared off into space. "She was so sick. And nothing we did helped and finally Toro gave up and they took her away and I don't even know where she's buried."

"What hospital did they take her to?

"Don't know. We hid. Toro said they'd put us in foster care."

"Do you know the date?"

"December. Christmas Day. Two years ago."

"There have to be records. Maybe we could do some research and see if we can find out where she's buried."

"Yeah, we could do that." Hanger wiped away the tears running down his face. "Where's your mom buried?"

"She's not. She was swimming in the sea and disappeared. I couldn't find her."

Hanger tipped his head and studied her face. "Yep. I knew it."

"What did you know?"

"Your mother was a mermaid."

Bella's mouth dropped open. "*A what?*"

"You know the story. About the mermaid. Who comes on land and marries and has babies and then one day she goes back to the sea and leaves her husband and children to mourn. Like your mom."

"That's a fairy tale."

"But it must be true. Your real name is Sirena. Ari says that means mermaid in Greek."

Bella tugged on Hanger's beat up baseball cap. "It's a common name on Eudokia." She wiggled her feet. "And I don't have flippers. What's yours? Hanger On's a street handle."

"My real name sounds stupid. Mama said it was special, but it don't sound special. The kids laugh every time the teacher says it." He stood up and brushed off the seat of his jeans. "We should go. Sun's coming up."

229

Bella glanced to the east. The sky had turned the color of a lemon peel. She rose, her muscles stiff from the cold, and tried not to think about how she would get down. "So what's your name?"

"Didn't Ari tell you? He got us our passports so we could go to Greece."

"I've only heard him call you Hanger."

He peered off the edge of the roof. "Wish we'd stayed there. It's a good place, Eudokia. But Toro insisted we come back so he can become a legit artist. Wants to be *famous.*"

"It's probably better you're here. Ari and Melissa are off doing her fieldwork so no one's at the villa now. And you need to finish school." She crawled up next to him. "So you didn't tell me your name yet."

He disappeared over the edge. "Mircea." He balanced half on the railing and half on the window sash and reached up his hand. "Grab on and jump."

She grabbed on tight. "It sounds sort of Greek." She closed her eyes and leaped. Her feet hit the metal platform, and the shock spread up her legs. She swayed. Hanger On caught hold and steadied her.

"*Stupida.* Always jump with your eyes open." He turned and bounded down the ladder, leaving her to stagger behind him. "Not Greek," he called back, "Romanian. Like my dad. My mama said it was the name of a great king. I looked it up on the Internet in school. Not great. Mircea was Dracula's daddy."

They reached the pavement. Bella had to run to keep up. "So what's wrong with being named after Dracula's father? Sounds cool to me."

"Mircea? To the idiots around here it sounds like a girl's name. The kids call me Mercy. They gang up and beat on me until I say 'Mercy.' They think it funny." Hanger peeked out into the street. "All clear."

He crossed over and disappeared around the corner. Bella moved forward to follow.

Suddenly, someone seized her by the hair and yanked her back. A stinking plastic garbage bag dropped over her head. She scrabbled at it with her hands as the bag was pulled down her body and wound tighter and tighter around her.

"Got her, boss."

Bella's stomach twisted and turned. Hanger'd been wrong. Kiro and his partner hadn't left. Helpless, she was yanked backwards, the heels of her sneakers scraping along the ground, then thrown head first over a rock-hard shoulder. Blood rushed to her head. The plastic stuck to her skin, cut off her air.

She wiggled her hand up in front of her face and pushed the plastic bag away. If she didn't do something, she would suffocate in this bag. She gathered her strength, arched her back and bucked and kicked, twisted and turned, getting a good taste of something foul in her mouth. She gagged and spit. Thrashed again, kicking and kneeing her captor.

The goon holding her grunted. "Damn. She's wiggly as an eel, Kiro."

"Hold on. The car's just around the corner."

The man shifted her higher on his shoulder and tightened his grip. She rocked back and forth, her belly bent over his shoulder, her head bouncing with every step.

With a huff, her captor stopped moving. "Hurry. Open the trunk. My arm's killing me."

She went cold. Stuffed in a trunk, she'd surely

suffocate. There wasn't much air left in the bag as it was. Bella dug her nails into the plastic desperate to tear her way out. But instead of the usual thin grocery store trash bags, this was a heavy duty contractor one. Her nails slipped on the gooey surface.

"Got it."

Click. The trunk lock snapped open. The lid squealed as it lifted up, and the man lugging her tossed her inside. She landed with a bone-jarring thud. The lid slammed down, then opened again.

"What are you doing, you idiot?"

"Gotta take her out of the bag, boss. She'll suffocate."

"You wanted her to stop wiggling."

"I thought you needed her to unlock Vernon's place?"

"Just need her hand to key in."

"So why we taking all of her?"

"For Vernon's edification. Now get in."

Car doors slammed. The engine roared to life and, tires thrumming beneath the thin floor of the trunk, the vehicle pulled away.

Bella stilled, Kiro's last words rattling through her brain. Vernon's *edification*? What did that mean? Was Vernon behind this? Punishing her for jilting him? Would he be waiting when his brutes delivered her dead body to him?

No, she refused to believe that. Vernon could be cruel and ruthless. But he'd never hurt her, of that she was sure. But then, where was he?

For a moment, battered, bruised, struggling for breath, she thought about giving up. The Siren was gone. Her kitties were gone. The two nasty men in the car didn't care if she lived or died. The man she loved had abandoned her. Worst of all, she'd let the people of Eudokia down. Villagers would die without a helicopter to rush them to the mainland in a medical emergency.

If only she'd controlled her temper, let Vernon have his surprise wedding. She could be sunning herself on a beach in the Caymans without a care in the world.

No. She'd been right to send him packing. Marriage was a partnership, not a fiefdom. And the fact that these men were threatening her life had something to do with Vernon's crime operation. This was Vernon's fault just like the last time.

All her muscles tensed. She would not be a victim again. Struggling against the cloying plastic, she twisted around and straightened her limbs as much as she could in the cramped trunk compartment. Her body heat filled the bag, and the stink of whatever it had held burned her nose. She flexed her legs. The bag was open at the bottom. She kicked her feet, but the plastic was trapped under her own weight.

She scratched at the plastic again, her efforts feeble. She needed something sharp. Wait—keys! She had the keys to Toro's place in her front jeans pocket.

Holding the plastic away from her face, she wiggled her other hand down to her side, stopping every few moments to rest, and searched for her pocket. Yes. She pulled out the keys and taking a big gulp of the foulness of the bag, she stabbed the biggest key through the plastic. *Pop.* In it went.

She stabbed again. Chill air seeped in, heavy with gasoline fumes. She didn't care. To her oxygen-starved lungs it tasted like nectar. She poked her fingers through the holes and pulled. The gap opened wider.

More air swirled in. The car turned a corner, throwing her to one side, and then slowed and came to a stop. A garage door whirred open with a rattling of metal.

She knew that sound. They were at Vernon's condo. This would be her only opportunity. She had to get out now, be ready to run. If she could reach the elevator before them, she could take refuge in Vernon's penthouse. Call for help.

With renewed energy, she tore at the rip. The hole opened enough for her to get her head out. Sucking in air, she pushed the stinking garbage bag down her body, freeing her arms, then her legs, and finally her feet. Now all she had to do was wait, poised to leap and run.

The car moved again. The garage door rumbled down behind it and shut with a loud clank. She wiggled around searching for a crowbar, tire iron, anything. But the trunk was empty and if it had an emergency release, it had been removed.

All she had were the keys. Heart pounding, knowing she had little to no chance of winning, she faced the latch holding the sharp end of the keys between her fingers, pointing out, set to jab the eye of the first laughing bastard to unlock the latch. The thrum of the engine stopped. Car doors slammed open and closed. Footsteps approached.

"Just bring the hand."

"Sure, bo—" An explosion rattled the garage. Then another closer to the car.

The trunk lid lifted. She came up keys first and stopped short. "Hanger?"

"Get out, Miss Bella. I only got two more cherry bombs. They won't stay hiding for long when they figure out I ain't NYPD Blue come to the rescue. Just a kid who knows how to ride a bumper." He seized her hand and took off, dragging her behind him as they scooted in and out between Vernon's cars.

Bella tugged him. "This way."

"Where?"

"The elevator. Up to Vernon's penthouse."

Hanger glanced over the hood of the limo. "They're getting up. *Vamos*."

At the elevator, Bella reached up for the keypad. A bullet smacked the door above her. Hanger tossed another firecracker.

The explosion rocked the garage. Keeping her head down, she punched in the code and prayed she'd got it right. There was a buzz and then the swoosh of the cab arriving. Yes! She'd done it.

The door opened, and Hanger pushed her inside. "Get moving. They're coming"

She hit the up button and drew back as a hand came between the door and the jamb as it slid closed. Hanger grabbed hold of the fingers and bent them up at an impossible angle. There was a curse. And then the arm was out, the elevator door closed, and the car was racing upward.

Bella leaned against the cold stainless steel, tremors running through every part of her body. *They'd planned to cut off her hand.* It was like being in some horror movie, the kind she couldn't bear to watch because they made her stomach twist into a thousand knots.

She glanced over at the kid standing next to her in his grubby jacket and paint-stained ball cap. She owed her life to this reckless street gypsy. The beasts who were after them—they'd kill the boy in a blink. She couldn't let that happen.

But how could she stop two vicious killers?

She bit her lip. Vernon would know how to handle them. It's what he did for a living. A chill shot through her. Or was Vernon behind this attack—punishing her for jilting him? Would he be waiting for his brutes to deliver her dead body to him? She pressed back into the corner of the elevator. No. She couldn't believe—wouldn't believe—the man who touched her so lovingly wanted her mutilated and killed.

The words she'd overheard rattled around her head. Kiro needed her hand to key in. If he were working for Vernon, wouldn't he already have access? Something wasn't adding up.

When the elevator door slid open on the penthouse floor, all she could do was stagger out into the steel-encased corridor. Hanger tipped back his ball cap and glanced around. "Hey, it's like a bunker up here. Vernon really is a badass, isn't he?"

"Yeah, right." Bella stomped to the penthouse door and placed her hand in the palm reader. "It *is* a bunker. Vernon has nasty friends. You just met some."

"Already knew Shark Tooth. He worked for Tuccio."

Tuccio's name sent chills slithering through her. The door opened, and they stepped inside. Behind them, the door slid closed with a click so loud Bella jumped. In front of them, the living room lay in the shadow, faintly lit with reflected light coming from the windows where the Manhattan skyline stood bathed pastel in the early morning dawn.

Her skin prickled. Nothing had changed since her

last visit, except the air was staler than before, the sweet-sour reek of spoiled food more gut-wrenching. She flicked on the lights. No Vernon rushed out to greet them. No warm arms reached out to comfort her and tell her this was all a bad dream. No brash crime boss sneered at her.

"Wow. Some place your guy has here." Hanger bounced across the room and stared out the window. "You can see forever."

She glanced back at the massive steel door. The bulletproof door might keep the killers out, but it also trapped Hanger and her in. All Shark Tooth and his goon need do was set up camp outside the door and starve them out. "Search the place. We have to find a phone. Call the police." She pointed to the left. "You go that way toward the kitchen. I'll take the office and bedrooms."

She headed down the hall, searching each room, the lump in her throat tightening with each failure. No landlines. Of course not. Why would Vernon have them? Untappable, untraceable cells were a criminal's stock-in-trade.

The last room was Vernon's. She stood in the doorway and peered in. The room was the same as she'd left it, the covers twisted in a heap on the bed. A ghostly trace of Vernon's distinctive citrus cologne still hung in the air.

Bella pressed her hand against her thumping heart. She'd felt safe with his arms wrapped around her. But she'd never been safe. He might look like a multimillionaire business executive, but he was a criminal. There would always be men, like the killers chasing her, wanting to bring him down.

Heavens! She swallowed hard. They might have already succeeded. Vernon had been missing over a week now—not answering his phone, his SUV missing, the penthouse abandoned. She gripped the door frame to keep from sinking to the floor and curling up into a ball. Vernon could be dead. That's why those bastards needed her to get into his place. She pictured the men downstairs pressing the keys on the elevator thumb pad. Soon or later, they'd get the right combo. It was only four numbers—2010—the year Vernon met her.

Somehow, she had to get help. Finding a backup cell phone was unlikely, but if there were one, it would be in here, or in his office.

Hollow inside, she forced herself to enter the room and peer into the top drawer of the closest piece of furniture—the nightstand. Vernon was surprisingly neat for such an impulsive man. Spare change rested in a small enameled dish beside a pad of paper, and in the back, the latest Jack Reacher novel.

She crossed the room and yanked open the drawer of the bureau, revealing rows of rolled up, color-coordinated silk ties. She scooped out a shimmering gold Cavelli tie and rubbed the silk against her cheek. It carried Vernon's distinctive scent to her nose. She inhaled deeply.

This was the tie Vernon wore to their celebratory dinner after she'd said yes. He'd been so handsome. She'd been so in love. And after dinner, they'd had so much fun with this tie.

She brushed her finger over the textured silk. Why couldn't he have been an ordinary man with an ordinary job—a garbage man, a carpenter, a store manager? She didn't want a life of luxury. She didn't need fancy cars and nights on the town. She needed him—Vernon—alive and safe.

Bella balled up the golden silk and tossed it across the room into the mess of bedding. She should have said no to his proposal and maybe none of this would have happened. She drove her hands into the drawer and tossed the ties about. *Ouch.* She stubbed her finger on something hard. A cell phone? She dug under the ties and came up with a square, leather-covered box. Not big enough for a phone. She shut her eyes and prayed it wasn't what she thought it was.

Her hands shaking, she flicked it open. Two Celtic knot wedding bands nested in the silk lining. She slapped it closed and shoved it back into the drawer along with her heart.

Bella staggered over to the bed and collapsed. No phones anywhere, just bad memories. She flopped over onto her stomach and pounded on the bed with her fists. They were trapped. With no way to call out, they could be here for what might be a long time. No one even knew where they were—except two murdering bastards who were desperate to get inside.

"Miss Bella." She turned her head. Hanger stood in the doorway holding a bag of chips. "Some place your Vernon's got here. It's like, amazing. Your guy has a whole room for a closet with millions of suits and shoes on this rack that rotates when you push a button. And the kitchen looks like it can fly. It's ten times the size of ours, and ours is nice. Stinks though."

He came in and bopped down on the bed. He took a chip from the bag and stuffed it in his mouth. He crunched down. "And there's a security room. State of the art. Live video cams of everywhere and a map of the world that has blinking lights all over it and a string of computers and monitors. Man, your lover must be paranoid." He took out a chip and offered it to her.

She shook her head and pushed herself up. "Usually he has several guards in there."

"Yuck." He wrinkled his nose and sniffed. "You stink of garbage."

"Oh, hell," She climbed off the bed, every muscle protesting, and peered down at the filthy sheets. "Go watch the monitors. See what those bastards are doing." She dashed into the bathroom and shut the door, turned on the shower and stepped under it. The goop and unidentifiable dirt stuck to her clothing and skin washed off and disappeared down the drain. She leaned against the shower wall, and let the hot water run over her.

A loud bang echoed through the door. Fear shot through her. She jerked upright, turned off the water, and grabbed a towel. "Yes?"

"Miss Bella." The door cracked open, and Hanger whispered at her, "Those guys. They figured out how to get the elevator going. They're on their way up."

Chapter 25

Bella studied the scene on the security monitor. A new guy had replaced the thug with the broken arm. This one was twice as large. He lounged outside in the vestibule like he had all day. Probably did.

She looked across at Hanger. Dwarfed in a Vernon-sized leather upholstered office chair, the kid was bent over one of the computers, his face scrunched up in concentration. She had no clue what he was doing, but at least it was keeping him occupied in a safe way. His original plan was to storm out the door and crush the brute with the marble statue of Archimedes.

She'd convinced him that she was not up to knocking out anyone. The fact that he agreed without a word of protest scared her. Either the crazy kid knew things were hopeless, or she really did look bad.

She felt sick. Her encounter with Kiro and his partner had banged her up more than she thought. Once the adrenaline had subsided, the pain had rushed in. A huge bump on her head throbbed. Cuts and scratches covered her body. She had garish purple bruises on her legs and her arms. Every breath set her side to aching. Something inside had been damaged when she'd been thrown like a sack of garbage over the goon's shoulder.

Bella laid a hand on the spot that hurt the worst. The damp of her half-dried T-shirt pressing against her skin sent goosebumps up her arms. Thank heavens, she'd thought to toss her wet clothes in the dryer while she toweled off. Unfortunately, there hadn't been time to dry them completely. She sniffed herself. No more garbage stink. If the thugs got to her, at least she'd die clean.

Bella wandered over to the huge desk in the corner of the room. This was obviously the hub of Vernon's off-the-books operations.

Gone straight, he'd said. Right. She fingered the traffic tickets tossed on top of a pile of ignored summonses and lawsuits and the urgent messages from criminal names even she recognized. A cheery thank-you card leaned against a framed photo of her in her red wig. She picked up the card and opened it. It was from one of the major ex-politicos in the city. He'd been indicted for corruption. What had Vernon done for him, she wondered?

She tossed the card down and went over to where Hanger sat. On the monitor above him, the image of the guard filled the screen. With his gun and its lethal-looking silencer resting at the ready across his chest, the man sat sprawled on the floor, staring into the camera.

The hairs on the back of her neck rose. The man looked like death personified. His eyes were black glass, deeply sunk into a face marred with shiny white scars, red-lined gouges, and a disfiguring burn mark running up the side of his neck and over his left cheek. The bald skin of his head was the color of dirty ice and lined with gray-purple veins. At some point in his life, he'd sported multiple piercings in his nose and ears and lips, but now he wore no jewelry, only the droopy punctures. He looked the kind of man who would cut off a hand under orders—Bella gripped the edge of the table to steady herself—a man who would kill without mercy.

Hanger rolled back the chair. "I still say we take him head on before his buddy returns. I could toss some of that sour milk at him."

Bella's heart thundered in her chest. "No. You are not invincible. He'd shoot the minute the door slid open." She changed the subject. "I checked the food. The stuff in the fridge has turned bad, but there's plenty of pasta and sauce and canned veggies to see us through for days. I even found a stack of frozen pizzas in the freezer. We can hole up here in style. Sooner or later, Toro or Fur Tree will answer the e-mails I sent."

"I doubt it."

Bella glanced at Hanger. "What do you mean? It said sent."

"I think there is a block on outgoing messages or something. Your e-mail's been sitting in the outbox forever. Mr. Boss Man probably didn't want his employees wasting time on personal stuff. And I can't figure out the password to get out on the Internet."

Bella peered up at the monitor. Glass-Eyes was picking his nose. "Maybe those guys will give up."

"Not these men." Hanger turned back to the computer. "Do you know who the shark guy really is?"

"Tuccio called him his protégé."

"Protégé Schmotégé. I guess ya could call him that. But their relationship is a lot closer."

"Closer?"

"Got the whole family history right here. There's a file called Family Business. Found this old *Daily News* newspaper article. Let's see." He moused over the screen. "Yep, here it is. Front page and all. Cosmo

Newell. The man was a major crime lord. Gunned down in the bathroom of his million dollar mansion in Saddle River, New Jersey."

"He was killed in his own home?" She hadn't asked Vernon how his father died. But if his father's enemies could murder a man in a place as well-protected as his own house, Vernon, who roamed everywhere with just one bodyguard, was an easy target.

Hanger clicked to the next screen. "Now here's the obituary." He scrolled down and read "Leaves behind three sons, Vernon Newell, Theo Tuccio, and *Cole Tuccio*. Vernon ever gab about his third brother?"

Bella shook her head. "No. Never."

"There's tons of info here about him. Vernon was like on his case. Guy went to Princeton. Got a law degree from NYU. Looks like Vernon paid for it all plus all his other diversions. Bills for restaurants and suits and stuff. But here"—he clicked open another document—"this is what I wanted you to see. Take a look at this photo."

Bella laid a hand on Hanger's shoulder and leaned in. The photo was a typical graduation picture, complete with silly cap, diploma hugged against the chest, and a sheepish smile. But there was no mistaking the face. She covered her mouth with her hand and swallowed down the bile. It was Shark Tooth Man with perfect teeth.

Hanger pointed at the image. "This Cole and the Kiro guy. Gotta be the same person. Don't ya think?"

Bella's throat was dry. "No. It can't be. Vernon would have said."

Hanger shrugged. "He does have that same weird

color hair. And doesn't Vernon have a dimple like that?"

A hole opened up inside her. It couldn't be true. She gripped the back of the chair. "Shark Tooth can't be that Cole. His name is Kiro."

"Kiro? Cole? Just names." Hanger turned to peer up at her. "We all have different names depending on who we want to be. You do. I do. So this clean-cut Cole lawyer character plays at being Kiro when he's a bad guy."

"Got to be someone else. The guy can't be a lawyer. What lawyer has filed teeth?" Inside, Bella knew she was stretching for straws. Anything to pull her out of the abyss of betrayal she felt. Vernon had a little brother—a nasty one. Was he nasty enough to have done Vernon in, or was he Vernon's agent?

Hanger leaned back in the chair and stared up at the screen. "All lawyers are sharks." He jerked upright. "Told you we needed to take out that guy."

Bella snapped her attention to the flickering images on the monitor. The elevator door slid open, and the subject of their discussion stepped out, followed by a man in a technician's coveralls.

She dug her fingers into the leather of the chair. "They won't be able to get the door open. Vernon told me it's foolproof."

"Nothing's *foolproof*, Miss Bella."

The kid's cynicism surprised her. She'd been cynical ever since her mother died. It was her worst fault. But her cynicism was hard won. She was more than a decade older. Hanger, for all his fewer years, sounded like someone whose dreams had passed him by. Some mothering urge stirred inside, and she wanted to give him the hug her mother hadn't offered her. She rested her hand on his shoulder.

He tossed it off and stood up. "We're so cooked."

She glanced at the screen. "But they're leaving—all of them."

"Give it a minute." He pulled a gun from the back of his waistband.

Bella threw up her hands. "Where'd you get *that*?"

"Found it in the drawer over there."

"Do you even know what to do with it?"

"Yeah, I watch TV." He gazed at her, suddenly very young. "If you make it out, tell Toro I'm sorry." He seized her arm and pulled her down under the table.

Kaboom. An explosion shook the floor. The monitors in the room flickered and went out. Something fell with a crash in the living room. Fire alarms blared, smoke billowed, and the overhead sprinklers came on. Bella's ears rang. Her eyes watered. There seemed to be no air.

There was huffing sound and out of the dust, two men wearing masks charged into the room, guns at the ready.

Hanger slapped her on the arm. "*Gas.* Hold your breath.*" Beside her, the kid fumbled with Vernon's gun. But a boot kicked it from his hands, and one of the masked men dragged him up by the hair. Hanger yelped and swung out his fists.

"*Enough.*" His captor thumped him on the side of the head with the butt of his gun, and Hanger sank to the floor and sprawled there like a crushed doll.

Bella scuttled farther under the table, sucking in the gas, feeling her throat closing in, knowing there was no escape, that her turn was next. Spots jumped before her eyes. She wavered, her body numb, her mind foggy. She hardly felt the hands that seized her, then dragged her forward and dumped her next to Hanger, who lay still on his back.

Was he dead? Had she caused the death of this innocent child? She rolled her head to the side, blinked the dizziness away. With trembling fingertips, she checked for a sign of life. A tiny pulse flickered in his neck. Yes. He lived. There was still a chance they'd survive.

She glanced up. Mr. Baldy and the so-called technician had their guns trained on her. She was going nowhere. But she didn't have to cooperate. Time was on her side.

"You idiot!" Kiro, his pale cold eyes just visible above the face mask, nudged her hard in her bruised side with the toe of his boot. "It would have been so much easier if you'd just opened the door. Now we have to hurry before the cops show up." He turned away. "Bring her."

Mr. Baldy lifted her up and carried her into Vernon's bedroom.

"Her hand here."

The technician wearing rubber gloves yanked her arm up. "Yuck, it's like handling a wet fish."

Mr. Baldy behind him growled, "Just blow the damn thing. We've only a few minutes."

Kiro knocked the technician aside and wrapped his hand around Bella's. His grip was like a vise. "Idiot. I need the papers inside readable. This will do." He pressed her hand against a blinking light. Nothing happened. Shark Tooth loomed over her and lifted an eyelid. "Tell me how to get into this safe." He slapped her cheek.

Despite the pain, Bella pretended she didn't hear. With luck, she might delay them until help arrived.

Behind him, the bald guy shifted from foot to foot. "Maybe she doesn't know, boss."

"She knows." Kiro gave her a shake. "Vernon trusted her."

Boom. An explosion shook the room and a foul stink followed. Screeches and yells filled the air. Kiro snatched her by the wrist and turned toward the door. Hanger appeared out of the smoke, took one look, and backed away. "I'll get help, Bella."

Idiot, who did he think he was—a knight in shining armor? Bella struggled against the man holding her, shouting at them to leave Hanger alone, her throat burning.

"Can't you idiots handle one kid? Go. Help Scuttle round up that piece of filth. Don't want him getting away. He's seen too much."

The man took off on a run.

Kiro yanked Bella around. "Now. It's just the two of us."

She flailed against him, kicking and twisting. But she was no match for him.

Shark Tooth tightened his grip on her wrist. "Be still, you'll just break the bone." He hauled her in and pressed her against his body. He leaned in, his breath hot against her cheek and ran his tongue down the side of her jaw. "Ah, yes. I remember how sweet you tasted."

"Don't." She jerked her head away.

"I like a girl with spirit. But right now, I haven't the time."

From the other room came a shriek of pain and the sound of something smashing. Kiro's head shot up. "Haven't you guys got the kid, yet?"

A voice called back. "He's got Scuttle trapped."

Kiro grimaced. "All I have is idiots around me. Can't subdue a miniature teeny bopper." He threw her face down on the bed, pressed his knee into her back. "Now you be a good girl." He picked up the tie she'd discarded and waved it in front of her. "So convenient of Vernon to leave this behind." He leered at her. "Appears you are as troublesome to him as to me." He yanked her hands behind her back and bound them together, then tied the ends to the bedpost.

For a moment, his hand rested on her butt. He ran it across gently and then gave her a hard slap. "Mmm. Maybe I want more than your hand." Then he stood up, pulled down his coat sleeves and strode from the room like he was off to a day in court.

****

It was over in minutes. Kiro stomped back in, shoving Hanger in front of him. The street artist had a swollen eye. Blood dripped from a cut forehead. Kiro tossed him to Mr. Baldy. The boy held up his head and glared defiantly, his lips clamped tight. The thug drew out his gun.

Kiro pushed the man's hand down. "No guns. We've made enough noise."

"But he blew up Scuttle's face with that concoction he made."

Kiro flicked his hand across his throat and turned back to the safe.

Behind him there was rustling, and then the goon took out a long wicked-looking knife, lifted Hanger's head, and placed the edge against his neck. The kid sputtered something.

"No." Bella gritted her teeth and twisted to the side. "Kiro. Don't."

He held up his hand and signaled his underling to wait. "The lady has a request?"

"I—I'll help you open the safe. Go with you. Do anything you want. Just let the boy go."

Kiro grinned and walked over to the bed. He curled a lock of her hair around his finger. "*Anything?*"

She nodded, her heart pounding in her chest. She'd kill herself before she'd let him touch her, but he didn't need to know that. "Anything."

"Sounds interesting." He untied her from the bedpost and pushed her forward. "So how's the safe work?"

She wiggled her hands. "I need my palm."

Kiro signaled his minion. "Keep the knife on the kid."

Bella glanced over her shoulder. The bruiser had Hanger's head tipped back, the blade pressed to his jugular. Nothing in that safe was worth a boy's life. Vernon had shown her how to open the safe months ago. "Everything that is mine is yours," he'd said. Inside, she knew, were merely lists of foreign bank accounts and a bunch of papers. But what Kiro would do with that data, she didn't know. All the passwords were inside Vernon's head.

She pressed her palm to the pad until the light in the panel flashed. Then she spit on her finger and tapped the flashing light to the rhythm of Avril Lavigne's *Complicated*. The light stopped blinking. She counted to eleven. And repeated the sequence. There was a small click, and the safe sprung open.

Kiro retied her hands together and pushed her to the side. "Leave it to Vernon to have some weird locking mechanism. How'd you know what to tap?"

Bella shrugged. "His favorite song."

"Oh, whatever." Kiro reached into the safe and pulled out the padded envelopes and neatly stacked papers, and stuffed them into one of Vernon's briefcases.

Bella glimpsed a tri-folded paper. It looked familiar. She crooked her neck. Blast it. *It was familiar*. It was the deed to the villa on Eudokia. Fists clenched to keep from grabbing it, she watched Kiro drop it into the briefcase with all the other papers.

The technician hustled into the room, his face blistered on one side, his eye swollen shut. He croaked. "Gotta go, boss. We've disturbed the neighbors. Guard's on his way up."

Kiro shoved in the last envelope. "Done. Cut their throats and go."

"No." Bella peered straight into his cold, pale eyes. She had to have that deed. She had to save Hanger. She had to find out what had happened to Vernon. "I'm going with you. Remember." She put as much enticement in her voice as she could.

Kiro stopped. His mouth turned into a smile, revealing his filed teeth. "Oh, what the heck. Bring them both."

Chapter 26

Vernon flopped over from his belly to his back. Water puddled around him. He was rotting to death in this cesspool. His feet had gone numb. His arms and legs refused to work. Skin was peeling off his toes and the soles of his feet.

He tried to picture what he looked like, but his brain could not imagine anything so real. The pain that had driven him crazy, now felt like a dull ache. He was no longer hungry or thirsty, and somewhere in the fog of his mind, he knew that was a very bad sign.

Most of the time, he slept, dreaming of stomping through snow drifts and floating amid icebergs, fleeing from the ghosts of the men he'd killed. He rolled over again and pressed his cold, hands to his ears. Still their voices whispered, begging for mercy.

Howls of the tortured rose up around him. The chains of men he'd held captive rattled. The worst was when Ari peered down at him, his mutilated hands stretched out as if to choke him.

He'd done a lot of bad things in his life, hurt a lot of people, but he regretted what he'd done to Bella's brother the most. The man had only been protecting his sister. He hadn't deserved to have his incredible talent destroyed. The world would be poorer without it.

He drew in a breath of the fetid air. Bella'd been right to reject him. Vernon Newell was a measly grub who'd sucked the life blood from the poor, the weak, the abused, the addicted—his father's clone.

He struggled upright and balanced himself on the wooden stumps that had once been his feet. The only thing keeping him alive was anger, hot murderous anger.

Cole was going to pay for this. After all he'd done for the boy. Giving him everything he'd been denied. Getting him the best education money could buy. Setting him up as a partner in a major law firm. The kid had no appreciation for how lucky he was to be free of their father's yoke when he was still young—before he'd been twisted.

But it had been futile. He leaned back against the wall. The cold cement pressed on the open sores, setting them to throbbing. His step-mother was right. There was something in his father's seed, some kernel of evil that no amount of goodness could fix. It had taken mere months for Theo to unearth that bit of dirt about his father's death and turn Cole against him— turn him into something worse than even he had been— a greedy fool.

A ghostly head that looked like his father hooted in his ear. He swatted at it, lost his balance, and tumbled into the water. He clawed his way up, water dripping down his face, fighting the madness that hovered. He would not surrender. Not yet.

One hand on the wall, he stumbled through the water, walking the perimeter. He had to keep his heart pumping, his limbs moving. Sooner or later, his brother would come back to see if he still lived. And he would tell him—he swayed, caught himself, and kept moving—he would tell him—damn, he'd forgotten what he meant to say. He leaned back against the wall and slid down into the filthy water.

A screech of metal echoed through the cistern. The noise cut through him like a knife. He pressed his cold, rubbery hands against his ears.

It was feeding time.

****

Kiro slammed the car door closed, opened the fast food bag, and handed Bella a greasy hamburger. "Dinner time."

Holding the burger in her bound hands, Bella took a bite and chewed. The soggy bun stuck to her teeth. The meat had the texture of granulated cardboard. She forced the mouthful down her throat, then dropped the tasteless concoction on the paper wrapper in Kiro's—or was it Cole's—lap. She refused to ask. "You forgot the ketchup."

"Figured you were spicy enough." Shark Tooth bit into his own burger as the car pulled away from the ratty-looking gas station. He chewed noisily and swallowed. "Well, it ain't a Commodore, but what do you expect out here in Natty Bumppo land."

"Who land?"

He licked his lips and tucked in his chin like a prosecutor judging a witness. "I see your knowledge of American literature is deficient, my Miss Bell. But no worries. It's not your brain, I'm interested in." He placed a hand on her thigh.

Bella shifted her leg, but his hand stayed put. She peered out the car window. They'd left the main road over half an hour ago and started up what could only be a mountainside. Trees and bushes, their limbs glaringly white in the beams of the headlamps, hugged the edges of a shoulderless gravel road that twisted and turned as they climbed higher and higher.

After years of living in the city, she'd forgotten how dark it could get out in the country. Not a street light or house light flickered in the blackness. The only lights came from the dashboard of the car and the high beams illuminating the empty road ahead. Every once in a while, they came to a place where the overhanging trees fell away, and she had the feeling that the road just dropped off on that side into a gorge or ravine.

She had grown up on Eudokia, where the only trees were olives and carobs and a few bent Aleppo pines. The higher you climbed the rocky hillsides, scented with wild sage and oregano, the farther you could see and the lighter you felt.

This place of dark and woods weighed on her. A heavy, wet dampness hung in the air, filling her lungs with a bone-chilling cold the rasping car heater blowing full tilt did nothing to dispel. A shiver swept over her. It looked like a place you'd dump dead bodies.

"You really should eat." Kiro played with a lock of her hair. "I'm going to need you all energetic when we get there." He pinched off a bit of the burger and held it to her mouth. "Eat."

She clamped her mouth closed and pulled back.

He readjusted his position so he leaned against her and whispered into her ear. "I believe you said you would do anything I asked if I didn't hurt the kid." He pressed the soggy burger to her lips. "Eat."

She shifted her head away and peered to the back of the car. "How do I know he's okay?"

Kiro let out a long sigh. "He's safe and sound. Even gave him a blanket."

"A blanket! It's got to be near zero in that trunk." She slapped the food out of his fingers. "Let him out."

"No can do, Mermaid." He rubbed the teeth marks on his hand. "He's bitten me one too many times."

"At least stop the car and let me check. He hasn't made any noise in hours."

"Thank the gods. His caterwauling was driving us all crazy. We'll be there in a few more minutes."

Bella froze. "Where's there?"

Kiro popped the burger morsel in his mouth and glanced at her from the corner of his eye. "The Pines."

"Vernon's castle?" She struggled to draw a breath. "Is Vernon there?"

He licked his thumb. "Should be."

"Alive?"

Kiro raised his eyebrows. "Was the last time I saw him."

Bella bit her lower lip. Vernon wasn't dead then. So what game was he playing? If he had sent his brother to terrify her because she refused to marry him, she would kill him. "What's it like—The Pines?"

Kiro glanced at her, threw back his head, and laughed. "You've never been? I guess you weren't quite special enough." He rubbed his hand up and down her thigh, each stroke moving higher. "I'd have brought you many times, Mermaid."

She jerked her leg away.

He tilted his head. "You did promise to do *anything.*"

Bella pressed her legs together. "Vernon will have something to say about that and how you've treated the boy. He likes the kid."

"Maybe," Kiro said. He gathered up the uneaten

burger and wrapper, lowered the window half-way and tossed them out.

Bella struggled to regain control. "That's littering."

"Just feeding the critters. Keeping them happy. It's dead winter, and they get mighty hungry out here in the mountains."

"Critters?"

"I must introduce you to my special guards."

He signaled Mr. Baldy to pull over. The car came to a halt on a sharp upturn, rolled back a few feet and crunched to a stop. "Turn off the lights, Roger." The head lights dimmed and died. Kiro lowered the window the rest of the way.

Cold air, pungent with the aroma of evergreens, seeped into the car. The fresh scent pricked Bella's nose and reminded her that Christmas was coming. Ari would be trying to get in touch. Toro too. They'd be frantic by now, calling the police. There'd be search parties. She hugged her arms to her body and glanced around at the thick woods. But no rescuers would ever find them here in the middle of nowhere. What had Vernon said about his fortress? That's right, it was surrounded by five hundred acres of nothing.

"Watch," Kiro said.

Bella jerked her head up. He winked at her and then leaned out the window and let out a long howl. For a minute, silence filled the dark. Then answering howls, deeper, more primitive than a city dog's cry, tore through the night. Over and over. Echoing. Coming closer.

The hair on the back of her neck rose. Shadows moved between the trees. *Thud.* Something hit the side of the car so hard the whole vehicle shook.

Bella glimpsed gaping teeth, black fur, and mad-looking eyes.

Kiro rolled up the window. *Thud.* The creature whacked the car again. He yelled at the driver. "Get moving." The car took off, wheels skidding on the gravel.

Mr. Baldy clutched the wheel and half-turned. "I hate when you stir them up so close to the gate. What if they follow us inside?"

"You got a gun. Just drive."

Bella couldn't stop shaking. "What were those things?"

He snugged his arm around her and pulled her up against him. "One of my papa's special projects—wolf dogs. He had them specially bred from Šarplaninacs, biggest dogs in the world. Makes you think twice about hoofing it out of here." He ran his finger under the tie that bound her wrists. "I really don't want to have to keep you tied up *all* the time." He leaned back and hummed an off-key version of the theme song from *Jaws.* The blue light from the dashboard caught him full face. Bella blinked.

For a moment, in the splash of light, he looked just like Vernon.

Chapter 27

Seconds later, the car crested a hill and came up alongside a high stone wall that in the beam of the headlights seemed to go on forever. Mr. Baldy slapped the steering wheel. "We're here, boss."

Kiro nodded. "Let them know."

The car stopped at an arched gateway blocked by heavy metal doors. Baldy honked the horn five times.

Bella leaned forward to get a better look at this place Vernon was holed up in.

Kiro pulled her back. "Relax. It will take a moment to get inside. There's quite an elaborate lock on the gate. Vernon trusts no one."

A loud thumping came from the trunk.

Bella jerked around.

"See, I told you your gypsy'd be fine." Kiro knocked on the seatback and the thumping stopped. "Keep your tighty whities on, boy."

An ear-splitting screech filled the air, and she turned back to stare as the gates opened inward to reveal a thick-walled, castle-like fortress built of flat river-stones, complete with parapets, battlements, and arrow slots. At each end stood a round tower. Lit only by the car headlights, the place looked unreal, like a set for a ghostly horror movie.

Bella glanced at Kiro. "This is it? The Pines?" She put her hand on the window and wiped away the condensation to get a better look. Camouflage-clad thugs stood on either side of the car as it drove past. Other guards, military-style guns half-slung, peered down from the towers. Vernon hadn't been kidding. He really did own a castle. And the guards really did tote AK-47s.

"Yeah." Kiro got out on his side, then came around and opened her door with the gentlemanly flourish of a man on a date.

Bella hunched back. Vernon was in there— waiting. She slid farther away from the open door. Would her former fiancé be smiling or wearing a sneer?

"Stop contemplating your navel, Mermaid. Move it." Kiro grasped her by her arm and yanked her out. Her foot caught on the bottom of the door opening, and she came down hard on her knee. Her jeans tore. Gravel scraped away the skin. Pain shot up her leg.

Behind her, the trunk lid snapped open. Hanger leaped out, jabbed Mr. Baldy in the eyes with his fingers and took off running.

Here was their chance. If she could get control of the car maybe they could escape. Ignoring the pain, she dug her knees into the gravel and pulled against Kiro's grip.

Shark Tooth yanked her up and gave her a bone-rattling shake. "My dear Mermaid, the kid's going nowhere. There's no exit from the courtyard. No way to open the gate without me knowing. No one comes here unless invited. Once you're inside those gates, the only way out is *through me*." Kiro's jaw tightened. "I've been kind to you because you seemed interested in entertaining me. Don't spoil the illusion." He gripped her arm tighter.

Bella struggled to free herself from the vise of his fingers. "Stop manhandling me. Your brother won't like it."

"Brother? You mean Vernon? He's no brother I'll claim. Now come along, Mermaid. This has nothing to do with Vernon. You're here because *I* want you here." He turned to Baldy, who was staggering to his feet. "Round up the idiot kid and put him in the game room. Try not to kill him in the process. It would hurt the lady's feelings. Use the Taser. When the kid's nice and tight, go fill the cistern."

Kiro dragged her up the icy steps, then shoved her to the side and entered a code on the keyed entry. She pressed her bound wrists to her chest. *Please let this be a very bad joke of Vernon's.* She glanced at the hard-set face of her captor, a mocking imitation of Vernon's. *Please let him be alive.*

The door opened to reveal a stone-walled, vaulted hallway. She gasped. Along the walls on either side hung a row of Ari's huge canvases—early works done right after he'd gotten out of prison, the ones Vernon stole from the villa in reprisal for Ari chasing him from her bed.

Ari had mourned their loss more than he had hers. It was one of the reasons she'd fled Eudokia all those years ago.

Kiro put a hand on her back and shoved her forward. "Move along."

"Wait. The paintings here. Are they yours?"

"Paintings?" He flicked his hand toward the walls. "Oh, this stuff. Hell, been here since I was a kid."

"They're quite good."

He narrowed his eyes and studied the paintings as

if it were the first time he really looked at them. "Think they're worth any money?"

Bella opened her mouth to say a fortune and then thought better. These paintings were Ari's and somehow, if she survived this, she'd get them back to him. The money would go a long way to making up for losing the TV job. She shrugged. "I have no idea. I'm a tattoo artist. Not an art critic."

"Never saw much purpose in hanging paint messes on perfectly fine walls myself," Kiro said as he opened the double doors at the end of the hall. Lights snapped on automatically, revealing a huge open-design living-dining room with a wet bar and sleek steel, glass, and leather furnishings at odds with the rough-hewn beams and rock walls of the castle. The far end of the room was an expanse of sliding glass doors which probably looked out across the mountains during daylight hours, but at the moment were inky dark. A doorway to what appeared to be a state-of-the-art kitchen lay to her right.

Not a house of horrors. A comfortable millionaire's retreat. The kind of place Vernon would own.

She glanced around for Vernon. But no toe-tapping, angry lover greeted her arrival. He'd been here though. She could smell his distinctive scent—the one imprinted on her since the day she'd first met him on the dock in Eudokia. She'd know it anywhere.

He had to be here. She moved farther into the room so she could peek into the huge, white marble and barn wood kitchen. Professional-quality stainless steel appliances wrapped around the outer walls. A polished oak table surrounded by chairs sat in a glass-walled alcove.

"Impressed?"

She spun around.

Kiro leaned against the door jamb looking for all the world like a man surveying his property. He held a sharp-tipped, ivory-handled knife in his hands—the knife from her nightmares. "Come here."

A chill started at the base of her spine and crept up her back. Her feet refused to move.

"Come here, Tattoo Lady." He twirled the knife. "Let me free your hands."

She glanced down at the gold tie binding her wrists and then back into his cold eyes. She had no illusions that the devil facing her would relax his control over her no matter how solicitous he appeared at the moment. One glance at his pale icy eyes was enough to make her stomach curl up into an ever-tightening knot. He was a shark pursuing his prey. He would kill her, and Hanger, in a second, if she tried to escape.

She swallowed hard. No Vernon was going to come save her. If he'd been here, he was now gone. She'd have to survive anyway she could. Hanger was depending on her.

If that meant she had to play along with Shark Tooth, then she would. Arms outstretched, she forced herself to step toward him.

He caught her by the hand and pulled her closer. With one swipe, he sliced through the silk. The tie crumpled to the floor like a dead snake. He lifted her right wrist to his lips and kissed where the tie had chafed. "I apologize for manhandling you the way I did. But the result"—he licked the spot he'd kissed—"will be worth it." He let her hand drop. "So you like the place?"

She rubbed the wrist he'd slobbered over on the

seat of her jeans and forced her mouth to curve into a smile. "Place is amazing. Have you had it long?"

"Been in the *Newell* family for decades. But it's about to change ownership." He padded over to the bar on the wall opposite the windows. "Sit down. Relax. Can I get you something to drink?"

Bella stood looking at him. This was the slimy thug who'd had her wrapped in a garbage bag and was going to cut off her hand so he could get into Vernon's place, and now he was acting all gentlemanly?

He turned around holding two glasses of golden liquid, and she glimpsed his filed teeth. Nope. Not a gentleman. This nice guy act was just that—an act. Everything about him was an act. He was probably a terrific lawyer.

"I said sit." He strode toward her.

She backed up and collapsed onto the black leather sofa. He handed her the glass. "You didn't specify. So I choose for you. I think you will like this."

He sat down next to her, the cushion sinking under his weight, and rested his arm on the seatback. His fingers stroked the nape of her neck as he sipped his drink.

Bella steadied her breathing. The longer she could keep up the pretense of being cooperative, the more chance she'd have to escape. But she was exhausted. It had been a grueling day with little sleep and a whole lot of terror.

She took a sip of the drink and gagged.

Shark Tooth tugged on a lock of her hair. "Do you like it?"

She held the glass in her lap. "It's quite sweet."

He drained his down. "Take another sip or two. It

grows on you."

She twirled the liquid in the glass." "What is it?"

"Melomel—a kind of fruity mead. Most women love it." He took the glass out of her hand and raised it to her lips. "Drink."

She closed her eyes and dipped the tip of her tongue in the mead. The cloying honey aroma assaulted her nose. She took a small sip and forced it down.

"And another."

She glanced at him. He was being overly insistent. Had he put something in it? She drew back. "I don't like sweet drinks. They make me sick to my stomach."

"This won't do that. Just make you relaxed. Another sip. Let it grow on you." He held the rim to her mouth and pressed.

She craned back and shook her head. "Really. Just the smell makes me nauseous."

"But I insist. It will help us get along much better."

She had to keep him talking until she could dump whatever was in the glass. "I'll give it a try. But don't say I didn't warn you when I vomit." She slipped her hand under his and took the glass. Pretending to sip, she pushed up from the sofa and wandered over to the windows. "Must be a beautiful view in daylight."

He trailed after her, halting behind so close his breath brushed her ear. "If you like trees." He glanced at her. "Enjoying the drink?"

She put the rim to her lips and took the tiniest of swallows. Maybe she could spill it over the balcony railing. Cupping her hand against the glass, she peered out into the dark. "What's out there?"

"Curiosity killed the cat, you know—among other things." He flicked a switch. Floodlights blazed on, illuminating the narrow balcony and the snowy tops of fir trees. Kiro slid open one of the doors, put a hand on the small of her back and pressed her forward. "Take a good look."

A chill wind whipped at her hair and tore at her clothing. Snowflakes, brilliant white in the floodlights, swirled around her. Down below, the earth fell away into a deep gorge blacker than black. Even with the balcony railing between her and the drop, she felt like she was going to tumble over the edge. Bella took a step back and smashed into Kiro.

"Don't like the view?" He nodded at the glass. "Drink it or you will find out just how high up we are."

Maybe it was exhaustion. Maybe it was anger. Maybe she just went crazy. She'd been bombed, terrorized, abused by this man. Her hand came up. The glass went airborne. Liquor splattered his face. "Enough of all these threats," she screamed. "The joke's over. Take me to Vernon *now.*"

"Vernon?" He actually seemed surprised. Shark Tooth wiped the dripping liquid from his face with his sleeve. "I thought you tossed him aside."

The words flew out. "Yes, isn't this what it has all been about? Your job is to torment me for rejecting your bastard of a brother. Well, I must say you've overdone it by far. But your whole family is crazy. Vernon's told me about your mother. Nasty lady. And your father had to have been ten times worse. And you. You're just a despicable little goat turd."

Kiro threw back his head and laughed. The sound echoed across the gorge. In the distance, the howls of the dogs answered back. "You think this is all a joke?" he sputtered. He stepped back and looked her up and down. "Nice bod"—he touched the healing cuts on her face—"but the face is a major turn off. I was willing—"

She pushed his hand away. "Don't you touch me."

He shrugged. "Fine. Come, Mermaid. We'll do it your way." He seized her by her shoulder and dragged her back through the glass doors, across the living room and into the entrance hall. He opened a door to the left and shoved her forward. "Down the stairs."

She twisted around. "Where are we going?"

Kiro's sharp-toothed grin grew larger. "We're going fishing."

Chapter 28

Clang. Vernon shook himself awake, but it was hard. The world of dreams was a much better place. Soon he would not wake up at all. He rubbed his aching head and then pressed his ear to the cold, clammy wall. Vibrations penetrated the fog of his brain. He rolled his shoulders and forced his unwilling body to push up tighter against the wall. A shuffling noise came from overhead and then the screech of the grate being lifted. A flash of light illuminated the cistern. He shielded his eyes and peered at his prison. The walls were green with slime. Water full of his filth covered the floor. Bags and wrappers and sodden food floated around him like an armada of decay.

A rattling came from above, and a hose snaked down. Water sputtered from the nozzle and then turned into a steady flow.

He scrunched closer to the wall. *Not more water.*

"Hello? Still there?" One of his brother's thugs, the bald one, moved the hose to the side and stuck his head through the hatchway. "There you are." He aimed the nozzle at him. "Phew. Need to clean you off. Kiro's orders."

Water pelted him, trickled into his ears, and flooded his eyes. Clamping the lids closed, he turned his head up and let the clean water fill his mouth. He swallowed. It was like swallowing liquid ice, so cold it burned all the way down and set him to shivering.

Damn it, Cole. If Theo were still alive, he'd kill him all over again for turning his little brother into a monster. He'd tried so hard to keep his little brother above the law, and all it had taken were a few months under that snake's tutelage to stir up the greed that was their father's legacy.

A spray of freezing water on his stomach knocked the thought from his head. He looked down. The water was rising at an alarming rate. In just those few minutes, it had reached his knees. He glanced up. Baldy was gone, but the hose hung down, wedged in the grate, spewing water at full blast. Damn, they meant to drown him.

He tried to gauge how long it would take to fill the tank, but his water-logged brain could no longer wrap itself around numbers—a very bad sign. Numbers were his forte. He watched the water level rise higher and higher. Forget calculations. Obviously, faster than was good for his survival. Once the water covered his chest, hypothermia would set in, and everything would just stop functioning. The actual drowning would be an afterthought.

He ran a finger over the mermaid on his biceps. He hoped Bella was happy, busy working, creating her amazing tattoos. She had been right. He was a murderous crook who deserved to die young. He would have preferred a bullet than this slow torture, but villains didn't get a choice. Somewhere his victims were cheering.

He stopped fighting and let his body drift with the current. His breathing slowed, each breath a little shallower, a little harder to draw in. The light from the opening above him reflected on the surface of the water as it swirled around him. In a way, it was beautiful, peaceful.

Inch by inch the water rose.

He was half-conscious by the time the water ringed his neck, lapped at his mouth. A few more inches. Water filled his ears, muffling the rushing sound of the pouring water. Then it reached his nose. The next breath would be his last. He shivered. He'd never been so cold. At least hell would be hot.

****

Bella peered down into the cistern. Vernon, his body deathly white, floated in the water.

Kiro's fingers clamped over the back of her neck. "Uh-oh. Guess we're too late."

No. Vernon couldn't be dead. She hadn't thought when she'd leaped in after her mother. Despite the panic pressing in her, she didn't think this time either. Willing all her strength into her legs, she shoved Kiro aside, filled her lungs with air, and jumped, another leap into freezing water tearing at the edges of her memory.

Splash. Water frothed around her. Pressure built in her eardrums. An electric bolt of icy cold shot through her. Blinking water out of her eyes, she swam to Vernon and lifted him. She brushed her lips against his neck searching for a pulse. Yes. He was still alive, but barely.

Bella flipped him over. Beneath his days-old beard, Vernon's skin was pasty white and shriveled, his lips blue. He looked dead. Only the fact that his eyelids fluttered and his pulse flickered kept her hope alive.

She rested the back of Vernon's head against her

shoulder, looped her arms under his armpits, and wished for a flotation device like the life guards at Coney Island used. He was a big man, and the water was frigid. After the spike of adrenaline that had enabled her to jump into the cistern, the shock of the icy water set her body shivering. Her teeth chattered. Waves from her dive slapped on the sides of the tank, each splash roaring in her ears like angry sea monsters.

She pressed her lips to his frigid cheek, murmured in his ear. "Don't die. I love you."

In slow motion, Vernon pushed at her arm with his hand. But the attempt was feeble, no more than a ripple against her skin. She tightened her grip. It was like holding on to a block of ice. How long had he been down here? In this temperature, she would have no more than ten to fifteen minutes before the cold stole all her strength, too. Vernon was already chilled beyond safety.

Bella maneuvered under the hatchway and called up, "He's suffering hypothermia. Throw down a ladder."

Shark Tooth's hyena laugh filled the cistern. "Oh, but this is so *delightful*. The brave heroine to the rescue. Like something you'd see on a TV show."

"Bastard." Bella leaned back to keep Vernon's nose above the lapping waves and, despite the deathly knot of fear cramping her body, treaded water. Her body shook with the effort. She hadn't been in water over her head since her mother drowned.

A scraping sound above drew her glance up. Kiro smiled down at her. "I'll be right back." The metal lid closed with a clash.

All light evaporated, leaving her and Vernon's still

271

body floating in the watery tomb. She clasped his head against her breast and cursed that she ever doubted him. He hadn't been terrorizing her. His foul brother had.

But Vernon flailed again, twisting like a fish in a net. Pulling her under. She sank below the water, came up sputtering. Using all her strength, she clung on in the pitch dark, sinking beneath the water and then scissors kicking herself to the surface again and again. She would *not* lose another person she loved.

The memory struck her like a needle piercing her heart. Her mother had taken her to Lamia on the mainland to buy goodies and gifts for Christmas. A special treat—they rarely left the island. But mid-voyage, her mother wandered to the back of the boat. Trailing after her, Bella saw her mother tip over the railing, her black hair disappearing beneath the white caps. She opened her mouth to scream for help, but the words stuck like a wet paper wad in her throat.

Then she was running, leaping, diving into water as cold as this cistern. She snagged a hand and held on with the desperation of a child. But her mother fought her, yanked and tugged, pulling her under, trying to take her daughter with her. Lungs burning, she let go.

One of the crew members on the boat hauled her out. But they never found her mother. She tightened her grip on Vernon as she sank beneath the water for the hundredth time and came up coughing and spitting. She would not let go again.

Clang. Light streamed down above her, but she had no strength to lift her head. A confusion of voices mixed with the constant sucking and lapping of the water. Metal grated on metal. A ladder came down. She gave one last kick. Her fingers found a rung, and she latched on.

Through the square of light, Kiro's backlit silhouette waved. "Rescue is here, Mermaid."

Relief flooded through her. At this point, she'd accept help from the devil. "Vernon. You need to get him out. He's near death."

"Wouldn't want that, would we?" Kiro leaned farther over. "So answer me this question, and I will grant you a wish."

Damn the man. This was no time for riddles. She was losing strength and consciousness. Her hand slipped from the rung, and Vernon slid farther underwater. She scrabbled for the ladder and with numb fingers, latched on again. "Hurry," she croaked, "I can't hold on much longer."

"Here's the question. So who should I save? You, my beautiful Mermaid, or my bastard of a brother who abandoned you and hurt you? Who destroyed your brother's art career?"

She glanced at the white face of the man who'd haunted her for years, who'd hurt her and who brought her to the heights of ecstasy. Who loved her with a passion found only in epic romances. If the tables were turned, he'd sacrifice his life for her.

Vernon's body shifted against hers. His words came as a breathless whisper. "Let me go, angel. Let me go."

Bella murmured into his hair. "Never, my love." She shouted up at Kiro, "Save him."

His head bobbed. "Your wish is my command." The ladder vibrated. Feet clanked down. Hands took Vernon from her grasp and lifted him up and out of the cistern. Bella squinted up as his legs disappeared from her view. She'd done it. Saved him.

The man on the ladder leaned down toward her. "You want the woman too, boss?"

She gathered her strength and reached for the man's hand.

"No. Get up here and get my brother upstairs."

The man dropped his hand and climbed up and out.

Kiro cupped his hands and called down. "Hey Mermaid, it's your turn to be the dying fish."

The ladder rose with a screech. Bella held on to the rung as long as she could, but her hands slipped off, and she fell back into the water with a splash. The cover slid closed and darkness rushed in. The water eddied around her, cold as the bastard's heart. Shark Tooth was leaving her to drown.

She sank under and let herself float. Would it be so bad? Water filled her ears, muffling the roaring noise of the water roiling in the tank. The pressure built in her lungs. Sparks exploded beneath her eyelids. Was this what her mother had felt at the end? All she needed to do was open her mouth. Let the water in.

Chapter 29

Vernon sucked in a lungful of warm, sweet air. It rattled around in his lungs and wheezed out. He tried to roll to one side and succeeded only in flopping like a landed fish. His arms and legs felt like dead weights, his hands and feet numb. He shifted his right hand against whatever he was lying on, and it was like moving a piece of wood.

He inhaled again, and coughed up phlegm. *Gah.* He turned his head to spit. A soft cloth wiped his lips.

"My turn to be the nursemaid."

Vernon half-opened his eyes, then shut them tight against the bright light. "Cole?"

"One and the same, bro. Never understood why you inspire such loyalty."

He searched his foggy brain. Loyalty? His traitorous brother wanted to talk about loyalty? He opened his mouth, but all that came out was a wet cough.

Cole wiped his face again, more roughly this time.

The cloth tore at his damaged skin. Vernon jerked his face away. "Stop, Cole."

"Kiro. That's the name Papa called me. My Macedonian one. What was yours again—*Veton.* Right?" He raised him more upright and stuffed a pillow behind his back. "There you go, bro. Better?"

"Co—Kiro—" Vernon coughed again.

"Tsk. Got some damp in those lungs from your stay in the cistern. Not built to be a fish, brother." Kiro rubbed his back.

Fish. Cistern. Vernon grunted and tried to lift his hand. It refused to move. He blinked his eyes open and glanced down. The palm and fingers were white and wrinkled. But the rest of his hand was red, swollen and covered in raw sores.

Kiro gave a short laugh. "Your feet aren't too good either. But you won't need them much longer, dear brother. All I need from you are the passwords for your accounts, and we can call it quits."

Vernon coughed again. Forced the word out. "Never."

"I think Bella would like it to be sooner than that."

A vision of an angel come to rescue him flooded his mind. Strong arms, inked with wondrous sea creatures, holding him above the water. Kissing him. "Bella?" The hollow feeling inside him exploded into hot rage. "Where. Is . She?"

"Ah. There's my brother. The one I remember. The angry one. The one I could never satisfy. You must be feeling better." Kiro reached behind him and caught up a paper and pencil. "Bella is playing mermaid right now."

"In the cistern?" Pain ripped through his fingers. Feeling was coming back.

"Ah. A brilliant deduction. I see your brain is starting to work again. Perfect." His brother tapped the paper with the pencil. "Now. Here's a list of your bank accounts. I'll read the number, and you tell me the password." He settled back on the chair. "Then when we're done, I will pull her out of the cistern. And I suggest you not delay much longer. I like to think of her as a mermaid. But really, she isn't any more waterproof than you are."

Vernon sucked in a breath and closed his eyes. He should have listened to Bella. Gotten rid of all his ill-won gains long ago—given them to that charity she thought so much of—what was it called? Mercy House.

The door flew open. "Boss, we've got a problem."

Kiro frowned. "I told you not to interrupt me."

"But—but there's a woman at the gate. Claims she's your mother. She won't leave." He hesitated a moment. "She's waving a gun at us and threatening to call the cops."

Vernon let his head loll back on the pillow. Step-mama to the rescue. The question was: who was she here to rescue?

****

Screech. The metal plate over her head slid open a few inches. "Bella? You down there?"

Bella pulled her head higher above the water. She'd been clinging to the inlet pipe for what seemed like hours, but probably had been merely minutes. Her fingers were only starting to wrinkle. "Hanger?" Reluctantly, she let go of the small nub of pipe that had kept her afloat. It had been serendipity she'd found it in the dark. She swam over until she was under the opening and blinked up into the light.

The plate slid over a little more. Hanger's worried face appeared. "*Qué mierda!* Gotta get you out of there." He disappeared. "There's nothing here but a hose."

"No ladder?"

"Not that I can see." He pulled the cover farther

open, and the hose flopped down. "Grab on, and I'll pull you up."

Bella shook her head. Hanger was a skinny thing at least half her weight even when she wasn't wearing waterlogged clothing, and there was no way she'd keep her grip on the slimy hose. Any strength she once possessed had fled. The cold had sucked it away. "No. I have a better idea. This is going to sound crazy but turn on the water and let the tank fill up to the top.

"*Bueno.*" He snaked the hose down farther into the water. "Now move away."

Bella grabbed the hose as water even colder than what she been floating in swirled around her torso and legs. She bit her lip to stop her teeth from chattering. A popping noise made her flinch. She called up, "That sounded like gunshots.

Hanger leaned over. "Yeah. Big commotion going on somewhere. It's how I was able to slip away. Nobody can keep me tied up for long."

"Do you know where they have Vernon?"

"Vernon's here?" The boy looked over his shoulder. "Makes sense he's part of these monsters."

"He's not. That Kiro—Cole or whoever—he's his brother. He had him trapped down here."

"Well, it looks like he rescued his brother and left you to drown. Sure they were not playing a trick on you?"

A chill bolted through her. She pictured Vernon cold, numb, unable to stay afloat. Within an inch of his life. That had been no trick. She was sure. And who knew what they were doing to him now? "No, Vernon would never—"

"Hush. Someone coming."

The cover came clanking back down, plunging her back into pitch darkness. She clung to the hose, inching her way up as the water rose inch by inch. She could feel the strength leaving her hands. How much longer could she last?

A few minutes later, the cover lifted. Hanger peered down at her. "Okay, I've scoped out the place. All the bad *hombres* are in the courtyard arguing. Some lady's outside the gate screaming her head off and shooting a gun in the air. Your Vernon is upstairs in a bedroom. Looking poorly. Face all white like. His hands swollen up like balloons."

Fear gathered in her belly. She was going to be too late. Bella sucked in a breath and reached up. But she was still three feet too low to reach the lip of the opening.

Hanger called down. "Got an idea." The kid disappeared again, but at least this time he'd left the hatch open. Bella clung on. If she stayed submerged many more minutes she'd be as numb and weak as Vernon. No help at all.

"Here. Grab on. It's from the chair they had me tied to." A kinked rope lowered toward her. "I tied this to the water pipe. It should hold."

She spit out a mouthful of water. "I hope I have the strength."

Hanger looked down. "The water's gotten higher. If you can get a foot up, I should be able to grab hold of your hand."

Bella grasped the rope and yanked. Her whole body trembled as she rose, her water-drenched clothes dragging her down. "I'm not sure I can do this."

A bang and the thump of footsteps echoed from

above.

Hanger yelled down. "The inmates are on the move. Maybe twist your legs around the hose."

She grasped the rope with one hand, locked her thighs around the slippery hose and with her other hand reached as high as she could. The water sucked at her waist and legs.

"Here." Hanger extended his hand toward her. Their fingertips brushed. He wiggled closer to the edge and stretched some more. "A few more inches."

She bent her legs and jerked upward.

Their hands met, and then he yanked her up and over the edge of the opening, the metal frame scraping her water-softened skin. She flopped on her stomach and gasped for air.

Hanger gave her a shove. "Come on. Move. We got to get out of this place *rápido*."

Bella rolled over and shut her eyes against the fluorescent light above her.

Hanger shook her. "No time to rest. Help me get rid of this rope."

She roused herself. "What are you doing?"

"Covering our tracks like they do in the movies. Hide this"—he handed her the rope—"and pull up the hose. The longer they think we're still under lock and key the better. I'll go see what our goon guys are doing."

Bella clutched the rope to her chest. Hanger was just a kid. If he got hurt, she'd never be able to face herself. She gave herself a shake, rubbed her arms and legs trying to get them warm and moving again. "This isn't a movie. Those men have real guns—"

"All the more reason to escape."

"But there's no way out. The place is surrounded by walls. Outside there's a cliff and a pack of wild beast things, and it's miles from anywhere." Bella grabbed the hose and started hauling it up.

Hanger peeked out the doorway to the stairwell. "It's a castle, right? So it must have secret passageways and stuff. Come on." He wagged his finger at her and took off.

She trailed after him. "I don't think it's that kind of castle."

"It's a crook's joint. Gotta have hidey holes." He dashed up the steps.

Somewhere above them a door banged closed. Men's raised voices echoed down the stairwell. A woman cursed.

Hanger was heading right into trouble. Bella took a deep breath and forced her numb legs to stumble after him.

Chapter 30

Vernon rubbed his eyes and rolled over. He was warm and dry and feeling much better. A quick glance at the sun shining in the window told him he'd been sleeping for hours. He surveyed his body. His hands and feet still stung, but they were much less swollen. He had a brief image of Bella kissing him, and then it was gone.

The door opened, and his brother stepped inside. "Good. You're finally awake. Let's finish our business before mom sticks her nose in it."

Mom. Right. Nina had arrived, guns shooting. Vernon narrowed his eyes. "So where did you stash her?"

"After she stopped attacking my idiot guards, I sent her to the store to get food. Told her you were sick. She's going to make you Macedonian chicken soup." Kiro sighed. "She swore she'd never cook it again after papa was killed."

Vernon shook his head. Kiro always could wrap his mother around his fingers. "Did she see your teeth?"

Kiro gave him a perfect-toothed smile. "Got covers. Can't go a-lawyering in my true guise, now can I?" He stuck out his tongue, then picked up the pad from the nightstand. "But we have more serious matters to discuss, Veton." He drew a pen out of his pocket and settled into the upholstered chair near the bed, looking for all the world like a corporate lawyer at a business meeting. "Passwords."

Vernon rolled back onto the pillow, his mind racing. He leaned up on his elbow. "Why should I give you anything? I worked hard for all that money. Did things that make me sick to remember. And I've taken care of you. I give you an allowance bigger than most CEO salaries. You have a fine career. Have you ever wanted for anything?" He glanced at his brother, with his curly white-blond hair and the dimples that always reminded him of a cupid. "No need to get involved in all the rot our papa raised us in."

"The word on the street is you're going legit. Giving it all away. So give it to *me*." Kiro leaned over him. "I want it all, big brother. The whole kit-and-caboodle. Everything Papa left you. All the businesses, the whorehouses, the greasy diners, the marijuana farms, the warehouses, the apartments. That island estate on the Caymans. That villa in Greece. All. Of. It."

Not Bella's Eudokia. Vernon shot up, wrapped his arm around Kiro's throat, and squeezed. "*Never.*"

Kiro struggled and kicked. His fingernails clawed Vernon's water-damaged skin, sending lightning bolts of pain up his arms. Still he held on, pressing just enough to cut off most of Kiro's air, but not enough to crush his windpipe. Being able to control his strength so precisely was what had made him his father's prime enforcer and what made him such a fantastic lover, but it was what made him weak in the moment. He should kill his brother for what he had done to him. But he couldn't. No matter how warped and twisted he was, he loved him.

He relaxed his grip just enough for Kiro to suck in a mouthful of air and spit out a curse. "Bastard. You want to go back in the cistern? Join your whore?"

Vernon's heart pounded. Bella rescuing him wasn't a dream? He yanked his brother's head harder against his chest. "What? Do you mean Bella? She's really here? In the cistern?"

Kiro nodded.

"Damn you." Vernon clamped his brother to him and rolled up to his feet. Kiro kicked his legs and twisted, but he'd always been the smaller, weaker one. Vernon hefted him forward. No way would he let go until Bella was safe.

Ignoring the shooting pains in his feet, he dragged Kiro to the door and glanced up and down the corridor. He had to get to Bella. She hated water. Hated the dark.

But he hadn't risen to the top of his father's crime syndicate by following his heart. He forced himself to take a deep breath and gather all his fury into a tight little bundle to deal with later. He needed to find his satellite phone and call for backup first. It would be foolish to rescue Bella and then not be able to escape the stupid fortress. It didn't take many men to hold it, and there was his step-mother still to face.

Pushing his brother ahead of him, he shuffled down the hallway and into his own bedroom. His grip slipped, and Kiro took the opportunity to jab him in the ribs with an elbow. Vernon huffed and gripped him harder. He couldn't hold on much longer. His battered body was failing him. Only red-hot anger kept him standing. He looked around. Where could he stash his traitorous brother?

There. He pushed Kiro into the bathroom and

slammed the door on him. Then he wedged a chair under the doorknob. "Stay put for the moment. Take a shower or something. Then we'll negotiate. I have a lot to say to you."

Kiro yelled and banged on the door, but the sound was muffled by the thick walls and heavy oak door. This had been their father's suite, and the whole thing was built like a fort inside a fort. Although the main purpose for the excessive soundproofing, Vernon always believed, was so his father could bang the maid while Nina and the kids slept down the hall.

He found his suit jacket and rummaged for his phone. Yes—his fingers brushed the aluminum case—it was still there. He pulled it out and dialed Gav's number. The phone rang and rang and rang.

A bad feeling spread like poison through his veins. Had Kiro done something to Gav? He thumbed the phone and jabbed in Lovisa's number.

"Vernon, that you?" Gav's wife's voice quavered with panic. "Where are you? Where's Gav?"

"He's not with you?"

"Haven't seen him in days. He went off to set up all your wedding plans and never returned. I thought maybe you took him to the Caymans with you. But he would have called. Tell me the truth. What's happened?"

Vernon exhaled, but the panic rising in his chest only tightened. Without Gav, he was truly on his own. "A kink in the plans. If you see him, tell him to get a bunch of the men together and get out to The Pines."

Lovisa's voice steeled. "If I see him, I'm telling him to head in the opposite direction. Away from you. I'm done with this life."

"Fine, Lovisa, fine. Tell him he's just been retired." Vernon jammed the phone back into his pocket. He'd tried to get Gav to quit when he'd married his beautiful housekeeper. But the fool man refused to leave his boss unprotected. It was a level of loyalty he didn't deserve. He looked over at the bathroom door. He bet Kiro knew what had happened to Gav.

Well, he was on his own. He had no way of knowing how many of his men Kiro had turned against him. Best to assume all. "Trust no one" had been his father's motto. It had worked for the old man for forty-three years. He could do worse.

He hauled his laundry bag out from under the bed. So here he was. One water-bedraggled man against the rotten crew Kiro had surrounded himself with. Not one of them had two peas for a brain, and with his mother thrown in, everything could get volatile quickly. How long would it be before she returned and took Kiro's side in the whole mess? For sure, she wouldn't take his.

What next? He dumped out the laundry and extracted his knife from the pile of dirty underwear. Fool brother. Kiro hadn't the sense of a flea. Not searching his luggage was a novice mistake.

The kid had no forethought. Totally impetuous. He'd never survive if he tried to manage the legal holdings. Not to speak of the illegal ones that came with a bullet in the gut if handled the wrong way. Mr. Cole Kiro Tuccio should just go back to being a paper-pushing corporate lawyer stealing from the willing rich.

He looked down. Naked wasn't going to do it, especially once mama showed up. He tore a pair of jeans out of his bag and yanked them on, followed by an old T-shirt and socks.

Shoes. He rummaged around the bottom of the closet, cursing at the time all this was taking, and stuck his feet into his old boots, ignoring the burning pain. Then he shoved the knife in the top of his sock.

He pictured Bella in that freezing water and sent her a mental message: *Hold on Bella, I'm coming.*

Vernon turned back to the bathroom door. Now what to do with the kid? Hell, Kiro was only twenty-three years old, had a whole life ahead, and he had a bad feeling that he would have to do some damage to his mother's cupid before this hellish bit of mayhem was over.

He sucked in a breath, fighting the congestion in his lungs. The damp and cold had gotten deep inside him. Phlegm gathered in his throat, and his body burned fever hot.

Right this minute, all he wanted to do was curl up in that nice warm bed and sleep. He was really too weak to be manhandling people. But that had to be done. So he'd do it just like he always had.

He knocked the chair away from the door, stepped to the side, and opened it wide. His brother came rushing out swinging a towel bar. Vernon extended his foot and sent Kiro tripping head first into the carpet. He put a knee on his back and pressed hard. Kiro twisted beneath him.

Vernon laughed. "Just like old times. I always could trip you up." He pressed until Kiro dropped the bar.

Kiro lay still for a moment. "You win. Let's go fish out your mermaid. But I want those passwords and a letter turning over the property you got from father to me in return."

He hauled his brother to his feet and shoved him toward the door. "And I am going to do that because—"

"Because Mama will make you when she gets back. I already gave her the lowdown." Kiro pulled away and headed to the stairs. He pushed open the door and started down the steps to the basement. "And you know she'll support me. She's always hated you— Papa's *real* son. Scion of the virtuous maiden he fell in love with back in that hole-in-the-wall village full of bandy-legged men stinking of sheep, and crones with hairy chins. He left you everything. Including his name. While Theo and me were always treated like second class bastards because he wouldn't marry her."

Vernon grunted. He knew the family history too well. It was engraved into his psyche. "She'd slept around behind his back."

Kiro looked over his shoulder as he pushed open the cellar door and entered the room above the cistern. "And he didn't do the same?" He bent down and slid the lid of the water tank open. "She was loyal in every other way."

"He was a cruel man. They deserved each other." Keeping a hold on his brother, Vernon peered over the edge. The familiar stink assaulted his nose and gave him the shivers. "Bella." Her name echoed in the chamber, but only the slap of the water answered. Vernon went rigid, every muscle tight. She couldn't have drowned. He seized his brother by the neck and shook him. "If she's dead, I'm throwing you down there and locking the lid."

Kiro's face went white. "No. There's a drain. Look"—he pointed at the wall—"over there. I'll get it. Let go of me."

Vernon released him. Kiro dashed to the wall and began turning a large faucet handle. Below there was a sucking sound as a small whirlpool formed in the center. He gripped the rim of the cistern opening. "This is too slow. Where's that ladder?" A shadow flitted behind him and the hairs rose on the back of his neck. He looked up to see Kiro swinging a metal pipe at his head.

It whizzed through the air straight at him. He ducked, caught it mid-air, and ignoring the tearing pain in his hands, gave it a twist and yanked it away. Kiro tipped, regained his balance, then tipped again. Hands flailing, he fell toward the open hatch.

There was barely any water left, and the ten-foot fall would kill him.

Vernon reached out and caught him at the last minute. He jerked him back and gave him a hug. Kiro might be a bastard, but he was his brother.

Chapter 31

Hanger peeked around the corner. "This way," he whispered.

Bella nudged up against him as they moved down the hallway. "Do you have any idea where we are?"

The kid crept toward a partially open door. "No. Place is like a maze." He pushed the door open a little wider and peered inside. "What the heck?"

She came up behind him. At one end of the small, windowless room hung a huge portrait of a man. Photos and plaques covered the other walls. "It's a shrine of some kind."

Hanger stepped a little farther into the room. "*Hombre* looks a lot like Vernon."

Cruel silver eyes stared down at her. Bella rubbed her wrist. "Must be his father. Looks vicious."

There was a creak behind her, and she whirled around.

"He *was* vicious." An elegantly coiffed woman stepped through the doorway and gave her a wry smile. "I thought I heard voices." Bella instantly recognized the woman wearing a clingy purple suit and an avant-garde hair-do. She'd seen her photo in Vernon's wallet.

This was the evil step-mother—Nina Tuccio.

The woman's red-lipsticked lips formed a pinched cupid's bow. "I do agree the resemblance is uncanny. Like father like son, as they say."

"But Vernon isn't vicious—"

The woman gave her a hard look, the kind a snake might use to paralyze its prey. "Isn't he?"

Bella shook her head. "No. He's a good man."

Nina Tuccio stepped closer. "Ah, you must not know my son well. Do you know how many bodies are lying dead at the bottom of that cliff out there with Vernon's name on their death warrants?" She took another step toward them. "Hundreds."

Hundreds? Bella shivered. She knew Vernon had done bad things—lied, stolen, wheeled-and-dealed with shady people—been in jail even. It drove her crazy that she could love someone like that. But murdering hundreds of people? It was impossible to conceive. Could a man who touched her with such love, kill over and over again in cold blood, and still have a heart left in him?

She swallowed hard and glanced back at the portrait of Cosmo Newell. Same white-blond hair. Same steely blue eyes. Same sexy lips. She ran her hand up and down her wet jeans. She should have let Vernon drown.

"Vernon killed him, too." Nina's voice sliced through her. "But I am not here to talk about vicious men." She lifted her delicate beringed hand and pointed a small gun at them. "I want to talk about you. Who the hell are you and how did you get in here?"

Bella stared at the black circle of the gun nozzle and then back into the cold black eyes of Nina Tuccio. Talk of being vicious. With parents like these, no wonder Vernon was the way he was. She had no doubts the stepmother from hell would kill them and add their bones to those in the gorge.

Beside her, Hanger shifted his weight from one foot the other. In a minute, he would do something crazy. She wrapped an arm over his shoulder and put her faith in motherly love. "Kiro invited us. We decided to tour the castle and seem to have gotten lost. Maybe you could show us back to the main hall?"

The woman tilted her head and gave her a once over. "Not Kiro's type at all, but I'm sure he brought you here for a reason." She waved the gun with a well-practiced arc. "Let's go ask him."

Gun held steady, she ushered them down the hall. "Turn right at the corner."

At the intersection, Hanger tromped on Bella's instep. Hard.

She whirled on him hopping on one foot. "Blast it! What was that for?" But he was already off running like a rabbit.

"Kids. Think they're immortal." The woman poked the gun into Bella's side. "My men will round him up. *You*—into the kitchen, please."

****

Vernon took one last look down into the empty cistern and dropped the cover. The metal clanged like a funeral bell. Bella was gone. Escaped. He followed his brother down the hall, glancing around as he did so. Where could she be hiding? There were plenty of cubbyholes and back hallways, but no way out of the fortress itself. He pressed his tongue against the back of his teeth. Wherever she was, he hoped she stayed there. Give him time to figure out how to deal with Kiro and his step-mom.

"Get your stinking butts in here this instant."

Kiro turned. "Mama, you're back."

Nina Tuccio waved the gun she was holding. "Into the kitchen, you two. Time we settle up."

Vernon gave her a nod. "Nina, nice to see you so soon again."

She smiled showing every one of her expensive implants. "No, the pleasure is all mine, Vernie."

He flicked his fingers at the gun she was wielding. "Nina, we both know you are not going to shoot me. That gets you and Cole nothing. My will does *not* include either of you."

She gave him a wink. "Don't need to kill you. I have something better."

Vernon stepped into the kitchen and despite his raging fever, turned cold. Bella sat strapped to one of the kitchen chairs, her wet hair wild about her face. A long scratch slashed across her cheek, and blood welled from a swollen lip. Old cuts and bruises marred her face. Behind her stood one of Kiro's thugs, holding a gun to her head.

He wanted to dive across the room, tear off the ropes, and hold her in his arms forever. Instead, he put his hands in his pockets and gave her a nod. If his beautiful siren had any love left for him, it would be gone in the next few minutes, but she might just walk out of this place alive. He glanced at the man holding her. Mikey Scuttle, his mouth twisted to the side, had once worked for him as a collector—until he'd kicked him off the staff for attempting to rape one of his tenants. The man had a pebble for a brain and a grudge a mile deep. He'd get no help from that quarter. "Hi, Bella. How do you like The Pines?"

She glared at him. "You fucking bastard. I saved your life and you left me to drown."

"Not me. Him." He pointed at Kiro. "*That* was my brother's doing."

His mother pulled out a chair. "Shut up and sit your butt down this instant, son." She turned to Kiro. "You too."

Vernon walked past the proffered chair and settled in the one to the left of Bella. He clenched his fists and avoided looking at the gun pressed against the pale, battered face he loved, and calculated the odds of reaching her before the stinking turncoat could pull the trigger. Not good—he unclenched his hands and ran his palms along the edge of the table—but he would die trying.

Kiro sat down to the left of Vernon and tipped back in his chair. "So what's to eat?"

Nina tossed a bag of chips and a tin of nacho cheese on the table.

Kiro's upper lip wrinkled. "Where's the Macedonian chicken soup you promised, Mama?"

His mother whacked him on the back of the neck. "Don't *mama* me. I stopped cooking the day your father died. Went shopping to give you time to man up and deal with Vernon here. But I come back and find some kid and *her*"—she tipped her chin toward Bella—"gawking at old Cosmo like tourists, and your brother sleeping like a baby." She slapped a file folder on the table. "So I'm taking over."

She sat in the chair at the head of the table where Cosmo used to sit and opened the file. "So Vernie, let's make this quick. You sign these papers. Then you can take your whore and leave."

"Won't be legal. My lawyer's not here."

Nina smiled. "But your lawyer is here. Kiro,

darling, is a lawyer thanks to you, and you've just retained him. Keep it in the family, my father always said. Your Miss Bella Bell will be our star witness."

She spread the papers out in front of him. Little yellow sticky notes stuck out of the pages showing him where to sign.

Bella licked the blood off her lip. "What am I witnessing?"

"Your lover boy here is going to pass his father's inheritance to me and his brother. Like it should have been done in the first place. Cosmo Newell had no right to cut off me and my children from our due. I put up with his abuse for years. I refuse to be under his so-called legitimate son's thumb for the rest of my life. And Kiro deserves his share, too."

Vernon made a show of reading the papers, turning each one over as he finished and straightening the stack every time. The only sound was his brother crunching at the chips. The thug holding Bella swayed in boredom. His mother glared, her red-polished fingernails tapping on the tabletop.

He came to the deed for the villa on Eudokia. Across the way, Bella gasped. The sound made every muscle in his body clench, but he turned it over and continued on until he reached the end. He put the last paper in place and then flipped the stack over. "Fascinating reading. Lot of interesting properties I own." He stared at his brother. "Who drew up these papers?"

Kiro tipped his chair upright with a slam. "I did."

"Really? Not Mama? Perhaps I should mention that she isn't here because I called her. Because I didn't. She's come out of her own self-interest." He tapped the stack of papers. "I think Mother might have had her own lawyer doctor them up a bit."

Kiro glared at his mother. "Did you?"

She slapped the table. "Yes, I made sure to get my share. You were going to leave me with nothing better than your father did. A pittance of an allowance."

"I gave you the Saddle River house and the villa in the Caymans."

"Ungrateful brat, after what I put up for you? Life with that bastard." She slapped him across the cheek.

Kiro pushed up from the chair. "Why—I could have had everything. Vernon was going to give me the numbers for the Swiss bank accounts."

Vernon waved his hand. "Relax. Didn't mean to start a family argument." He leaned back in the chair, folded his arms behind his head. He glanced at Bella. "Sorry that you have to witness my happy family life. But none of this matters. I'm not signing anything over to anyone. It's mine and I'm keeping it."

Nina and Kiro turned in unison to stare at him.

Nina's hand lifted and pointed at Bella. "Then she dies."

"So kill her. I still won't sign."

"Perhaps, I was a bit unclear in my language. She dies *slowly*." She nodded at Scuttle. "Hold her hand down on the table." She pulled a knife out of the holder on the counter and came alongside Bella. She placed the sharp edge on Bella's pinkie finger. "Sign or I'll cut off her fingers one by one, then her toes, then her nose, and her ears. Until you wish her dead." She twirled the knife in her hand. "You know the routine, Vernie. You were the knife guy."

"Damn it, yes." He grabbed the heavy table by the

edge and tipped it up and over. The table flipped with a resounding crash. The corner caught Nina on the side of the head, and she fell backwards. Lunging, he dove for Bella, knocking her chair back and into the thug's stomach. Scuttle collapsed under their combined weight. His gun went off. The bullet whizzed past him and struck Bella.

Blood blossomed and dripped down her forehead. Vernon's insides turned to mush. Was she dead? Had he killed her?

Vernon pushed back her hair and found the wound. A graze, thank goodness. But she didn't deserve to be hurt at all. He reached for the knife in his sock. But before he could cut her free, Scuttle pushed the chair aside, tipping Bella over, and plunged a knife toward his chest. Vernon arched backward, twisted away from the driving blade, and in one fluid motion, drove the side of his hand into the man's neck. It was a killing blow. The man groaned and fell back, struggled to draw breath, and then went still.

A sob broke the silence. Vernon looked up. Kiro sat with Nina in his arms, tears running down his face. The former beauty queen's head hung off-kilter like a broken doll's. Kiro spoke between sobs. "You've killed her. You've murdered my mother."

She'd been his mother, too. Vernon blinked back tears and glanced down. Scuttles' gun lay within reach. All he had to do was pick it up and put a bullet in Kiro's brain. It's what his brother deserved for what he'd done to Bella. It's what his father would expect him to do.

His hand crept toward the gun. If he killed him, he could keep his empire, keep his money. Bella would be safe. His fingers wrapped around the grip. He lifted it. The snake slithered in his stomach. Bile crept up his throat.

Kiro peered up at him with tear-filled eyes. Vernon squeezed the trigger. If he killed his little brother, he'd be worse than his father.

In his lap, Bella moaned softly. He stared at his brother, then pocketed the gun and forced himself to shrug. "Nina had it coming. Let Bella and the boy walk out of here, and I'll sign everything. Give you the passwords. You get it all."

"Everything? The accounts? The deeds? The villa?"

Vernon waved at the papers scattered across the floor. *"Everything."*

Kiro eased Nina's body down and rose. He nodded. "Deal."

Vernon cut Bella free. Then he rose, wet a wad of paper towels, and held it to Bella's head. Her eyelids twitched. She'd come round in minutes. He pressed his lips to hers and then drew back. She wasn't for him. He'd almost killed his brother. He had murdered his mother. Nina may have favored her own boys, but she'd given him as normal a childhood as could be expected under the thumb of his father.

He glanced over to where Nina and Scuttle lay still in death. His inner snake writhed. Bella was right. He was a bad man. He turned back to his siren and lifted her in his arms, knowing this would be the last time he held her close. He didn't deserve this beautiful, caring woman, who'd faced her demons to rescue him. Not after she'd seen him as he really was—a murdering monster. Not after all his love had brought her was terror and hurt.

He had to let her go.

Chapter 32

Bella woke with a splintering headache. A taped-on gauze pad covered her forehead and hung down over one eye. For a moment, her mind was blank, and then she remembered: the concussive gunshot, the burn across her brow, a curtain of blackness, and then coming to and hearing Vernon and his bastard of a brother wheeling and dealing away her villa on Eudokia.

Bella pushed herself upright and waited for her head to stop spinning. Stone walls and heavy beams overhead told her she was still trapped in the fortress. Vernon's suitcase lay open on the floor. This was his room then. She wrapped her arms around herself and shivered.

When he'd entered the kitchen, she'd thought he'd come to rescue her. But his voice had been so cold, his face so hard. He'd looked just like his father. She touched the bullet gash. The bastard would have let her be mutilated and killed to keep his dirty money. Nina had been right. Vernon was a killer. Like father, like son.

She had to find Hanger and escape before Vernon came back. She tossed off the covers and stopped. Something stank. She glanced down. Yuck, she was still in the clothes she'd worn in the filthy cistern.

Forcing her battered body to move, she stood,

wavered a bit, and then rifled through Vernon's suitcase. She came up with sweat pants and a sweatshirt. With the pant legs and sleeves rolled up, they would do. She tugged them on, inhaling the faint scent of his distinctive cologne, and fought the memory of his lips on her.

Stupid. Stupid. How could she have ever loved him? The man was a murderer. He killed his own mother, and probably that guard. Nina said he'd been his father's *knifeman*—she didn't even want to think what that meant.

Bella walked to the window and looked out. In the distance, snow-covered mountains rolled across the horizon. Below, the gorge lay hidden in shadow, the stony outcrops and bent pines littering the almost vertical slope. She touched the glass. Hundreds of bodies were buried down there, and the man she loved had put them there. She picked up a heavy vase and threw it at the window. The glass cracked into a million pieces, just like her heart.

The door slammed open. Kiro stood there, hands resting on his hips. "Good, you're alive and breaking windows. Come. Time to leave."

"What? I'm not going anywhere with you."

"The kid's in the car waiting. Get along with you. You're a fish gone bad. Time to *vamos* and all that."

"I don't think—"

"No thinking needed." He strode toward her, seized her by the shoulder, and aimed her toward the door.

"But Vernon—"

"Has his own problems." Kiro shoved her out the doorway and down the hall.

She glanced into the living room as they passed.

Vernon stood out on the balcony, the glass doors open behind him. Cold air wafted through and ruffled his hair. For one moment, she hoped that he would turn around, take her in his arms and explain it all away. But he never looked. "What's he doing?"

"Contemplating his navel. *Move.*" Kiro gave her a hard shove, and she tripped forward into the entry hall, past Ari's paintings, and down the steps.

In the courtyard, a smallish rust-covered car probably belonging to one of Kiro's thugs waited, the engine running, white steam rising from the tailpipe. Inside, Hanger grinned at her.

"Say hi to your sidekick." Kiro yanked the door open and pushed her in. She landed half on top of Hanger. The door slammed, and before she could right herself, the car zoomed out of the yard and through the gate. She straightened up as the gates clashed closed behind her. She swiveled around and peered back through the rear window.

The car rounded a curve, and the trees fell away momentarily, revealing the massive stone walls and turrets of the castle. On the balcony, she glimpsed the figure of Vernon leaning over the railing. Then the car swerved around another curve, and the castle disappeared behind a wall of trees.

****

"They're gone."

Vernon turned around. His brother was sporting his filed teeth again. "So all's well in the Tuccio family."

Kiro rocked back on his heels. "So it seems."

"Then I think you should leave, too. Get back to whatever entertains a new billionaire crook. Hope you don't get too bored."

Kiro interlocked his fingers and gave them a crack. "I have my future all planned out. Meanwhile, you are welcome to stay here as long as you like. Commune with your ghosts."

Vernon nodded. "You are all generosity."

Kiro gave a little bow. "Fine, then I'll be off. Got to give Mom her grand funeral, you know. Too bad you won't be there. But then, you don't do funerals, do you?"

Vernon turned back and stared out into the ravine. "No."

"And I'll keep an eye on your little tattoo artist for you. She's a doll. A real heroine. Should be in the movies."

Vernon gripped the railing. "You promised to leave her alone."

"Yes, I did. But she may have different ideas now that she's seen you for the murdering bastard you are. Goodbye, brother."

Vernon waited until he saw Kiro's SUV exit the gates and head around the curve of the mountain. In the distance, one of the guard dogs howled. He looked down into the gorge. How many bodies had he tossed down there for his father? How many fingers had he sawed off under those cruel eyes?

Bella had been right. His father's money and property were tainted. He was tainted. He should have gotten rid of all his father's inheritance years ago. Given it all to good causes. Gifted Ari and Melissa the island. Gone to work like an ordinary Joe and been satisfied. He'd been too greedy—had wanted it all. Thought he'd deserved it for what he'd suffered as a child.

He climbed over the handrail and stood on the edge of the balcony, looking down. There was no question where he belonged. He closed his eyes, and let his grip on the railing loosen.

At the last minute, he remembered Kiro's words. Could he trust him to stay away from Bella?

Chapter 33

The roar of a car engine coming up behind them caused Hanger to jump up on his knees and peer out the rear window. "That bastard Kiro's behind us, and he don't look happy."

A gray Land Rover pulled alongside and started to pass them. Hanger clung to the seatback. "There's no room to go by here. He's going to force us off the road."

Bella slumped lower into the seat. "I supposed he's in a hurry to spend all his new-found blood money." She tapped the driver's shoulder. "Pull over and let him by." The car jerked farther to the right, and she snatched on to the door handle. "Hey, watch where you're going. There's a huge drop off on this side."

"No room to maneuver," the driver yelled. "I should have stuck with Vernon. This brother of his is crazy."

At that moment, Kiro's SUV nosed past them. There was a screech of metal as the bumpers met. The tires squealed as their driver did what he could to slow down and stay on the road. But the road was too narrow. Kiro's vehicle bumped into them again.

Hanger reached over and pulled the seatbelt around Bella. "Safety first." The two cars swerved again. He snapped on his own belt. "*Idiota.* Shark Man's going to kill us." Seizing Bella by the arm, he held on tight as their car careened crazily, tree branches and brush scraping the side.

Suddenly, they broke out of the pines and into the open. Below them stretched the gorge. Across the way, the castle hugged the top of the cliff. The driver gunned the engine. The right wheels dipped into the soft gravel shoulder and caught. For a moment, Bella thought they'd make it. Then Kiro's much bigger vehicle roared past, driving them closer to the lip of the gorge.

Their car shuddered once. Twice. Then it went over the side of the shoulder and slid toward the cliff edge.

Their driver did his best. He stepped on his brakes and steered to the left. But the car was too far down the embankment. Gravel scudded under the wheels as the car hesitated and then tipped to the side and crashed down the talus slope.

Trees and rocks smacked into the sides. The windshield smashed. Brush whizzed past. Dust and fumes and bits of flying debris filled the air.

Bella bounced and swayed, her head whipping back and forth, the seatbelt choking her, as the mangled car slid down the mountainside.

At the bottom of the gorge, it rolled to a stop in a cloud of dust, listing to one side.

"Get up. Get up." Hanger slapped her lightly on the cheek. "Hurry."

Bella shook her spinning head and glanced around. Everything was tilted. In the front seat, the driver lay sideways, the air bag deployed, his head bloody. "The driver?"

"Nothing doing." Her seatbelt unsnapped. Hanger tugged on her arm. "We got to get out before Kiro gets here."

"What?" She shook her head and peered up the hill. The Land Rover was parked above them. The sight of Kiro looking down was enough to get her moving. She let Hanger push her up and out of the broken side window. She reached back and hauled him out, then followed him through a clump of brush. They took shelter behind a craggy boulder.

From the road above, Kiro yelled down, "Still kicking? Good luck, my friends. I let the dogs out before I left. Vernon is never going to know what happened to you." He cupped his hands and howled. From the woods beyond, a deep-throated bay answered. Then another. He shook his head and stepped toward his vehicle. "Dying in the crash would have been a better way to go." He jumped in the SUV and took off.

Something rustled in the brush below them. Bella wrapped her arms across her chest and shivered. "I hate dogs."

Hanger held out his hand. "I like dogs, but not ones big as elephants." He nodded toward the ravine. The rustling was closer. "*Vamonos.*"

Bella took his hand, and the kid, using surprising strength and clever positioning of his feet, half-pulled, half-pushed her up the slope to the road. At the top, she leaned down, hands on her thighs and sucked air in and out. Her heart pounded in her chest.

Hanger gave her a shove. "Can't stop now. They're still coming."

Bella raised her head. Her leg muscles cramped. Her breath caught in her lungs.

Down below, two large creatures emerged from the thicket and stared up at them, growling. She'd never seen such big dogs in her life. They stood chest high, big boned, thick legged, covered in long, matted hair. Around their necks were iron collars studded with metal spikes. She pointed. "What the hell *are* those things?"

"Man-eaters. Move."

She gulped down a breath. "We'll never outrun them."

"Try or be eaten." Hanger gave her another push. "Run. Toward the castle."

Bella summoned up the remnants of her strength from her adrenaline-drained body and took off at a run, forcing her weak knees to bend and her struggling lungs to breathe. Hanger's feet thumped behind her.

She risked a glance back. Predators after their prey, the huge creatures bounded up the slope and came after them. She gasped as another dog dashed out of the trees from the other side of the road much closer to them, its mouth open, its sharp teeth looking for all the world like Kiro's. She ran faster, an untied shoelace threatening to trip her with every step.

There was a whine. She peered behind her to see that Hanger had stopped and was tossing rocks at the creatures. He must have hit the near one, because it had circled back and joined the other two. He yelled over his shoulder. "Keep running. I'll slow them down."

Bella faltered. She couldn't leave the kid behind. He'd done so much to help her, and it was all her fault he was even here, his life at risk. The dogs would tear him apart for sure.

She glanced around for something to stop them, but all she could find was a thin branch from a pine tree, the needles still attached. She looked at the glowering dogs. It would be like warding off a wolf pack with a feather. But she had to do something.

Heart beating wildly, Bella swept the branch in front of her and loped back to where Hanger stood.

The dogs circled around them, growling, saliva dripping. Eyes red. Teeth bared. Hackles raised. Tails held rigid. Ears flattened. She took a stance behind the boy, her pine branch clutched tight to her body.

"I told you to run," Hanger said, his young face scrunched up.

"I couldn't leave you." Bella watched the dogs as they moved in closer, sure now of their prey. She put an arm around the boy, a lump of unswallowable fear in her throat. "Maybe if we play dead? I heard it works with bears." One of the dogs leaped out at them and snapped his teeth. She jerked back. "Or maybe not."

One nipped at Hanger's legs. He shrank closer to her. Another snapped so close Bella could smell its rancid breath. She closed her eyes and waited for the next attack, for the teeth to sink in.

"*Stoy!*" The voice was rough, guttural, the language foreign. But she'd have recognized it anywhere.

The dogs recognized it, too. They froze and turned their heads in unison to face the newcomer.

Vernon came up behind her. "Stand still. Don't look in their eyes." He clicked his tongue, and the dogs sat back on their haunches, their ears flipped toward him. He stepped in between them and the dogs. "Walk slowly back to the castle. *Very slowly.*"

Bella glanced at Vernon. His face was drawn, his eyes sunken. He looked like a man whose whole world had collapsed. She wanted to throw her arms around him and soothe away the pain she saw in his eyes.

She clenched her fists. Was she crazy? Vernon didn't love her. He would have let Nina and Kiro kill her. He'd probably sent Kiro after them in the Land Rover to do just what he did. After all, they were witnesses. But still. Deep down, she couldn't believe the gentle man she'd loved was lost. He'd said she could save him once. She held out her hand. "Vernon?"

He turned his back to her. "Start walking."

All the anger and fear and pain she'd been carrying inside ever since he'd gone missing, boiled up and poured out. She shook her fists at him. "I hate you, Vernon Newell. You should have let those beasts eat me." She punched him in the arm. It was like punching a stone statue. "I'm going to the police. I'm going to turn you in for murdering your mother and all the rest."

Vernon didn't move. Didn't look at her. But one of the dogs growled. He held out the back of his hand to the beast. "There's an old pickup truck with keys in it in the garage. Take it and go."

Hanger clasped her hand and tugged her back. "Come."

She gave a huff and turned away. Her last glimpse of the man she'd once loved was of him standing rigid, hand outstretched, surrounded by a pack of man-eating dogs.

Later, as she sped down the drive, the tires of the battered pickup kicking up gravel at every turn and rattling over every bump in the road, the thought struck her. If he were as bad a man as she thought, why had he put himself between them and the dogs?

Chapter 34

Daniela pushed the door to the empty store open, and Bella followed her inside. "I've been looking and looking for a place for you," Daniela said. "And then *Tío* Paco at Christmas dinner starts complaining about his wacky tenants and how they'd just taken off without paying the last of their rent and I thought of you. Besides, I need you back tattooing. Every day we get a girl with a gang mark or abuser's name sprawled across her."

Bella glanced around the interior of the storefront. It would need to be completely redone. The plaster was cracked and chipped, the old tin ceiling rusty, and the floor a mess of crumbling linoleum. But the location was good. Not as great as where the old Siren had been. This place was on a side street, but still near to the Bedford Street subway, and the bus stopped on the corner. Her customers would find her.

Bella peered into the small bathroom at the back. The hexagonal tiles must date from the turn of the century. Painting. Re-tiling. New fixtures. She'd have to comb the second-hand furniture stores for a sofa and tables for the waiting area. She let out the breath she'd been holding. The work would be good for her. Time to start over.

She walked to the front and smiled at Daniela. "It will do. I'll take it."

Her friend clapped her hands. "*Bravo.* I'll tell my uncle. He's wanted a tenant in here for ages, but everyone said it was too small. And you get the apartment above, too. I know it's a mess, but everything in the kitchen works, and it has lots of windows. The place just needs elbow grease to shine it all up, and someone with a good eye for design to redecorate it." She gave her a big hug. "It needs *you.*"

Bella hugged her back. "I can't thank you enough for finding this." The empty place in her heart warmed a bit. She had friends. So many good friends. Daniela. T-Crew. Orange Man. All reaching out to help her get back on her very shaky feet.

She clenched her hands in her skirt. "I'll be glad to have my own place again. Living at Toro's is like living in a clubhouse. No privacy. The kids are in and out at all hours. The reek of spray paint everywhere. Got to be bad for the lungs."

Daniela wrinkled her nose. "*Graffiti.* Don't understand what people see in that stuff. Looks like an eyesore to me. Some of it is pure vandalism. Did you see the rot someone's sprayed on the door to the apartment?"

Bella shrugged. "Street art is part of the local scene. I like to think of it as being created by magical gremlins giving us a peek of another dimension." She pictured Hanger hanging over the bridge support. "Some of it's very good, and compared to other things those young people could be doing, relatively harmless."

"Harmless? Do you know there's a picture of you on the side of a building down toward Bushwick?"

"Me?"

"Yeah. Red hair. Fishtail. Big boobs."

"I'll kill him."

"Who?"

"The kid. Hanger On. He's got a crush on me ever since Vern—well, ever since I've been living with him and Toro." She twisted the fringe of her silk scarf around her fingers.

"You ever hear from Vernon?"

"No." Bella kicked at a piece of broken vinyl. "So what color should I paint this place?"

Daniela put her hand on her shoulder and gave her a pat. "Something happy, Bella. Something happy." She gathered up her huge woven bag. "Got to go. You let me know when I can bring the girls around to help you with the cleaning and painting."

"Will do." Bella waved goodbye and turned back to study the shambles that would become the reborn Siren. The space was as long as the old Siren, but much narrower, with only room for a table and maybe a tattoo chair or two. It was going to be tight and cozy.

But nothing wrong with cozy. It would be a while before her clientele built up to what it had been before the bombing. She'd start small. She'd have to. Orange Man had donated some equipment and an old tat table. Enough to get started. But she'd miss her tat machine and her kitties.

Bella bit the inside of her lip. No use pining for what was gone; all that led to was a bigger ache in her heart. She unwrapped the cleaning supplies Daniela and she had bought, and rubbed her palms together. Time to put on her thrift shop jeans and get to work. The Siren was going to rise from the ashes.

Bella picked up the broom and began to sweep.

****

She was half-done sweeping when the door opened behind her. Bella whirled around. She was far from ready for potential customers to see the place. But it was Fur Tree standing there, his arm wrapped around a huge portfolio, a large duffle bag over his shoulder. He licked his lips. "I have come to apologize."

Bella spread her arms wide and hurried over to him. She gave him a hug. "No need. The Siren was failing. I was failing. You were right to move on. Where you been working? No one at T-Crew could tell me where you'd gone."

He jerked out of her arms, knelt down on the floor, and opened the portfolio. Her sketches spilled out. The ones she'd created for *Secret Ink*. The snarling dragon. The intricate Celtic cuffs. They spread over the dirty linoleum as surprising as if he'd pulled a pink rabbit from his baseball cap.

"Where did these come from? I thought they'd burned up in the explosion."

"Not these." Fur Tree put his fingers on the top one. "These are from your LA notebook."

"My notebook? The one I lost?" She fell to her knees next to him and shuffled through them. "I don't understand?"

"I found it. The notebook. On the sidewalk where you dropped it. And I kept it." He sucked in a deep breath. "Then I stole your job. When you were hurt. After the explosion."

She drew back, her stomach an aching knot. "The TV job? *Secret Ink*? How could you do that to me? That job would have made all the difference. I could have—" She stopped. The once confident young man looked broken. His shoulders curled in. The skin under his eye trembled.

He gathered up the sketches and handed them to her with shaking hands. "I told them today—that I stole your work. Insisted they hire you again. That Avery guy. He was thrilled about having you back. They start filming the pilot in a week. There's plenty of time for you to work with the cosmetic team." He stood up and hefted the duffle. "From what I saw, the show will be a great success. You'll have all the money you need to do whatever you want with this place."

She clutched the sketches to her chest. "Fur Tree. Thank you. Do you know what this means? It's not just this place you've saved. You've saved the villagers on Eudokia. Now I can help Ari pay for the helicopter that flies them to the mainland when there's a medical emergency."

"*Dios mío*. I never meant to hurt you"—he closed his eyes and swallowed—"to hurt anyone. Certainly not Ari who did so much for me and T-Crew. Or your village." He took a step back. "I can never make up for what I did. I thought Vernon a bad man. But I'm worse. Much worse. I pretended to myself that I was doing the right thing. That I could do a better job than you. At least, Vicious Vernon made no excuses for what he was." He slipped on his ball cap and turned to go. "I can never make up what I did to you. But—if you ever need anything, just ask." He slid the duffle strap higher on his shoulder. "*Adios*, Bella.."

She couldn't let him leave. The boy was young. He'd learned humility, and she'd learned that sometimes forgiveness came too late. Vernon was gone from her life. She couldn't give him the forgiveness he needed. But she could forgive this boy—show him the kindness Orange Man had shown her.

Bella lowered the sketches. "You have a place to tat?"

Fur Tree tipped back the ball cap, his young face drawn, his normally rich brown skin ashy. "No, I quit Freddie's when the TV show gave me your contract. So no more job." He rubbed his hand on the duffle strap. "I told T-Crew what I did, and they've kicked me out. No more home either."

"Stay."

"Huh?" Fur Tree stared at her, his eyes wide.

"Stay here. Help me get The Siren going. Together we could finish the renovations in no time."

"You'd want me after I—"

"Yes." She held out her hand. "Let's shake on it."

He shifted from one foot to the other. One toe poked out of the torn end of his canvas sneaks. "I'm not sure—"

"Seconds ago, you said if I ever needed anything to just ask." Bella walked over to him. "Well, I'm asking. I need help to get this place cleaned up." She handed him the broom. "It's a messy job. But when it's done"—she opened her arms wide—"it's going to be the best tattoo parlor in Williamsburg. In the world!"

Fur Tree laughed. "How can I say no to that?"

Bella clapped her hands. "Good. It won't be a picnic. You'll have to sleep back there in the filth until the apartment is up to speed. The shelter might just be more pleasant." She bent down and picked up the portfolio and sketches. "But seeing how well you tat, I think I'll be getting a good deal. So what do you say?" She reached out her hand again. "Ready to dive in with a Mermaid?"

"You're too good, Bella. Too good." Fur Tree let the duffle bag drop, then he took her hand in his and squeezed. "I promise with all my heart to never betray you again."

Chapter 35

Vernon yanked his cap down over his eyes and leaned against the wall of the building. The rough brick caught at his shabby jacket. The cold air off the river cut through his worn flannel shirt. Through the plate glass windows, he could see Bella on a ladder splashing paint as yellow as the Mediterranean sun on the walls. He glanced down the street. Where was the truck? The last thing he wanted was for her to see him. But he had to make sure Kiro did as he'd promised.

There. Finally. He straightened up as the white and orange rental van worked its way through the traffic and stopped in front of Bella's new place. The brakes squealed, and some hireling got out with a clipboard and went inside.

He watched Bella, her mouth going a mile a minute as she signed the paperwork and came outside, crossing her arms across her chest for protection from the gusting wind. She opened the side door to the upstairs apartment and stepped aside.

Another man got out of the truck, went round back, fussed with the hasp and yanked the tailgate open. In minutes, Bella's belongings were streaming out and disappearing up the stairs. Her red sofa, her queen-sized bed, boxes of her clothing and books. Ari's paintings. All of them. The ones from the penthouse and the ones from The Pines. He'd had to do a bit of maneuvering to weasel those from Cole. But luckily, what his brother knew about art would fit on a nail head.

Vernon sighed, and then turned and hurried down the street. He had a job to be at, and it wouldn't do to be late. His new boss was a stickler for promptness.

Concentrating on making it to work on time, he didn't see the trap until too late. A huge man with a floppy hat that shaded his face stepped abruptly into his path. Vernon no longer carried a knife, and he'd sworn off violence, but it took all his willpower to not throw a fist and take the man out. Instead, Vernon swerved aside and found himself being manhandled into an alley and shoved face first into a pile of trash bags by a bunch of sneaker-clad guys wearing balaclavas. The stink of reeking garbage filled his nose.

He went limp and waited. If these guys wanted him dead, he'd be bleeding out by now. They dragged him farther back into the alley.

The seam in his jacket ripped open. One of his sneakers came loose and was left behind. His ball cap disappeared. At this rate, he'd be denuded before they were done. He twisted against their grip. "Stop. My wallet's in my left pocket. Take it and go."

There was a rumble of angry Spanish. Someone socked him in the jaw. Someone else walloped him on the butt with a bat.

He swallowed a groan. Okay. It wasn't money they were after. Which was just as well as all he had in his wallet was a twenty-dollar bill.

Under the shadow of a fire escape, the big guy seized him by the shoulder and threw him against a wall. The air whooshed out of him. Vernon slumped over and slid down to the pavement. He stared at his masked capturers. He didn't need to see their faces. Those baggy jeans and down jackets covered in silver and red paint stains were a dead giveaway. He knew each and every one of them. "Okay, T-Crew. This is idiotic. You can't assault a man walking down the street. I bet police are on their way right now."

There was a sprinkling of laughter, and then Toro and his crew threw off the balaclavas.

The big man standing behind the T-Crew guys pushed up his hat. "Nobody saw us. Nobody coming to rescue you."

"Gav." One of the knots inside him loosened. "I thought Kiro killed you."

"Seems not to have succeeded. Gave it a good try, though. It was touch and go there for a while." He pulled up his shirt and showed the jagged scar crossing his stomach.

"So what's with all this"—Vernon sat up a little straighter and rubbed his jaw—"beating me up?"

One of the twins—he thought it was Solo—kicked him in the shin. "Bella."

"Shit." He rubbed his leg with his other hand. "I gave her back her stuff."

Gav loomed over him. "You think it's stuff she wants?"

Hanger swung the bat back and forth. It was black and shiny.

Vernon narrowed his eyes. "That Zeya's bat?"

The kid tightened his grip on the neck. "She couldn't be here so she sent her bat along to help out." He pointed it at Vernon's balls. "Told us where to hit you, too."

"Better you smash my head in."

Hanger grinned. "I think the *cojones* more appropriate."

Vernon pressed his back against the wall. "Do your worst. Bella doesn't want me, guys. She hates me." He glanced at Hanger. "You heard her."

Gav raised an eyebrow. "You never did understand women, boss. They say no when they mean yes and hate when they mean love."

"That's what I always liked about you, Gav. Everything is black and white, just in reverse." Vernon pushed up to his feet. They would either knock him down again or not. And he was pretty sure there'd be no killing or even bloodshed, notwithstanding the angry faces surrounding him.

There was something about Toro's eyes, a softness that didn't fit with his rigid jaw and firm wide-legged stance. "Well, everything is dirt gray as far as I'm concerned. I'm down here in the gutter with you guys now. No lady wanting me." He patted his pockets. "I've got nothing. In fact, if you don't stop this foolishness and let me go now, I will have less than nothing. He yanked down his jacket. "I'm going to be late to work."

Gav laughed. "Work? You?"

"Yeah. That's what poor slobs have to do if they don't want to end their days in a flop house."

"You got a job? Bet it's running numbers, selling dope, or pimping some runaway."

Vernon seized Gav by the collar. "*Wrong.* I'm a *carpenter*. I'm installing kitchen cabinets and stuff."

Gav peeled away his hands and stared down at his blisters. "It's true then?"

"Yeah. It's true." Vernon shoved his hands into his pockets. "I hope you didn't want your old job back."

Gav shook his head. "No way. Lovisa forbid me to ever see you again. I've got a chauffeuring gig. I get to drive bachelorettes to their parties and brides to their weddings."

"Nice." Vernon tried to push past.

Gav blocked the way. "Speaking of weddings… Seems to me and these guys here you owe us a wedding."

Vernon gave them all his nastiest glare. "Don't look at me."

Hanger glanced at Toro. "But we got a plan, right?"

Toro smiled. "That we do."

Chapter 36

Bella inhaled the scent of fresh paint and varnish. The new Siren was everything she dreamed it would be. Bamboo flooring gleamed underfoot. Goldenrod yellow walls gave it a warm, welcome feel. Half-walls separating the waiting area from the two tattoo stations made the small area seem spacious. Her phone rang, and she slipped it out of her pocket. She thumbed it on. "Ari."

"*Ti kanes*, Sirena?"

"I'm fine." She spun around, taking in the secondhand oriental rug on the floor, the bench with washable cushions for waiting clients, the counter made from leftover flooring. "Really fine. The new Siren is done. Ready for business. I wish you could see it. It's gorgeous." She unlocked the door and turned over the cardboard sign so it read "Open." It would be a while before she could afford neon.

"Send photos. A trip to New York is not in the plans right now." There was a shuffling on the other end. Melissa came on. "You might want to come here—I had the baby. It's a girl—Stamatina, of course. After your mama. You're an aunt."

Bella sank down on the bench. "An aunt?"

Ari laughed. "*Thea* Sirena. Has a ring to it."

"Blast it, Ari. Don't call me that. Remember how we always called all the old ladies in the village *Thea.*

Makes me feel ancient." She bit her lip. "The baby came early? I thought it was due a month from now?"

"Well, she did surprise us. But thanks to you sending that money, we helicoptered out and got to the hospital in time. She's a little thing, but feisty, just like her *Thea*."

Bella clasped her hands together. Her brother had a child, a family. An emptiness opened up inside her. Something she'd never have. She peered around the shop. But she had this, her art, her business. It would be enough. "So she's healthy?"

"Very. We'll be taking her back to the island the end of the week."

She would have to tell him. "Ari—have you gotten any paperwork about the villa changing hands?"

There was a long pause. She could hear the baby crying in the background, and Melissa shushing. "No, why would I?"

"It's been deeded over to—Vernon's brother, Kiro Tuccio. I have no idea how long it will take before he takes possession."

"Why wasn't it in your name? Did that bastard Vernon break his promise to me?"

"He broke a lot of promises. But he did give all your paintings back. That should help some."

"*Sto diavolo,* tell me what's going on there, Bella." Angry as he was, her brother's voice seemed very far away. There was nothing he could do to fix the mess she'd made. And he knew it. She'd let him down. A horde of nasty-minded criminals would take over the villa on Eudokia. Melissa and Ari and their new baby would have to leave.

The shop door opened, and Henri Avery peeked in.

"Open?"

Bella spoke into the phone. "Look, Ari, it's a long story. I'll fill you in tomorrow. The television producer for *Secret Ink* is here right now. Got to go. Take good care of my niece."

She stowed the phone in her pocket, gathered her skirts and stood up. Henri crossed the waiting area and wrapped his arms around her. He gave her a soft squeeze. "I missed my little tattoo artist. You feeling better?" He kissed her on the cheek.

She kissed him back. "Fully recovered."

Henri grinned at her. "I was so happy to learn that Fur Tree had just been taking your place while you were recovering from that bombing." He patted her rump. "Now you can finish my tattoo. I want it ready so I can show it off on the set. We start filming next week."

Bella looked up into his soft, kind face. There was no fire, no passion. He was no Vernon, just a good man. She could do worse. "Come on back. You can be the first customer in the new Siren."

****

Vernon stared into the trash can. "This isn't going to work."

Hanger moved the cardboard box closer. "It will. I'm sure."

"You weren't there when I let her think I wouldn't stop Nina from cutting off her fingers." When she learned he'd been his father's knifeman. He peered down into the can. "You sure these ain't rats?"

"Too hairy for rats. See if you can get the little sick one first."

Vernon reached in. "*Ouch.* Damn things bite."

"Gloves."

He pulled his work gloves out of his back pocket and reached in again. He scooped up the tiny gray creature cowering against the side of the can and lifted it out. "Looks like a rat to me."

Hanger twisted his lips and held up the carton. "It's a kitten. Got a furry tail."

Vernon shrugged and dropped it inside.

Hanger flapped down the cover. "One down. Two to go."

He glanced at the mewling kittens cowering in the can. "Sure one isn't enough? These two don't look friendly."

"You got a lot to make up for. And that Avery guy is chasing after her now. Taking her out to dinner at expensive restaurants. Taking her to plays. Can you afford that on your carpenter salary?"

"Okay, okay. Makes a man long for a life of crime." He leaned over and chased the kittens round and round the can with his gloved hand. "Come here, you little goblins. Damn, they're fast. *Oww.* And nasty." He pulled up his hand with a kitten clinging on, its claws sunk deep into the bare skin exposed above the top of his glove. "Get it off me."

Hanger extracted the kitten and slipped it into the box. "Now the other."

"How come it didn't claw you?"

"'Cause I'm not Vicious Vernon. Animals can tell those things."

"Yeah, right." Vernon bent down and wrapped his hands around the remaining kitten, lifted it up and held it in front of him. Eyes just a slit. Ears barely showing. Totally helpless. No bigger than the palm of his hand.

With one squeeze, he could crush the life out of it. But he wouldn't. That man, the one that could kill, no longer existed. That man had died when he'd seen the horror in Bella's eyes. Now he banged nails into wood and sanded rough edges until they were satiny smooth. And he loved it.

He lowered the kitten into the carton. "They're all eyes and whiskers."

"And they will all be dead if you don't hurry over to Bella's with them." Hanger whacked him on the back.

Vernon hefted the box and headed down the street. Visions of Bella kicking him into the gutter or calling the cops filled his head. At the corner traffic light, he stopped. This would never work. He'd never even get his foot in the door. Weight shifted inside the box and a pitiful meowing began. The woman standing next to him huffed. He knew what she saw: a mean bruiser of man in dirty work clothes disposing of some unwanted pets.

A particularly plaintive squeak emanated from the box. She tipped her head. "Wha'cha got in there, man?"

"Kittens." Vernon sucked his lower lip. Hanger better be right. They'd better not be rats.

The woman frowned. "They okay?"

Vernon shifted the carton to the other arm. They would be. Bella would care for them. She was so motherly, big hearted. What did it matter if she kicked him out—she'd keep the kittens. He gave her what he hoped was a sincere-looking smile. "Yeah, they're going to be all right. I'm taking them to a good lady who rescues cats." *And maybe—desperate men.*

The light changed, and he hustled across the street

and down to the new Siren. Lights shone through the plate glass windows onto the sidewalk. Good, she was still open.

A group of college-age kids spilled out the door. A young girl in tights and a puffy white jacket examined the bandaged wrist of one of the guys. "You had to go and get a mermaid, didn't you?"

The youth sporting the new tattoo grinned. "It's her specialty. No one does mermaids like Bella Bell. It's quality work. *Quality.*" The proud owner displayed his carefully wrapped wrist like a badge of courage, twisting it this way and that. "And she's so gentle, didn't hurt a bit."

Vernon clutched his fingers tighter around the box. Gentle? Not the Bella he knew. Not the Bella he had to face. He rolled his shoulders where her masterpiece, the winged siren, spread across his back. All the beautiful things he selected so carefully over the years that made him feel like there was some good in his rotten life—his entire art collection—except for Ari's paintings—Kiro had shipped to auction.

But his brother couldn't take away the art covering his body. He adjusted the box. If kittens didn't melt her heart, at least he'd always have Bella's stunning work gracing his body and the memory of her hands tatting the design on his skin.

He slowed. After all, despite the hopes of T-Crew, the chance of her ever touching him again was almost nil. Why would she want a mother-killer like him? He swallowed down the bile roiling in his stomach that made it impossible for him to think or eat or sleep and called after the departing customers. "Bella's the best. Spread the word." Pumping up her business was the least he could do for her

The youths pivoted and gave him a thumbs-up. "Will do, man. Will do," they answered back. Then they ambled down the street and left him standing alone in front of The Siren. Vernon sent up a prayer. "Be gentle with me, Bella. Be gentle." Then he pushed the door open, setting the little bell on the back to dinging, and stepped inside.

Bella stuck her head out from what had to be a bathroom in the back. Her hair had grown. Black ringlets tumbled around her face, making her look more real, more like the woman she was meant to be—strong, proud, no longer in hiding. "*Vernon?*"

He held out the box. "I—I found these kittens. They need help. I thought"—he set the carton on the floor and stepped back ready to retreat—"well, you're good with cats."

Small peeps and cries sounded through the cardboard. Bella straightened. "Kittens?"

"They're very small. One's sick. They were found at the building where I'm working. The mother disappeared. The boss ordered them thrown out. I saved them."

"Thrown out?" Bella came forward, lifted the flaps, and stared down. "Oh, the poor babies. Their eyes are barely open. Just days old. I'm going to need to feed them." She glanced at the clock. "The pet store is closed by now. Bring them up to my apartment. We'll have to make do until I can get out and buy proper formula."

Vernon hefted the carton again and waited for her to lock up, his heart thudding so loudly he was sure she heard.

Bella took the keys from her pocket. "It's after closing time. You were lucky to find me here." She opened the graffiti-covered door to the apartment next to the shop and hesitated. For a moment, he thought she'd take the box of kittens from him and tell him to get lost. But she didn't. Instead, she headed up the stairs.

He clutched the box in front of him like a shield and trailed after her, soaking in the view of her hips swaying in that special Bella-way he loved. Heat flared through him. His cock throbbed. He couldn't wait to kiss her, tell her he loved her, explain everything he'd done the minute they got inside.

Stopping on the landing to unlock the door, she peered back over her shoulder. "I have a date."

She had a date.

The words sluiced over him like an avalanche of ice. His body went rigid. He struggled to breathe. No kisses. No hug. Hanger was mistaken. This wasn't going to work. She'd keep the kittens and toss him.

He gripped the box tighter and followed her through the dark living room. But she hadn't ejected him yet. He just had to remember to keep his mouth closed. Every minute he spent in Bella's company, inhaling her scent and watching her move, was a gift. Even if he never touched her again, he'd have the memory to keep him breathing through the long sleepless nights.

Bella flicked on the light, and Vernon had a better view of the apartment. The place was in rough shape. Stained wallpaper on the walls. Worn carpet on the floor. Half-opened cartons shoved here and there. Obviously, she'd put all her time and money into getting the new Siren up and running.

He glanced around. Had she opened the small white package—the one from him? He couldn't tell.

"Put the box down on the floor."

Vernon placed his burden down on the dirty yellow kitchen tile and kneeled beside it.

"Wait here." Bella disappeared and then returned, carrying a stack of towels. "Luckily, I still have some kitten formula, and I found several orphan feeding bottles tucked away in my old knapsack. I've rescued kitties before." Her voice hitched. "We can take turns feeding them."

His heart caught on that *we*. Maybe she would cancel the date and stay. Maybe they could talk. *Maybe—*

She handed him the towels. "It's going to be a long night. They'll only take a tablespoon every two hours or so. Make a little nest for them on your lap. You can hold them and keep them warm while I make up the formula."

Vernon settled on the floor and crossed his legs. He loved Bella when she was bossy. He loved when she knew just what to do. Damn it, he just loved her.

He glanced at her turned back, the muscles of her neck rigid above the collar of the silk blouse she wore, her jaw twitching. It would take more than just loving her to win her back, though. He flicked a piece of dirt off his jeans. Back at the castle, she'd said she hated him, and she'd meant it.

He adjusted his legs. How could anything he said fix that? He took a deep breath. Better to listen to Hanger and focus on the kittens. He fluffed a towel and laid it in the hollow of his folded legs. Then he added another for more padding. Their little claws were razor sharp, and his essential bits were pretty exposed in this position.

He peered into the box. "Okay, guys. I'm coming for you." Carefully, he lifted each kitten out of the carton, avoiding the claws as much as possible, and placed them in the notch between his legs. They crept around on their bellies, decided it was better than anywhere else they'd been, and settled into a warm mass of matted gray fur right where he didn't need to feel any warmer. He raised his hand like a wary school boy. "Like this, Bella?"

She craned her neck in his direction. "Just like that." She bit her lip and turned away. "Looks nice and cozy and warm."

Vernon rested his spine against the battered kitchen cabinet and watched her boil the water for sterilizing, whip up the formula mix, and heat it in the microwave. He ran a finger over one of the kittens' heads. He could feel the hard bone of its skull, the knobby bits of its spine poking up. Even matted and grimy, the fur was soft as feathers. A low hum vibrated through him. Silly thing was purring.

"See, he likes you." Bella squatted down beside him, her gypsy skirt floating around her, enveloping him in the enticing scent of her signature bergamot, but with something new mixed in. He liked it. His cock hardened under the kittens, and he was glad for the extra toweling. Lust had no place in the conversation they needed to have, as much as he wanted to kiss his way back into her heart.

She passed over a tiny curved bottle of milk. "Don't tip his head up. Just put a drop or two on his tongue. You don't want to send it down his windpipe and choke him. Once they get the idea, they'll start to suck on their own. But you have to have patience."

Patience. He'd never been a patient man, but if that's what it took to win this woman, he'd be patient. He'd sit and he'd wait and he'd do everything she said. He cuddled the kitten against his stomach and worked the nipple tip into its mouth.

Beside him, Bella encouraged the sickly kitten to suckle. She looked like a Madonna—he glanced around—a Madonna in a trash pit. She was sitting on a rotten filthy floor, probably in a mess of cockroaches, next to a man wearing shitty clothes from the thrift bin and holding a rat-like creature that smelled like the garbage can he'd rescued it from.

His kitten sucked the bottle dry. Feeling mighty proud of that small success, he picked up the other and inserted the nipple.

Beside him, Bella shifted her legs. "I think we might lose this one." She put down the bottle. "And I really do have to go out this evening. It's too late to cancel. He's already bought the tickets, and they cost a fortune."

Vernon glanced over. The kitten in her hand looked dead. Its head drooped to one side. Milk dribbled from its mouth. Bella's chin rested on her chest. She looked defeated. He wanted to wrap his arms around her and tell her it was all right. Instead, he reached out and took the kitten from her hands. "I'll work with it. See what I can do. You go. Meet your date."

She handed him the tiny bottle. "Your chance is as good as mine. But you can't save them all, Vernon." She pushed up from the floor. "And this—this together thing. Don't read anything into it. I'm just helping the kittens."

He pressed his back against the cabinet to keep his body from collapsing. "Yeah, I get that."

And then she was gone. Off with another man. Off with someone who could buy expensive tickets and dinners out like he used to do. His stomach tensed. His resident snake shifted, waiting to feed on jealousy and vengeance. But he was no longer that man. Willing it back to sleep, he rolled his shoulders and settled back on the hard floor.

It was going to be a long night with no hope at the end.

****

The apartment was silent when she got back. Bella peered down at Vernon. He was sound asleep, half leaning over, his neck crooked at an awkward angle. Poor man, he was going to ache when he woke up. She lifted the kittens off his lap one by one and put them in the warm cozy box she'd prepared for them. Their little bellies swelled with milk. The weak kitten seemed more alert. She peered into the box. The kittens mewed for a minute, and then curled up in a quivering ball next to the hot water bottle she'd tucked under the towel. They'd sleep for a while longer.

She glanced at Vernon again. The ex-crook had done a good job keeping them alive all night. She would never have credited him with the staying power.

Bella heated up a pot of coffee, poured herself a cup, and studied the man at her feet. What was she going to do with Vernon Newell? She'd told him she hated him. But she didn't really. Never had. Which made having him here damn uncomfortable. Damn complicated. Because despite everything, she still loved him.

She loved his strength, she loved his passion, she loved the way his mouth tipped up when he smiled, and she loved the boyish wonder he'd never lost despite the vile upbringing he'd suffered. But most of all, she loved his courage.

She put her cup down and patted the top of his head. She owed him. She'd relived that moment in the castle kitchen over and over. She'd be dead if he hadn't flipped the table and killed his stepmother. He'd done that to save her.

She studied his worn, drawn face, lined with the burden of guilt he carried. Underneath all the bluster and scorn, he'd loved his backstabbing stepmother.

And the idea that he killed and dumped *hundreds* of bodies in the gorge? Now that she had time and distance and was no longer terrorized out of her skull, she realized nobody, not even a billionaire crime boss, could kill that many people and not get caught by the police. Scheming Nina turned her against Vernon just at the time he needed her to trust him the most.

And then there was this. She drew the envelope out of the kitchen drawer. She'd found it a few days ago in the oddly shaped white box labeled cryptically "Extras for Bella" in Vernon's messy scrawl. It was the deed to the villa on Eudokia and all the land that hadn't been incorporated into the reserve her brother had set up. It was dated December of last year—long before the ill-fated engagement party. It might have been in the packet of papers on that kitchen table, but he hadn't deeded it to Kiro. He couldn't. It had already been hers, fair and square, signed and stamped by the Greek authorities.

And the other paper. She drew it out of the envelope and looked at it again. She still couldn't fathom the amount of money he'd given away. Twelve zeros—that was billions of dollars. Donated to Mercy House in her name.

She peered down at the sleeping man in his tattered clothes and unkempt hair. It didn't look like he'd kept any money for himself. She'd heard from Hanger that he was working as a carpenter, and the rough callouses and the broken fingernails painted the rumor real. From multi-billionaire to scratching-by-carpenter. From vicious killer to kitten-savior. It seemed impossible. If she'd read it in a novel, she wouldn't believe it.

For a moment, she hesitated. Was the old Vernon with the too-big ego and the life-is-a-joke chip on his shoulder truly gone? She stared at the tired, scruffy man stripped bare of artifice and glamor, power and ruthlessness, lying on her kitchen floor, and knew the answer.

Bigger-than-life Vernon Newell had been a role he'd been thrust into, a mask he hid behind. Without the power, without the wealth, he was just a man who hurt and worried and wore his guilt close to the skin—a man willing to risk everything to start his life over to win her back—this was the man she loved.

What was it her grandma always said? Sometimes you had to stop what you were doing and begin anew to find the truth of things. She looked around at her crummy apartment so like the one she'd lived in when she first arrived in New York.

She was starting over.

He was starting over.

They could start over together.

She knelt down in front of him and dropped the papers in his lap. Then she took the beloved face in her hands and brushed her lips along his. Blast it, she had missed him.

She deepened the kiss and pressed closer. He was warm and gorgeous and smelled right—not of some rich man's cologne, but earthy and sweaty like a man who earned his living through hard work.

This was the man who completed her. Henri Avery might treat her like an exotic morsel to wine, dine, and entertain, but he would never satisfy her. She was a one-man woman, and this beaten-down, guilt-ridden man was the one who made her blood sizzle.

Bella gave a little sigh and kissed Vernon again. It was like acting out Sleeping Beauty in reverse. Instead of a princess, she would wake a sleeping prince who'd battled his way through wicked stepmothers and vengeful brothers to reach her.

The third kiss did it. His eyes flickered. His muscles gathered beneath her. His lips firmed, and he pressed back.

"Bella," he whispered against her lips. "*Bella?*" His hands slipped around her waist and snugged her against him.

Every part of her body came alert. Her skin tingled. Reservations melted away. "Yes."

Vernon pulled back and stared at her, a question in his eyes.

She waved the papers at him and then tossed them aside. "You crazy, crazy man." She kissed him again, trailed her lips down his cheek, rough and unshaven, licked his neck and tasted the salty sweat of him.

He twisted under her. "Wait, Bella. We need to talk."

"Talk? Sure. Let's see. *I'*—her fingers fumbled at the buttons of his shirt—"*love*"—the cloth was so worn they slipped out like a knife passing through butter—"*you.*" Shirt open, she pulled up his tee and found his nipples. She sucked one and then the other, inhaling the taste of him. *"And you"*—she drew back, smiled and then leaned in and sucked the nubs, while her fingers grabbed the golden hair on his chest and tugged gently—"*love me.*" Her hand slid lower. "Your turn. Say *yes.*"

His cock hardened under her palm. "But Bella."

"Nooo." She put a thumb against his lips. "I only want to hear you say the magic word. *Yes.*" She tongued his nipple.

Vernon's head tipped back. She gazed up at him. He licked his lips and said the only words she wanted to hear. "Yes, I love you. I've always loved you. I will love you forever."

Bella tore at his jeans button, unzipped his fly and released his hard, long cock. He was hers and he was under her control. "Talking over."

****

Vernon knew what was coming. Bella looked like a goddess, her lips wet, her eyes bright, her hair curling every which way, and she was kneeling between his legs, ready to take him in. It was his job to pleasure her, not the reverse. But he had no will power left to prevent it. Later, he would blame it on the kittens keeping him awake all night. Right now his aching body would take anything she offered.

Bella circled the head of his penis with her lips,

licked and tasted. She lowered her mouth and took him farther inside. His hips jumped, and his hands twisted in the frothy fabric of her skirt.

His breath came in gasps. She slid her mouth up and down, grazed him with her teeth. He bucked, bucked again, and then he could hold back no longer. It had been too long. Over and over he spurted into her mouth. Her precious mouth, so warm, so tight, so perfect. His hands fell numb onto the floor, his head flopped back. He shook and convulsed once, twice, three times.

She'd undone him.

Vernon took a sharp breath. "That was—that was torture."

She slapped him on the stomach. "Good. It was what you deserved."

He righted himself. "But you—I didn't—"

"Didn't give me pleasure?" She licked her lips. "How little you know me."

"Oh my beautiful siren." He pulled her against him and buried his face in her hair. "I don't deserve you. Never have. Never will. You are the most forgiving person I know. After everything I've done to destroy you, your brother, your business, your whole fucking life." He waved his hand at the dilapidated kitchen. "Reducing you to living like this. You should be kicking me out the door. Not letting me hold you in my arms. Letting you take me to heaven with your mouth, Bella. Don't you know I've never been honest with you? Even the kittens were a ruse."

She put her fingers on his lips. "Hush. I'm the one who hasn't been honest. I let guilt and fear and resentment grow until the wall around me was so high nothing could reach me." She pressed her palm against his chest. "Not even your love. I shut you out when what I was really shutting out was myself. I blamed myself for everything. For being weak. For not fighting back. My suicide attempt after my mother drowned. My brother's imprisonment. My father's death. Your brother—"

"Wait. My brother?" Vernon tipped up her chin and studied her face. "What did Kiro do to you?"

"Besides bombing The Siren, killing my kitties, almost drowning you, threatening Hanger, and terrifying me to death?" She glanced down.

"There's something else?"

She let out a breath. "When I was kidnapped by Tuccio. Kiro—he touched me, made me kiss him, do things—it was abuse. I know that now. But he said I had asked for it. Dressing as I did, flaunting myself, sporting tattoos. He made me feel like a piece of trash. I was tied up. Helpless. And you didn't come." She pounded on his chest. "*You didn't come.*"

"Oh, Bella." Vernon rocked her in his arms. "I was looking in all the wrong places."

She undid the top buttons of her blouse. "He—he carved his initial into my skin. It left a scar." She touched the fish tattoo above her breast.

Vernon hugged her tighter and pressed his lips to the tattoo. "Why didn't you tell me?"

"I should have." One of the kittens mewed. Bella pulled out of his arms, reached into the box, and ran her fingers down its back. The kitten circled and resettled atop the others. "But it made me feel weak and powerless. That's what abuse does. I felt vulnerable—and I blamed you."

Vernon stretched out his legs. There was a gaping hole in his jeans. But it was minuscule compared to the hole in his heart. He'd failed her. "You should blame me. All I ever wanted was to protect you from the hell I lived in and from my family. But how could I when I couldn't even protect myself? Damn it. You had to save *me* from my own brother." He rolled his shoulders. "I couldn't kill him, Bella. I let him take it all. He's the new crime boss on the east coast. He won't last long in that world." Vernon turned his hands palm up. "But I am done with it. I'm a working man now. Living in a flop house. Living straight." He inhaled deeply. "Living poor. And I can't believe I'm saying this, but being ordinary—well, it's okay."

"Just okay?" Bella put her hand in her pocket and pulled out a ring. The engagement ring. The diamond siren sparkled in the dawn light creeping through the window. "*Ordinary* can be very special."

He held his breath.

She cocked her head and winked. "Ask me again, *Mr. Ordinary.*" She picked up his hand and placed the ring in his palm.

Vernon clasped it in his fist and pressed his hand against his heart. "Marry me, Bella Bell, and join me in living an ordinary life. I won't be able to take you out to fancy dinners and opening nights on Broadway. We won't be whizzing around town in a limo or vacationing in the Caymans. My boss doesn't provide paid vacations. But I can promise you one thing. I can give you an extraordinary kitchen re-do."

Bella glanced around the room and smiled. "An irresistible proposal." She leaned in and whispered in his ear. "Yes."

It was the sexiest sound he'd ever heard. Yes was his new favorite word. He was going to spend his life saying yes to this woman and getting her to say yes back.

He picked up the ring and slid it on her finger.

"Oh, Vernon." Bella threw her arms around him. Her fingers wove through his hair. Her lips brushed his. It was a sweet kiss. A get-to-know-you initial date type of kiss. The kind of kiss they'd never shared before, not even when they'd first met on Eudokia. He'd been too experienced. She'd been too excited. He tipped his head for a better angle. She moved with him, her lips melded to his—warm, soft, tender.

He shifted back and studied the woman in his arms. The morning sun shone in through the window gilding her hair, illuminating the curve of her cheek, the slant of her nose, the sweep of her eyelashes. The combination was so familiar and yet, so new and wondrous.

Bella had always been a beautiful woman, the kind any man would be proud to have strut beside him down the street. Now, as if someone had ripped away bandages from his eyes, he could truly see the precious woman he held in his arms—a living one-of-kind masterpiece, powerful, unique, completely herself.

He could never own her or force her to his will. Love wasn't about possession. It was about opening up the most vulnerable part of himself and letting her in. The barriers he had built up over the years to protect his heart from being torn apart by his father, by his stepmother, by the horrible things he been forced to do—all the walls around his heart crumbled.

Heat rushed in. His heart swelled and pounded

against his chest. His lungs expanded with something more than air—with joy. He buried his face in her hair and inhaled the scent of her. He feathered kisses down her neck. "I'll love you, Bella Bell, until my dying day."

She peered into his eyes. "Of course you will. And that will be a very long time from now, Mr. Ordinary." Cupping her hand around his ear, she whispered in the sexy, breathy voice he adored. "Speaking of a long time—" She ran her fingers down his chest and rubbed her tush against his most sensitive place, making her meaning clear.

Vernon wanted to go slow, show her how much he cherished her. He needed to get her off the filthy floor and find the bed, then make love to her with all the skill he could muster amidst blankets and pillows and sheets. But his bossy Bella wasn't having it.

She yanked the sleeves of his flannel work shirt down his arms and off. His tee ripped over his head. Her fingers wiggled beneath his waistband and shoved down. He toed off his sneakers, lifted his buttocks, and let her strip him bare.

His wild-eyed Greek seductress was still fully dressed. He reached out to unbutton her silk blouse, and the roughened pads of his fingers caught on the fine cloth. He jerked his hands back. How could he touch her? He was no longer a manicured, pampered man of wealth. He was dirty, rough, stinking of sweat, no better than a bum. "My hands—"

"Don't you dare stop. I can't wait for you to touch me with those hard-working hands." Bella rose up on her knees, tore the blouse over her head, then slipped out of her skirt and bra and the lacy little panties he loved to collect.

One eyebrow cocked, she seized his hands and placed them on her breasts. "Take me to heaven. Now!"

Vernon's breath caught somewhere deep in his throat. His heart thumped so hard it hurt. This beautiful exotic woman with her glorious tattoos—this living work of art—had said yes.

Brushing her silken skin with his fingertips, he traced the flowing lines of the siren tattoo lower and lower until he reached the apex of her thighs. He settled his hand between her legs and touched her soft folds. She was warm and wet and ready. Placing his hands around her waist, he lifted her up and slid inside.

"Yes," she moaned, leaning down and kissing him. "You are so perfect." Then with a gentle sway of her hips she drew him in deep, and he was lost.

They had made love hundreds of times before, professed their love over and over. But this time it was different. All his defenses were down. Every long slide in and out reduced the entire span of his poorly lived lifetime to nothingness.

Only joining with this woman mattered. The warmth and softness of her, the tight, wet welcome surrounding every inch of his cock, stole his thoughts until sensation took over and they were joined mind to mind, body to body, skin to skin.

When she came, he prolonged it, slowing the rhythm and changing the angle, until Bella's head tipped back, and she convulsed around him, then tumbled boneless on top of him.

He clasped her to him and thrust harder and deeper into the clenching heat of his siren. Every muscle in his body quivered. His blood churned. His heart banged against his ribs. When he came, he exploded, and this time, she came with him. For the first time in his life, Vernon lost all sense of himself. There was no him, no her, only them.

Vernon collapsed on the kitchen floor wrung out, a completely new person. Bella lay atop him, glorious in her nakedness, Aphrodite and Hera and Eos all wrapped up in one amazing woman, her hair tickling his nose.

A mewing came from the box beside them, and Bella lazily lifted her hair out of her eyes. Then she pushed up on her elbows and gave him a Cheshire-cat grin. "I was wrong, Vernon. There is nothing *ordinary* about you."

Epilogue

"*Ouch.*" Vernon picked up the cat crawling over his head and placed it on the floor. A second purring feline attacked his toes.

Beside him, Bella stirred. "Did you forget to close the bedroom door again?" She turned toward him and ran her fingers over the winged siren that emblazoned his chest.

He caught her hand. "I have to get up and go to work, wife. Got to rip out another kitchen today."

"Good."

"Good?"

"Better than ripping people off." Her finger swirled over one wing and then the other. "Wait. Look here." Her finger stopped.

He glanced down.

"There's a blank spot right here under your heart. And I know exactly what I am going to tattoo there."

He imagined her fingers tracing the design onto his skin and grew heated. He hadn't gotten a tattoo since she'd finished the one on his butt over a year ago. Even a short time under her needle would be heaven. He touched the space. "What will fit in this tiny spot?"

She laughed. "A baby siren."

He rolled over and looked into her eyes. "*A baby—*"

She nodded. "Yep, I'm pregnant."

Vernon's heart thudded in his chest. "How will we support a child, Bella? Kids cost a fortune to raise. All we have is this rundown place, my new carpentry business, and you're just getting The Siren going again."

She tugged the hair on his chest. "Worrywuss. The business is going to do just fine. Your cabinets are fantastic." She snuggled closer. "The TV show I worked on—*Secret Ink*. It's been renewed for another season. I've been asked to design tattoos for the new members joining the cast. It's not a fortune, but it will help." Bella placed his hand on her stomach. "This is our future, Vernon. We may not have a ton of money, but we do have a ton of love. We're going to share that love, you and I, and raise a child who will grow up to be compassionate and loving. Just like his daddy."

Vernon rested his hand atop hers. "And extraordinarily wise like her mother."

A word about the author...

Zara West loves all things dark, scary, and heart-stopping as long as they lead to true love. Born in Williamsburg, Brooklyn, Zara spends winters in New York where the streets hum with life, summers in the Maritimes where the sea can be cruel, and the rest of the year anywhere inspiration for tales of suspense, mystery, and romance are plentiful. An accomplished artist by training and passion, she brings a love of art to every book she writes.

In a life full of misadventures, she has had sunstroke on the top of a Greek mountain while doing ethnographic research with shepherds, been stranded on the banks of the Rhine with no money and one chocolate bar, and while she has never been kidnapped, she has been abandoned on an uninhabited island in the middle of the wilderness for longer than she wants to remember.

In her spare time, when not writing award-winning books, magazine articles, and flash fiction stories, Zara tends her organic herb garden, travels widely, and whips up ethnic dishes for friends and family.

A member of RWA, Zara is a published author of both fiction and non-fiction. Her short stories have appeared in several anthologies, and have received awards from Women on Writing, Stone Thread Publishing, Tryst Literary Magazine, and Winning Writers. Her novels have placed first in the Pages from the Heart and the Romance Through the Ages contest, second in the Touch of Love Contest and long-listed for the Mslexia Award.

http://www.zarawestsuspense.com

Thank you for purchasing
this publication of The Wild Rose Press, Inc.

If you enjoyed the story, we would appreciate your
letting others know by leaving a review.

For other wonderful stories,
please visit our on-line bookstore at
www.thewildrosepress.com.

For questions or more information
contact us at
info@thewildrosepress.com.

The Wild Rose Press, Inc.
www.thewildrosepress.com

Stay current with The Wild Rose Press, Inc.

Like us on Facebook

https://www.facebook.com/TheWildRosePress

And Follow us on Twitter
https://twitter.com/WildRosePress